Totally Bound Publishing books by Aurelia T. Evans

Single Books
Calling the Dragons Home
Red Queen

Arcanium
Fortune
Carousel
Aerial
Ringmaster
Contortion
Spider

I0526278

Anthologies
Wild After Dark: Intervention

Collections
Frost Bite: Gravedigger

Arcanium

FUNHOUSE

AURELIA T. EVANS

Funhouse
ISBN # 978-1-78686-397-3
©Copyright Aurelia T. Evans 2019
Cover Art by Erin Dameron-Hill ©Copyright April 2019
Interior text design by Claire Siemaszkiewicz
Totally Bound Publishing

FUNHOUSE

Chapter One

She was freezing in spite of two layers of pants and three layers on top—four, counting the scarf. But despite a rough post-holiday month with her husband—first holiday living together, first holiday married—a glimmer of something like contentment glowed in her chest. Joseph had his arm around her, and they were sharing one of the best hot chocolates she'd ever had. It felt like when they'd first started dating—all the reasons he'd eventually asked her to marry him, in spite of everything, and she'd said yes. He was her person, and her own personal heater as they walked through the traveling circus.

According to some of their friends, Arcanium had come to town several times before. Neve couldn't believe she'd never heard of it. A circus-slash-carnival with freaks, steampunk and horror? It was so totally up her and Joseph's alley. How'd they miss it all those other times?

It was small and cheap-looking from the outside—such was the travail of a nomadic business, she was sure. At a distance, Arcanium was just clusters of tan canvas tents and wooden booths — easy to erect and tear down. The fences were solid and good quality, and the gate entrance was beautiful, but the limited rides were, at first glance, a weak offering.

That is, if a person didn't get close enough to notice that the carousel was one of a kind, each mount custom rather than generic or cheap and delightfully weird, with a squid, spider and a few saddled men to accompany more traditional mounts. Parking lot carnivals had higher Ferris wheels with brighter lights, but sometimes one of the performers or oddities would creep into a swing with someone to give them a good selfie from the top. And although they hadn't visited yet, Neve was looking forward to the haunted funhouse.

Heck, she'd come back for the hot chocolate alone. She didn't care what their special chef of odd delicacies might have put in the drink, whether it was cricket legs, coffee extracted from civet droppings or cocaine. It was amazing and warmed her up from the inside, where Joseph couldn't reach.

Walking with him through Oddity Row was an exercise in trying to figure out which one was the humbug — and how they faked it — and which one was real. The best part was that it didn't matter.

If the oddities were real, it was a testament to the awesome variety in the gene pool that hadn't been, or couldn't be, completely eliminated. As the only pale redhead in an immediate family of tan brunettes, recessive genes and genetic anomalies had been an amateur fascination since elementary school.

But if the fakes were just that good, kudos had to be given to the person responsible for such exceptional, consistent illusion.

The Bearded Lady, the Man Made of Stone, the Human Spider with all her lovely spiders and insects, the snake charmer with all her wonderful reptiles, the Sphynx, the Cyclops, the mermaid, the Rotting Man… And those only tapped the surface, since many oddities were walking out and about, mingling with the guests.

Neve had thought freak shows had been mostly banned and eliminated in favor of acrobatic performance art and gross-out sideshows — which she loved, too. But she was oddly thrilled that an actual freak show still existed outside cable TV, whether the freaks were real or not.

"You want to ride an elephant or go to the haunted funhouse? I hear it's nice and dark in there, sometimes even sexy." Joseph kissed her forehead, his lips lingering there.

There had been plenty of oddities and performers who were as sexy as they were strange, like the harlequin clowns with their painted monster faces and their raunchy vaudeville pantomime. Like the contortionist in latex, with the dragon fire-eater led behind her on a silver leash. Like the Human Spider in leather and bound in white rope into her web. Like the strongman and the snake charmer showing off their bodies by limiting their costumes. Skimpy attire was par for the course in a circus, but Arcanium walked the line between teen-appropriate and adult, obeying the letter of the law, if not the spirit.

But Neve could only really tell sexy based on other people's reactions and the empirical facts right in front of her, like clothing types and movement, the way Joseph's pupils dilated and his easily red face flushed to his hairline.

Bodies were just bodies to her. Anatomical curiosities, sometimes walking pieces of art — and quite a few pieces of eccentric art were walking around the circus. Neve had always seen bodies differently than most. That had only been confirmed after her beautiful white wedding. She loved bodies, and she loved Joseph's. But it wasn't quite the same way he loved hers. His expression as he looked at her now gave her an all-too-familiar pang in her chest.

"Sure." She hoped her smile appeared sincere, because she didn't want the good day to sour like New Year's Eve all over again. "I'm looking forward to the scary more, though. If you want romance, why not win me a Cthulhu and ride the Ferris wheel with me?"

Joseph's eyes crinkled when he smiled. It lit him up like a yearlong Christmas tree. When he wasn't smiling, he had what would be called Resting Bitch Face on a girl. On a guy, it was just a scowl. But she loved the furrows and his strong brows as much as she loved his smile.

"Sounds like a plan," he said.

One stuffed tentacled elder god later from her amateur baseball pitcher husband found him and Neve waiting in line for the Ferris wheel, which, like the carousel, looked so much better up close — with gears and scrollwork over the enclosed swings and integrated into the wheel structure itself, like a giant faceless clock mechanism reduced to skeleton plates and cogs.

"Mind if I join you?" A short woman in a feathered bustle and sparkly red corset and shoes walked the fence around the ride as though she wasn't wearing four-inch heels on a railing no wider than two fingers. When she flipped to the ground, her barely contained breasts quivered from the landing, lending credence to Neve's theory that most of Arcanium's people were actually glued into their costumes.

Joseph checked with Neve, as though he thought she'd be threatened by a beautiful, bosomy woman joining them. Why he thought she didn't know he noticed other women's tits as much as her own was beyond her. They were his favorite parts, after all. Neve's only rule was *Look, but don't touch*, but he still got jumpy about the *look* part now and then.

Neve nodded in encouragement, happily allowing the Arcanium performer to tuck her arms into both of their elbows like Dorothy in Oz, the very embodiment of ruby slippers. As soon as the ride was ready, she stepped up into the enclosed swing and beckoned them to follow.

"Either of you afraid of heights?" she asked.

"If that's a subtle way of asking whether we can rock the swing at the top," Neve said, "how about no?"

The woman laughed. "I'm the tightrope walker. I had to get over my fear of heights pretty quick. It helps when you know you won't fall."

"I'm fine on a Ferris wheel as long as it's stable. How long have you been a tightrope walker?"

"A few years now, not long after I joined Arcanium. I started as the magician's assistant, but they like you to have multiple skills around here." She sat next to Joseph, across from Neve, and she crossed her strong, shapely legs to nudge Joseph's knee with her shoe.

"I'd think it would take just that long to learn how," Neve said.

"Apparently all you need is the right motivation." The woman's smile was dazzling, especially with the deep red lipstick she wore to match the corset, shoes and scarlet pigtail falls that fountained out on either side of her head. "No net."

"Seriously?" Neve said.

"This place isn't for the weak of heart." She kept her arm hooked around Joseph's next to her, but her harmless flirtation seemed directed at both Joseph and Neve together.

"I can take a lot, but I don't like the idea of falling. Some of my worst dreams are of falling," Neve said. "You know, the ones where you jerk on the bed when you wake up because you died hitting the ground."

"There are some good kinds of falling," the woman said. "Here we go."

Neve kept a hand on the edge of the swing. As long as she sat still, she was fine.

It was interesting to see Arcanium from above. From here, she could see the caravan of semi-trailers, recreational vehicles and pickup trucks huddled together on the other side of the big top tent. The funhouse gargoyle poised above the haunted house entrance, ready to startle the unwary. She watched children riding the placid elephants, watched the carousel spin. Guests and performers mingled in the crowd, the monsters and freaks almost indistinguishable from the average people around them from this height.

"Want a picture?" The woman stood up to shift around to Neve's side. "You're not going to get a better shot in all of Arcanium — not while it's open anyway." She winked, with long false eyelashes that appeared to be made of fine, tiny black feathers.

Neve handed her phone to Joseph to take a high-angle picture as the woman sidled close, her breast against Neve's. She kissed Neve's cheek during one of Joseph's pictures.

"Just a little souvenir," the woman whispered in Neve's ear. Then she shifted back over to Joseph's side and handed the phone to Neve.

Kudos also went to whoever was responsible for the makeup and manicures, because those were exceptional as well. Neve worked in a lab, where long nails and latex gloves didn't mix, so she always loved looking at other people's nail art—right up there with enjoying other people's tattoos while not interested in enduring one herself.

Neve scrolled through the pictures Joseph had taken as the Ferris wheel did another rotation. She smiled. The woman's lipstick had left a blood-red lip mark on Neve's cheek.

"Love it. Your turn, Joseph." She set her Cthulhu stuffie on the seat in preparation.

As soon as the Ferris wheel stopped again at a good angle over the circus, Neve raised herself up, and the woman tucked herself close to Joseph.

"Want a souvenir of your own, sweetheart?" the woman asked.

"Absolutely," Neve said, although she quashed the first irrational pangs of jealousy.

The woman kissed Joseph soundly on the cheek, leaving another mark behind, then smiled for the camera.

Not for the first time, Neve thought she was being grossly unfair and had been for a while. She recognized Joseph's body language—not to mention the less subtle bulge in his jeans.

From the beginning of their relationship, she'd warned him that while she loved him to pieces, loved the closeness they had when they kissed, she didn't seem to have what other people called a sex drive. She got more excited by kittens or the good pizza place near his house than the conclusion of date night.

They'd been traditionalists, which meant no sex until the wedding night, but there had been plenty of red flags before. Like when he'd been hot and bothered after a make-out session, and she'd just felt warm and fuzzy inside — no urgency, no regret they had to stop, no challenge in waiting. When she was younger, she'd thought she just hadn't found the right boy. Now she'd found her soulmate, and six months in, they were subsisting on unenthusiastic once-a-week sessions.

At the beginning, they'd told themselves she just needed to get used to sex for it to start feeling better. Then he'd tried being more romantic, which had never been the problem. They'd bought marital aids — which was nice, but that was all.

She'd sworn to herself she would never be this person, never put her husband through a sexless marriage. It wasn't like she'd ever been particularly conservative. She and Joseph were middle-of-the-road Christians, and she had a bit of a pagan streak to accompany it. Most religions were pretty clear about how cheating really wasn't okay — hence her *no touching* rule. But as long as she simply wasn't interested in sex, would it really be so bad to let him seek it elsewhere? Say, if this woman's flirtation weren't so harmless. There was certainly biblical precedent.

Neve forced herself to keep grinning and took the pictures, pretending it was all in fun. Now wasn't the time to make a scene over something best aired in the office of a marriage counselor.

"It's been wonderful to meet you," the woman said. "Don't forget to tag Arcanium in anything you post. We mostly depend on word of mouth." She licked her lips then reached into a small purse at her side to apply a new layer of lipstick.

"How should we tag you?" Joseph avidly watched the lipstick's progress, hiding his erection with his coat.

"Sky High Maya," the woman said. "I'll admit, not as catchy as the Human Spider, but it does the trick. Hope to see you both again at the performance tonight or down by Oddity Row."

Neve hugged her Cthulhu to brace against the cold, because Joseph kept looking back at Maya as she vaulted over the barrier to the ride and headed toward the midway.

"She kind of looks like you, don't you think?" Joseph said.

Neve laughed. "Sure. Except for the cyberpunk falls, darker skin, darker eyes and being seven inches shorter."

"No, I mean shape. You're both kind of the same curvy."

"You mean she's busty," she said.

"No, it's not just that. I mean, yes, she's top-heavy and so are you. I mean…" Every time he tried to backpedal, he just got Italian red and even more tongue-tied.

Neve patted his shoulder in sympathy. "Your bigger brain isn't getting much of the blood right now, is it, honey?"

Relief came out as his own laughter, and in a parody of Maya, he held out his arm for her to take the crook of his elbow. They strolled back through the midway toward the food court and fortune teller tent.

"It was supposed to be a compliment. I can see you wearing something like that—not in the middle of winter to visit the circus, but maybe for a more private performance," he murmured near her ear where Maya had whispered to her. "Our own little three-ring circus. You bring the corset, and I'll bring the flogger."

"I think I'd like that."

Her wardrobe had never been particularly provocative, with the exception of the sweetheart neckline on her wedding dress, because Joseph had wanted that. But when a girl was 'top-heavy' most of her life, she didn't need a low-cut top for men to notice her. It had been a point of private embarrassment, bewilderment and sometimes guilt ever since puberty, when she'd started growing much sooner and faster than the other girls, earning catcalls and commentary from boys and even men who should have known better — back when she'd still just wanted to play soccer and do ballet and not have to adjust to a new body and what it meant.

But in the effort to kickstart their love life, Neve had discovered a love of sexy costumes and lingerie — when she found something that fit — and she wasn't averse to some of the basic S&M they'd experimented with, either. All of that was Endorphins 101. The only problem with those little experiments was that they still hadn't led to the kind of sex Joseph had been going for.

"Would you?" he said, his lips brushing her neck like a kiss.

That whisper in her ear was supposed to do something to her. She could tell, because he always squirmed when she did it to him, and he did it to her when he was in a mood.

When they reached the fortune teller tent, he guided them not to the entrance but behind it. There weren't a lot of places to hide from other people in an open circus, but he chose the side where fewer people would see them, a dead zone between Oddity Row and the fortune teller.

"God, you're beautiful." Joseph stroked her cheek, which must have been as flushed as his, but from the cold. "I don't tell you enough. They don't know what you look like under those winter layers, but I do, and I keep seeing you in all the girls' tiny costumes. Dancing, flirting, tumbling, walking a tightrope... It's hot."

She knew what he liked, and she met his kiss as he opened his coat and pulled her against him, accepted him when he unbuttoned her coat, too. Their thick coats provided cover as she brought her hips against his erection and he palmed her breasts. He'd come once just from handling her breasts, nearly smothered between them at the time, which she thought might qualify him for something in the realm of fetish. It didn't bother her in the slightest.

It was comfortable for her to have him there against her, holding her, but it just wasn't hot, and no matter how she tried to pretend it was, he could tell. Maybe she had to know what it was like to enjoy sex to fake it.

In fact, realizing she was faking it just frustrated him more, which sent him right over the edge to angry. And she hardly blamed him.

But she couldn't explain in a way he could understand that he *did* turn her on. He lit up something wonderful and exciting in her, but it wasn't lust. She wanted the former to be enough, or at least she wished she could fake the latter well enough to make both of them happy.

Hard to do when any suggestion of sex these days made her stomach drop and her throat tighten. Dread wasn't much of an aphrodisiac in the bedroom — or out of it, when one's husband was trying to be young, impetuous and frisky like a teenager in a sexy circus that was *supposed* to drive people this kind of crazy.

Joseph sighed, leaning his forehead against hers. He kept his hands on her breasts, under her sweater but over her bra. He had big hands that couldn't hope to hold all of her, which was apparently how he liked it. He gave her all the back rubs she wanted to help her

17

deal with the backaches, and when she didn't have access to a heavy-duty sports bra, exercise was out of the question unless she wanted to risk boob punches and pain. Her biggest problem with them, though, was entirely how others reacted. But she could stand her husband's attachment if it meant he hadn't noticed the way she'd stiffened.

No such luck.

"I just don't understand it," Joseph said, eyes still closed. "I don't know what else I'm supposed to do."

"I'm trying, Joe. It's not you. You know that. Please don't leave." She reached after him as he withdrew, adjusting his coat back around him. "We can go back to the car and I can take care of you…"

"It's not about you taking care of me."

Neve glanced around to see if anyone had heard him, because he wasn't whispering anymore.

"It's about being able to take care of you," he said. "It's about sparks and chemistry. And let's face it, baby, we might not have it."

"You used to love kissing me."

"Back when I thought you loved kissing me back."

"I do," she said.

He turned away, pinching the bridge of his nose. "When you're more afraid I'm going to ask for sex now than back when we were dating, something's wrong."

"Well, if you didn't pressure me by expecting it to be mind-blowing every time, maybe I wouldn't get so tense. I love you, Joseph, but you can't turn me on and off like a light switch."

He whirled back around. "I can't turn you on at all. And we've done everything right, haven't we? Counselors, doctors, switching things up. But there's just nothing! You're a fucking gorgeous woman. I want to make love to you all the time, and you feel *nothing*. If

I'd known we were going to go dry so early in our marriage, I wouldn't have..." He stopped, running both hands over his buzzed head.

"What? You wouldn't have married me?" Neve was suddenly cold all the way down to the bone, hot chocolate heat long gone. "As I recall, we had similar discussions before the wedding, and we still went through with it."

"That was when we still thought *something* would work."

She threw her hands up. "So that's it? You want to toss a whole relationship out the window, not because I *won't* have sex with you, but because I can't enjoy it as *much* as you? All the other aspects of our marriage—our Netflix binges, late nights, experimentation adventures, the fact we're so *good* together—none of that means anything because I don't have, or really need, earth-shattering orgasms? That's the hill you're going to kill our union on?"

He sighed. "Look, I'm really mad right now. I'm going to go cool off. You go ahead and do a fortune telling. We can discuss this later, when we're less upset. And frankly, when I'm less horny."

Neve tried to smile, but it died halfway through.

He took her face in his hands. "I love you, Neve, and you're my best friend. I just... I don't know how the sex part is going to work with us."

"Neither do I. But don't you think six months is too early to call it quits?"

"Maybe earlier would be better for both of us. But I'm not wanting to quit yet. I'm just frustrated."

She nodded, not quite meeting his eyes. "Sure. Go on, then. Cool off. I'll see you at the funhouse."

"It's a date." Joseph walked back toward the midway, hunched over with his hands in his coat pockets.

Neve stood behind the fortune teller's tent alone for much longer. It was too common a fight for her to cry over it anymore, but she continued to foster that niggling doubt that, though he wasn't handling the issue well, she was really the one at fault here. After all, why shouldn't someone expect their spouse to be more than happy to have sex with them, especially in the early honeymoon phase? It wasn't supposed to get stale before it even started, wasn't supposed to be scheduled until they had children.

Variety was natural, of course, and Neve defied normal in her family in many ways, but she would have been just peachy with a normal marriage. She was used to succeeding at whatever she put her mind to — not just succeeding, but being exceptional. Sex was the only thing she'd ever wanted that she couldn't do all by herself, so maybe it wasn't such a surprise that that was where she failed so spectacularly.

What made this whole thing even worse was that she'd be fine the way she was. After everything, despite her willingness to try new things, she was beginning to think this wasn't something she could change — no matter what she did, how she worked, what new ideas she conjured from self-help forums. This was what she was, and she wanted that to be okay, because when she and Joseph were doing anything else but trying to enjoy sex — and even sometimes during — she was so stinking *happy*. And she'd thought he was, too. But maybe things had always been more unbalanced between them than either had believed.

She'd been more or less honest about her nonexistent sex drive — as much as she could have been when she'd never had sex before. But Joseph had never indicated to her until today that the rest of the partnership had been in any way inadequate or didn't compare with his sexual needs. If it was bad enough that he wished they'd never married, then who was the real dishonest one here?

No. Now was no time to start the blame game. This was *their* marriage, so it was *their* problem.

Maybe she needed to start thinking even farther outside the box to satisfy them both and keep him in her life. There was always a solution. If she couldn't find one, it was usually because she wasn't looking at the problem from the right angle.

Neve rallied herself, the way she had since her older brother first told her girls couldn't be mad scientists. She'd come to Arcanium for fun. There was no reason to stop that now just because of a little fight.

There was already someone in the tent when she went back around, so she turtled herself in her lovely, warm scarf and waited, watching one of the guests at the picnic table try a fried grasshopper. Amusement eased her tension.

A couple stepped out of the tent with matching expressions of wonder and bafflement. That probably spoke well of this particular fortune teller. She wasn't sure how she felt about the whole flimflam profession, but they were an amusing diversion to challenge her mind, and a good fortune teller, like a good magician, always kept her guessing. Knowing the trick just wasn't as fun these days, although she'd loved solving the mysteries as a kid.

"Do come in," a male voice called from inside the tent. "I have my own space heater. I think you'll appreciate it."

"Oh." Neve entered the tent behind the couple and tied the tent flap closed. "I don't know why I expected a woman. I've seen all kinds."

"I hear that a lot." But although he probably did hear it multiple times an hour, he didn't appear annoyed by the repetition.

With the thick tent canvas surrounding them and a tent flap that probably stayed closed more often than not, the space heater he'd enticed her with had warmed pretty much the whole room, which was bigger than she would have expected. The fortune teller stood by a pair of small, velvet-draped parlor tables. The rest of the space appeared to exist solely to create ambience and give the incense plenty of square volume to suffuse. Beads and scarves hung from the conical ceiling, and behind the palmistry tables hulked a sideboard decorated with salt lamps, candles, carved wooden idols and crystals, including a nearly glass-like crystal ball and what appeared to be a highly included clear quartz skull. A low, winged armchair had been angled on an oriental rug in the corner, but it was empty.

On the second table, the fortune teller had arranged a phrenology bust, several hands of old tarot cards for the visitor to select and what looked like a steampunked Magic 8-Ball, which made Neve giggle.

The fortune teller grinned when he saw what amused her. "You like that? It was a gift from a crafty fan. At least two of my oddities are going to enjoy this. Do join me. It's warmer at the table."

"*Your* oddities?"

"I'm but a humble fortune teller by day, but behind the curtain, Arcanium is mine. Have you enjoyed your visit so far?" He remained standing like a gentleman until she'd taken the seat opposite him.

"I love it, especially Oddity Row. I've heard the haunted funhouse is one of the best, too, so I'm looking forward to that."

"I pride myself on doing well with what I'm given. But not everything went well during your visit today, did it? Trouble in paradise." He placed his right hand palm up on the table.

She offered her hand palm up as well, but he turned it around to move the wedding ring on her finger, a small diamond inset within the platinum band rather than displayed in a setting — that way she could wear it under her latex gloves at work rather than string it on a necklace like some of the married women who worked in the same lab.

Joseph's parents had protested it wasn't enough, that she could absolutely ask for a bigger rock because he could afford it. But Neve had told Joseph exactly what she'd wanted. It was only a symbol, a small diamond as enduring as a large one.

"How did you — Oh, never mind." She laughed to conceal embarrassment that stopped just short of humiliation. "I shouldn't be surprised when you do that. But you heard us, didn't you?"

"My ways are often mysterious, my dear, but they can be quite mundane as well, if you permit me the confession."

"Were we that loud?"

"You were that close." He nodded to the sideboard. "The canvas is thick, but it's certainly not a wall."

"Please tell me you weren't with a customer," Neve said.

"Despite all my training to tell you what you want to hear…"

"Oh God." Neve pulled her hand from the fortune teller's and covered her face.

"They've already forgotten it." The fortune teller came around the table and knelt in front of her. He took her wrists, parted them. "There now. No need to cover

23

such a pretty face. I manage dozens of people in this dramatic profession. Scandal doesn't scare me away, and it shouldn't make you so ashamed."

"It's not the issue so much as the venue." When he let her go, she unwound her scarf. Turned out space heaters and embarrassment did wonders for fighting the winter chill.

"I completely understand. But let's start again, love, as though none of the trouble outside ever happened." He placed both hands on the table and beckoned for hers. "A blank slate, in return for a moderately overpriced fee that you may place under the Fantastic Mr. Magic 8-Ball."

"Sounds reasonable." She paid him then offered her hands again.

He bent over them, stroking over the lines in the palm with his thumbs. The way he shifted them independently but with purpose made her suspect he was ambidextrous.

Her friends often found the things that intrigued her odd. For instance, she'd noted he wasn't wearing a stitch of clothing above his black leather pants, if accessories didn't count as clothing, but the possibility of him being ambidextrous fascinated her more. Good-looking half-naked men could be found everywhere, but perfect ambidexterity wasn't so common.

"Ah, a scientist but not a skeptic."

"Is that not something you see often?" she asked.

"Believe it or not, artists challenge me the most. The right-brained guests who pass through my tent tend to be far more open to the experience of the supernatural or divine."

"I believe it. I don't know if you're really supernatural or not, but you're interesting—and beyond that, does it matter?" Neve shrugged. "Besides, 'supernatural' is a misnomer. What we call 'supernatural' is all too often just 'natural' we can't explain. Algebra would probably be called numerology if you go back far enough. Chemistry would be alchemy. We think that because we know so many things now, we must know almost everything, and therefore anything we don't know must be 'magic'. I'm confident we'll eventually understand the things we attribute to magic or to aliens or to God, but I think it'll take a lot longer than we think."

"Quite a blasphemous tongue for a believer." It was hard to tell whether the ankh charm he wore on his necklace or the crystals around him signified he was pagan or whether those were all just figments of his persona, but she didn't detect contempt.

"Not really. Just because I say God operates within natural laws He existed in before He turned around and created them for us doesn't mean I'm saying He isn't there or that He isn't God or isn't powerful. Believing scientific principles hold up—and if they don't, that they'll be adjusted to accommodate new knowledge—and believing in God isn't a contradiction from where I sit."

"A rousing thesis for why the analysts who present me their palms tend to have more faith than the relativistic creatives." The fortune teller caressed her lines again in a manner she was sure had earned him his share of blushing maidens. "I'm being overly simplistic, of course. There are a variety of factors that influence why a customer believes or does not believe in me."

"Have you ever convinced someone who didn't believe in you that you were the real thing?"

"What a delightful question. Yes. I'm unusually convincing."

Neve leaned in with an arch of her eyebrow. "Then convince me."

His grin deepened without broadening. He had striking eyes—hazel, with light enough brown that it created the illusion of a golden glow. They were bright against his darkened skin. If he insisted on spending his time half-naked even in the dead of winter, it was no wonder he was so sun-kissed. Strangely, despite the fact he looked at least ten years older than her, that much sun hadn't yet translated into dark spots, freckles or the leathering of his complexion.

"Yes, ma'am. Well then, you're not the eldest of the four children in your household. Despite—or perhaps because of—the chaos you grew up in, you're far happier when it's quiet, which was why you chose a profession where you work alone, albeit with other people near you, and where you don't need to speak often."

"No way." She grinned. The corners of his eyes showed smile lines that reminded her of Joseph, although his were not as pronounced. "You don't even know my name, and I'd swear Joseph didn't say it, so you couldn't have googled me beforehand."

"Do you see a computer in here? Where would I put a phone in these pants?"

"Touché."

"I should say so. I take it you're a fan of the eldritch and weird?" He nodded to her stuffed Cthulhu, who she'd set next to the phrenology bust.

"Lifelong. My parents figured it out early when I started digging up worms at four and searching the woods behind my grandparents' cabin for wendigo, witches and werewolves when I was six. Lord knows what I would have done if I'd found one."

"You wouldn't have done anything. The witch might have found you charming enough as a ginger…"

"Hey, I have a soul," she said playfully.

"Our Bearded Lady is the closest we have to a redhead, and she has more heart than the rest of us, so you'd be hard-pressed to convince me of her lack of soul. But regardless of beauty, charm or soulfulness, the wendigo and werewolf would have swallowed you right up." He still held her hands, although he wasn't even looking at them anymore. She liked the familiarity of the contact, the comfort of it.

"Are you telling me those are real, too?"

"Have you not met my werewolf yet? Of course not. You planned to visit the funhouse afterward. But you will meet him. And I'm employing dark arts just by reading your palms, love. That makes me a witch, doesn't it?"

"I meant 'crone', but I suppose when the supernatural becomes natural, it tends to lose its mysterious appeal."

She was already feeling so much better. The reading was worth it for the conversation alone. As he'd pointed out, she didn't speak much at work, but preferring silence most of the time didn't mean she didn't have plenty to say. And it often seemed easier to say it with a stranger than with friends. It wasn't until she'd met Joseph that she'd realized she could be talkative with people she knew, too.

"I hope not, my dear. There's still wonder to be found in real magic." He pulled away from her palms, leaving them deliberately on the table to indicate she should keep them there.

"I'm often awed by nature. No mystery needed," she said. "Walking through Oddity Row awed me. Even if just the insects, spiders and snakes are real, that's enough wonder for me right there."

"Oh, many of them are quite real." He straightened from where he'd been rummaging through one of the sideboard drawers. His smirk was gone, replaced with a quiet seriousness that sobered her. "I may sometimes embellish, but I rarely counterfeit. In fact, if I were plainer about what was real and what isn't, many of my guests would experience far more discomfort than they'd enjoy. There's nothing wrong with a dramatic flourish to soften the blow."

He brought two short, white candles to the table and placed one in each of her palms then bent her fingers up to hold them. He blew on the candle in her right hand. A dancing flame burst to life on the clean wick. He maintained his more solemn expression, but he gave her a wink before he blew on the second to light it as well.

"Cool." Sometimes it was the littlest things that impressed.

"Thank you." When he spoke, everything he said seemed the epitome of sincerity. Even the humor had an undertone of absolute truth. Like the rest of Arcanium, one didn't expect greatness, but Neve was surprised she kept encountering it.

"How very kind of you," the fortune teller added, with enough of a pause between that and the previous thanks that it seemed to be about what she'd just thought rather than said. "Now, I'm nowhere near the open flames in your hands, am I? Nothing up my sleeves." He spread his bare arms. "There's nothing under the table, because your hands would block any mechanism I might use to manipulate the candles."

"I'll take your word for that."

"You shouldn't take my word for anything." He leaned back in his chair in a display of casual bravado, showing how far away he was from the table and the candles. A mere flicker wouldn't convince her of anything, because even a focused blow from a distance could influence flame. But she thought he wouldn't limit himself to that, impressive small magic notwithstanding.

"Your right hand represents your head. Your left hand represents your heart. If I lie, nothing will happen. I'll make every effort not to lie, but if I do, neither flame will change. If I speak the truth, the flames should change. Often, both will change, but you do not always recognize the truth in both head and heart, as I'm sure you understand."

"We're talking metaphorical heart here, right?" Neve said.

"Metaphorical heart," he agreed. "Are you ready for me to begin?"

She nodded. The warmth in his voice was mesmerizing. She wondered whether he did hypnotism.

"I do private sessions now and then. I'm not averse to using the skills in my fortune telling."

"Arcanium likes multiple skills." She sounded distant from herself. She didn't think she felt especially suggestible. Just…relaxed. Open to suggestion, but not enslaved by it.

"Exactly. Now, my dear, do I speak the truth? You're a newlywed, just half a year."

The flames in both hands neither flickered nor guttered. Each flame lengthened to nearly longer than the candles themselves.

"Wow."

"Wow, indeed. Your husband is older than you by more than five years. True or false?"

Both candle flames lengthened once more.

"While I'm being honest, I cheated off of your conversation. You're a mature, even-keeled, steady young woman who wouldn't enjoy someone juvenile or thoughtless. And I extrapolated based on the sound of your husband's voice."

The candle flames remained long for a few additional seconds, so it must have been true.

He stood up from his chair and began to pace near her — just another way to show that he wasn't directly manipulating the candles in any way. She trusted her experience that the candle magic was a trick, but he was really good at driving her crazy trying to figure out how it worked without anything in his hands or connected to him.

She also found herself fascinated by the way his muscles played underneath his skin. When she looked at people, she saw their cross-section — skin, muscle, organs, bone. It didn't freak her out like it would some people. The human body was a fascinating thing. If she hadn't been afraid of accidentally killing someone, she would have become a doctor rather than work as a research lab tech. Rats were less of a moral dilemma for her than people.

"Your love of horror was what first drew you to your husband, yes?"

She nodded after the candle flames lengthened, but mostly on her heart side. "I was at a *Rocky Horror Picture Show* midnight party with friends. I went as Magenta. He came as Riff Raff with another group of friends. Then he asked me out to a haunted house. When he wanted to celebrate Christmas Eve with *Nightmare Before Christmas* and *Krampus*, I knew we were in it for the long haul."

"You didn't incorporate it into the wedding, because you wanted to keep it traditional, but you've planned to incorporate a chestburster theme to your first pregnancy announcement."

Neve nearly threw the candles away, but the head candle's flame was too high for her to trust that it wouldn't set something on fire. "Okay, how could you possibly know that? I'm not pregnant right now, am I?"

He shook his head. "No. I'm just amused by the plan."

"There's literally no way you could know that. I haven't written it down anywhere. We haven't discussed it with anyone else."

"I am exactly as advertised, love. I can see your past, your present and your future. Far be it from this flimflam artist to advertise falsely."

Now he was repeating things she'd thought but hadn't said. Neve finally felt safe enough to set the candles on the table. One of them dripped wax onto the velvet.

"It's magic," the fortune teller said.

"But *how*?"

He laughed. "Science has not yet determined how this nature works. There's much left for it to discover. After all, it took till almost the end of the last century to realize that a woman's clitoris was much more than what they saw on the outside — a gross oversight after studying the human body all these decades and centuries. Was it because they feared female pleasure or because they deemed it irrelevant?"

She shook her head. "Shameful is what it is."

"But irrelevant to you."

"Okay, now we're heading into personal territory. I'm sorry we fought outside your tent, but it was supposed to be private. Why are the candles flaring like that?" She started to stand, but the fortune teller placed a hand on her shoulder to urge her to stay. She slowly lowered herself back down.

"Your heart and head know what I said was true. You believe yourself incapable of enjoying pleasure the way other women do."

Neve narrowed her eyes, trying to detect any trace of mockery—or worse, intent. She wasn't used to a man talking with her about sex without his gaze crawling over her breasts and mentally undressing her. She didn't understand it, but she recognized when it was right in front of her.

Instead, the fortune teller was solemn once more, neither pitying nor suggestive, and his attention merely passed from the candles to her face—nowhere else. It was strange to her, as weird as his oddities. For a moment, she wondered if he was gay, except gay men seemed to get distracted by her boobs, too, so she wondered next if he was like her. Except she remembered his thumbs on her palms...

Even his smile was somehow serious this time, as though he'd again heard the whole thought progression.

"Why not ask me for the truth, Neve, and let the candles confirm? It's no coincidence you and your husband exploded outside my tent, nor is it a coincidence the problem escalated here in Arcanium. I know you want answers—answers that all your other advisors couldn't give. You've tried psychologists, a marriage counselor, a sex therapist, an endocrinologist. Everything came back normal, and every experiment failed."

Neve stood again. This time he let her. The candles blazed as though they were torches, but he didn't look at them. He faced her, and somehow she couldn't storm away, storm out. She couldn't tell if he was just that good at cold reading or whether it was all real.

It can't be real. She had an open mind, but when most magic was merely a collection of clever tricks, what were the odds this wasn't? Was she really supposed to believe Arcanium was the circus with the real thing?

But he'd called her by name, and neither she nor Joseph had used it.

"You needn't look so spooked, love. I'm just a humble fortune teller, and it's all for entertainment, isn't it? I've seen your love lines. Romance is in my wheelhouse, so to speak. I'll be honest, but you don't have to take me so seriously." He nudged her chin, a sweet, sexless gesture that reminded her of her older brother at the wedding. That just left her more confused than before.

"Was marrying Joseph a mistake?" That faraway quality to her voice had returned. Thoughts swirled a few inches higher than her head, but she didn't think the fortune teller was hypnotizing her anymore.

"No."

The rush of pure relief left her shaky. Neve nearly collapsed back into the chair.

"Why do you believe it was a mistake?" He slid back into the chair across from her, the lengthened firelight only increasing the impression of glowing eyes.

"I've been worried we're on the brink of a quick turnaround divorce. Silly to be so relieved because a fortune teller told me it was okay, I know." She dabbed at the corner of her eye to catch the tear before it smeared her eyeliner. "Might as well read my horoscope for advice."

"You misunderstand me, my dear. Just because it wasn't a mistake to marry your husband doesn't mean it was meant to last."

Following the same chemical path as relief came the sickening, sinking feeling that the ride was dropping too fast. But this was no ride, and now that she'd started, she wasn't certain she could stop — or that she should.

"My dear, a feat that fails is not failure in itself. A mistake would have been marrying your sweetheart in spite of hating him. Or if he'd hurt you or cheated and you thought marriage would protect you from those things. You married for love. That is not failure."

"Do I love him?" she asked softly.

"Do you?"

"Do I really love him if I can't…" She had trouble saying it with someone who wasn't Joseph. She gestured vaguely to her hips.

His eyes sparkled with mirth. "There are many facets to love. But you never questioned the depth and sincerity of your love for him until he did."

She reached across the table to cover his hands, which were loose fists on either side of the truth candles. He raised his eyebrows but didn't withdraw.

"We've done so much to figure out how to make it work, but there doesn't seem to be any way to make me… What's *wrong* with me?"

"Neve, they couldn't find anything wrong because there is nothing wrong with you."

She pushed her chair back away from the table, where the head candle had remained the same but the heart candle's fire burned so high and hot that the bottom half of the flame was blue. Wax dripped down the side of the heart candle like blood. She blew both candles out. The tent was suddenly silent.

"What do you mean there's nothing wrong with me? Of course there's something wrong with me. We wouldn't be searching for solutions if there wasn't a problem."

He stood and stepped around the table. "Oh, there's a problem in your marriage, but its source is not your lack of interest, nor is that a symptom. Your asexuality is innate, inherent, genetic, irreparably bound to your mind and body."

"Even if it's coded into my DNA, sir, rather than a hormonal imbalance or benign tumor, that doesn't change that something's wrong. Sexuality is part of being human. Sex is what keeps our species going, growing, changing, mutating—keeps us variant and strong. Without it, what does that make me? Less than human?"

"What poison have you been listening to, love?" He stroked her hair back from her face, tucked a stray lock behind her ear. "If you want to make a scientific argument, there are plenty of biological and anthropological reasons for a person to be celibate and absent average sexual desire, just as there is for the opposite. And as you've already noticed, I abhor normal the way nature abhors a vacuum."

"I don't mind being weird, but is it so wrong to want to be normal in some ways? This is my marriage we're talking about, marriage to someone I love, but I don't know if I love him enough to even call it love anymore. And if I can't love him enough, I'm going to lose him."

"You've already considered many other options than fixing what isn't wrong," the fortune teller said. "Has *he* considered any other options other than fixing you?"

Neve racked her brain for some sort of answer for him, some way to defend Joseph from what seemed like unfair targeting on the fortune teller's part. He couldn't understand why this was so important to her—that it was part of her job as a wife to make her husband feel at his best whenever she could, that her deficiency contributed to his own sense of deficiency, that she wanted to please him with her pleasure more than anything, just as he wanted to give her pleasure with his. A certain disconnect between timing and preference was to be expected, but they hadn't anticipated such a profound disconnect, and there was no way he could have known in the beginning that none of their experimentations would bear fruit.

"You think I don't understand, but I understand so much better than you know," the fortune teller said. "I'll admit, though, that I'm biased toward those who believe themselves to be freaks."

"Is that what I am?" Neve asked.

"You're not average. You are uncommonly lovely, intelligent, articulate and you aren't driven by the same lust that fuels the rest of us, which some would call a blessing. There are much fewer entanglements in the name of love than there are in the name of lust. You're not normal, but you're far from a freak. But whether you're a freak or not, you feel like one, and he does nothing to assuage that feeling. He blames you for his sense of inadequacy, and you blame yourself for something over which you have no control. There is no reason why you and your husband can't be happy that you found each other without this matter getting in the way, but I'm afraid such reconciliation seems unlikely."

"Why?" she asked.

"Because you and he have done everything you could think of to change you. You've done nothing to try to change him."

"But I'm the one who's wrong." Her throat felt thick, as though a prickly seed had lodged itself in the center.

"No, you're the one who isn't normal. *He's* the one who's wrong."

She dabbed again at the corner of her eye with her fingertip, willing herself control over her emotions. She had to endure a certain amount of turmoil from her husband, but she didn't have to pay the fortune teller for the displeasure. She'd already humiliated herself in front of him enough. No need to add crying to the list.

She didn't reach the tent flap in time to escape. A strangled sob wrenched through her throat before she could stop it.

Nothing was going the way she'd wanted it to. Arcanium was supposed to have been a good date, something that reminded her and her husband of why they loved each other, why they'd gotten together in the first place. Visiting the fortune teller was supposed to have made her feel better after her fight, not worse. And a silly fortune wasn't supposed to upset her this much.

But the fortune teller wasn't doing what he was supposed to do either. Psychic predictions were all about tall, dark strangers and coming into inheritances, prospects looking good in the near future, no shaking hands with southpaws. If he'd wanted to get the most out of her, he would have told her that change was possible, that she and her husband could still make their marriage work if they saw someone on the quarter moon while Mercury was out of retrograde, after sacrificing a pear to the chicken gods — with his help.

A psychic wasn't supposed to tell her there was no hope for her marriage, no hope for change.

"Neve. Please." The fortune teller placed a hand on her shoulder. "It is my nature to meddle, but my intentions are neutral, believe me."

That was an interesting way to put it. But she still should have known better than to open her heart to a confidence man, albeit one who considered himself chaotic neutral instead of lawful evil. And a fortune teller should know to stick to fortunes rather than attempt armchair psychology, as though she and Joseph hadn't tried real psychology on so many levels.

"Do not leave this tent angry," he said. "There's more yet I can do for you that has nothing to do with the heart line or your heartstrings."

When she turned back around, no effort to duck her head could hide that she was fighting a losing battle against tears.

The fortune teller frowned. He opened the leather bag he wore on his belt to pull out a white handkerchief. She would have taken it, but he eased her hands away. Instead, with the care of someone accustomed to working around makeup—though he wore none of his own, not even eyeliner to match the leather pants—he gently caught each tear that fell over the edge of her eyes.

"Sweet Neveline. Not wanting sex is far from the end of the world."

"How do you know that name? Only my dad calls me that. It's not my real name, not anywhere online."

"I know." He folded the handkerchief then tucked it back in his bag. "There, no damage done."

She took a cautious step back. "Who are you?"

"Bell Madoc, the owner of this circus and quite good at my job. Not average at all, I'd say."

"How can you know these things?"

"Because I am expected to know them. I apologize if I overstepped what you believe should be my boundaries. I get carried away with my own understanding and penchant for dramatic flourish."

She swiped at the last of her tears and prayed that would be the end of it. "You weren't *entirely* wrong. I just hope you are."

"I'd rather you didn't hope I was wrong. I would rather you embrace what you are."

"I think it's normal to want to change things about yourself." Neve sniffed as she undid the buttons of her coat. Between the space heater and the emotional upheaval, she was actually starting to overheat. "Look, we'll deal with the sex issue eventually. We have to. It's important to him, and it's important to me. No offense, but despite your 'neutral' intentions, we're not going to make our decisions based on the recommendations of a fortune teller."

"Wise. Although I hope you are kinder to yourself in pursuit of change."

His amusement had returned, as though solemnity were nothing but another part of the show. And it probably was.

"I'm sorry I cried. I'm betting weepy customers aren't your preference."

"Tears, like screams, signify an emotional reaction, one entertainment is meant to evoke. You needn't apologize. Finances are the primary strain upon a relationship. Intimacy is a close second."

She sighed. "I enjoy it in my own way. But when I experience him enjoying it, I feel like I'm missing something important, unable to understand why he feels so much and I feel so little. I wish I could enjoy sex the way he wants me to, but there's just nothing. Most cases of asexuality have a cause. If it's not an obvious one, then there must be an unobvious one. I don't intend to stop looking." She hugged her stuffed Cthulhu. "I've been here God knows how long. I don't want to dominate your time, and I certainly don't intend to pay for more than the original price. I have to thank you for such a wonderful circus and carnival experience, though, at least before my personal problems decided to take over."

"It was no trouble accommodating you, and I wouldn't dream of charging extra for a few minutes over. But while we're on the subject, Neve..." He curled his fingers around her wrist before she could leave, his knuckles nudging her stuffie. "What if there *were* another way for you to change your capacity for sexual pleasure?"

"Is this where you take out Love Potion No. 10 and say it can be mine today with five easy payments?" She would hate it if that were so. It would cheapen the whole confusing time she'd spent with him.

But she felt strange with his hand around her wrist, stranger as he slowly drew her back toward him. He wasn't forceful, but he was undeniable, his bright eyes intense over cheekbones cut from glass.

There was that sense he was hypnotizing her again. She was lightheaded, breathing shallow, but there was another quality underneath—one she couldn't put name to.

"What if I told you that you just found the only natural loophole to an unchangeable sexuality? I would have preferred for you to stay as you were, but you're far more useful to me this way."

"I don't understand." Neve tried to ease her wrist from his grasp, but he somehow used the attempt to bring her closer still.

"You're a woman of science, yes? What would you say to another experiment? I doubt an elder god would mind his present position."

Bit by bit, Bell had eased her close enough that the stuffed Cthulhu was caught between them. Bell suddenly seemed very naked. And she seemed quite clothed, layer upon layer, yet not enough for how close he'd somehow brought them. Close enough to dance. Close enough to kiss.

Men had come this close before, had lowered their gaze from her eyes to her lips. But why had her own gaze been drawn down the line of his cheekbones to his mouth, the slightly parted lips, to the hooded eyes, to the movement and shift of the muscles of his arms, shoulders and neck? And this time, a cross-section was the farthest thing from her mind.

When she trembled, only part of it was from nervousness. "What are you doing?"

"Let me kiss you."

She was almost certain she was supposed to reel back. Instead, her mouth went dry, and a kind of tingling urge underneath her lips seemed to draw her closer. It was horrifying and exciting at the same time, but she didn't know what it was, didn't know where it came from.

"Let me kiss you, and you'll know what your husband wants you to feel. I wouldn't ask for more than testing a scientific theory. Just a kiss, and you can be on your way with your husband—not fixed, but altered."

"What the hell are you talking about?" It came out a whisper, because he brought her wrist to his mouth and saluted it, the way a gentleman might kiss the hand of a lady, but this action was far from that of a gentleman.

"Permission, my lady?" He smiled against her wrist.

There he went again, saying things as though he knew exactly what she'd been thinking. At that moment, peering into the uncommon dark amber of his irises, she could believe he was actually reading her mind.

Her face suffused with heat, heat that seemed to sink down her spine with little electrical shocks that weren't painful at all.

Bell threaded his fingers through her hair, pushed the rubber band from her ponytail to let the rest spread loosely over the shoulders of her coat. She loved when people played with her hair, when nails would scratch over skin, especially during the winter months when no amount of conditioner kept her scalp from itching. His caress over her head and the light pull of each follicle had the old familiar comfort, but also a whole new sense of intimacy that no closeness had ever inspired before.

"What are you doing to me?"

"What you should ask, my dear, is what I've *done* to you." He angled her head as effortlessly as he'd pulled her in, as though their very closeness now was just another illusion.

But in being so close to him, she wanted something more than real, something she didn't have words for. She was certain, as she was that the Earth revolved around the sun, that Bell knew what she wanted — and that he wanted to show her.

She tentatively slid a hand over his shoulder at the base of his neck. He was even more of a furnace half-naked than Joseph was fully clothed. He felt like fever to her cold hand, but she couldn't escape how smooth and soft his skin was, like good leather over the defined, surprisingly hard muscle underneath, but no mistaking it as anything but warm, living flesh. She'd never been quite this fascinated by the texture of skin before, although she'd enjoyed the sensation of leather when she and Joseph had experimented with S&M play.

An experiment, he'd called it.

"Yes," she whispered.

The kiss was chaste, just a touch of his lips to hers. Her awareness narrowed to his thumb on her wrist, his fingers over her scalp and the sensation of his lips brushing hers.

The stuffed elder god fell to the ground.

Bell pushed her coat back as he wrapped an arm around her waist, and when he brought her hips to his, she couldn't help the gasp that parted her lips. He didn't waste time, didn't give her an opportunity to think about what was happening to her. The closest thing she could compare it to was the shock of adrenaline that followed the best jump scare in her favorite horror movies, the ones that made her think her heart was going to stop.

She had once loved making out with Joseph, although prior to him, she hadn't much enjoyed tongues in her mouth. There was a theory that kissing was an immunological booster, exposing oneself to another person's microbial biome and gradually inoculating oneself to a different environment. Mouths were supposed to be one of the germiest places, after all. A human bite was more dangerous than a dog bite. All of that was the unsexy, scientific side of romance. No one was ever going to hire her to write romantic sentiments. She couldn't think of many greeting cards that went 'Let's make our immune systems stronger together.'

In practice, however, making out with Joseph was good for her because she liked the contact, liked the closeness, liked becoming a part of him. And if the scientific theories behind it were a contributing factor, she made sure to save that for when they weren't fooling around on the couch or in bed with his hand up her shirt. Before they'd married, he'd laugh whenever she'd mention it during, which would kill the mood —

albeit in an amusing way. After they'd married, he didn't laugh anymore. Talking about that kind of thing was just another way in which his wife might as well be an android when he'd thought he'd married a woman.

Right now, not a single biological thought entered her brain, which was suddenly filled with sensations too big for her, feelings ready to burst like grapes under a heel. But she didn't know whether it would be painful, or where it was going to burst.

Bell was achingly slow, still gentle, but when he ran his tongue along the tip of hers, she nearly died. Some part of her might have, because she weakened against him. Her hips shifted against the front of his pants, and her breasts pressed to his chest. She parted her lips to take him deeper, to suck the length of his tongue, suddenly making a connection between their kiss and his cock twitching in its confines against her hip.

With Joseph, she'd known how to move against him to make him moan, to give him an erection, to bring him to his climax. She'd memorized his groans, followed where he'd guided her, learned his pleasure the way a foreign student learned English. She'd done what needed to be done, because she loved giving him pleasure.

Now she understood. She understood that other women did those things because their bodies told them to be a complement to their partner's. Her hips were drawn to Bell's, her tongue to his, her lips to his. She moved her hand from his shoulder to the back of his neck, pulling him closer because *she* wanted him closer, not just because *he* wanted her closer. For the first time, she understood the push and pull of selfishness in a kiss, in the art of making love — one partner balancing what they wanted with what the other wanted, and sometimes those innate desires meeting in a spontaneous moment of equally shared lust, giving in the act of taking.

It was a revelation. She understood. She understood the songs her sisters listened to, the songs Joseph listened to, the songs her parents listened to. She'd always preferred instrumentals and movie soundtracks, but when she'd found Joseph, she'd finally understood the love songs.

With Bell, she finally understood the lust songs.

She chased his tongue, bit his lip. She'd always thought describing lust as hunger was just a metaphor, but she was surprised to learn that it wasn't. She wanted flesh in her mouth, wanted the taste of him over her tongue, could smell his sweat, craved something salty.

Neve had cultivated a repertoire of sounds that the men in her life enjoyed—based off of their own, based off of movies, based off of porn she'd studied despite her general distaste for the loosely termed 'art'. As Bell massaged her scalp and met her tongue with his with each pass of their kiss, she learned which sounds were her own because they weren't calculated anymore. They weren't chosen and disseminated like Halloween candy, treats to avoid a trick. Each sigh, each moan— which he rewarded with a deepening of the kiss, a moan of his own or pulling back until his lips merely grazed hers and she had to chase him again—were her own, of their own accord.

Neve didn't think she'd ever been this out of control of her own body's responses. She wasn't a person, of flesh, blood and bone. She was sensation, the quickening of her heart, the drive inside her to press forward, to take more and more and more from him. But now that it was her body that wanted it rather than her wanting to please, she was paralyzed on how to begin, only that she didn't want this kiss to stop, didn't want this terrible, wonderful chaos to end.

She shrugged her coat off. Then she smoothed her hands over the godlike planes of his back and canted her hips closer. The erection that pressed back excited her.

So this is pleasure. This was what they meant, this susurrus of sibilant words that people used to describe these fundamental biological urges that she'd literally never had—not to this degree, not to this intensity. Just the promise of his cock against her abdomen was more intense than any orgasm she'd ever given herself.

Now she wanted to know what an orgasm was supposed to feel like.

She brought her hands to the front of his leather pants.

He stepped back, stopping her.

As soon as the sexual contact ended, everything else rushed back.

Neve jerked away from Bell, covering her mouth. She'd been so swept up that she'd forgotten what she was doing and with whom.

She'd nearly forgotten her own name. Biological urges had almost driven her to do more than kiss a man who wasn't her husband—already well over the line between a harmless experiment and unacceptable intimacy.

She began to understand why Bell had said that a lack of sexual interest could be seen as a blessing.

Neve backed away, holding her hands in front of her in case Bell tried to follow. He didn't, so she felt safe grabbing for the things she'd discarded on the ground. "Why did you— Why would you do that?"

"I needed to show you."

"Not like that, you didn't."

"You agreed to it," he said. "I wouldn't have done it if you hadn't agreed."

"I agreed to a kiss. One kiss. You could have let me figure it out on my own. Or you could have told me to try being with my husband tonight. You didn't have to do it this way. For God's sake, you know I'm married."

"As when I used the candles, I needed you to trust that what I was saying was completely true. I needed you to return to your husband with conviction. He could have been good enough for you, but he isn't. He doesn't deserve you. However, you should have what you want, and you've decided that you want him." Rather than advance on her, he backed away to his chair on the other side of the parlor table.

"I trusted you. I thought you were like me."

He actually laughed. "Why would you think that?"

"Because men stare at me. You didn't. Not until you started to…" Before, she couldn't say 'sex' or 'making love', and now she couldn't find it within her to say 'kiss'. At the rate she was going, she wouldn't be able to say anything unless it was pre-approved by a nun.

"I have discipline other men lack. Not to mention I can tell when a woman isn't interested, so I proceed to not pursue her, which by some men's estimation is a Herculean trial. In your case, some might argue that's not hyperbole. But someone—something—like me doesn't know what it's like to lack sexual pleasure. We are creatures of pleasure, you see. Forged in fire, we are not slaves to our passions, as man is, but we are defined by them."

"What the heck is that supposed to mean?"

"A smart woman like you should be able to find out. All you need to know, gingersnap, is that your wish has been granted, and I wanted you to be certain of it."

Neve alternated between wanting to run out of the tent and turning back to the fortune teller, swallowed back the impulse to ask for the catch—because none of this made any sense. She'd said fifty times that she wanted to enjoy sex with her husband, and forty-nine times, he'd said she couldn't. Then suddenly there was this loophole.

"You. You did this," she said. "You altered something inside me, just like you could hear my thoughts. Because you *were* hearing my thoughts, weren't you? There's no way you could know some of the things you know. No earthly way."

"I do admire that open mind of yours, my dear. More people could stand to have one. Now, go and reunite with your husband for that second honeymoon. I'm sure you'll both be thrilled. You'll be able to satisfy him, but do you really think he will ever satisfy you?"

He kicked his legs up onto the table and crossed them at the ankles, his heavy boots thudding against each other. "Of course, there's an alternative. You could stay with me. Arcanium more than satisfies, little girl. You haven't yet begun to tap the surface."

No, he wasn't leering, but she didn't like the way he looked at her now. Proprietary. His smirk was a touch too wide, and the glow in his eyes took on new meaning, because he *had* done something. She was almost certain of it now. And that just brought up the question of what else he could do.

Thinking about Oddity Row gave her a chill.

She shook her head, backing slowly toward the tent flap, this time the way she would walk away from a predator—not taking her eyes off of it in case it decided to strike.

"Very well." He nodded in farewell. "Thank you, my dear."

"Thank you." Neve believed in being polite to powerful people, powerful things, but she fumbled behind her for the tie to the tent entrance.

"You're most welcome."

She stumbled out into the circus proper, startled by the bright afternoon light, sunbeams diffused through thin cloud cover that told her it would likely snow later. The forecasts had said it might sometime that evening or during the night. She could smell it in the sharpness of the air, under the enticements of the food court and the scent of canvas, large herbivores and leather.

Out in the light, what had just happened already seemed distant, more benign, like the lancing of a boil. But it had happened.

She was…cured?

Neve closed her eyes and thought of her husband. Thought of the way he'd kissed her after the Ferris wheel, the way he'd whispered in her ear, caressed and fondled her breasts in the middle of the circus where anyone could have walked around the tent and caught them.

Her nipples tightened under her bra. She had to resist the urge to touch them, stroke all around them, pinch them until they were dark pink. Joseph had liked to do that, but it was a little uncomfortable, so she hadn't understood when he'd asked her to do the same to him. She pulled on the straps of her bra to create a small measure of friction, but that just made it worse, like scratching a mosquito bite. Lord help her, was this what it was like for everyone else all the time? How did anyone manage to get anything done?

But it confirmed that what had happened in the tent was real. She *wanted* Joseph's hands on her breasts, wanted him to kiss her for more than closeness or health benefits, wanted him to lead her to the car and push her into the back seat, wanted their heated bodies to fog up the glass. The thought of him kissing her inner thigh, of his cock entering into her, filled her not with discomfort or dread but with such a strong pang of need, she once again initially thought she was hungry, except the hunger was lower.

She adjusted her bra straps again then fought to hide her smile. Joseph was going to get the shock of his life.

Neve couldn't find him waiting for her outside the food count.

He might have wanted to work off some steam by throwing more things, so she checked the midway, but he wasn't there either. She peeked into Oddity Row again.

She hoped he hadn't gone into the haunted funhouse without her. If it was as scary-sexy as he'd said, maybe that could be their foreplay before she surprised him — maybe in the funhouse itself, if this hunger grew any more intense.

When she was hungry, she ate. When she was thirsty, she drank. She wasn't used to having to deny herself basic human needs. Satisfying sexual urges wasn't a basic human need. It wasn't even technically a drive, despite the common language for it. Neither she nor anyone else was going to die if they didn't get sex, and the human race would continue if she didn't procreate. It was a species imperative, not an individual one. She knew that, but it was amazing how strong something she didn't need could be.

She walked the whole length of the midway this time, straining to find him among the crowd.

On the way back to the food court, she caught movement behind one of the midway booths out of the corner of her eye — a flash of red, a long gray peacoat. The peacoat, at least, she recognized, as well as the loose plaid scarf she glimpsed as she crossed beyond the line of the midway. She could see behind every booth from there.

The woman was nearly hidden within his open coat, but it was impossible to deny what they were doing. They muffled their moans with furious kisses. He pumped his hips up into her, holding her by her thighs and pressing her against the back of the booth, which must have been constructed better than it looked, because if it had been slipshod, it would have been rocking and creaking like a swinging gate. But it held the woman, withstanding Joseph's forceful thrusts.

There was nothing loving about their coupling. He was fucking her, pure and simple, wasn't doing anything that spoke of consideration or tenderness, and she didn't appear to care.

She adjusted her legs around his waist, and Neve caught flashes of bright red glitter. The woman wasn't wearing the red falls anymore. They lay in a heap on the ground next to them. Her real hair was a bird's nest of near-black and streaks of red, but Neve hadn't recognized her until the corset was exposed. *Maya of the high wire. Sky High Maya.* Did she know she was fucking a married man? Did she know the same woman she'd flirted with and kissed was that man's wife? Did that matter to her, or was she a slave to her own pleasure as much as Joseph?

It would have been so much easier to hate Maya, but there was no ring on Maya's finger. She was guilty of poor judgment, of aiding and abetting. Joseph knew about the ring on his own finger. He'd opined about the failure of their marriage, but that had been worlds away from serving Neve papers. They were still married, still bound to each other and no other, nor had they agreed to widen the circle of what constituted fidelity in their marriage the way Neve had been considering.

She'd thought this man loved her. Love might not have been enough to keep them together, but it should have been enough to keep him from stepping out of their marriage before its end.

Somehow, the fortune teller was right again. She fought the urge to laugh and cry at the same time.

Neve heard them as though she were right next to them, nothing but air and distance to obstruct the low gasps and groans of sex, of pleasure, of growing desperation. Neve knew that quality of Joseph's groans from their dark bedroom. He'd tell her how good she felt to him, that he was close, that he was going to come...

He whispered in Maya's ear the way he would whisper to his wife. Maya hooked her arm around his neck and rode him faster, one of her breasts exposed over her pulled-down corset. She kissed him with passion Neve couldn't have hoped to fake.

Neve couldn't look away, turned on and horrified at the same time, watching her husband feeling all the things she'd wanted him to feel with her — the things she could have felt with him later that afternoon or evening. She'd wanted him to clutch *her* thighs, press *her* breasts to his chest, tweak her nipple, kiss her as though he needed her to breathe, kiss down her neck, sink his cock deep into her while she rode him back.

But she watched helplessly as the man she loved completely — and she could swear what she'd felt for him had been a kind of love, intense and inexorable, unconfused by sexual desire — made himself filthy on and inside another woman. She couldn't imagine easing his cock into her now, not after Maya's wetness had mingled with his pre-cum. She couldn't imagine kissing him again when she'd never be able to forget how he'd kissed Maya, exactly as he'd kissed Neve in the past. He seemed to gather the corset glitter in the creases and lines of his palm, as though if he were to touch Neve, he'd smear that red glitter all over her with the memory of the other woman he'd touched.

Neve thought she was going to throw up.

He clutched at Maya's hair, dug his fingers into her thigh under her feather bustle. He didn't have to concern himself with bringing Maya off first, because Maya panted open-mouthed into his kiss, shaking in his arms, her hips and abdomen rolling through her climax. Joseph wasn't far behind. He slammed into her as his own pleasure pangs shot through him. He couldn't quite muffle his grunts in her shoulder.

"That bastard," Bell murmured behind her.

She spun around. No one was there.

When she turned back, Joseph had tucked himself back into his shorts and was zipping up his jeans. Maya adjusted her costume then picked up her falls, shaking out any stray twigs and leaves before pinning the falls back into her hair. Her smile was as dazzling as when she'd taken pictures with them on the Ferris wheel, oddly sincere and even guileless for a woman who'd just helped a husband cheat on his wife. She kissed his cheek again, this time not leaving a mark. Most of her lipstick had smeared over and around her lips, but in a way that still worked for the mad Queen of Hearts look she'd chosen, which probably explained why she said 'thank you' — Neve could read her lips — and left just as she was, returning to the midway.

Half of the lipstick had ended up on Joseph's mouth, though, and some on his neck. He spat on his fingers and rubbed away at it, probably wishing for a mirror.

When he started to use the tail of his shirt, he saw her.

Neve's first instinct was to run, run back to Bell and ask him what she was supposed to do. But whether he was fake or real, depending on a fortune teller was a bad precedent to set.

She'd stood up against her brothers, her father, against fellow students, teachers, coworkers. She could stand up against her husband—the man she should have been standing up against the world with. She wasn't going to run. That was the lizard hindbrain talking. She was a human woman at the beginning of the twenty-first century. She wasn't going to run from her own cheating husband.

Every step she took was like a mermaid's on land—walking on knives, except the knives went straight into her heart—her metaphorical heart. Funny how a metaphorical thing could hurt so much.

Recognition, shock, shame, anger and contrition passed over Joseph's expression like watercolors.

"Neve, I—" He tucked in his shirttail, wiped his mouth with the back of his hand, but he had no way of knowing that he hadn't wiped off nearly enough of the lipstick. It was such a vibrant color, even a little would have been obvious to her. He kept adjusting his shirt, his scarf, his coat, trying to put himself back together, back to how he'd been before Maya, as though that would somehow take it back. "I—"

"Keep trying, Joseph. I'm just dying to hear you make it my fault. I'm waiting with bated breath for the lecture that you're a man and men have different needs, even though I've offered to fulfill them at every turn—more than other wives who aren't interested in sex, I'm damned sure. But not to your satisfaction, which is why you had to look to other women, right? How many others have there been? Wait, don't answer that." Neve held up a hand to stop him from protesting. "It doesn't even matter. Whether it's a hundred women or one, it doesn't matter. You can't deny the one, Joseph, because I saw it. I saw everything."

"I was upset when I left, and I was still..." He gestured to his hips, much the way she had when she'd tried to indicate to Bell that she was deficient. "We crossed paths, and she—"

"Forced you behind the booth at knifepoint?" The laugh that bubbled up from her throat like blood was mirthless and sounded like crying, although her eyes stayed dry. "You don't even know," she said through laugh-sobs. "You don't even know what happened. God, I would have given you everything you ever wanted! And right now, I can't even look at you."

"Neve, I—"

"I don't want excuses. I don't even want an apology. I don't want you to say another word. We're going home and you're sleeping on the couch until I can look at your face without wanting to scratch it out."

She strode toward the Arcanium entrance, seething herself sick. The crunch of winter grass behind her indicated that Joseph followed, wisely doing what he'd been told.

If only she could slam the Arcanium gates shut behind her. The clang would be briefly satisfying and final. Between Maya's dazzling smile, the memory of Joseph sinking into the woman, and Bell's warnings and inexplicable power that had helped her too late, she didn't think she'd ever be able to come back here again.

Chapter Two

The snow came that night. Neve usually had to wake up before the sun rose, so she liked keeping the curtains open to catch the dawn. The night looked blue when it snowed. The layer of white reflected midnight into full-moon brightness, which angled into the bedroom, falling upon the half-empty bed. It felt so much larger without Joseph there.

It had taken her a while to get used to sharing a bed with another person, but after six months, she missed having someone there. She reached out but encountered nothing except more sheets and the duvet. She spread her legs like she was making snow angels, but there was nothing there. She didn't take up much space while sleeping. Having room to stretch out was overrated.

Especially since she desperately wanted someone in that bed. She'd put his pillow and a quilt on the sofa, and he'd showed penitent initiative by using the guest bathroom instead of the master. She couldn't call Joseph in now and reward him for his indiscretion. She still saw him with Maya every time she closed her eyes, which was not conducive to sleep, nor had it been beneficial to her appetite that evening. But while she usually preferred to sleep cocooned in the duvet and clothed in warm pajamas when it was so cold outside and in the bedroom, she kept having to fold the covers back to let her skin breathe.

Neve finally just took everything off but her panties. But being naked under the sheets, while cooler, made the sensitivity of her skin all the worse.

If she'd thought that the feelings in Arcanium were an anomaly caused by some kind of love potion aerosol that would temporarily induce sexual arousal in even the most impenetrable of asexual individuals, that doubt could now be set aside. Her instinct-driven desire hadn't abated. Just as she couldn't control imagining Joseph fucking the tightrope walker, she kept imagining herself in Maya's place, sometimes with Joseph, sometimes with Bell. The thoughts eddied around and around and around in her head.

When she tried touching herself, smoothing her hands over her abdomen and plumping her breasts, Neve bit her lip. Touching herself tonight was like touching herself for the first time, or how she imagined normal people felt touching themselves for the first time. As it had been with Bell, the feelings were so much *bigger* than she could have anticipated. But unlike when she was with Bell, it didn't quite turn off her mind. She overthought everything—every movement of her fingers, every intensified sensation. Although she'd slept naked in this bed before, she couldn't convince herself to take her panties off and touch herself there, though everything ached in what could have been pain if she hadn't wanted more of it.

She might as well get used to this, though—this ache, this dissatisfaction, this near distress. She was still married, and unlike Joseph, she believed in that vow. People dealt with sexual frustration every day, right? It was just distressing for her because it was new. And if this wasn't going away, she'd surely get used to it just like everyone else.

Neve flopped over onto her stomach and forced her eyes closed, leaving her top half and one leg uncovered to cool her down.

She'd always thought herself so distant from this particular vice. She hadn't believed she was judgmental about those who succumbed to it, and perhaps she wasn't as bad as some. But now she knew that the reason she'd always been able to withstand this temptation was because she simply hadn't been tempted. Chocolate cake and pizza, a warm bed on a cold morning when there were things to do, idleness in boredom… All of these things had been more tempting to her than sex.

People believed in divine retribution, karma, the Rule of Three and other moral laws like them for a reason. People wanted to believe justice would prevail, one way or another. They wanted to believe that even if a murderer wasn't convicted, something horrible would happen to them anyway. People liked balance, fairness, even if they didn't want to contribute to it themselves.

But most religions didn't have a system of retribution meant to occur in a person's lifetime. Karma was applied to the next life. For those who only lived once, judgment came after the life lived, and if one believed the Gospels, it had nothing to do with sin. Levels of hell and purgatory had been developed because of man's innate sense of justice, not God's. Yet God had conquered cities for slights, and Jesus cursed the fig tree because it wouldn't bear fruit out of season. People wanted to believe in the lightning.

Science had its own law of returns, albeit an oft-misunderstood one — that for every action, there was an equal and opposite reaction. Of course, most physics principles were only true in a perfect vacuum, and as Bell had mentioned before, nature abhorred a vacuum.

Neve didn't think the world was that simple. She didn't believe in consistent or instant karma. She didn't trust a justice system run by people. She believed humans placed the weight of sins on scales, not God. But she was a human animal like everyone else, and she couldn't help but discern patterns — real and false — like the rest of them.

It was difficult for her to view gaining the experience of pleasure right before her husband cheated on her so that she couldn't *use* it as a mere coincidence. Perhaps this carnal frustration was punishment for not being wife enough to her husband, that he would stray from her just to fulfill the need that she now denied him on principle. And she couldn't help but wonder whether she'd been cursed with the very thing she hadn't understood was so difficult for other people to control, just so she could finally understand — and then some.

With her brain well into contemplating the cosmic and scientific implications of the last twenty-four hours, she doubted she was going to get much sleep. If there *was* any justice in the world, she hoped Joseph was having just as much trouble, if not more.

She punched her pillow then flipped around onto her back again.

"Well, aren't you just the tastiest little thing?"

Neve gave a little scream, hurriedly covering her top half with the duvet.

Part of her expected to see Bell, although she didn't know why she would expect him at her bedroom window in the middle of a snowy night well after the circus had closed, when he was probably too tired to do anything but sleep. She didn't know how she could expect anyone at her second-story bedroom window. And she'd sign a sworn affidavit that she would never have her window open in late January.

Yet her bedroom window was open, and a man perched on its edge like a hybrid between a gargoyle, an owl and a very creepy person.

At first she thought the reason for the smoothness of his color was because of the shadows. But then he shifted and her eyes adjusted at the same time. In addition to sitting on the edge of a previously unopened window in the middle of winter, he was completely naked. The dim, blue, reflected moonlight illuminated the steam that emanated from him. Though his knee was propped up to conceal his front, the extent of leg and buttock exposed proved he wasn't wearing a stitch.

She bit back the part of her that wanted to invite him in out of the cold, a perfectly rational act of hospitality. But a strange man at her open window at midnight was not a perfectly rational thing at all.

Neve wasn't a hundred percent sure she was awake. This seemed like the kind of dream she'd have, trying to fall asleep as she had been—a tall, large, dark stranger with eye sockets so black, they were the darkest part of midnight.

"I usually don't visit someone while they're awake, but I so rarely sense sexual frustration as keen as my own. It's an awfully big bed, and it smells like a man. Does he not satisfy you?"

"Who the hell are you?" She wasn't fond of swearing, but she was tired, angry and, yes, unsatisfied. "How did you even get up here?"

There was a baseball bat under the bed and a gun in the closet safe, but to get them, she'd have to either emerge nearly naked from under the covers or drag the heavy duvet with her. He'd be able to catch her either way. She considered yelling for Joseph, but she still wasn't certain any of this was real, and she didn't want to need him for anything right now.

"It's his loss if he cannot satisfy a woman like you." He spoke in chocolate — warm, dark, rich, with the hint of a foreign accent she couldn't place, although it resembled the mild Middle Eastern accents she'd encountered at school and sometimes heard at work. "Let me in. I'll show you how a man should treat a woman. With me, you'll know satisfaction. With me, you'll never again be satisfied by another."

"I have my phone. I'm calling the police. And if you come any closer, I'm going to get the baseball bat and crack your kneecaps right after I hit a homerun on your balls."

"You don't have your phone." He spoke with absolute certainty. "And if you were going to go for a weapon, you would have already. I don't think you're afraid of me. I think your body is so distracted that you don't have enough in your head to be afraid. And that's good, woman. Shall I take up more of your mind?"

He lowered his bent leg. And though Neve couldn't see details, she didn't need to. She could see clearly enough to notice that he was definitely without any kind of covering, and the winter cold had done nothing to diminish his sexual frustration.

In such little light, Neve couldn't be positive. It could have been some kind of trick to the angle, but his full, high erection looked like it was the width of his wrist. She didn't think that was anatomically possible — and certainly not something that would be comfortable going into anyone.

But the sight of it bobbing near his thigh made her ache — and not in preemptive pain. Her lips went dry even as she salivated. Her clit twitched in odd little pulses that felt like some kind of atavistic signal, a primitive *I want* with which her cunt agreed. Her panties had already been damp from frustration, but she felt new wetness drip out.

"I'll create oblivion between your thighs, bring poetry to your lips, fire to your skin. Your body is a finely crafted instrument, and I am a master musician. Invite me into your cool, empty bed."

He brought his hand to the base of his cock, stroked himself slowly. It didn't feel like the kind of frantic perversion of a public voyeur or peeping tom. He was deliberate, the action a supplement to his words, a display of his wares.

"I have everything you've ever desired, everything you've ever fantasized about. Let me in, and I will be the fulfillment of every dream, any dream. Even now, your body makes itself ready for me, craves me. You are starving, but I am a feast, and I offer myself to you. No woman should ever go as unsatisfied as you are right now. I can practically taste the salt on your skin, the sweetness between your legs. It fills the very air, no matter how the cold tries to chase it away. You needn't suffer any longer. Let me in."

If it was a dream, it was the most intense sex dream she'd ever had. Even she had sex dreams now and then, of subjects that seemed eminently unsexy upon waking. She was capable of orgasm, so she would sometimes suffer through a meaningless one, clutching the sheets and willing it to be over.

If this wasn't a dream, it was utter madness. She'd had time to grab her phone from the nightstand drawer. She'd had more than enough time to get the baseball bat from under the bed, even with the duvet. She could do it now. He'd trip over that cock on the way to her.

But his words caressed her as though they were fingers, awakening every part of her that he spoke of. She remembered when she'd thought Bell was hypnotizing her. Neve couldn't shake the idea that this man might be doing the same thing — that he was more than just a man murmuring sweet nothings to her as he masturbated.

"Let me in. Or cast me away. But do something, woman. Don't torture me like this, able to see you, smell you, taste the mist of you but not touch, not feel you against my body. I'm as hungry as you are. So very hungry, my love. Please…" He bowed his head. The silhouette of his hair suggested it was loose and long, tangled into locks that draped past his elbows. Neve thought he was almost familiar, but she couldn't think of anyone she knew who looked like that, or anyone who could possibly be packing what he had between his legs. Scrubs and lab coats could hide a lot, but she wasn't sure anything could hide *that*.

Neve felt frozen, mesmerized by his strokes, by the way he seemed clearer and clearer to her each time he passed his hand over the shaft, as though lust attuned her senses to him.

Her breathing was loud but shallow. She'd fallen slightly forward, still using one hand to hold the duvet over her front, the other one braced on the bed between her knees. The position made her feel even more sexual, waiting for him to come up from behind and push her panties to the side, push every huge inch of that impossible cock into her cunt, where she'd take it — and gladly — because her need was even closer to painful, her wetness soaking through and smearing against the tops of her thighs. All this was impossible, but it felt so damn real, too strong to be a dream, too *strange* to be a dream, even as strange as dreams could be.

Every time she thought she'd regained control of her tongue to tell him to get out of her room, to go away, that she was definitely calling the police now, that her husband was just downstairs, he would stroke himself again, and the action would erase the board of her mind.

"At least let the covers fall. Let me see more of you. I crave the sight of your body as much as the sensation of it against my flesh. Show yourself to me."

In spite of the cold, sweat dripped down the back of her neck and the valley of her spine. She struggled to gain control over these all-too-strong, all-too-new aches and pangs of what seemed like unfiltered, unadulterated lust — just as dangerous as anything else pure. Whimpers spilled from her pressed-tight lips as she tried to hold back.

"I cannot enter unless you allow it. I cannot harm you or even touch you if you don't let me in. What harm would there be in showing yourself to me? You want to. Your nipples harden and your belly tightens at the thought of me seeing you — the thought of another man seeing what your man cannot appreciate. Even my gaze upon you will be better for you than twenty hours under his hands."

This is not normal. She didn't know what normal was, but this couldn't be it. People weren't prostrate on the ground at concerts by their favorite bands. People weren't moaning in ecstasy when their favorite song came on the radio. *I really don't think this is normal.*

"Who *are* you?" It was all she could manage to say before another pang of need cramped through her abdomen. She shook her head against another whimper.

"I'm the best sex you've ever had." His answer came to her as a promise. "Let the covers go. Lose your inhibitions. I uncovered myself, showed you my lust. I'll show you more if you show me yours."

She let the hand holding the duvet drop to the bed, hoped that giving in a little would ease some of this ache. It didn't. A sob escaped her.

It didn't help that when she lowered the cover, he doubled over with a groan of his own, and he quickened his hand over his erection.

He spoke of tasting her, but his own desire seemed to thicken her air as she breathed. As each breath entered her, it weakened her resolve. The snow-strewn breeze fluttered the curtains, struck her newly exposed skin, but though she marbled, her nipples tightening further, it had little effect on the heat inside her. She didn't need the covers when she had his gaze.

"You *are* a tasty thing, aren't you?" The muffled slapping sound of his hand over his cock was loud in the quiet room, unbearably obscene. "Painters and poets dream of such a muse."

"Neve, is that you? Are you watching something in there?"

Neve had left the bedroom door open a crack. Now the man at the window jerked his head toward Joseph coming down the hall. The door closed on its own, locked with a definitive click.

"I know you're mad at me, but I thought I heard you crying. Are you all right?"

Neve turned from the closed door to the man in the window.

In the darkness of his eye sockets, she saw Maya's dark hair, Joseph's fingers tangled through it. She saw Joseph grasping Maya's body as though to imprint her upon his memory. She'd known their marriage had cracks, but she hadn't imagined how broken it was, that she couldn't swear her husband had been faithful just yesterday or the day before.

"You're even more beautiful when you're angry," the man whispered.

"Neve?" Joseph tried to open the door, with no success.

"He's not even a man. He doesn't deserve a woman like you. Do you know what a woman like you deserves?"

Her legs shaking, Neve lowered herself back onto the bed, parted her knees and slid off her underwear. "Come here," she said softly, "and show me."

"Your wish is my command." The man climbed down from the window, his steps muffled by the carpet. But his body whispered, skin brushing skin. She couldn't deny him as some dream figment. He was too large, blotting out the snow, a looming shape advancing upon her like some kind of monster. But though she thought she might hyperventilate, only a little of it was from fear.

She was going to do this. She had just invited a stranger into her bedroom, a man who otherwise would be considered a total pervert for masturbating himself uninvited at her window. She should have been calling the police — or at the very least, setting aside her anger and shouting for Joseph to help her, save her. But after witnessing her husband break their vows, break their marriage, the marriage was over. She didn't want

Joseph anymore. She wanted this. She wanted this more than she'd ever wanted anything in her whole life.

He stalked toward her bed like a predator, his cock even larger and more daunting the closer it came. He climbed onto the foot of the bed, crawled over the duvet, his knees and fists pressing deep into the mattress with a profound creak at every inch forward. He was shadow and furnace heat. She was afraid that his touch would leave blisters behind, but he arched over her, keeping himself away to the last. Even his cock, drawn down by its weight, didn't reach her from how he positioned himself above her.

When he stroked along her cheek and into her hair to cradle the back of her head, she somehow didn't catch fire. He caught her cry just in time, slanting his mouth to slide his tongue along hers. She felt branded, not blistered, by his hands, his lips, his tongue, claimed in a matter of moments.

He might as well have locked a shackle to her neck. Nothing he did would ever be enough.

"Neve, please," Joseph called through the door. "I'm kind of worried now. Just tell me you're okay and I'll go back downstairs."

The man's hair waterfalled over his shoulders to brush her chest like fingers. She reached up through the locks, strands clinging to her hands, to hold him in the kiss, to keep him close. She drank the soft groans he gifted her, licked and sucked what he offered. She had no idea what she was doing, and she didn't care. She'd become the creature, the animal that humans were before civilization demanded its rules and rituals. She didn't care that it was messy or lacked finesse, and neither did he.

Just his mouth, hand and hair brought her to the edge then pushed her over to fall, body clenching and tensing in a primitive rhythm she recognized but had never experienced like this. He bit her lip, sucked it with relish, then covered her mouth again to muffle her cry as she came. Her hips lifted from the bed, but he still kept himself away from her, laughing as he avoided the contact she instinctively sought, her need to fill the hollowness made unbearable by her orgasm.

"It's been a long time for you, hasn't it, if just my kiss can bring you to your climax? I barely have to try. How long has he left you unsatisfied?" He nudged her nose with his then dipped down to her neck. He covered her mouth with his hand before she could cry out. "Shhh, woman, unless you want him to hear. Of course, if you do, I can make you scream louder."

"I've never… It's never felt like…"

"Tragedy, tragedy. His shame is my delight."

She ran her tongue over his palm, taking in the salt of his pre-cum and the strong musky scent of him caught under the curtain of his hair. "Let him hear."

"With pleasure." His smile warmed his words further.

Then he kissed her neck, using his teeth to call a flush to his tongue. He lowered his hand to stroke her lips with two fingers. She anticipated his intent and opened her mouth for him again. He stroked his fingers over her tongue, a mimicry of what he would do to her, either in her mouth or her cunt. Not that two fingers were enough to compare to his cock, but the comparison was apt enough for her palate. Her mouth watered as he thrust to the knuckle, where she ran the tip of her tongue across the creases before his palm.

He bit her neck then the swell of her breast above her nipple, but he avoided the taut, aching bud to bite the underside. A pained groan followed when he abandoned her breasts to bring his mouth lower.

Oh God. Just thinking about it felt dirty. Joseph had performed oral for hours on her, employed every trick he already knew and a number of them he'd had to look up. But in the end, they'd given up on that and contented themselves with using a vibrator if he needed her to come. From the strange man's kiss alone, she'd already experienced a tremblor multiple orders of magnitude greater than one of her old orgasms.

He was gentler on her abdomen, little deliberate licks down her to navel, to the soft belly below. He inhaled like a dragon preparing to breathe fire.

"Your skin is sweet, love, but you smell dark and wicked where you want me. Shall I taste such wickedness from its source? Would you make your angel fall for you?"

He still hadn't brought his body against hers, hadn't given her the closeness and intimacy she needed more than sex, had needed all of her life and knew so much better than the pleasure torturing her like a sadist with thorns under her skin. Before she could beg for more than the parts of him he'd allowed her, he licked a line up her inner thigh to her folds. He swiped through them with the tip of his tongue, dragging his lips along, before closing his mouth over her clit and pressing his deft tongue to the hood in a soft, luxuriant suck.

She clapped her hand to her mouth to contain her cry on her own, not quite ready for her husband to hear her, despite what she'd said to the man making the music he'd promised. Her flesh flamed, prickled with the intense heat emanating from his expert mouth. If she had wick, he would have lit it and melted the wax down in a matter of minutes, like Bell's truth candles.

Neve clawed at the sheets with her free hand. The other she made into a fist, gagging herself, though she dug her teeth into her fingers. She tried to find an anchor for what she was feeling, for the swell of emotion and sensation, but there was nothing to hold, no way to hold it in. Her cry sounded like crying, like sorrow keening through her fist. Underneath the nails of her other hand, she tore through the sheets as though she had claws. Tears seeped from under her eyelids, and her arousal dripped out of her to dampen his chin. He broke away from her clit to nudge her thighs wider with his shoulders and probe her cunt with his tongue. Whatever he tasted there, it made him moan, a more powerful vibration than anything mechanical she'd tried.

"I can't." His pained admission sounded as much like sorrow as her cries. "Damn it, I can't wait anymore."

He raised his head from her cunt, wiped his mouth like a cat after a feast. Up close, she could see him a little more clearly, and the sense she knew him became stronger, but the fog from their bodies in the cold room had grown thicker, obscuring him in waves.

"If I had the endurance, I would take all night to have you. I'd savor you slowly, make it last. But I've waited too long, held myself back from so many. I can't hold back from you anymore, not when you taste so dark, my delicious, rich pomegranate. How I'd make you last…if I wasn't so fucking hungry."

Her skin felt the truth of his words as he bit his way back up her body, growling and leaving marks. Sharp pain was something she already knew she liked, and she arched into every bite. But more importantly, he dragged his body against her. Every fine hair and cell of her flesh nearly screamed in its own miniscule orgasm. She wrapped her arms and legs around him, urged him up, urged him against her, curved her body to fit his.

Holding him was like holding hot marble covered in a thin layer of velvet. He was unexpectedly hard, heavy, impossibly dense, though he moved with the ease of someone half his weight. His flesh yielded just enough for her to believe he was a man.

The darkness in his eye sockets burned as he looked down at her, his hips slotted against hers and the base of his cock settled between her folds. It was even hotter than the rest of him, nearly as hard, somehow bigger when she couldn't see it and measure it for herself. She trembled as he canted his hips in simulation, watching her reaction with something like curiosity.

"You can take me. You can take all of it, love. Don't fear that."

She'd only had her husband, and not often, not long when he was inside her. All men seemed small in comparison to this stranger, and that wasn't necessarily a good thing. A woman was made to pass much bigger through the canal, but that didn't mean it wasn't painful to endure, and that kind of pain might just be too sharp for her.

Even plastered against her as he was, he somehow found space to smooth his hand up her side to her breast, taking a moment to enjoy the give of her, far more yielding than him, all of her softness and curves pressed to the hard planes of his large body.

"I'm sorry," he whispered.

"For what?" There was so much of him to touch, and though he was hot and heavy over her, she didn't mind how she'd sunk into the mattress, didn't mind how shallow her breathing was. She wished she could see him, wished she could have him underneath her, facedown, to study the play of muscle in his back, his shoulders, the flex of his buttock and thigh. She used her sense of touch as well as she could in lieu of sight.

"For this." He didn't have to reach down and position himself. He shifted back, tightened his muscles as though he could direct himself by will alone and pressed the head of his cock to her entrance.

It was like he'd brought a fist there, and she tensed, in spite of the rest of her body wailing and pleading for the god on top of her to lavish her with every inch of generosity he offered. She was sure he'd apologized because he was going to rip her open from the inside, rip apart his promise just like her husband and leave her torn after exorcising his pleasure and denying her her own—a victim for her cuckold and cheating husband to put back together, the last insult.

But as he shifted forward, the weight of his cock sank him into her, and though she felt strain, there wasn't tearing or stinging or pain. Far from it, the deeper he went, the tighter she clenched around him, not just around his cock but around his body. Her mouth dropped open as she tore lines down his back.

He dominated her with his kiss once more, savage as a counterpoint to the patience of his cock, which seemed to take forever to reach the base. She expected him to have to hold back, only enough room for a few inches to fit comfortably, especially as tight as she felt around him. She was stretched thin, with agonizing arousal alight across nerves she hadn't known existed. But he kept entering her, and she kept opening for him. He filled her emptiness, a hollow always waiting just beyond where he entered her.

This isn't normal. He was too big, and he was too far in. He should have hurt her, through microtears or something bigger at a part of her so rarely used, or just from him hitting her cervix, lengthened though her cunt was from arousal alone.

But she could hardly complain when it felt like the ecstasy written about in books that never described reality. She kissed him with her own hunger, her own starvation, raised her hips to take him deeper, deeper, deeper, until finally he reached his end.

Air shuddered from her lips as he pulled back from her again.

"I'll hold out as long as I can," he whispered.

"Neve, if you don't answer me, I'm going to find the key and break in. I value your privacy, but I'm seriously worried."

"I'm sorry." The man didn't let her ask why again.

He peppered her with kisses, shallower this time, less possessive, so she could focus all her attention on the possession he'd taken between her legs. He wasn't slow anymore, although he started gentler, just a rolling of his hips to snap him back all the way inside. But as she realized he wouldn't hurt her, she parted her thighs more, lifted them to bring her knees to the back of his ribs, and his thrusts grew stronger. Each one nailed pleasure deeper inside her flesh, driving her breathless, head spinning, eyes fluttering shut, though she didn't want to close her eyes to him.

It was as though his cock was the only thing inside her, filling her beyond its already exceptional girth. Pleasure stretched out from where he fucked her, tendrils of excruciating, exquisite, impossible arousal that seemed to come *from* him.

Then he climbed onto his knees, changing the angle and forcing her hips up with him. Her breasts shifted toward her chin. She let go of the man to hold them down, not anticipating how the press of her palms over the protruding nipples would awaken them again, happily accepting her in replacement of his chest against them. And without him to kiss her, there was nothing to conceal her moans.

He dug his fingers into the flesh of her hips, used the leverage to thrust himself deeper at this new angle — harder, harder. His thighs struck hers with bruising slaps. His groans were low, as though they originated from all the way down where he took her. Every time he pushed in, however, his cock seemed to reach all the way to her throat, pushing out her moans in time with his claim.

"Neve, what are you doing?" Joseph was right up against the door, rattling the doorknob. Then, after a beat, "Who's in there with you?"

"Not you," the man rumbled.

Joseph stopped trying to get in, and footsteps hurried away down the hall. He'd be going for the house key.

"Hurry." She grasped his forearm, pulling on him to urge him on.

"Don't worry about him. You're mine now." He overlapped her fingers with his to massage her breast then brushed the corner of her mouth with his thumb. "There's nothing he can do. Time to sing for me, love."

He rocked his hips, forcing her to arch in order to take him all. She shouted, writhed when he brought his thumb from her mouth to her clit to rub the hood and sometimes over the sensitive nub itself. She'd never understood why women would scream unless they were faking, but now she tossed her head from side to side on the pillow, unable to hold back or keep quiet. With the window open, the whole neighborhood had to hear her. Maybe someone would call the police and report a domestic dispute…or a murder. She didn't care. There was no space for her pleasure with him inside her. She had no choice but to release it.

"I can't..." He doubled over again, sliding his hands under her back to arch her himself as he thrust harder, and she kept expecting it to hurt, but it never did. Instead, it kept feeling better and better. She gathered sheets up in fistfuls, her breasts moving back up toward her chin without her holding them, but she didn't need to breathe anymore. She needed to come. She needed it more than she needed air, more than she needed to function, more than she needed to think. She'd give anything, even her soul, for him to make her come as strongly as the storms inside her promised she would.

He slammed in hard enough to hurt now, but as he came, he took her face in his hands and pressed his forehead to hers as though in grief, growling like a beast as he snapped his hips, grinding into her.

Neve screamed to wake the dead, her whole body bowed up as though in spasm. Climax was like the thorns from before raking over her insides and outsides, tearing her raw, and still she asked for more. She thrashed as much as she could with him inside her, with him holding her head. He ground into her and she ground herself back over him, clutching, clenching, tightening, but everything about her was soft and everything about him was hard. And he was the one who tightened around her, swallowed her from the inside out, sucked her in — he the black hole and she the star whose light he devoured.

Her heart raced, skipped. Air sucked out of her lungs. For a second, she ceased to exist. She blinkered out, her limbs laden as stone and the light at the end of the tunnel nothing but religious ecstasy — light, heat, lust, a second that lasted forever.

Neve slumped in his arms, at the mercy of his not inconsiderable strength. He panted, great heaving breaths, like a bear after a fight. He closed his eyes, his forehead still on hers. When he withdrew his cock from her, he made a sound as though removing himself from her cunt was physically painful, as though the thorns he'd sent through her had wrapped around his cock as well.

The bedroom door unlocked, flew open. Joseph ran into the room, took in the dim tableau of a giant, wild man over her, both of them naked, the fog in the room still steaming from their skin. Neve couldn't move yet, shaken to the bone. She wondered what he thought of her, limp on the bed, undignified, tousled, bent upward on the man's thighs, her breasts heavy along her collarbone, her mouth slack, her legs spread wantonly on either side of the stranger.

The man raised himself up, flipping his hair back, his teeth bared.

"Neve!" Joseph pointed at the stranger in accusation. "You bastard, what did you do to her?"

"Get out!" The darkness of the man's eyes glinted, lightning over a night sky. Joseph flew from the room, striking the wall out in the corridor with a terrible crash that made her suspect the drywall hadn't survived. The door slammed and locked once again.

The coiled tension in the man's limbs loosened, but he was far from relaxed. He hung his head, his hair tickling her breasts and belly.

"Not that I'm upset, but how exactly are you doing that?" Neve knew things moving on their own was impossible, but after seeing it twice, it was damn hard to deny that it had happened — which meant she'd met a psychic person who could spontaneously change her sexuality in the span of a second and a wild, sexual beast with the ability to move things with his mind both in one day. What were the odds, really?

All of a sudden, she remembered where she'd seen the man before.

He jerked up in surprise, tension shooting through him once more as he stared down at her. "You're alive."

"You were *almost* that good, but not quite." She managed to twitch a finger, which snowballed into closing her hands into loose fists. "Nothing to be ashamed of."

"You're alive."

"You said that already." As soon as she could prop herself up on her elbows, she did, narrowing her eyes. "Did you expect otherwise?"

"You're welcome."

What were the odds that the strongman of Arcanium would be at her window just hours after the fortune teller had made her sexually voracious? She hadn't recognized him because his hair was loose, and he'd seemed less…animalistic while posing like a bodybuilder for the audience outside his oddity tent. She and Joseph hadn't lingered long with him. Feats of strength didn't usually impress her, but the snake charmer appealed to both her and her husband—her because of the snakes, him because of the charmer.

Yes, what were the odds? And what were the odds that the voice she'd heard in her head, clear as day, had come from the aforethought fortune teller mere seconds after said strongman was surprised he hadn't killed her with his cock?

Something weird is going on seemed like an understatement.

The man in her bed crawled back, tilting his head—a cautious beast.

"Mind telling me what's happening, or are we just going to freeze to death?" Neve managed to lift herself upright, bent her knees to push herself back, but she still didn't have the energy for it, so she just sat there on her bed, a damp spot underneath her, her legs parted to a lewd degree, but after what he'd just done, she couldn't convince herself that now was the time to cross her ankles like a lady.

Her aunt would call her scarlet. Her grandma would call her a slut. She'd call herself a cheater, and she was pretty sure turnabout hadn't been the proper way to get back at Joseph for doing the same thing to her.

Even now, though, anger flared up inside her at the thought of her husband, despite what he'd entered in on. No, she didn't think she was getting over this, which meant he'd get his wish, too. He'd get his divorce. He could fuck any woman he wanted. And she could fuck every other man in the world if she damn well pleased. She'd fuck the one in her bed again if he kept looking at her like that while her legs were open, her breasts pressed against her thighs, the nipples still hard and sensitive and the rest of her still on a hair trigger.

"The police are on their way!" Joseph called from outside the bedroom.

"Damn you, Bell." The man looked over his shoulder, though there was nothing at the window. "Why would you do that to me?"

"You're welcome. Now, take her. She's one of ours."

"What the hell —" she began.

"I'm sorry."

The last two times the man had said that, he'd followed it up with mind-blowing sex. But given how he'd responded to giving her that mind-blowing sex with the assumption he'd climaxed her to death, Neve shook her head as the man turned back to her, the darkness in his eyes more menace than mystery.

"No —" she began.

He had quick reflexes and long arms, and he placed his hand on her head before she could back away or crawl to the other side of the bed. He could bend cast-iron skillets, pull phone books apart, so he could do anything to her, and maybe it hadn't been such a good idea to invite him in.

But with just his hand on her head, already she wanted him inside her again — this dangerous, savage strongman, a man who thought he could kill her with the power of sex alone. Maybe the next time he'd be right…

All these thoughts passed through her head in a matter of seconds before exhaustion sank upon her and she collapsed to the side. The last thing she remembered was being gathered up in his arms, a burst of cold and a terrible leap from a terrible height.

Chapter Three

She woke up in a bed she'd never slept in.

Tan tent canvas stretched out high above her, and crates were piled almost to the top on one side. To her right, huge cages held two pacing big cats — a lion with a thick, dark mane and an even larger tiger. Their tails flicked with irritation. The tiger bared its teeth in a snarl as a man passed by their cages. When his red leather jacket pulled back, Neve glimpsed a black whip holstered in his trousers. From a distance, and as bleary as she was, the man looked like the devil.

Neve jerked upright, the covers falling away. She was wearing a silky beige nightgown, thin and slinky enough to be called a negligee. Someone had dressed her since she'd been taken — and not for comfort. She might not have been naked, but she pulled the covers back up to her chest.

The unfamiliar bed she was in had no headboard or footboard, just a soft mattress, soft covers — and her. The devil in the red jacket barely paid attention to her, though the bed was the most unusual thing in the room, which was either a back room for something in the circus — likely the big top where they did their performances — or just used for storage.

But as her thoughts caught up with what had happened to her, she started noticing other people there, wearing their own leather, lace and latex. She was definitely back in Arcanium. There, the contortionist and the fire-eater. There, the tallest man and shortest man. There, the Human Torsos — a woman without any limbs at all, who was in the company of the Tattooed Man, and a man with strong arms that functioned as his legs.

The devil in the red jacket left, but the rest of the circus folk slowly gathered around her rather than dispersing. They each found a place to stand or settle, from the Man Made of Stone and the furry gargoyle with bat wings sitting on the crates to the Human Spider reclining on a pink, floral chaise longue that seemed almost as out of place in the tent as the bed.

The Bearded Lady's skirt jingled with little bells sewn into the fabric, and she'd woven her thick, chestnut braid over her shoulder with what looked like tinsel. Her beard had been tied in three places with silver bells. She made so much noise as she approached that if the circus folk had been doing something performance-related that justified their costumes, it had likely concluded before Neve had regained consciousness.

The cadre of clowns passed by the foot of her bed, and the younger of the two male clowns smiled. The line of his lipless mouth stretched well beyond the mouth painted on his face, all the way from ear to ear, and with the sound of a thousand cracking knuckles, he revealed multiple rows of thin, needle-sharp teeth.

Neve screamed, scrambled back and fell out of the bed with another shriek. The Bearded Lady kept her from hitting the ground completely, grabbing her under her shoulders and helping her to her feet.

"Don't worry. They won't bite." The Bearded Lady steadied her, but Neve jerked away from her, too.

The woman's warm hands on Neve's bare skin reminded her that the silk she'd been dressed in stimulated everywhere it brushed over her. The lace she'd once been fine wearing now itched, because it was rough where she wanted velvet soft. Under the silk that held her breasts, her nipples had tightened. The tent wasn't as cold as outside, but she didn't think her nipples were tight because of low temperature. As sensitive as she usually was to chilly weather, her body seemed to have become sensitive to something else entirely — contact.

Even her own. Rubbing her arms against the slight chill made her more aware of all the other bare skin in the room, from the Bearded Lady's fine fur over her arms and chest, to the Human Spider's long arms and legs, to all the half-naked men. In fact, now that she looked around, the man in the red jacket had been the only one wearing anything to cover his torso. The rest of them wore leather or cotton trousers that left nothing to the imagination, not that Neve would have needed imagination to know what they looked like underneath. There was a definite bulge in every man's pants — every last one.

"You're going to be all right," the Bearded Lady said. "You're probably hungry. The golems should be bringing you food here soon. You've slept all day and evening."

Neve's stomach growled at the mention of food. But bringing her arm down to press against her belly shifted the negligee over her skin all over again. Neve made a fist against the prickly feeling she recognized now as touch starvation, touch sensitivity, a burning desire to have all the men in the room open their trousers and bring their cocks against her skin, because that would at least gutter the flames.

Thoughts that had never considered entering her head for the vast majority of her life intruded upon her with a manic intensity that made her feel insane, even more so with all the attention on her.

What are they waiting for?

"I don't know whether we met when you were last in the circus, but I'm Kitty," the Bearded Lady said. "I know you need a lot of time to adjust to what's happening to you, but Bell's on his way, so I'm just going to say this now and hope you retain some of it before he gets here. You wished yourself in. Since you're the very picture of confusion, I don't think you meant to. You made a wish, Bell granted it and now you have two wishes left. Whatever you do, don't try to wish yourself out or wish punishment on anyone here. Bell won't let you go, no matter how you word it, and he won't take kindly to any wish that might hurt his people. But you're one of his people now."

Kitty stroked her hair in a comforting, maternal gesture, but she misconstrued why Neve pulled away from her again. She held her hands up and away from Neve as though calming a spooked mare. "So although you won't *feel* all right, you are. Okay? Just don't make another wish for a while, or you may like what happens even less than this time."

"And what exactly happened this time?" A short, slight man with pale skin and long black hair twirled a chair around, straddled it like a Fosse dancer. "She's a pretty little thing, but she doesn't look much like our sort. What kind of special talents are you hiding under that dress, little girl? Not that it hides much…unless that's your talent."

The Short Man snorted.

A rock struck the pale man's shoulder.

"Ow. What gives, Spider?"

The Human Spider brushed the dust from her hands. "Last I checked, that kind of talent was common as corn around here. No need to be vulgar."

Neve would climb back onto the bed, but she'd have barely any clothes on, surrounded by other half-naked people and on a bed while her body overheated and clamored for relief, so she didn't think that was a good idea. However, surrounded as she was, every potential exit was easily blocked by someone from the circus.

"Someone mind telling me what the hell is going on? Nothing's been right since I came to Arcanium, and I have no idea how I got back or why." *Or what happened before that.*

The last twenty-four hours were either a dream or a blur, and she wasn't positive what was happening now was real either. She didn't feel like herself. The heavy threads of arousal pricking like dull sewing needles through her again only enhanced that feeling.

"What's the last thing you remember?"

There was no mistaking that voice, the smooth darkness of it as much a caress as anything his hands had done.

The strongman emerged from the shadows near the red curtain opposite the exit.

Her body recognized him just as much as her brain did, but it had none of the same caution. Her breasts hurt in want of his hands. Her clit remembered his mouth and throbbed at the sight of his beautiful form moving through the shadows and low, golden light of the lanterns.

"You. You did this to me." Neve looked around for something to protect herself with as he came toward her.

She took a cue from the Spider, grabbing a larger rock from the ground. Most everything was covered with a biodegradable layer of sawdust, but the ground underneath was discernable through it — brown grass, dirt and rocks.

"Woman, I didn't mean to — "

The Spider wasn't the only one who knew how to throw. Neve had pitched all through college and for the Sunday school softball team. She could have won her own stuffed animal in the midway, but she liked it when her husband won her things she knew she could get for herself.

The rock hit squarely at the base of the strongman's sternum. He grunted, clapping his hand on the imprint of sawdust where the rock had hit him. When he pulled his hand away, blood had smeared over the skin and on his palm. The strongman looked up, but he wasn't mad. If anything, he looked impressed.

"Ho! Strike one!" the pale man crowed from his chair. "I could watch that all day. And she hasn't even had training. Want to make it three strikes, princess?"

She ignored the pale man, took a few steps toward the strongman and picked up another rock. "You didn't mean to *what*? What exactly were you apologizing for?"

She didn't wait for him to answer. She wound the pitch and threw.

The strongman caught the rock just before it hit his chest. He clenched his fist, muscles and tendons flexing, veins bulging. When he opened his hand again, the rock trickled out as coarse sand.

"Neve... That's your name, isn't it?" The strongman continued toward her, no longer concerned about being thwarted.

But despite the display with the rock, she didn't feel threatened. She just felt angry. A little scared. But mostly confused, and angry because of it. "What the *hell* is going on?"

Kitty regarded the strongman with visible caution. "Mikhail, I'd keep a good distance if I were you."

"Bell!" The conjoined twins were close to the big cat cages, and both of them were looking over their shoulders at Neve, at the strongman coming for her, with identical fear in their eyes — the sort that came from experience, like realizing someone was standing too close to a hornet's nest.

"Stay away from me. Don't touch me. I want to know what's going on. Why did you bring me here?" Neve crouched to find another projectile, but when she stood again, the strongman was close enough to reach her.

"Mikhail, don't!" Kitty shouted.

He took Neve's wrist and twisted it — not to break the bones but to make her drop the rock she'd found. Then he yanked her against him, her whole body flush to his, hands and forearms on his chest, her cheek just above the blood she'd drawn.

"I need you to calm down," he rumbled above her head. She hadn't understood how tall he was until now, since she'd first seen him on an elevated platform and last experienced him horizontally.

If he had been anyone else, she would have pushed herself away. But once she was against him, she couldn't bear the thought of not having his skin on hers when it was everything she'd needed since she'd woken up.

In the golden light, far more of him was illuminated, from the way he appeared carved from redwood to the tattoos that crisscrossed his chest and arms and the parts of his legs she could see. His long hair was thick, blacker than the ink on his body, and he wore even less than most of the other men, the leather briefer on his legs to display his musculature. And based on what she'd seen of him, he was either significantly smaller while not erect or something else managed to conceal him. Like, say…magic. It was difficult not to consider that possibility at this point, although she was open to more likely ones — any other reason why she couldn't take her hands from his chest, mesmerized by actually seeing the hard planes she touched. Her anger hadn't dissipated, but now lust flared up to match it.

She ran her tongue over his salty skin, raising herself on her toes to lick up the sternum to the hollow of his throat. She caught his Adam's apple between her teeth in frustration, but she couldn't hurt him too long, not with his hot, broad hands heating her through her thin nightgown until it was as though it wasn't there.

Something like a growl vibrated through where she sucked at his skin. He tightened a fist in her hair to ease her head back then dipped down to kiss her. Their hips slotted perfectly together, his cock struggling to grow against her. A combination of really tight pants and magic, she concluded hazily. That had to be what kept the extent of his size hidden. It was the only explanation.

"Oh, bollocks." A curse and a groan in equal measures from the pale man, but it wasn't the only one she heard — just the only one she could discern out of the sounds from both men and women in the room.

"Get away from her." Nails painted dark red closed around the strongman's neck and pulled him back with strength as preternatural as his own.

The snake charmer tore him from Neve's arms and threw him toward the bed. The strongman somersaulted onto his knees then leapt to his feet before he reached it.

The charmer wore little more than a tiny leather bikini and a python over her shoulders like a feather boa — the same thing she'd been wearing when Neve and Joseph had visited. She, like the strongman, was taller than Neve had thought. Without the heeled gladiator boots, she would have been a few inches taller than Neve, but with them, she stood eye to eye with the strongman. Her long brown hair and her skin tone were lighter than his, but there was something similar about them, about the way they held themselves, the discernable strength in their figures — not simply superhuman, but exaggerated timeless elements of what was considered feminine in the charmer, masculine in the strongman. They could have been Adam and Eve, the Man and the Woman. And now Neve was starting to understand why her husband had been so smitten with the snake charmer.

Even so, Neve tried to dart around her to go after the strongman again. Without him, the hunger had returned, and she wrapped her arms around herself against the pangs. She wouldn't die from them by any means, but if she didn't know better, she'd think something was seriously wrong with her.

This is not *normal.*

Kitty grabbed Neve's shoulders to hold her back. "I know you want to, but you can't go to him."

"Don't *touch* me." Neve wrenched away from her.

Kitty held her hands up again, wincing at her misstep, but she kept herself between Neve and the strongman. "He's dangerous."

"How?" Neve stopped trying to go to him, but not because she didn't want him anymore. "How exactly is he dangerous?"

"He's an incubus." The snake charmer fixed her gaze upon the strongman as she answered. "If he touches you, he has you. If he has you, he'll fuck you. If he fucks you, he'll eat you — which means he'll kill you. And we don't touch Bell's people, not without his permission and without extreme care to protect them, do we, Mikhail?"

Mikhail shook his head like a lion shaking his mane. "She invited me in. I touched her. I had her. I fucked her. I fed upon her. Yet she's still alive."

"So you came to my bedroom window to kill me?" Neve looked around for bigger rocks. She wasn't used to pitching at a head — well out of the strike zone — but she could certainly try. "That's all it was? A lot of pretty words to...what? Get me to serve myself to you on a silver platter?"

The snake charmer looked down at her. She narrowed her hazel eyes, more like Bell's than Mikhail's, peering over Neve as though searching for an answer in what was exposed of her body. "That's what we are. It isn't personal."

"Well, it is to me. Doesn't *anyone* have anything I can hit him with?"

"How did you survive?" The charmer turned from Mikhail to face Neve more fully. "You shouldn't have survived, not with the way Bell starves us."

"Sure she's not succubus herself, Lady?" The pale man bit his fist in theatrical agony. "With the two of you in the room, bit hard to pinpoint where the lust is coming from, and she's quite a piece."

The charmer tilted her head. "I don't smell anything from her except her own desire. She's no demon. How did she survive? Mikhail should leave none alive."

The python around the snake charmer's shoulders slithered through her shampoo-commercial hair. It stared at Neve from the side as though imparting its own suspicions.

Neve loved snakes, but she respected them. And when both woman and snake stared at her like that, like predators sizing up prey, Neve knew to back away and make no sudden movements. She crossed her arms over her breasts, which did nothing for the cleavage showing but at least hid the press of her nipples against the silk.

But the charmer didn't attack. She whirled away at the shuffle of Mikhail's feet across the sawdust and pointed her painted nails at him. "You stay away from her. You think I can't feel how you pull at her, how you've wrapped your spell around her so tightly she hurts? She can take her pleasure from any other man in this circus, but I'll punish you myself if you take another step closer. I thought we were past this, Mikhail. Past these dangerous obsessions — obsessions you know will have you under the Ringmaster's lash and possibly under Bell's guillotine."

"Am I really supposed to believe that you're incubus and succubus? Actual demons?" Neve said. "Are you serious?"

But when she peered back into the previous night, dreamlike and ragged though the memories were, calling the strongman an incubus made too much sense.

She'd known deep into her tangle with the strongman that what he'd been doing to her wasn't natural, even if she wasn't sure what normal was. Then there'd been her final orgasm, the way he'd scratched and scraped her insides raw, hollowed her out with his fullness, *pulled* from her like a fisherman removing the organs from his catch. There'd been the moment when everything ended. Then there'd been the leap from the window, his bare skin in the dead of winter without any fear of frost.

Neve believed in evidence. The evidence told her that either this entire circus was colluding on the greatest practical joke in the history of illusions, all to fool one person they'd chosen at complete random, or that the strongman and the snake charmer were what they said they were — which meant the fortune teller was what he'd said he was. And not all the people in the tent around her were what they seemed to be — or maybe they were *exactly* how they seemed to be.

"Deadly serious," Bell said from behind her. "But like I said, Neve, you're a smart girl. A healthy skeptic, not a skeptic for skepticism's sake."

Neve stopped backing away, stopped covering herself, stopped looking for a weapon, but she didn't turn around. "Why would you do this to me? Because the rest of the world doesn't suffer like this. It can't. And why would you do that just for him to kill me?"

"I didn't want him to kill you," Bell said. "I wanted to prove that he couldn't."

"But he thought he was going to."

"You shouldn't judge him too harshly for that." He was closer to her now, the coolness of his breath on the back of her neck. "He starves because I deny him free rein with any woman he chooses. I restrict my demons from calling police attention upon the circus, so I can't allow them to form a pattern of deaths. It was easier to find you by making you easy for him to find, easier to explain that he could slake his lust on you and you could slake your lust on him without fear of death. The pain you feel now isn't because of me, Neve — or at least not directly. You have no idea how safe you were before you asked to change. The pain is from *him*. In that way, I'm afraid you suffer the same pangs of desire as my incubus and succubus — and several of my humans."

"Kitty said I made a wish." She was usually quiet, but some things needed to be processed aloud. "She said it with significance, implying that you granted wishes. Whether sorcerer, demon, jinn or witch in disguise, wish-granters in the stories need a spoken wish. I don't remember making one — or at least I don't remember saying that I wished something, unless your brand of wish-granting only requires you to pull from someone's spoken desires."

"I require an explicit wish, but you don't remember it because you made it idly, as so many do." He combed his fingers through her hair, pulling it back behind her shoulders.

Neve struggled not to close her eyes from the sweetness of the feeling, less primeval and raw than how the strongman made her feel.

"You may not remember the wish," he said, "but I do. I'll remember it long after you've left Arcanium, my dear. Shall I refresh your memory?"

"Please."

"I do appreciate politeness." He stroked the curve of her ear to the lobe. She bit her lip.

Then she heard herself, as though speaking into her own ear. *"I wish I could enjoy sex the way he wants me to."*

"If you had simply wished you could enjoy sex, you might not be here now," Bell said. "I might have left you with an average woman's sex drive as a gift—not an improvement on who you were, just a change. But your choice of phrase made it impossible for me to resist. Not just enjoying sex, but enjoying sex the way *he* wanted you to. And he wanted you to enjoy sex the way almost any man would want a woman like you to. I'll admit, several of my own people inspired the execution—the Spider, the sex demons themselves, my Maya."

The Spider sat up at the mention of her name, one set of arms crossing over her corset, the other set of hands clenching into fists. She didn't say anything, but she stood from the chaise longue and left without looking back.

Neve couldn't dwell too much on the Spider or on the incubus and succubus. Bell's own curious word choice distracted her. "*Your* Maya?"

When Neve turned to face Bell, she was somehow still surprised to see Maya there, taking his hand when he stepped back from Neve. She wore the same red corset Joseph had pushed down from her breasts. A different skirt, though, black tulle instead of feathers, with fishnet stockings and the same heeled ruby shoes, same red and black falls, same Queen of Hearts face makeup, no longer smeared. She met Neve's eyes without any semblance of shame.

"I remember you," Maya said brightly, although she wasn't smiling. "You're from the Ferris wheel, right? I never forget a redhead."

Neve wanted to smear that makeup and tousle that hair for an entirely different reason than Joseph. "Do you forget the husbands you cheat with?"

"Excuse me?"

"I saw you." Neve didn't yell, but heat rose in her cheeks and ears, because everyone else could hear, no matter how softly she spoke. They were all silent, watching and listening with the avidity of a soap opera audience. "I *saw* you with him."

"With who? That guy you were with?" The only thing that saved Maya from a full-on chick fight—which Neve was *not* beneath doing—was that she looked genuinely nonplussed. She stepped away from Bell, slipping her hand from his. "You didn't sit together in the Ferris wheel, and you didn't get defensive when I flirted with him. He didn't get defensive when I flirted with you. I assumed you were friends or related. And I checked for wedding rings. I always check."

"He might have taken his wedding ring off after we split up, but we were wearing wedding rings on the Ferris wheel." Neve held up her left hand. She couldn't be too judgmental about Maya having sex with her husband, given the glass house she'd built, but a thick, platinum wedding band was hard to miss.

"No." Maya shook her head. To Neve's surprise, tears actually started swimming in her eyes. "No, that's when I checked. That's when Bell gave his permission for me to…"

Both Maya and Neve looked from each other to Bell, who raised his eyebrows slightly. Not subtle alarm, but intrigue. Curiosity, and all the more insulting for it.

"You told me to go out and have fun," Maya said. "When I indicated who I'd like to have fun with, you encouraged me. I didn't see a wedding ring on the Ferris wheel or when we went behind the booth. You *wanted* me to fuck him, because you wanted *her* to see it."

"And you wanted me to see it after you changed me so I wouldn't say no to the incubus at my window,"

Neve finished for her. "*You* orchestrated all of this. You had to have known what I was going to wish for before Joseph and I reached the Ferris wheel, which was before I even knew I wanted to go to the fortune teller's tent. How far back did you know?"

He clasped his hands behind his back like a patron before a piece of art rather than a contrite school boy, but the intrigue in his expression faltered. "As soon as you entered Arcanium, I told Maya to leave the tent and have her fun. She's my magician's assistant and apprentice. That's why I keep a chair for her in the corner."

Neve felt sick, and it wasn't solely from her proximity to the incubus. "But she's not just your apprentice or assistant. You called her yours. And not for a little bit of fun on the side, or else she wouldn't have needed your permission."

"I asked her if I could kiss you, as well," Bell said. "We both stray, as long as it is with foreknowledge."

"Foreknowledge... Such as two people, in what was apparently an unhappier marriage than I thought, entering your circus, and you finding a way to tear them apart by lying to your own lover? Not to mention lying to the person you sent to fetch me, making him think he was going to kill me. I might never let him touch me again, because now I know he was willing to."

"He is what he is. There's no need to punish him for that," Bell said.

"So you reward him instead?"

Bell arched his eyebrows higher at the snake charmer's interjection, amusement a cold, gleeful glint off the amber in his eyes. Add the Spider's abrupt exit into the mix, and he'd apparently pissed off at least four women with one plot. It would have been impressive if Neve wasn't so damn furious.

"True, you starve him more than you starve me," the snake charmer said. "Most of your trespassers are straight men. What doesn't go to the clowns most often goes to me. But I've never developed an obsession with two of your women, never nearly killed another one of your men because they happened to be fucking my obsession. The Ringmaster has never had to discipline me. I've danced for you, performed for you, kept Mikhail satisfied when it was too much to take. I suffered Bale's worship without ever being able to touch him until you fulfilled his wish to sacrifice himself to me. I've done everything for you, followed every rule. And you give this gift to *him*?"

The python snapped at Bell. Neve jerked out of staring at a mesmerizing succubus gathering power around her like gold coins in a vault, power that crackled with the same electricity Neve remembered in her bedroom, when it had steamed from the strongman's body.

The snake charmer stalked away, following the Spider out of the tent.

Despite all the power Neve had sensed around the succubus — power inextricable from desire that had nearly shaken her legs out from under her — she had a bad feeling that the fact the snake charmer had left instead of confronting Bell more physically spoke to Bell's greater power rather than the charmer's self-control.

Kitty had already moved out of the succubus' way, joining the conjoined twins, but disapproval had brought a frown to her pretty, furry face. The twins were both side-eyeing Mikhail, fear in the set of their shoulders, the knitting of their foreheads. Two men came up from behind them with their own comfort, holding the girls' hands, holding each other's hands.

The gathered power left behind by the charmer dissipated, although not enough for the flush to leave anyone's faces. Maya adjusted her corset, shifting her thighs against each other in exactly the way Neve wanted to do. It was oddly comforting, knowing she wasn't the only one.

"You could have just taken her," Maya said quietly. "After she made the wish, you could have whisked her away like you've done before. But no, you had to make sure everything crumbled in your wake. You had to entertain yourself by manipulating everyone around you. Which isn't news anymore, but then you made me a party to the misery. You actively misled *me* into having sex with a married man for his wife to witness."

Either Bell didn't see it coming or he let it happen. Maya was a short woman, but she had powerful arms. She landed a solid punch right in the hollow under Bell's prominent cheekbone.

A few of the people in the tent laughed, some of them uproariously, but Neve wasn't one of them. She brought her hand to her cheek in involuntary sympathy as Bell reeled to the side. And she waited for Bell to retaliate. All that talk about protecting his people and punishment that could include death by sex demon… She couldn't imagine how bad it would be for someone who struck him.

When Bell straightened, he touched the blood dripping from the corner of his mouth, but he didn't hit her back, didn't rain down hellfire and brimstone or call for a public flogging. However, the amusement and curiosity had been stricken from his face.

"Over and over, you bring people into Arcanium in personal, painful ways, and I'm your favorite spectator.

You do it for yourself, but you love an audience." Maya's eyes were red, and tears streamed down through the makeup now, but it was of such good quality that it barely smeared. "We keep telling you there's a better way, but you never take it. You do whatever will be the most interesting. and we know you will, so I don't know why we still try to get you to change. That's on us. But you made me part of it this time. And you did it exactly the way you shouldn't have. You should have known better!"

She shoved him, voice catching on the 'better'. Bell stumbled back, still doing nothing to stop her.

Maya swallowed against whatever had thickened in her throat, gathering herself up as well as someone so extravagantly and sexily costumed could. "You're a fucking psychic. You do know better. That's why you hid their wedding rings from me. That's why you didn't tell me about my part in the plan. It was stupid of me to think you cared — or that you ever could. Well, you still get a little of what you want. I like Arcanium too much to leave now. But we're done, Bell. We're done."

"Maya." Bell reached for her, but Maya backed away and took the same path as the Human Spider and the snake charmer to the back exit.

"Wow, Bell. Do you think you could piss off any more of us with this one brilliant move of yours?" Kitty said, still protective of the conjoined twins.

Mikhail had moved away from them, though, away from the bed, toward the part of the tent with the Tall Man, Short Man and the gargoyle on the crates. In the shadows, his eye sockets were dark again in a way shadow alone could not account for, but the set of his neck and shoulders suggested he'd been chastened rather than Bell.

"I'm sorry you had to meet us like this, Neve," Kitty added. "I suppose it's better than abject terror, which some of our new members experience. Still, we're rarely this fractured all at once."

Bell ran the back of his hand over his mouth, wiping the blood smear away, but the motion didn't hide how his fingers trembled. "She's still here. She didn't leave."

"Yet I imagine you're going to have to conjure up another trailer to sleep in, unless you want to sleep in the big top bed you've created." As soon as Kitty made sure the conjoined twins were okay, led away by the two acrobats, she adjusted her skirts. The jingle bells sounded cold in the emptier tent. "You'll notice I have no sympathy."

"You have no room to talk, Kitty, given with whom you bed yourself."

"He never pretends he's not evil. We're absolutely on the same page. Everything he does that's not evil is the pleasant surprise I wake up next to. But if you insist on describing yourself as neutral and not actively malicious, maybe don't trigger your girlfriend in the process of traumatizing another recruit. And maybe don't take the people you use for granted, because Lady Sasha and Lord Mikhail don't have to stay. They can wish themselves out anytime they want, and they've been with you long enough and served you so faithfully that you would let them out, unless you wanted a full-on mutiny among your demons. The Ringmaster can leave. *I* could leave."

"You're not ready to leave either," Bell said. "This is your home, Kitty."

"No, I'm not ready. I don't have anywhere else to go." Kitty crossed her arms. "But Maya does. You already set her free. Why would you ruin that by taking advantage of her?"

"I take advantage of everyone. How often has she taken advantage of me in return, for which I was perfectly willing to give her advantage?"

Kitty glared. "You're a fool. And until you realize that, I'd get myself that solo trailer if I were you. Do you want me to go over the rules with Neve, or did you want to botch that up, too?"

"I'll botch that up, too, thank you. Go follow her. Maya will need you to speak to." Bell put his hand on Neve's shoulder, and although the touch brought the aching and restlessness back to her muscles, Neve didn't jerk away. Angry men with power were unpredictable. He hadn't struck back at Maya, and he'd let the charmer and the bearded lady talk back, but they'd been there for years, and Neve knew a little something about seniority.

"Let's just say I notice a pattern among your favorites," Kitty said. "If you're going to do that to your women, Bell, maybe you should stick to casual. Once again, Neve, I'm sorry you had to see us like this. We're normally much more welcoming after the initial trauma. Should I send a golem back with food?"

"I'll take care of it," Bell replied shortly. "Thank you, Kitty."

She went out the back exit with the rest. While everyone had been distracted, a few others had left as well, either to do whatever circus folk did after a circus closed or to avoid any collateral damage.

Bell coughed, brushed his cheek again. The swelling and discoloration faded as though it had never been there.

"You fucked up, man," the pale man said gleefully.

"Yes, I appreciate you vocalizing what I've already heard in everyone's minds," Bell snapped. "Go drown yourself in your mermaid's tank, Lennon, and leave me be."

"Welcome party's over, boys. And I thought it was going to get real interesting after Mikhail touched her." Lennon leapfrogged over the back of the chair, pushing it over, but he caught it with his heel before it could hit the ground. Another acrobat, then.

"Don't you even think it, Moss." This time Bell directed his venom to the Short Man. "You were never anything but a diversion."

Moss rode the Tall Man's shoulder on the way out, unshaken. "And she'll need plenty of diversions if Mikhail and Sasha keep getting their dander up. It can't hurt my feelings if I don't want anything more. You'd do well to learn that."

Neve shifted out from under Bell's hand now, because there was no one to witness her doing it except Mikhail, who was still in the shadows. "So this isn't common?"

Bell deflated, the strong lines of him somehow weakened, but he shook his head, blinked hard — although not against tears, against something else he kept inside. "No. Nothing about this is common. They'll understand eventually. They'll understand why I needed you, why I needed you the way I collected you. Mikhail, please leave. If she wants you, she'll follow the scent you trail behind you even with your tail between your legs, but right now, I can't stand the sight of any of you."

"Do you know what you've done? You can't have me bind myself to a human then deny her to me," Mikhail said.

"Watch me. The same rules inside Arcanium apply. She isn't yours just because you're bound, any more than the Creature can own the Spider because he bonded with her."

"You fucking bastard." Mikhail grabbed the chair that Lennon had straddled and threw it against the crates, shattering the wood into kindling. "I'm not angry at her. She didn't know what she was doing. But you did." Mikhail pointed at him, an accusation he clearly wanted to make more physical. "You know I won't leave as long as she's here, as long as I've got a taste for her and can have her more than once. You hooked me on her so I wouldn't leave. And you're keeping me so Sasha doesn't leave, because no matter how angry she is, she wouldn't leave me behind. You've got everything figured out, you conniving son of a slaughtered pig."

After Mikhail stalked out, Bell and Neve were the only ones left in the tent other than the big cats in their cages — except they weren't big cats anymore. Sometime during the arguments, they'd become human and wrapped blankets around their nakedness. Well, that was one way to safely keep big cats in a small traveling circus. It probably also saved them some grief from animal rights activists — especially if the animal rights activists were the ones who ended up in the big cat cages.

Bell rubbed his face, sighing. "Well, that could have gone better."

"If you hadn't used magic to protect me, Mikhail would have just killed me, wouldn't he? And you wouldn't have lost a second of sleep." The same privacy that made him feel comfortable enough to show his weariness meant she didn't have to protect his ego anymore.

"It wasn't magic that saved you but the wish and the qualities the wish imparted. But if I hadn't granted your wish, my incubus and succubus would have considered you such pleasant company. Do you know how rare it is for them to spend their time with a person they aren't interested in because that person is completely unable to be stimulated into desiring them? You would have been one of the safest people in the world for them to be with. Pleasant for me to be around as well. Sex occupies much of many minds. It's uniquely peaceful to spend time near a mind that isn't occupied by such a drive. Granting your wish changed everything, made you uniquely irresistible to Mikhail, but I ensured the same transformation would protect you."

"What exactly did you do to me? Because this isn't normal. Right? *This* isn't normal." She stroked her upper arms as though cold. Really, she just needed the friction.

"No. It's not normal. But you already know about me and normal. Besides, you didn't just wish you could enjoy sex. You wished to enjoy sex the way a man wants a gorgeous woman to enjoy sex. You'll find that's far from normal. But you'll learn ways to live with it. All of my oddities learn."

"It hurts." Neve used her nails next. She didn't want to scratch through the skin, but it was hard to restrain herself.

He led her from the tent with his hand a few inches from her back, not touching her. The warmth from his palm drove her forward, especially once they stepped outside, where her skin pebbled, tightened like canvas pulled over a frame. "It hurts because Lord Mikhail made contact. Distance and time are the only things to slowly heal that ache, unless you exorcise your need with another man—or with Lord Mikhail himself."

"I'm *not* going to him." Even as she said it, her abdomen spasmed in protest, almost like one of her really bad cramps. "And I'm not going with *you*, so don't think you've got someone else to warm your bed with your lover out of it."

"I force granted wishes on the people of Arcanium. That's all I force upon them. I'm quite insistent on that point."

He walked her around the other side of the big top tent, away from the carousel and the animal enclosure, away from the funhouse, the midway and Oddity Row. They headed for the caravan, a piecemeal collection of RVs, trucks, trailers and semis that clustered together at the edge of the circus.

"Don't be alarmed by how out in the open, haphazard or unsafe everything looks. The nature of Arcanium means that my people, even some of my demons, can be vulnerable to outsiders, so the incubus, succubus and clowns are my first line of defense against trespassers."

"What's the second line?"

"Me."

"But if your power is in the wishing, how do you defend Arcanium? You can't force someone to make a wish." But she realized as soon as she said it that she was wrong. There was plenty a man like Bell could do with predatory demons on his side. Fates worse than death weren't hard to come by with people who smiled like the clowns.

Bell smiled, too, as she answered her own question. So he *was* psychic. That wasn't just a trick. She wondered if he could really see the future as well.

"I see the future as it could be, as well as the future as it will be. There's plenty of room for error. And some slices of the future I'm not permitted to see."

"Was Maya hitting you in one of those slices?"

She didn't expect him to answer, but he glanced down at his boots and said, "No. It was fixed in the tapestry. Unchangeable."

"But knowing it would happen, you could have ducked."

"I know how this works, Neve. Very few humans do. It all seems so simple to you because you experience time as progressive, linear, the effect of each moment created by all previous causes. That's not how I experience it. A great deal of the future is flexible, but there are things I cannot change, though I can cause them."

"You're right. That makes no sense to me."

"I'm not a man, Neve. By which I mean I'm not human, in case you were in doubt. I look like a man, more so than most of the others, but I'm not. I'm jinn."

"Under what mythology? Arabian demons, genies, some kind of angel…"

That earned her a proper smile, nearly guileless. "I do like it when I don't have to explain everything. We exist in most mythologies under different names, but I'm no demon. All demons are jinn, but not all jinn are demons. I'm fireborn, not hellborn."

"The distinction is important to you."

"It's important to you. Believe me, Neve, you don't want a demon running Arcanium."

Some of the trucks, trailers and RVs were newer models, the kind of vehicles Neve would expect Bell and other demons to demand for themselves, but a surprising number of them were modest, some downright small or beat-up, like they were on their last legs. Kitty implied that Bell could conjure whatever vehicles he wanted for transport. Neve would be curious to know why he chose the ones he did, whether it because of some internal pecking order between humans and demons, whether it was just a way to camouflage themselves—if they appeared too rich, they could attract thieves—or whether there was a different logic that determined his choices. This time, Bell didn't answer her unasked question.

He led her to a relatively small trailer, clean and new. He opened the door then gestured her in.

"This will be yours. I've provided you many books on subjects I believe you'll like, but people brought into Arcanium against their will aren't permitted the use of a phone or computer, at least unsupervised. And you cannot step outside the borders of Arcanium, as defined by the fences. To do so will result in an extremely uncomfortable, paralyzing sensation and five lashes from the Ringmaster's whip. He's not like your husband with a flogger, my dear. His hand is merciless. While Arcanium is on the move, you must stay within your trailer. Once it's set up, the circus is free to you, but the fence is as far as you can go."

The interior of the trailer was paneled in dark wood like an old-fashioned study. A tiny kitchenette and living area faced the equally tiny shower and water closet.

Those spaces were small to accommodate the large, surprisingly luxurious bed in the back. Bookshelves, constructed with barriers that would keep the books inside while the trailer was moving, lined the walls on either side of the bed, and cabinet wardrobes were built into the partition.

"Kitty already warned you not to test my patience by attempting to use one of your last two wishes to leave Arcanium or hurt anyone under my protection. No matter how intelligent you are, there is no way to outsmart me—like, say, wishing you'd never come to

Arcanium or wishing I'd never been born. I've been granting wishes for centuries. I've heard every attempt to thwart me, Neve, darling, and you're not going to be the one who comes up with the perfect word selection. I'll find every loophole and make you regret wasting a perfectly good wish."

Neve's attention kept returning to the bed and why Bell had given her such a good one.

He was behind her, his breath cool on her shoulder, and she was tingling again, knowing how close he was. Regardless of what he had done to her, what he could have done or the way he'd offended everyone else, none of that affected how he could kiss, how his body had felt against hers. And since she wouldn't let Mikhail near her again…

"Tomorrow, we'll be traveling. A golem will bring you dinner tonight and take care of you until we arrive at our new destination. You won't have to worry about being a part of the circus until next Friday. Nothing too strenuous. I actually didn't bring you in for Arcanium so much as the Funhouse season approaching."

"Isn't your haunted funhouse up all year? I didn't get to go through…" Neve stopped talking. She didn't want to think about why she hadn't visited the haunted funhouse.

"I'll explain more when you've had your chance to rest, adjust and get your bearings." His voice had gone husky. She wasn't the only one who wanted in that bed. "You're safe here, Neve. I need you to know that. But it won't always be easy to do what I need you to. No, you don't have to respond. I know how much you hate me right now, despite what your body wants and what it feels I can offer, but I like you, Neve, and have no desire to torture you. I'd rather you view this as an opportunity."

"An opportunity?"

"To experience something new, something you would never have had if you hadn't wished it. There was nothing wrong with what you were, but there's nothing wrong with what you are now. It's just new." He pressed a kiss to her shoulder then withdrew before she could whirl on him, either to take a page from Maya's book or draw him to the bed. "And as a scientist, don't you want to explore?"

Chapter Four

She searched every inch of her trailer during that first night.

No doubt Joseph had reported what had happened to the police. The logical progression from there was academic — either the police would believe she ran off with the stud she'd cheated with or they'd believe he abducted her. She wasn't concerned about Joseph right now — she wasn't there yet. She mostly worried about how her friends and family would suffer, not knowing what had happened.

But while there were all kinds of things in her trailer, a phone or computer weren't among them. She could put a note on the window saying she was kidnapped, but Neve already saw the futility of that, and she wasn't in the practice of doing things she knew would fail just for the sake of doing *something*. No, she wasn't really looking for escape, because she doubted she would succeed. She just wanted people to know she was okay — relatively speaking — not dead in a ditch somewhere or trapped in some maniac's basement.

Maybe she could tell them she went on a self-discovery pilgrimage, contact her work and leave on good terms so she could get another job in the future without burning valuable bridges.

There was nothing in the trailer to help her, not that she believed Bell would overlook any means of communication, given how meticulously he'd furnished the small home for her. She'd mostly just needed something to do while unable to sleep, some form of active meditation to *not* think about where she was, why she was here and what Bell had planned. There was a place for everyone else as performer or oddity in Arcanium, but aside from some ballet until she'd gone curvy, she didn't have much in the way of natural circus-specific talent. And she really didn't want to think about what Bell wanted to do with someone made to enjoy sex, given the reputation of the performing arts throughout history.

Bell had told her that consent still mattered, but there was no ignoring how he'd fundamentally altered her willpower. How many of the yeses she'd given already and would inevitably give in the future would be because of what Bell had changed her into? She was going to have to figure out where she stood on that and soon, because her body and skin were just as restless and needy now as they had been before Mikhail had arrived in her bedroom window.

Going through her trailer and getting to know her space provided a modicum of distraction.

The book selection on the fortified shelves was eclectic but mostly to her taste. When she was in bed, the left wall held books meant to stimulate her brain, keep her learning, questioning — works by journalists, political scientists, economists, psychiatrists, medical

doctors, historians. To the right were works of fiction—
some of literary merit, some mindless. There was also a
whole row of old and new romance and erotica, a pair
of genres she'd mostly dismissed. She wondered
whether her new interest had also changed how she
consumed a typical romance plot, which seemed
dependent on readers rooting for a relationship
because they put themselves in the place of the
heroine—something she'd never quite been able to do.
It would be an interesting experiment, but she was
thankful Bell acknowledged the other parts of her so
thoroughly.

The left wardrobe held other gowns like the ones she
wore, nothing that could be called proper clothing. She
checked the drawer underneath and found entirely
impractical underwear. She'd been going to work in
scrubs and lounging in yoga pants for years now, but
there wasn't a pair of sweats or a cute oversized T-shirt
to be found, just negligees with varying necklines and
hemlines, a few with sleeves and a few without. The
only thing of comfort was a large, thick terrycloth robe,
which she put on now, although the cold wasn't
bothering her the way it had before Mikhail had come
into her bedroom and made her forget about it.

Lingerie, silk and lace, all meant to show off her body,
but nothing seemed Arcanium's style—too light, too
sweet. She didn't think any of it was intended for her to
wear in the circus, although it disquieted her that Bell
thought she should wear it as casual, off-duty clothing.

Then she opened the right wardrobe and got a look at
some of the costumes Bell had in mind. She
immediately shut the door again. They weren't much
better than the lingerie, and at least one of the costumes

was comprised of dozens of hands groping the body they'd cover.

Don't want to know. Don't want to know. There'd been some deep red velvet, some black leather, but they'd been so spare, she wasn't sure they were still street-legal. She'd worn fetish gear before, but that had been in private. There wasn't anything private about circus exhibitionism. Still, she was more disturbed by her body's reaction to the thought of everyone viewing her as a different person than she was — a woman who made herself up for the purpose of their admiration — than she was at the shocking lack of modesty, even for Arcanium.

But that was part of the problem, wasn't it? She used to avoid cleavage like the plague unless it was for the benefit of her husband. Was this new excitement hers — the kind she'd have if she'd come by her sexuality naturally — or Bell's? Or was it Joseph she could blame for this, since she'd framed her wish around *his* desire, not hers? Had *he* wanted her to flaunt herself more?

Whether or not the desire was hers, it made doing anything in that little traveling cabin difficult. She tried taking a shower, but though she felt better emotionally after all that hot water — in a stall barely big enough to hold her hips but somehow *just* big enough for her to maneuver without sticking a limb out in the process — a shower still left her naked, with a large bed to fill and nothing but sexy clothing to wear.

She compromised with the terrycloth bathrobe, although she still felt very naked underneath it, and she'd been this close to inviting the staff person who came with dinner up into the cabin if he hadn't looked completely dead inside. Neve wondered how long the crewman had been there if he'd grown that indifferent.

Still, his lack of interest kept her from making a fool of herself.

The more she mulled about it over dinner, the more she thought the question of whether her desire came from Joseph or from Bell was likely moot. She'd done everything she could to change her asexuality, but what she'd wanted had no more bearing on her sexual sensitivity than it did now. One was given to her by the Creator, the other by a jinni. Either way, her sexuality had always been out of her hands. That hadn't changed.

The only option for her, as she saw it, was to adapt — adapt to Arcanium, adapt to the changes wrought upon her. She was partial to stability, not change, not chaos, but if she didn't adapt, she was going to lose her ever-loving mind and probably get punished with the business end of the Ringmaster's whip. She didn't want that. Ergo, she wasn't going to step out of line unless she saw a genuine out, unlikely though it was.

She put the dishes on the kitchenette until she figured out where to take them, but on the way back to bed, she caught sight of a long plastic tub under the frame. Neve knelt to pull it out.

"Oh."

Neve had owned plenty of marital aids, but the collection here dwarfed hers — in more ways than one. She didn't know whether to be amused, offended, touched or excited. Her body seemed to know its opinion on the matter. Her folds grew more sensitive, thickening with a rush of blood flow. Her pussy clenched out a new draught of wetness to cool in the errant breezes through the robe. There were a few standards in the container, like a plain, trusty vibrator, a rabbit vibe, a wand, but the rest...

Neve wasn't used to blushing this hard when she was by herself. She'd bought far more realistic toys that fostered equally realistic expectations between her and Joseph. When a girl had trouble wanting sex, more extreme options didn't seem prudent.

She didn't even have names for some of the things in the tub, wasn't sure where some of them were supposed to go or what they were used for. What made her blush the worst were the toys she knew exactly what they were for, though she'd never considered anything quite so esoteric. For instance, she'd never needed dildo models of dragon or werewolf cocks before, and tentacle porn had never been her fetish. But there they were, lovingly wrapped with the other extra-large toys, nestled next to a convenient saddle to which she could attach them.

Only two days ago, the thought of some of these toys anywhere near her would have made her cross her legs in protection. She didn't know what to do with herself when she was brought to a keen edge just by imagining herself setting one of those exotic toys onto the saddle and sinking down over it, imagining herself taken by monsters instead of toys, remembering how afraid and fascinated the strongman's cock had made her.

She didn't know how long she knelt at the foot of her bed, trapped in a loop of her own weird, down-the-rabbit-hole fantasies. She picked up the plain vibrator. It would have been her go-to for taking care of herself before. But her clit made its preference known when she set the plain jane down and trailed her fingernails over to the other side of the tub, the intimidating side.

The strongman had intimidated her. She hadn't thought he would fit, and in reality, he shouldn't have. Simple physics and biology should have prohibited it.

She didn't know whether the same magic that made Mikhail's cock fit inside her would do the same for three-inch-wide dildos. Hell, that dragon cock had a base of four inches, if she wasn't mistaken. But she didn't have to take it all in. She'd had to go half with Joseph for most of their marriage, using positions to make sure he didn't go too deep.

She wasn't used to this much physical anticipation unless she'd put in a late-night pizza delivery order. The more she dwelled on the toys in front of her, and the more her fingers trailed over the hyperdetailed ridges and veins of both the anatomically human and anatomically not, the more her mouth watered. Firm silicone yielded a little under pressure, and the matte finish gave them a velvety texture. Holding them made them warm. Add lubrication, and they might as well be real. Even better, she didn't have to sacrifice her dignity to ask anyone to fuck her so soon into being brought into Arcanium when she didn't want to give anyone the satisfaction of watching her submit so soon.

She had to be better than that. Surely she could be better than that. Surely, if consent mattered to Bell, she could control when and with whom she made herself vulnerable — and not based on some primal urge or an incubus' magic calling her in like a siren.

She'd waited until marriage before having sex and not all of that was because she wasn't positive she was going to enjoy it. Sex was special to her. Closeness was special. It had always been rare, a precious commodity for her to give, as valuable as the ring she still wore. No matter what her clit and cunt were telling her, she didn't *want* to screw her way through Arcanium to find the right person to settle down with. The very thought made her horny as hell, but it also made her feel cheap, the very thing she'd fought against for most of her life, when she'd wanted to be taken seriously for her brain but people kept looking at her body and assuming she had only one thing in mind. Half of the men she'd tried to date in high school and college hadn't actually realized she knew four-syllable words in addition to the four-letter ones they liked to use with her.

Neve lifted out a nine-inch, bright purple dildo, one with a thin layer of what felt like jelly on the outside. She stroked over it, caressed it. Then, before she could lose her nerve, she fitted it over a vibrator that attached to the saddle. Her ears felt like they were on fire, but her mouth watered so much, she couldn't resist anymore. She slid her lips over the head of the dildo, moaning as she took it in, her hands on her floor, as though she were fellating someone sitting in front of her.

In the past, when she'd made that sound while sliding inches into her mouth, it had been a performance. But there was no one here with her now. Anything she did, she did for herself. Now was the time to determine what *she* wanted when no one else was around, without pressure to be what someone else wanted or needed her to be. She probably wouldn't be able to unlearn her impulse to perform, but the pressure was definitely gone, which left her feeling lightheaded, unusually embarrassed, unusually giggly and more than a little excited.

Slowly, with the terrycloth rasping over her skin like sandpaper in comparison to the silk, she untied the robe and slid it down her arms, leaving herself naked. Already, her breathing had grown shallower. Although she was still tentative, she wrapped her slender fingers around the shaft, testing how it gave over the firmer vibrator underneath. She moaned again, twisting her mouth over the head of the dildo until it reached her throat. She swallowed, expecting a gag reflex, but none came.

The way he wants me to. Apparently, Joseph hadn't liked her gagging when she tried to take him all the way in. It was difficult to resent him that. She hadn't liked gagging either.

"Mmmm." She swirled her tongue around the artificial slit, imagined a man's answering groan, the jerk of his hips at the absence of her mouth around him. "God, I want you. You don't even have to do anything for me. I'm ready now."

It was strange to speak to no one, but she wasn't wrong. And she could imagine she was speaking to the man she was sucking off, because she knew who she wanted that to be, even if she refused to go to him. She wanted him in her bed right now, his darker skin and black hair on her white sheets, his cock erect and ready for her like the one she stroked now. Except he'd be hotter and harder, and she'd be able to kiss him, stroke over his abdomen and chest instead of tracing the wood-grain tile on the floor. She'd be able to see him in her bed the way she hadn't been able to in the darkness of the bedroom. The lights were on in here, her body and all its inglorious imperfections, as well as the things about her that distracted from those imperfections, on equal display.

She felt silly, dirty, helpless as she took the dildo into her mouth again. She brought the saddle up with her, moved it to the bed so that her knees wouldn't hurt so much as she knelt.

Splayed out on the bed like a boudoir shoot just made her wetter. There was no one in the room with her, no one able to see through the blinds, yet she felt on display, watched by many male eyes, gazes dragging over her skin like the hooks of a rake, the way she'd always felt men's eyes. But those eyes had never been allowed to see her, and now these imaginary men did. They got to see her deep-throating a huge purple dildo to its middle and reaching down between her legs to slither her fingers through the folds, whimpering like a kitten at how her juices clung to her fingers. Would she even need lube? She decided better safe than sorry.

She put a towel under the mount then set out a container of water-based lubricant and a few other toys on the bedspread, like someone picking tools from a tool box.

She poured the lube on the top of the dildo. The bulbous cockhead wasn't as big as the strongman's, but it was about twice as wide as Joseph's, and there was no magic here.

"Now," she whispered, closing her eyes and willing herself somewhere else, with someone else. "I need it now."

The cock was too long for her to stay on her knees to take it in, to her chagrin. She crouched over the tip, gripping the bookshelf to hold herself upright, then brought the head of the cock to her clit, rubbing herself with it until she tossed her head back with a groan and impatiently pushed the dildo through her folds to the entrance of her cunt. She was clenching already, grasping, and she nearly cried as she lowered herself onto the purple cock. Her cunt seemed to yawn around the wide head, with the same fundamental satisfaction, clung around it like a snake consuming its prey. That's how she felt — dangerous, powerful, taking in something so big, already close to coming.

With her head still thrown back, her wet hair brushing her shoulder blades, she rode just the first few inches, but her hungry cunt wasn't content with a bite. Half-inch by half-inch, she lowered herself until she had to adjust the saddle to bring the dildo forward — too darn big to ride, even though Mikhail's had been bigger. It was better on her hands and knees.

Lube and her own juices trickled forward to tickle her clit. She gasped, writhed, stretched, purred, set her own pace, took the dildo exactly as far as she liked, riding it deeper than she would have guessed possible without magic. She was so turned on, she didn't think she'd be able to touch her clit without coming.

She wasn't wrong. Neve pinched her nipple, and just after twisting that little, hard nub for a few seconds, she let out a prolonged moan and pushed back against the dildo, filling herself as her climax gripped it and rocked through her like hot bathwater. She fucked herself through it without trying to extend the orgasm. She already knew her cunt wasn't finished with the cock whose soft exterior she squeezed so hard that she was surprised it didn't burst.

She continued to ride, moving her hips more than her torso. She wished someone's fingers would dig into her hips, her thighs, grab her subtly swinging breasts and keep her clit throbbing with each rub and twist over her nipples, because now she moved her own hand away. She circled her navel, imagining a tongue dipping in before moving farther downward, where dark ginger hair framed her pink folds and shiny, swollen clit. She used some of the lubricant and her own arousal to wet her fingers before stroking along the length of her stretched-thin labia up to her clit.

She gasped, shifted her position to make it easier to stroke. "Oh my God…"

Neve fumbled for the vibrator, wondering how intense that would be in comparison to before, but she closed her fingers around the cluster of sculpted red tentacles instead. And all of a sudden, her mouth wanted to be filled. She wanted two cocks, maybe three, maybe four—thick meat over her tongue and thick flesh in her cunt, stroking, stroking, stroking…and everything felt so *good*. Her body was awash in pleasure she didn't know a human being could endure—as big and intimidating as the strongman's cock, as impossible to take. Yet she had, and she'd survived.

The tentacles stuffed her mouth, muffling her cries, her swears, and she'd taken the purple dildo almost to the base by now, the silicone balls striking her fingers every time she bottomed out. The jelly coating of the dildo masked just how wet she'd become with its own noises. She stroked her clit like she had the head of the cock, round and round, mostly indirect, but sometimes a tap, a nudge, a press into her pubic bone and the sensitive cluster of nerves there.

"*You're such a slut,*" she imagined someone saying to her in an unmistakable, animalistic growl. "*Look at you. But you're my slut now. You'll take whatever I give you, and you'll come for me when I tell you to. And you're going to come…right…now.*"

She thrashed over the purple dildo, nearly rocking the saddle clean off the bed, nearly choking herself on the tentacles, but this time her orgasm wasn't its own foreplay. It shattered in her as terribly as a crystal vase on concrete floors. She rubbed her clit frantically, telling her climax to keep going, keep going, she was almost there, almost to that perfect point of satisfaction, just a little more, just a little more...

Neve spat out the tentacles and really did sob this time. A single burst of satisfaction, brief but there — then not. As her orgasm subsided, she knew she hadn't been satisfied. How many more times would she have to do this? One? Three? Fifteen? She wanted hands on her, a mouth, but all she had was silicone, lube and fine craftsmanship.

This time she reached for the vibrator, tried and true. As soon as her clit could stand rough, rumbly stimulation, she worked it the way she had hundreds of times before. And she did come, squelching around the now well-lubricated dildo again, but she lifted herself off it and collapsed, alternating between sighs and sobs, because it still wasn't enough.

* * * *

Neve opened the door for Kitty, who took in her tousled appearance, flushed face, hastily tied robe and very clear projection of frustration. Then the Bearded Lady's nostrils flared, likely catching the unmistakable scent Neve had gone nose-blind to.

"Oh dear." Kitty stepped back, gesturing to invite Neve out. "You haven't left your trailer since we arrived. Bell wasn't distressed — not about you, anyway — so I left you alone, because sometimes new folk need their space. But the circus opens again tomorrow. I wanted to give you a chance to visit the real Arcanium before you deal with crowds."

"Please don't tell me it's Thursday." Neve attempted to rake her nails through her hair to tame it, but she caught on a number of snags that told her fingers weren't going to be enough.

"It's Thursday *morning*, if that helps. The golems make a good communal breakfast. There are some vegetarian and vegan options, too, ever since Elizabeth joined us and brought her dietary principles with her."

"Changing people's bodies is okay, but he respects dietary principles?" Neve swiftly grabbed a brush from the bath tote and undid most of the damage. Then she retied the robe and knotted it so she wouldn't accidentally flash everyone. It would have to do, because she had no interest in doing any more at the moment.

"Don't try to understand or reduce Bell into one or even several boxes. I've been here longer than any human, and I've yet to make sense of him or stop being surprised, for better or worse. Have you been having some…trouble?"

Neve stepped down out of her cabin. There was definitely magic at work, because the robe was good enough for her, although traces of snowfall still lingered on the grass. Kitty's low neckline and flowy skirt could hardly be supplemented by her hair — she was more Lykoi than Bigfoot. Yet she and Neve crunched over snow and dormant grass with no need for additional layers. This answered a few questions she'd had on her first visit. It was actually refreshing, though — the winter sharp on her skin, crisp down her throat and not making her utterly miserable. She'd never been able to enjoy winter weather before.

"Why did no one tell me?" Neve said.

"You didn't give us a chance to. The fault isn't yours, since your welcome was hardly welcoming. But now I guess I have to warn you that if you've been trying to alleviate that particular pressure yourself, I'm afraid it's not very effective."

"That's not a relief, knowing it isn't just me. Providing a small fortune in sex toys seems cruel either way."

"Is that what he did?" Kitty appeared to be trying to hide a laugh, but Neve didn't think it was at her. "I assume he had his reasons, but I doubt cruelty was one of them. He doesn't provide a complimentary toy basket with every new recruit, although things would certainly be livelier if he did. I'm sorry, though, that it took you three full days to figure out that it doesn't work in here. The sex demons' magic has a very specific end in mind. It's not you."

"Oh, I'm pretty sure at least part of it is me." After dozens upon dozens of attempts to make a toy satisfy and doing things she never realized she was capable of doing—her own inventiveness and depravity shocking if she hadn't been so single-minded—she'd lost count of how many orgasms she'd had. Clearly lost track of how many days had passed. She wasn't sure when she'd last eaten, but her stomach told her it was longer than it should have been.

This was how addictions started.

Sometimes she'd been too rough, pounding a too-large toy too hard inside, keeping a wand against her clit beyond the point it was painful, as though she could punish her dissatisfaction into submission. Maybe part of it was the sex demons' magic—and that was a whole other barrel of infuriating—but she really thought the other reason was in the wording of the wish.

Wanting sex the way he wanted… Maybe Joseph hadn't wanted her to enjoy sex solo, hadn't wanted her satisfied alone—some sort of primeval misogynistic pride that paralleled his irrational need for her to have only mind-blowing sex with him. She could thank him for the mind-blowing, she supposed.

She felt five seconds from succumbing to the flu. Her skin itched and gritted in that strange, ill-fitting feeling she got after pulling an all-nighter. Her eyes were gummy, her mouth fuzzy and salty, her thighs smeared. She hoped Kitty couldn't hear it, bad as it felt.

And all because it was difficult to sleep when she wanted sex this much. It was dangerous, the sheer depth of her desire. The pit of it seemed bottomless, but she didn't *want* any other outlet. It was one thing to imagine being called a slut, but she didn't like the idea she might be one. Not at all. Like the butt of a mean joke—strung out, a junkie for sex and no rehab in sight, just plenty of enablers, men willing and ready to take advantage, standing in line to be her drug.

Hard not to view it as a cruel twist of fate, in which Bell was fate and his twist a razorblade dildo.

She wasn't in any state to be good company right now, but Kitty didn't seem to mind.

"Has Bell told you what he wants with me, or was he just hoping to add a bicycle to the line-up?" Neve asked.

Kitty laughed. "You'll be happy to hear we're very supportive and nurturing of a bicycle culture around here. Seems he might have made your sensations more intense, though. I haven't seen anyone this miserable about not having sex before—not even the prisoners, who sometimes go without for weeks due to whatever limitations or afflictions plague them at the time. But I recommend you avoid them until you're absolutely sure what you want and don't mind doing those things with people who don't deserve better than shit under your shoes."

"Who are the prisoners?" Bell's standard for punishment didn't seem to be oddity-based, and she didn't expect or want it to be. It would undercut everything he said he stood for. "For that matter, how do I tell what demons to avoid? Everybody looks like everyone else — in the sense everyone looks odd, not that they look the same, of course."

"Of course." Kitty appeared to enjoy Neve's turn of phrase, too. "We don't tattoo the prisoners or mark them as undesirables or anything, but they hold themselves apart. A few have transitioned into Bell's crazy family, but you'll know because of how comfortable they are with you, whether they can look you in the eye — or directly at you, as the case may be. Apparently, you can look like an orangutan and still all some men see is a pair of breasts."

Kitty led her into the big top tent from its entrance. Neve hadn't stayed for the evening performance, so she hadn't seen the ring yet. The two men who she'd thought were acrobats held hands as they pointed at a pair of trapezes. The African-American man lifted his chin with a smile as Kitty and Neve passed.

"Seth and Lars, our aerialists. They're like you, wished in by accident," Kitty said. "It enhances the wonder and magic of their performance, but Bell can do other things with you that aren't necessarily tied to the wish or simply tangential to it. He's good at that."

"What did they wish?" Instead of looking over her shoulder at them, which would be rude, Neve called them to memory from the brief glimpses — young, athletic, lean, a contrast of light and dark but otherwise similar in frame. She licked her lips at the thought of them kissing each other before kissing her in a trio of shared moans.

"Seth wished Lars would stick with him on a matter of importance to him at the time. Now they're physically incapable of separating. Things started shaky for them, like it does for most, but they've found their peace with it."

"What did you wish?" Neve realized the implication of the question only after she said it, though she hadn't meant it that way.

Kitty didn't seem to mind. "I just wished myself in. Arcanium's a good place if you're already a freak, too, human or demon. Not all demons can hide as well as Bell and the Ringmaster. For even the best of them, the illusions still let the monster through."

"Like the clowns? All three or just the one?"

"All three, and yes. Stay away from the clowns. Caroline, our carousel engineer, is the only human who gets along with them. They're complicated creatures, more monster than demon, but they *are* demon, and they'd rather eat you alive than play nice. Most of the other demons are mild-mannered, as you've no doubt discovered. You don't even have to be careful around the incubus like the rest of us." Kitty didn't miss a beat, so she must not have noticed how Neve flinched. "The other demon you have to watch out for is the Ringmaster. He's the only hellborn demon Arcanium harbors and the one most deserving of the name."

"And he's your lover."

"Yes." Kitty didn't elaborate. "You likely won't have to deal with him more than once or twice in your tenure here. Although if you're partial to getting whipped, he wouldn't refuse to indulge you."

"Are you? Partial to the whip?"

"No." Again, no elaboration.

Neve took the hint. "Neither am I." As far as she knew, that hadn't changed.

"Maya is. That's the only reason I bring it up. Before her, we never added that caveat."

This time, Neve chose discretion and didn't ask.

"The rest will poke and prod you, except Ciarán. But Moss, Lennon, Lady Sasha, Lord Mikhail, the Horned God… They won't do more than talk. Bell's policies make it very difficult for a demon to be demon-y, and most of them are part of Arcanium voluntarily because they aren't inclined to be demon-y. Besides, it's not the demons you have to worry about. Bell's the most dangerous, especially if you make a wish without realizing it. You should probably stop saying the W-word entirely. You only want to use it when you have a damn good reason, otherwise he'll make you regret it, and you'll be out one of the three. I sometimes forget, because I already used all of mine."

"And you're still here." Neve stopped outside the red curtain she now knew led backstage, where she'd awoken in the strange bed.

"Some people wish themselves out. Maya wished herself free and stayed, so she can leave whenever she chooses to. The Lizard Man wished himself out and got eaten because that's what he wanted. If some of the people working here wished themselves out now, Bell would probably grant their wish, but almost everyone's too nervous to ask, and Bell's not inclined to let people out before they do. I'm at Bell's disposal now, since I didn't use the last of my three to leave, but I don't have any more options outside Arcanium than I did when I arrived. It's more my home than anywhere else I've been, and I'm not sure I'd like what Arcanium might become if I wasn't here. Perhaps that's just vanity."

Kitty smiled crookedly then opened the side of the curtain for Neve to enter. "Aside from his granting, Bell's as careful with humans as the demons are. In the end, it's the humans you have to watch out for—the guests who think they're owed something from circus folk or who don't like freaks, and the prisoners who got trapped here because they did something wrong and aren't afraid to take it out on the rest of us. The Ringmaster punishes them if they do, but even if you get hurt, Arcanium has ways of saving its own—unless Bell doesn't want them saved."

They passed the contortionist, whose man knelt at her feet. He wore sweats instead of red leather, but apparently the pet thing wasn't just for the benefit of Arcanium's guests. The fire-eater was half covered in burn scars that extended into his mouth and over his scalp. Where he hadn't been burned, he was amazingly smooth, also athletic in build. He lowered his eyes from her and continued to eat in silence when the contortionist tapped on his collar. The contortionist grinned in greeting.

"Where exactly do I fit in?" Neve said. "I'm not an oddity, and I wouldn't know how to perform if I tried. I *feel* punished, but I'm not, am I?"

"No, you're not." Kitty motioned for a black-clad crew member to serve Neve.

Neve smiled at the crew behind the scrambled eggs table, but they didn't smile back.

"Don't mind the staff," Kitty said. "I'm all for treating support well, but the golems are soulless."

"You're kidding."

"I'm not. They're worker ants for Arcanium. Don't throw darts at them or anything, but they are literally here to serve. You don't have to be polite, because they don't have feelings. They're a little more animated when the circus is open, but otherwise Bell doesn't have them expend the energy."

"You're kidding."

"I'm really not. Coffee?"

"I'm a scientist. Coffee is never a question."

Kitty poured her a cup. Neve added the cream and sugar herself then chose an English muffin and jam from the rest of the buffet and followed Kitty.

Kitty led Neve away from the folding picnic table where Lady Sasha sat, snakeless, at one end and Lord Mikhail at the other, at a diagonal to maximize the distance between them at the same table. Lennon, Ciarán and Moss sat at the table next to them. All three had black eyes Neve hadn't seen during the welcoming party, black all the way to the edges. Lennon gave her a salute.

Kitty sat her at the other side of the table from Maya, who was eating alone and reading a paperback thriller with solitary determination Neve understood and respected. Across from her, the Human Spider ate her own English muffin and fruit, also reading, also determinedly solitary, and a bit ungainly with all her limbs attempting to fit at the picnic table.

They weren't ignoring each other. If they had been, they'd be sitting like Lady Sasha and Lord Mikhail. But their being alone together seemed somehow choreographed. It reminded Neve of when she and Joseph had sat at the same dinner table and eaten in silence in the midst of mutual irritation but also unspoken understanding and respect, neither of them relocating to the living room couch to eat truly alone.

Kitty slid onto the bench across from Neve. "As far as your place in Arcanium goes, you're not voluntary, so you can't cross the threshold the way some of us can. But within the borders of Arcanium, you're given certain freedoms, benefits, that the prisoners can't claim. Most of the prisoners sleep in a semi-trailer, a few in older trailers. Most of the involuntaries who aren't being punished live much like you do — reasonable privacy, space and a less painful existence, with an ability to take pleasure from life and to exorcise the desire that the sex demons create. The Rotting Man may have the same sexual frustration as you on the days he still has his dick, but do you think any of us have touched it?"

Neve snorted coffee through her nose, partially spraying the table. She coughed until she was sure she wouldn't choke.

"For the longest time," Kitty continued, as though Neve hadn't done anything undignified, "no one would let Misha, our sword swallower, near them because he had a tendency to spit blood and first came into Arcanium because he'd been an asshole. He's been forgiven his trespasses since, so he's on a level with involuntaries like you — like the Spider, like Christina, like Seth and Lars, like the twins, Joanne and Jane. Don't worry about which is which right now. They're mirror twins, so you'd have to look at scars for differences, and they wear their names around their necks."

Kitty glanced over at a table that appeared filled with misfit toys who just ate their food and didn't look at anything but their plate. "Most of the prisoners didn't used to eat with us, at least after the last influx, but now they do. They'll keep to themselves."

Neve had no particular inclination to hang around people with what appeared to be sucking chest wounds and limbs in sore need of amputation. A man who looked like a hybrid between a human and a Sphynx sat across from a woman who drank her protein shake through a straw, because that's all she could fit past the thick vine growing out of her mouth.

"If any of them bother you, kick them in the balls, hit them over the head with something and call for Bell. If he doesn't come himself, he'll send someone on his behalf. Or he'll help you kick their ass yourself."

Kitty stabbed a piece of sausage with more vehemence than a dead pig deserved. "They'll all be forgiven eventually, as soon as they acknowledge what they've done and atone — not for their sake, but for the sake of those they victimized. Colm, Riley, Melanie and John... They're on their way. As long as the prisoners serve Arcanium and its people, they work toward their redemption. Of course, they've been known to backslide."

She clenched her teeth after swallowing, but only for a moment.

Neve thought about how Kitty had entered Arcanium already the Bearded Lady, probably a victim many times over without having to step foot in a demon's lair. About how she was a demon's lover by choice, one she freely called evil. About how she'd said people were imprisoned in Arcanium for attacking freaks for being freaks — although what else people expected from a freak-show circus was anyone's guess.

A Human Spider with multiple limbs, a contortionist able to knot herself into ungodly positions, a fire-eater with burn scars... None of those things were quite like being a hairy, bearded woman—not being made into one, but actually *being* one. And she'd never wished for that to be taken away. Neve was sure there were many contributing factors to why Kitty was still Kitty, but it couldn't have been easy, even in a freak show, to have her natural oddity compared to the oddities forced upon people.

Even Neve had been relieved Bell had made her new freakishness less visible. If Bell could make a tightrope walker of Maya and aerialists of Seth and Lars on the basis of nothing more than bringing them into Arcanium, Neve could visualize quite well all that Bell could have done to her in addition to putting her on the opposite side of the sexual sensitivity spectrum.

After all, nothing apparently stopped the Rotting Man from wanting sex.

"After you eat, come by my oddity tent," Kitty added. "I live there full-time when we're not traveling. We can talk hair and makeup. I usually keep costumes in my tent, but Bell told me you have some of them in your wardrobe, so go ahead and bring those with you. You might want to freshen up a bit before you come over." Hints of amusement returned, tugging on the corners of Kitty's eyes and moustache. "Open a window or something."

Neve resisted the impulse to kick Kitty in the shins. "Where's Bell?"

"Not here. He's been scarcer the last few days."

Neve glanced at Maya then back at Kitty. Kitty nodded as she brought her coffee up to drink.

So much to ask, but it would be considered gossip and not a bit sweet-spirited. Neve held her tongue on that, too.

She also determinedly didn't look in Lord Mikhail's direction. She felt him, the way a person feels hearth fire against their backs. She'd prefer pretending he didn't exist, but she couldn't deny fire, and there was no air conditioning backstage to save her. If she were wearing anything decent under the robe, she'd shed it, because it was suddenly stifling, but she didn't even have a pair of panties as a barrier.

The scenario that kept playing in her head now was Mikhail striding up to her, throwing her onto the picnic table, parting the robe into a makeshift blanket and rutting furiously with her for everyone to see — like animals who didn't care about each other's pleasure, only about the satiation of their own. But Neve knew she'd feel all the pleasure, any pleasure that could be had, because that was Bell's design.

A girl up for anything, ready for anything, anytime... That's what men wanted from her, her husband no exception, and that's what she was. The natural redhead with big tits and an ass, with the voice of a submissive, an experimental nature and a body so full of lust she would exhaust a sailor who'd been at sea a whole year. At the foundation, it seemed all too clear what Bell wanted her in Arcanium for, and none of those reasons involved her doctorate.

She wanted so badly to forget Lord Mikhail was there, but she couldn't. And somehow she could tell that part of the reason she couldn't stop thinking about him, couldn't stop yearning for him to touch her, couldn't stop imagining the very specific things she wanted him to do to her, was because he couldn't ignore her either. He called to her without saying a word, whether he meant to or not.

A slam made everyone on her side of the room jump and turn toward the sex demons' table.

Lady Sasha pressed her hands against her head, her fingernails curled into her scalp as though she were holding her brains in. Lord Mikhail had struck the table as he stood, glowering first at Lady Sasha then at Neve.

Neve experienced his anger the way she did his lust, because the former was clearly spiked with the latter. He was wearing jeans instead of leather pants, but they served the same purpose in holding his cock down, semi-tamed without room to swell, grow, to stretch out for what it wanted. Instead, he stalked away, bent over like a hulking monster rather than a man.

"Lady Sasha's been giving him as much of a cold shoulder as Maya's giving Bell," Kitty said softly.

"I didn't mean to cause so much trouble."

Kitty blinked. "You didn't cause this, sweetie. Don't even think that. The pieces were all there. What Bell did to you was just the—"

"Catalyst," Neve mused, suddenly shivering.

"Yes. Lord Mikhail and Lady Sasha's relationship has been tempestuous from the beginning, as has Bell and Maya's." Kitty stroked her beard in contemplation. "But if the incubus and succubus continue not speaking with each other, Arcanium's going to get a lot more…interesting."

* * * *

Neve tried not to squirm from how good it felt for Kitty to brush her hair. Even when she'd been asexual, someone else brushing her hair had felt amazing. At least now she was clothed, albeit in lingerie. She didn't know whether she was allowed to ask for yoga pants and T-shirts here if they hadn't already been provided, and if Bell was pissed off, now was probably not the time to inquire.

"What did you mean when you said Arcanium's going to get more interesting?" Neve asked.

"Every time I mention Lord Mikhail or just say the word 'incubus', you tense up. Are you sure you want me to answer that?"

"Why are they called Lord Mikhail and Lady Sasha? I thought they were stage names at first, but all of you keep using it."

"That's what they are. Yes, we started out using their titles to fit in more with the Renaissance and medieval fairs, but where they were born, they *were* nobility."

"And how exactly do incubi and succubi become noble?"

"You'll have to ask them, sweetie. We don't talk much. It's not personal. They start emanating, we start lusting and it turns into a self-perpetuating lust bubble that's a bitch to pop when we can't have sex with them and they can't have sex with us."

"But I can." Not quite a whisper, and not for dramatic emphasis — a vocalization of thoughts that hadn't come to a particular conclusion, or at least one that Neve liked.

"But you won't," Kitty replied, blessedly neutral. "As for why things might get interesting, you have to understand a few things about our sex demons. They aren't just Arcanium's protectors. If all Bell wanted was muscle, there are far better monsters. While having sex demons tends to invite trouble in some areas, it creates the atmosphere Bell wants — like alcohol or ecstasy during a party, I guess." Kitty arranged Neve's wet hair over her shoulders. "Your hair color is quite striking without my help. I'll bet it was carrot red when you were younger. Do you want to leave it the way it is or deepen the red? I'm excited to have another ginger in the circus, but really, we can do anything you like. Maintenance is a lot easier in here than on the outside."

"I'd rather keep it the way it is, thank you." Neve valued her natural color, especially after reading an article that suggested red hair was slowly going extinct. The world could stand a few anomalies for a little while longer.

"Okay. I asked because it affects the hue of your makeup."

"You know what Bell wants me to do?"

Kitty nodded then pulled out the hair dryer. "We discussed it before you came here. The Spider was originally assigned to the haunted funhouse, and he wants you to take her old spot. It'll be dark, atmospheric, and I wanted to make sure I had the right shade of green."

The hair dryer halted the conversation. Kitty was as skilled and efficient as any stylist, accustomed as she apparently was to extreme hair and makeup styles. She found the waves in Neve's hair and drew them out with more drama. She trimmed here and there, dry styling, to add an edge without taking away the softness of Neve's features.

"The alluring atmosphere of Arcanium comes from sex demons' frustrations. They abstain until a trespasser crosses their path while they patrol in the evenings, or unless Bell finally takes pity on them and lets them loose outside Arcanium. Incubi and succubi are irresistible by nature, but most feed every night or so. They don't drive you insane because they don't emanate nearly as much frustration. Bell has Mikhail and Sasha hold out as long as they can. Their frustration maintains the circus' sexual tension, charges it and us. Then, during and after a feed here in Arcanium, it's a bit like a sex bomb goes off. Good thing they only feed afterhours, or else we'd start having guest orgies instead of the odd couple here and there finding semi-private places."

"Bell legally drugs his customers with sex magic. Got it." Neve was just trying to find where Bell drew the line, since he wallowed quite happily in gray areas. He needed a yes, the way the incubus had needed her to invite him in. Like the incubus, however, he had no problem at all rigging one.

"Casinos and department stores pump oxygen into their buildings. Real estate agents bake cookies to make a house smell like home. Fried fair food makes you nostalgic, and winning chimes make you want to spend money at the midway. It's really no different. The incubus and succubus try to keep it at a nudge rather than a push while the circus is open. That way customers aren't climbing into Lord Mikhail and Lady Sasha's tents and humping them like dogs. Afterhours, they don't have to be so careful and controlled. But in the absence of trespassers or Bell's permission to leave, they've always had each other. It's significantly more effective than solo sex, though significantly less effective than feeding from a mortal. It takes the edge off for a short while, and it's physical contact, something they hunger for as much as we do. Without that, who knows how taut that tension's going to be? Or what happens when it snaps before they're able to feed."

"What do you think will happen?"

Kitty finished applying foundation and powdered Neve's face. "You aren't going to like my answer."

"It's going to intensify, isn't it?" Neve's breakfast sloshed in a stomach that had just gone cold. "It's going to get so much worse."

"You really do have lovely eyes. You picked all the good traits when they were handing them out, didn't you? If you detect a note of envy, that's because it's there."

"I didn't get everything," Neve said quietly. "I suppose it's a matter of opinion."

"And isn't that just the truth Arcanium teaches us. But I do have my own opinions, my own childhood fantasies. I wanted to grow up to look like you." Kitty tossed Neve's styled hair back and forth then touched her smooth, unhairy cheek. "Sorry, sweetie. I didn't mean to put too much on you. There's all kinds of beauty in Arcanium. You're just a kind that goes straight through my heart like a knitting needle."

"Oh, I have an idea what people see when they look at me. They don't get tired of letting me know, even though it's none of my doing. I'm ambivalent about how I look, to be honest. Prouder of my academic accomplishments. But I didn't get the ability to feel sexual pleasure, for one. I didn't feel anything sexy about this place when I visited. Now I'm all the more aware of just how much I didn't feel. I don't have experience. I don't have a filter, strategies, nothing. It's excruciating now, and you think it's going to get worse?"

"Do you mind advice from another bicycle?" As Kitty bent to apply the eyeshadow, her long beard tickled Neve's hands. "We all had to find a way to deal with it in here, no matter how reluctant some of us were."

"Were you reluctant?"

"No. Mostly I was surprised by just how *many* men wanted to sleep with me. I can thank Lady Sasha for that. Without the push from a succubus, I'm not sure half of the men I've had sex with would have had the guts to ask. I'd had sex before Arcanium, don't get me wrong, but the general opinion of the men I slept with was that they were doing me a favor, so they could get one off and feel superior and charitable about it. No, thanks. I'd rather be exotic, an unspoken wish or fantasy — even sometimes a fetish, to a point. You'd be surprised. Most people are."

"But the Ringmaster…" Neve didn't know how to phrase the question, because she didn't know the full nature of their relationship.

"He's my primary these days but far from my only." Kitty painted a pale lip gloss over Neve's lips, which was distracting, as was the fullness of Kitty's more generous breasts over her corset, but Neve forced herself to focus on the words. "I prefer to seek other company outside the circus, although I'll stay in now and then. Maya prefers the people within, although she'll sometimes solicit guests. I'm sorry if that's painful for me to mention."

"It would be easier to hate her," Neve muttered. "She's here and he isn't. But I just really hate my husband right now."

"I'm sorry about that, too. Arcanium doesn't lend itself to resolution of outside conflicts. It has its moments, but marital strife isn't one of the exceptions. There. Test makeup done. What do you think?"

"Depends what it's for." Neve laughed in spite of the nausea and the fact her lips didn't want to smile. "Am I supposed to look seasick?"

Kitty grinned as she rummaged through Neve's costumes. She pulled up the gray-handed dress. "It'll look much better in a dim green light, trust me. It's supposed to be a touch of haggard, but theater makeup has to be more dramatic than regular to get a similar effect under bright or dim lights. Your coloring is like Elizabeth's. I have to go more gray and soft with you, with your red hair instead of her black, but both of you take to color really well, as well as a lack of it."

Kitty hummed in quiet happiness as she held a few other outfits up, some which appeared to not have enough structure to hold Neve in. "We've had Lady Sasha for decades, but I don't think Bell's gone the vampire route so plainly, even when it was fashionable a few years ago. It was wonderful to sew in velvet. Lady Sasha does all our leather, so she has plenty of work, but what I provide is usually simpler and smaller. I think he wants a Dracula's bride out of you eventually."

"Is that what the hands dress is for? *Dracula* plays and movies sometimes have hands coming out of beds for Jonathan."

"No, the hands are for something else, but that's a delicious thought, isn't it?"

"Depends on whether I have other outlets, I guess," Neve replied, lowering her eyes.

"Ah, yes, outlets. You don't have to pick the one Bell clearly groomed you for. That's your right. Maya and I have multiple outlets. Caroline has her two men. Christina and Troy are basically exclusive, although true monogamy tends to be rare in Arcanium. The Spider's got a stronger sex drive than me or Maya, but she mostly sticks with the Creature—the winged monster, who you'll probably meet at the funhouse. If you're like her and take issue with demons, Carlo, our legless Torso, rarely says no. Poor baby is dead-center bisexual and randy as a tom with both sex demons working their magic on him. Misha's kind these days. And the stone-skinned man, Victor, is a former lover of mine. We wanted different things, parted amicably. Seth and Lars are with the twins when they're not with each other, but all four have taken other lovers. You don't have to have both men together, although based on Maya's description, I do recommend the experience at least once."

Neve shook her head, laughing because she didn't know what else to do. It *was* funny, like a good girl listening to a worldly friend during a makeover. "It sounds ridiculous to say, because Joseph strayed and I did the same to get back at him, but I'm married. I'm monogamous, and marriage means I'm taken. Unless Bell knows a good divorce lawyer, I'm stuck with a ring" — she held up her left hand — "and no outlets."

"Christina, our limbless Torso, was married. She's been declared dead, but she took off her ring long before that. Arcanium's not the world, Neve. Your age is suspended. We produce no children, fear no disease. I've long suspected time itself runs a little differently. No one finds us unless Bell lets them, and until we wish ourselves out or Bell releases us, we can't leave. Even those of us who can cross the threshold must always come back. Arcanium's not the world. You're not married in here."

"I made a vow. It has a few cracks in it, but the bond was still made before God. And with jinn and demons here, it's hard not to believe God exists, too, right?"

"Suit yourself. Though if there's a God, He has yet to smite any of us," Kitty said. "I just mean you have options. They're not good options, but the best thing anyone can do in here is take comfort where they find it, and with the incubus and succubus working their magic into the soul of Arcanium, sex is inevitable. If you're crawling out of your skin, sweetie, you might have to stand before your Maker and admit to your weaknesses, because you're right. It's only going to get worse from here."

Chapter Five

Bell entered backstage as the golems were handing out breakfast tacos to the cast. He was as pretty as ever, summer-skinned in his leather trousers, but there was a drawn quality to his face, discomfort in his neck and shoulders. He glanced at Maya and Kitty where they sat together, but he didn't argue, and neither woman tried to castigate him any further.

Instead, he directed his attention to Neve. "I see Kitty's made you up for the day. Are you ready for what I have in store for you?"

Neve finished the last few bites of her taco, pulled lip gloss from the front of her dress, applied it then handed the tube to Kitty. With a burlesque flourish, she shed the robe that had hidden her from anyone's new-girl-in-town curiosity. As she folded the robe over the table, a few wolf whistles and delighted laughter rose in response.

She didn't know yet how it went with a haunted funhouse, but the gray-handed dress fit her like a body glove — comfortable, breathable jersey on the inside, with the rubbery hands covering every inch of the outside, seeming to hold her breasts, caress over her shoulder, grope her back, hips, ass, thighs. She'd done *Rocky Horror* costuming, so this was tame in comparison, if a bit exposed for nine o'clock in the morning and with everyone staring at her. Showing skin wasn't uncommon around here, but it felt strange to join their number.

Her reveal brought a smile to Bell's lips — and not a sad one. "Not every new member exhibits such enthusiasm."

"I'm not enthusiastic. I don't know what to expect, so I don't know how to feel yet."

"You know, people might be more 'enthusiastic' if you didn't abduct them, literally and figuratively strip them down, make them transform like some goddamn horror show then tell them they have no choice but to do what you say," the Spider said, still not looking up from her book. "Just a thought."

Neve raised an eyebrow at him.

"Every secret organization has a trial by fire. It's tradition," Bell said.

"Do you know why?" Neve asked.

"I do." His smile deepened. "Do you?"

"When organizations make membership difficult, prohibitive or exclusive, people work harder to get in, even if the organization itself is frivolous and not worth the currency paid. And when people share the same traumatic conditions of membership, they grow closer, form a bond, a tribe, based on that shared trauma. They succeeded, survived, where others failed, and no one else can know how they suffered. It forms the foundation of the Greek system, school pride, the military, gangs. It's a way to break down individuality and resistance, forge community and force rapport more efficiently — and it works."

"It must be interesting, seeing the moving parts," Bell said.

"I could say the same of you."

"It's all I've ever known," he replied. "You're fortunate I'm quite taken with intelligent woman and surround myself with them, else I'd be threatened, love. Even intimidated."

"Maybe you could stand to be intimidated." As Neve passed the table, the Spider, still not looking up, raised her fist. Neve bumped it.

Lennon, Carlo, Victor and Moss added their hooting and hollering to the fray.

"Oh, do try." Bell offered his arm the way Joseph once had.

But Bell wasn't her husband. His skin wasn't her husband's skin. She already knew direct contact would be like introducing a live wire to a rain puddle but she took it anyway, swallowing as her body reawakened.

Bell led her out of the big top. "You'll have plenty more to distract you in a few hours. Pace yourself."

"How am I supposed to do that? You made it impossible."

Out here, she couldn't close her eyes, breathe and keep completely still on her clean sheets to minimize stimulation, which was how she'd slept at all last night. But she'd woken keyed up, her libido shot with espresso from her dreams. Knowing the toys close at hand were useless to her made each and every one of them taunts. It had taken a cold shower to calm her nerves down enough for her to put on the costume and go to Kitty for makeup before breakfast rather than after — Neve's choice as a morning person and Kitty's prerogative as a person who didn't need much sleep.

Thinking about Kitty with the Ringmaster as soon as she'd seen the rumpled cot hadn't helped matters. She'd had to follow her time in Kitty's tent with a few minutes out by the food court picnic tables, which were frigid without the patio heaters on, just so she could eat her first breakfast taco without innuendo burning through her brain too far.

"Not impossible. Your brain's inexperience with these sensations is part of the reason you suffer. It's interpreting these foreign feelings as pain. To feel pleasure and not reach satisfaction can frustrate, but the foreplay stage is as important as the act of sex. I've offered you a world of foreplay, a way to sink into the warmth of your pleasure without an orgasm cutting it short. Once you're able to recognize what you're feeling better, you'll no longer react as though in distress. You're not in pain, my dear, and you're not going to die from orgasm denial, despite what many men will try to tell you."

"This isn't pleasant."

"Not yet. But I aim to please."

"I'm not going to fuck you just because Maya isn't."

For a moment, Neve thought Bell was going to strike her to the ground, and who knew what he would do after that.

Then he took a breath and continued to lead her to the funhouse as though he hadn't needed a beat. "That wasn't a veiled invitation into my bed. I'm a helpless, harmless flirt. It doesn't have to mean anything just because your mind's becoming acquainted with the gutter for the first time."

Neve stopped him, slithered her arm from around his and stepped back, but not to run. She couldn't run from him, but she could know where she stood. "Bell, should I be afraid of you?"

"No one's ever asked me so directly. I suppose it depends what you're afraid of."

"Don't equivocate. You're not just upset about Maya. You're furious. Is that something I need to watch out for? Are you going to hurt me if I ask too many questions?"

"I'm angry, but you needn't fear my anger unless you seek to sabotage or destroy my circus. Do you intend to hurt Arcanium?"

"No."

"Kitty imparted many valuable pieces of advice. You should be *careful*, but if you're good to Arcanium, you need fear nothing from me. I'm not going to take out my feelings about Maya on you or any other member of the circus. I simply experience it, the way you experience lust as it washes over you and threatens to pull you under. However, I don't fear that it will, nor should you."

He held out his hand, not to take hers but to indicate that they could walk side by side. Neve nodded, locked step with him. The haunted funhouse was just ahead, its reputation far exceeding an underwhelming exterior.

"Are you furious at Maya? At me?"

"Kitty was right," he said. "Your inclination to blame yourself for things you didn't do is a curious one. I'm neither furious with you nor with Maya. I experience anger when I think of her, but she is not the cause."

"Are you?"

He looked up at the roof of the funhouse in silence. The Creature slowly crawled onto the edge to peer down at him, as though he'd been waiting. The strange gargoylian monster licked his teeth, his glimmering red eyes unreadable.

"No," Bell finally said. "Not completely. Now, it's time for you to let your questions receive their answers in other ways, not that I wish to discourage your innate inquisitiveness. You are rare company, Neve, and the ease with which you choose to speak honors me. But once you enter the haunted funhouse, I trust you to figure the answers out for yourself, observer that you are. Are we agreed?"

Neve nodded, cautious of the gargoyle and his wicked smile, but despite his angle, he didn't leer, which made Neve feel safer.

"Ladies first."

She entered a corridor that remained as black as pitch until Bell closed the door behind them. Then the funhouse came to life, dim lights illuminating the way and a soundtrack of horror screams and creepy string music rising through the halls. It was like walking through a ramshackle trailer home, with thin hallways and hollow floors, but this one kept going and going.

Light, shadow, strobes and subtle architectural alterations messed with her perception. Trying to determine what was wrong about the funhouse structure hurt her brain, which briefly made her forget about the costume she wore and the desire tingling under her skin like an itch she couldn't scratch.

As she turned the first corner, a light switched on to illuminate the blonde girl with ivy coming out of her mouth. In her closet-sized diorama, the vine had been integrated into a parasitic forest. Brownish green vines thick as serpents and rough with bark wrapped around her legs and up her blue and yellow cheerleader skirt. Thinner vines curled out of her ears, budding with small, viper green leaves. The ivy in her mouth muffled her screams, but nothing covered her eyes, which were filled with fear. The vines she suffered all the time weren't just hidden among the rest of the tableau. They'd taken root, joined with the rest of the plant life to torment the girl, swaying her among them. It was a cross between *Evil Dead 2* and *Bring It On*, and if Neve had seen this before she'd been pulled behind Arcanium's curtain, she would have thought it was amazing. The sinking in her stomach came from realizing it was still amazing, but terrible at the same time.

She moved on from the ivy woman. A dark corner — darker than it should have been, as though Bell had some kind of mechanism for blackening shadows — concealed most of a monster except for his furry head. Horror movies had trouble making werewolves scary, but when the creature lifted its head and showed bright, silver-moon teeth threaded with strings of saliva, real life was far more effective. It emerged from the darkness like a body from water, chains clanking as they slid against each other. Heavy iron wrapped around the wolfman's neck, but nothing held back its long arms as it started after her.

Neve screamed as she scurried away.

She wasn't afraid it would really attack her. She knew this was a funhouse. But if she didn't give in to the fear, haunted houses and scary movies wouldn't be nearly as fun. Getting scared was the point.

The werewolf roared after her, lumbering, though it was lean enough it could have run faster, could have caught her and torn her limb from limb. He didn't look like a man in a costume. There was a terrible reality to his shape, his musculature, the fur over his arms, chest, abdomen, face. Like the structure of the funhouse, it was just real enough to disturb. But the werewolf caught up short at the end of his chains. He growled, ferocity and hatred mingling with a kind of evil glee in his dark, glittering eyes. Then he backed into the darkness, gathering his chains around him once again.

Unconcerned that the wolfman or anything else would hurt him or try, Bell maintained his own slow pace — like a god stepping through the carnage of a battle fought in his name. He raised his chin to encourage her to go on, his smile indulgent.

Neve turned the next corner without him. This tableau was larger, a small bedroom blocked off by glass and filled, body on body, with disease — suppurating sores, boils, necrotizing fasciitis that appeared to dissolve the flesh like slow-burning paper as she watched. Huge, evil-looking sewer rats the size of small cats clambered among them, nibbling at the lesions.

Neve crouched to peer closer at the people at the bottom of the pile, at the way the pus, lymph and blood smeared on the glass. No, they weren't faking. There weren't prosthetics here.

That was the trick, wasn't it? That was the humbug — that there was no humbug, but everyone thought there was. Everyone thought it was latex, corn starch and food coloring, all the best go-tos for a horror makeup artist. But this was real human misery. She'd seen some of these people eating breakfast this morning. That man with his forearm hanging from a mostly virus-eaten elbow? He'd been having his coffee. Ivy Girl had had vines growing out of her from both ends, but she'd been able to drink her smoothie, able to walk without blood dripping down her legs.

Did that mean it didn't feel as bad as it looked, or did that mean it was worse in the funhouse than it was in the rest of the circus? So there was the everyday torment, then the special torment Bell brought out when company came over and paid for the privilege. The practical side of her thought it was quite the system Bell had set up. The human side of her was horrified. The inner child, however, was fascinated with this new kind of haunted house, where the horrors were real but where she knew she was safe.

Already, she'd adapted to the horrors of Arcanium faster than she'd adapted to the changes in her own body.

"Help me," the man mouthed. Myoclonus twitched his body and the bodies over him like death throes, but Bell wouldn't make it that easy for them.

"I'm sorry." She wasn't sure whether he could hear her through the glass. "I can't help you."

Bell came up behind her and urged her back to her feet.

"Whore."

The man spat bloody phlegm on the glass. Neve jumped back.

"Don't take their epithets to heart, my dear." Bell put his hand on her shoulder, but she shrugged him off. "I never punish without a reason. Believe me."

Mindful of his suggestion to save all questions for the end of the funhouse, she continued, although she wondered — if the people in the haunted funhouse were the prisoners, the punished, then why was she here?

Was she safe, or was the safety he'd promised only to lull her into a false sense of security?

Around another corner, a man too tall and too slender, with his head brushing the ceiling, took up the entire corner, skewing her sense of perspective all the more. His expensive suit had been expertly tailored to his dimensions. His skin was the color of white greasepaint, eerily smooth, and he had no face, just lumps and dips where his features should have been, like bleached leather stretched over a grinning skull.

He reached out for her with long, long fingers as she passed him. He had four knuckles on each finger instead of three, and they made little cracking sounds as he closed them over her shoulder. Neve ducked under his touch. The thin man followed her, stretching and grasping like fog.

"Holy crap." She scrambled down the length of the hall, giggling madly on the edge of hysteria. She pressed her face against the wall to convince herself to stop, but it took a minute, and she kept having to look behind her to make sure the thin man wasn't coming after her.

The funhouse seemed to go on forever, longer than Neve would have expected for its size, each corridor and turn expertly arranged to make best use of the space available.

There was one turn where the whole wall was shadowed.

"That one is yours," Bell said.

But she couldn't tell what was in that darkness, and he wanted her to keep going, keep taking in the horrors that he'd made.

In spite of herself, she had to admit — it was a hell of a funhouse. Like the rest of Arcanium, it was much better than any expectations, better in its details than from a distance. But she would have enjoyed it much more if she'd believed it was fake. Neve tried to convince herself that there were crimes and sins deserving of such an end, otherwise there wouldn't be a hell, but she couldn't. No one deserved hell on Earth. Not even the worst of men deserved some of these torments.

A man had barbed wire wrapped around his limbs, piece by piece, down to his fingers. A machine tightened each section of wire bit by bit until, one by one, something sliced through. Blood dripped like sand in an hourglass onto the tiled floor and down a drain. The man's lips were cyanotic, but he didn't die, though he looked like he should have.

A man with scales over his body—not scale armor like a crocodile or alligator, but the smooth plates of a serpent—sat on a throne adorned with snake skins. He wore a leather loincloth over his waist, but his lower body was all snake, a giant king cobra with a man's torso and arms and face. His thin smile glinted with fangs. A body that appeared half-digested lay slumped at the foot of his throne.

A man posed among mannequins. Parts of his outer flesh and even a section of his skull had been removed so that he looked like an anatomical figurine.

Another bedroom-sized diorama held a collection of people who were the sum of each other's parts. Where they lacked one, another person was sewn to them with thick black thread to make up for the lack. Neve counted seven separate bodies, but not the correct total of parts. Naked but covered with half-leotards that matched their flesh tones, they were a rubber band ball of people, a gruesome sculpture. She hadn't seen them backstage, but it was probably difficult for them to move on their own, hard to do *anything* on their own. They clutched at the taut iron chains that held them in place.

She continued, peering into each window as she reached it.

A man was half-melted, a candle made of human fat and tissue, the soundtrack to his tableau one of sizzle on a skillet.

A cage encircled the head of a woman with self-inflicted scratches on her arms and legs. Her girlish dress was stained brown, red and black with unidentifiable fluids. The rubber room was torn and stained as well. The woman's eyes were bloodshot, her teeth broken, her tongue chewed, scarred, infected. She screamed, pounded against glass, bloody murder burning in her eyes.

The man Neve recognized as Carlo hung upside-down from the hall ceiling. He swung like meat from hooks that appeared to have been put into his hips. Fake legs had been made up to look as though they'd been sliced off of him. In this case, Neve knew it was makeup, because she'd seen the stumps where his legs ended, and they were smooth, not scarred, which meant they were probably congenital.

The hall was too narrow. She'd have to duck under him or plaster herself against the wall to pass without touching him. Neve knew the gag before it happened, but she still jumped when Carlo opened his eyes wide and shouted at the top of his lungs, reaching for her. He laughed, though, when she screamed.

"Hey, pretty lady. Maybe I'll get *my* hands on you next time." He winked. "Right now, the blood flow's all going the wrong way, but you sure do test it."

She dissolved into giggles again, holding her hand over her heart. "You know, they say if you look at things upside-down long enough, you start seeing things right-side up."

"I've never done this long enough for that to happen, but Bell keeps it from becoming a problem. Keeps blood pumping where it needs to be." Carlo ran his hands over his chest then a little farther down, but he resisted his clear impulse to touch. "Except that. Something about crotches at eye level needing to be controlled. Can't complain, though. This place is the only place I really calm down. When there's not a guest coming through, it's like meditation. Hey, boss." He nodded at Bell as he passed.

"I don't suppose you're going to turn me off while I'm in here, too," Neve said.

"Not with what I have planned for you. Go on. More to see."

A still living and breathing man lay spread like a feast on a fancy dining room table while a polite and refined cannibal horde ate him.

A chainsaw-wielding man in a butcher apron stormed down the corridor after her, stopping only once she turned the corner.

It went on and on and on, until…

Three men had been tied down onto metal piping in front of them. In the Ringmaster's hand rested a cat o' nine tails. When the light in his tableau came on, he raised the whip with a livid happiness that would haunt Neve far more than any of the gore. He laid into the backs and legs of the men in front of him, sparing none of his strength. The violent sound of the heavy whip striking each man with deadly accuracy was somehow worse than the screaming.

Daylight seemed doubly bright after the persistent darkness and strain on Neve's eyes.

Bell stepped out behind her with clear pride in his work. If he'd been going for evil, then he'd done splendidly.

"Can I ask questions now," she said, "or am I to contemplate the mysteries while you trap me with the rest of the prisoners in your house of horrors?"

"As you already know, not all of the people who work in the funhouse are prisoners. A few of our prisoners reside on Oddity Row or walk the circus, and some of my oddities and performers participate in the funhouse. Carlo you've met. The Serpent King also isn't a prisoner, and he's one of my few temporary oddities. You'll see more of him in due course when we start our Funhouse events."

"That wasn't the funhouse?"

"Different sort of Funhouse, love. Don't let the torment of some make you believe that I put you on their level. You'll have your own torments, I suppose, but don't we all?"

"You believe yourself tormented?" Neve asked.

"All those who walk the Earth and beneath it are tormented. To live is to struggle."

"How very Buddhist of you. Are you just saying that because you're not presently having sex with someone and you think that means you suffer?"

She regretted it as soon as she asked, but instead of looking like he was going to kill her with a thought, he laughed.

"Perhaps you believe close-to-omnipotent beings shouldn't or can't have troubles, but you'd be wrong. You might also think that because an immortal doesn't die, he cannot possibly experience pain. If, like Carlo, you take your hours serving in the haunted funhouse as an opportunity for contemplation, I think you'll discover that being immortal has its own tribulations when everything else, even the Earth itself, is mortal."

"So you're functionally omnipotent and immortal. Good to know. They didn't cover that in the Quran."

"I am limited only by the limitations I give to myself." He brushed the little hairs at the back of her neck that had resisted the ponytail she'd put up while Kitty had done her makeup. "The modern world has not sought demigods for many an age. It just wants a man with magic in his hands." He slid his fingers up to the rubber band holding her hair back and pulled it loose.

She leaned her head back into his fingers, but though he arranged her hair over her shoulders, he didn't pursue anything more, only led her to the funhouse entrance and gestured her back inside.

This time, the extra shadows weren't present, and the soundtrack and strobes had been turned off. It was just like walking down a black-painted hall. When Neve passed Ivy Girl, she was sagging into the vines, resting, although the blood dripping down her thighs and from the corner of her mouth was real.

"The Gentleman will be your guardian. He played that role for the Spider, and he's more than happy to do the same for you." Bell nodded to the tall, thin, well-dressed man in the corner. The Gentleman raised his long fingers in a creepy, insectile wave.

"Is he an actual Slenderman or just something you created? I thought he was made up as an experiment in urban legends, not an actual mythological thing."

"The Tall Man—quite different from Ciarán, by the way—has been a figure in many tales of terror throughout history. The faceless horror is another.

157

Slenderman and creations similar to him are basically the progeny of the original bogeyman. I did not create him. He found me. Like the clowns, he prefers children, so I provide him teenagers to provoke. Unlike the clowns, his feed is far less messy. He's not necessarily harmless, but in this environment, he's controlled."

"If he's not harmless, what does he do that isn't harmless?" Neve glanced over her shoulder, disquiet like ice chips in her lower abdomen. "He doesn't have a mouth, not like the clowns. How does he feed?"

"Oh, he has a mouth. It emerges. But though the clowns feed upon the body, the Gentleman feeds on the mind, soul, spirit—whatever you want to call it. One can die of fright, of course, but fear and hopelessness ravages in other ways, and the Gentleman enjoys these ways. Here in the funhouse, he can't feed properly, but he has plenty of opportunities to happily graze, so he remains. Most monsters love easy meals, and the Gentleman is no exception. Neither is the Creature, although his feed doesn't have the Gentleman's deleterious effect. It's much more work for him to *cause* fear the way the Gentleman does without effort."

"Monsters, then," she said. "They're not demons."

"No."

"Difference, please? This is fascinating."

Bell smiled. "Monsters aren't born of fire, nor are they immortal or invincible. They're beasts shot through with what your kind would call the supernatural—magic inside them like veins of gold in stone. Some believe they come not from the evolutionary chain but from the minds of man, as much a product of his presence as pollution—the manifestations of his fears, his furies, his hatreds, created like dark pearls over the course of centuries."

"A precipitate of human imagination. Interesting."

"You have no idea."

She'd been so distracted thinking about where things like the Creature and the Gentleman belonged in the great biological tree of life that she'd barely noticed Bell maneuvering her into the wall of shadows, shadows that settled around her like a blanket. She didn't notice until his breath was warm against her cheek and he ran his hands up her arms to lift them above her head.

"Bell..." If he kissed her again, she didn't know whether she'd be able to tell him to stop. After five days without anyone touching her and no hope for satisfaction on her own, with a man's hands now on her skin and his body not an inch from hers, her dress so short and easy to discard, the darkness ideal for a man to take her without anyone else seeing them... It all sounded like the perfect handbasket to hell right now. Just shove her against the wall, push up her dress and slip into her without preamble or aid, kiss her breathless, touch her everywhere, take her. Smooth as a good margarita.

He didn't kiss her, but there was indescribable tension to his body, a sense in his position that he wanted to. "You should ask our odd chef to make you one of his tequila worm margaritas, if that's to your taste tonight."

Neve didn't know what to do as Bell continued to lift her hands up toward the ceiling, bringing himself closer. She was afraid he'd use that against her, but though he was playing with the fire he'd lit, he hadn't blown on it or added kindling. Not yet.

"Do you call him an odd chef because he's a chef who's odd or because he's a chef who makes odd things?" She hated how breathless she was.

"Yes." There, the press of his lips to the corner of her mouth. But then he retreated from the darkness into the light behind him. Sweat gleamed over his forehead and his neck, though the funhouse was cool. Except for that and the dilation of his pupils, he seemed otherwise composed. "Don't be alarmed."

Despite his warning, she still gave a little cry as several hands grabbed hers. Then, from all sides, others grabbed her body, her waist, her ankles, her knees, her thighs, her breasts, her shoulders, her hair. Large hands, slender hands, strong grips, fondles, caresses, all at once. A light switched on, dispelling some of the shadows. It bathed her in grayish green light that matched the tone Kitty had set near her eyes.

The dress—which had been nothing but prop hands hanging from the cotton jersey—came alive and connected to a mass of writhing, stretching, reaching bodiless arms clamoring for her from all directions, seeking to pull her down into whatever abyss they came from. The prop hands weren't rubbery anymore. They flexed, kneaded her through the cotton, every last one of them the hands of a persistent lover. They strained, yearned, savored her flesh. Moans, male and female, low enough to be appropriate for horror but easily confused for pleasure, made up the soundtrack that played by her little open tableau.

The hands pulled her head back by her hair, caressed her throat with a threat, squeezed her breasts and taunted her nipples with their palms, clutched at her thighs—but nothing direct. Hands brushed just underneath the bottom of the dress's skirt, but no farther. The hands over her breasts could only use their palms in broad strokes, but no fingers on her nipples.

"We have to keep our funhouse teen-friendly. We show gore because they assume the gore isn't real. But when we go too sexy, that's when we get complaints about little Johnny getting an eyeful of pornography. I can *suggest* ivy running from one end of my cheerleader to the other, but it's okay as long as she suffers. I'm afraid I can't have you feeling pleasure so obviously. No direct contact. And that should satisfy your scruples as well, right, Neveline? No adultery with amputated limbs."

"You really are a bastard, aren't you?" She clenched her teeth against the sudden, unexpected stimulation from so many hands at once, when Bell's had been the first since the strongman. When she so wanted to be touched, but more. *More.* But she couldn't ask anyone to do that for her, and she couldn't get what she wanted from disarticulated arms, because Bell wouldn't allow her that.

"I was born of fire. It's impossible for me to be a bastard." But he was back to his old amusement. "You'll find no satisfaction here, my dear, but I won't leave you so unsatisfied forever. Until then, it's your own resistance that denies you, not me."

"We all have our struggles." Neve fought not to moan with the soundtrack, which stimulated her ears the same way the hands awoke her skin in a hundred thousand mini fires to join the one that Bell had lit. "Sex is apparently mine either way."

Bell sighed. "Human self-denial is something I will never understand. If you didn't deny yourselves so often, I wouldn't have to grant so many wishes. Calm down, appendages. You have all day."

"You son of a bitch." When she tugged against the hands holding her arms, they held on all the harder.

"Also impossible, my dear. Ah, this brings back so many memories. You remind me of Lizzie up there, spouting obscenities at me. Can I trust you not to scream for help if I let you have your tongue? No soliciting guests while working."

"I'm not going to scream for help, but I may be screaming death upon your head by the time the day is over."

"Well, that's available at the end of the day, too, should you want it." Instead of flirtatious, though, he sounded reserved, the amusement slowly dissipating. "I've already told you there is pleasure in the foreplay, in anticipation, in knowing that you will not be satisfied. Use this time to revel in the pleasures you were never able to know. This tension you feel does not always have to be snapped."

He brushed her chin with his thumb, smiling when the hand near her neck swatted him away. "They'll also protect you from anyone who thinks that because these appendages get you, they should, too. The Gentleman will move any gawkers and voyeurs along. In every way but one, you will be taken care of. Just relax, love, and enjoy the ride."

Chapter Six

Neve was going to lose her God-given mind. This was worse than trying to take care of herself with the toys under her bed.

Every weekend Arcanium was open, that was three straight days of teasing, of tiny shocks to every cell in her body overloading her senses.

The hands became more grasping and groping as customers passed, but when darkness returned, they softened yet intensified their efforts, the fingers slipping under her skirt just short of her panties. No matter how she tried to dip, how she sometimes begged in a whisper for them to just touch her, stroke through her folds, rub her clit, fuck her pussy, they always stayed just short of what she needed. They obeyed Bell, not her, and they had only two directives — to drive her crazy and to keep anyone else from finishing what they started.

And people did try. No matter how desperate the hands made her, Neve was astonished that people would try. The arms lunged at boys and men who laughed at their own daring. The fingers curled into hooks, blunt nails tearing at exposed skin. The visitors would yank their offending hands back, as though they'd tried to pet the nice tiger in the zoo and were surprised they'd gotten scratched. A few of them had the nerve to call her 'bitch' for it. If the guests didn't go on their own, the Gentleman came around the corner, his long arms and legs oddly graceful, to chase the lingerers off.

Then there were those who just stood there, staring — some slack-jawed, some with their hands in their pockets as though she wouldn't know what they were doing when they moved like that. She felt forced into another man's fantasy — an object, not even a participant. It was cheap, dirty, reductive in the way she'd always feared.

She'd tried telling a few of them to stop, but they never did. If anything, that made them more brazen. However, with the Gentleman's help, none of the voyeurs stayed with her long enough for the sight of hands all over her to bring them to completion, and the subsequent horrors in the funhouse were hopefully enough to deflate what they'd managed to grow.

Even so, it was as though she was slowly being stripped away to a body alone. It resembled the way she'd felt when the strongman had touched her, except this was her own sexuality rather than incubus magic grating her down. It left her raw as a scraped knee by the time the hands released her at the end of her shift.

The hands had fallen off her dress after the first day in the collective. Now, when she left the funhouse, she tied up her hair and walked to the food court in just the jersey dress. More often than not, people didn't make the connection unless they got a good look at her makeup. Sometimes they asked to take selfies with an off-duty circus performer, and she'd smile — tired but genuine, as long as they didn't get grabby — but they usually left her alone when she was in civilian clothes.

And when they didn't, the Gentleman would come out from the funhouse. He was even freakier outside it because he didn't look any more normal under less atmospheric lighting. Or the chef would come out from his booth with a meat cleaver. Or Kitty would interfere, putting herself between Neve and any man who thought that she was available just because being touched was her job and she had cleavage for days.

Honestly, even though she was ready to have sex with just about anyone after her shift, she was so overstimulated and tired of hands on her, she wouldn't have been able to stand most anyone actually touching her. The idea of some random Joe squeezing her tits like bike horns and shoving his dick in her wasn't appealing at all.

Neve thought it was a good thing that just because her libido had been switched to high, she wasn't willing to literally fuck anyone. Bell hadn't made her some kind of unicorn — a living, breathing woman who would never say no. If she could still say no, she was still more or less herself.

Even so, she slept a lot when Arcanium was closed. The sex dreams were getting ridiculous — more and more graphic, more and more weird — but she slept as much as she could, until long after the sun had crossed the zenith of the sky.

While awake, she balanced on a blade's edge of sexual explosion, fighting to keep from falling back into the infidelity that had drawn her into Arcanium. Tears gathered in her eyes like a river behind a dam. Most days she could hold it back, but the littlest thing could set it off—a girl holding her father's hand, a happy couple staring at each other with that honeymoon gaze she remembered well, the rare old couple conversing with casual ease.

She usually only got like this after too many nights of not enough sleep. She'd had no idea how nonessential biological urges could have such a toxic effect on a person. It gave her a little empathy for her husband wanting to dissolve the marriage, but blue balls still didn't excuse everything.

Neve found herself thinking more about her husband to pass the time, going over everything from courtship to cheating in sequence through the filter of new experience—weighing her unintentional crimes against his, weighing his needs and desires against her incompatibilities, searching for a way to make his infidelity make sense. She saw signs Maya might not have been the first, but if she were honest, those few incidents were far from unquestionably damning.

She kept thinking of her husband and what he'd done, what she'd done, in part because Lord Mikhail kept showing up in the food court after his evening performance. She was equally afraid of him and of herself when she started seeing him out of the corner of her eyes more often in the shadows, steam rising from his body and his breath catching the light. Sometimes steam was all she could see, but she'd know he was there. The iron needle inside her pointed to him every time, quivering the closer he came. He didn't approach, but it was bad enough he haunted her periphery.

Then Neve caught sight of the fingerprints and handprints — large ones — in the dust on the edge of her trailer roof.

She closed the trailer door and stepped back. Christmas lights were strung on posts all around the caravan. The angle and quality of light gave her the perfect view of every smudge in the dust all around her trailer, densest around her bedroom window. He wouldn't be able to see anything through the blinds, but just being there...things he might have heard her doing to herself...

Neve spun around, but no one else was there except Lennon having a smoke behind his trailers and Carlo walking with Misha. Both human men bore obvious erections, which may have been the reason they were walking as quickly as possible. Carlo got around just as fast as anyone else on his arms. At some points he outstripped Misha.

Neve blushed anew when she thought of why they might be so eager.

"I know you're there." She didn't have to shout, and she didn't want to call attention to herself from the rest of the cast. "Come out."

Lord Mikhail emerged from around Troy's trailer as though he hadn't been hiding. His trousers contained his cock far better than Misha's or Carlo's — another point in the magic leather column.

Neve put her hands on her hips. "You need to stop this."

"I'm well within the rules. I haven't overstepped them once." Lord Mikhail came closer, slow out of caution rather than deliberation. "I haven't forced myself upon you, haven't forced you into my bed, haven't so much as touched you."

"You've been stalking me. It was one thing when it was just in the food court. That's a public space, and you have as much right to be there as me. But how often have you been on top of my trailer?"

His silence answered her question.

Neve covered her face with her hands. "Oh my God. Really, you need to stop. You need to stop following me, and you need to stop calling to me. You think I can't tell? It's like a rope around my spine pulling me to wherever you're waiting. You might as well be whispering in my ear."

He crossed his impressive arms. "If I were pulling you in, you'd be certain of it, because you wouldn't be able to resist. But I'm not *trying* to call you, and *you're* calling *me*."

"Excuse me?"

"Do you think this has been any easier for me? To be told that there's a woman who I can't kill within my grasp, and then that woman won't look at me because I assumed I *would* kill her?"

"Was I supposed to *not* be offended by that?"

"I was born ravenous, like the rest of my kind. There are so many who walk this world hungry, Neve. You haven't the slightest idea what it is to be immortal and *always* hungry."

When he tried to look her in the eye, his gaze wandered lower, almost tangible. Her body couldn't hide under a dress the way he stared at her.

"Bell harnessed us perfectly, little girl," he said, forcing himself to look away. "You've experienced my touch. I am in your skin, in fiber and bone. You cannot shake me off like water from your hair. I can't stop calling to you any more than you can stop yourself from breathing. It's my state of being, nothing conscious or deliberate."

"You may not be able to help what you are," she said, "but neither can I, and a victim will never be okay being a victim. And as your almost-victim, I'm not going to let you touch me ever again."

His eyes were burning dark coals behind the curtain of his hair. "It is in a victim's nature to die. You should have died that night. It would have freed you. Don't look at me with such hatred. This torment doesn't only ensnare *you*. Your death would have freed me as well—to move on, to form new attachments, to crave new bodies. But no matter where I go, no matter how I satisfy myself, as soon as I return to Arcanium, your scent permeates the circus. It calls to me wherever you are. The more you need sex, the more inexorable the call. I'm drawn to your scent as a starving man to cooking meat."

She crossed her arms under her breasts, eyes narrowed slightly in suspicion. "If you can't die, you can't starve."

"You know *nothing* of desire that carves its way through your belly like acid, lust that dries your mouth and brings your cock up hard to your abdomen without relief for months…years…an ache as deep as the mouth of hell. You think I enjoy the way the fire forged me? Neither Sasha nor I took well to the slaughter of seduction. Born from the same flame, we shared the same weakness, yet we still must feed. The Creature and the Gentleman may do so with impunity, but Sasha and I must abstain? Would Bell refuse his precious humans their food for weeks at a time without respite?"

He faced her again, opening his arms until there was nothing about his body that was hidden. "Then to bring *you* into the circus, calling to me like a banshee in a cave, even louder than the Spider, yet I am no longer permitted use my influence to convince you to let me into your bed."

Neve wiped sweat from her temple, over her upper lip. She was surprised her nipples hadn't poked holes through her dress. Every time she tried to tell him to back away, her tongue weighed heavy, arousal a hot stone between her thighs.

"I'm married," she managed to whisper. As though he were like the other men who propositioned her in the food court and pretended to not see her ring.

"That didn't stop you before. That hasn't stopped you from being Bell's good little girl, satisfying him with your subjugation. And that didn't stop your man from submitting to Sasha's magic, releasing himself deep within Bell's woman instead of you."

When someone else said it so baldly, Neve's chest panged so hard she worried she was having a heart attack. "Stop talking."

"Let me in, Neve. You torture us both."

"You torture yourself. I'm not your spitted feast, your long pig, something you can discard the bones of when you're done. I can't have sex with just any man, knowing he doesn't give a damn about anything but his own release, knowing he'd kill me a thousand times if he could, without hesitation." Neve backed away. "You don't even know me. You just want to fuck a hole. Well, find another one. And stop haunting my trailer. You're making it difficult to sleep."

"It's an invitation that brought me to your bed in the first place, Neve, so don't lose your temper with me. That was *your* trespass, *not* mine."

"And I deserve death because you make it near impossible to resist? Does *anyone* say no when you do that?"

"Sometimes. But the 'no' always changes."

The darkness in his eyes glowed dark red, almost imperceptible in the black. She didn't know how he called darkness into his eye sockets, because the angle of the light didn't support such shadows. She could only guess what the coal glow within meant. Born of fire, indeed.

"You called *me* out here," he said. "I would have stayed in the shadows and continued to wait, as is my right. Because it's a matter of time, woman. It's only a matter of time. How much more frustration do you think you can withstand?"

"I'm saying no. You don't get to have me."

"Then why are you coming closer?" His deep voice had become a purr. "Why do you reach for me?"

She looked down. Somehow her feet had taken five steps forward without her knowing. And her hands were creeping forward in the air, fingers stretched to meet him.

"Stop," Neve whispered. She fought to keep herself from touching him, stumbled backward and used that momentum to fall against her trailer, three arms' lengths from him.

"I can't," he said, emphasizing each word. "I will always call to you, as you will always call to me, and the call will get stronger the closer we are. That is my nature as lure and yours as prey."

He was a celestial body, drawing her into his orbit, gravity screaming at her to come closer, that he would finally satisfy. Angels and demons weren't supposed to be too far off, one breaking off from the other — at least according to her religion's theology, which didn't account for jinn. Hers only had demons, angels, the Nephilim if you squinted. And if her theology was wrong about the origin of demons, about jinn, what else did it fail to account for?

He wasn't just getting to her body. He was getting to her mind, and that she hadn't expected. He'd been all charm at her bedroom window. Now he'd shed his charm and replaced it with substance—prickly and desperate, but substance nonetheless.

She hated when people assumed she wasn't intelligent. She hadn't assumed he wasn't because of his looks but because of what he was. What need did an incubus have for intelligence? Yet despite the distraction he had to be experiencing, as keen as her own, he was keeping up with her. Given that men's faculties tended to drop as their cock hardened, Neve wondered whether he'd surprise her even more when he wasn't frustrated.

"You can tell me to go away," Mikhail said, "but I'm not bound to your requests for greater proximity. I've been here much longer than you. I know my boundaries. Do you?"

"Fine." She was vaguely aware she was scratching her arms like a dope fiend in withdrawal. Walking away from him and toward her trailer door was like walking away from a dealer. God, how pure what he offered was—in the sense that it wasn't pure at all, in the sense she'd never felt dirtier, happy as swine to smear herself with the filthiness of every inch of his temptation. "But you can't come in unless invited, right? Like vampires. Well, I can't stop you from hovering like a lovesick psycho, but you can't follow me in."

She stepped up into the trailer, clutching the frame against the almost pain of turning her back on him.

"I do not know why your kind denies what it needs, especially when there is no danger to you. How much more peace could you have if you simply let yourself be, if you understood how pathological your need to control yourself is, when you were never meant for chains?" It was as though he spoke right next to her ear, but when she looked over her shoulder, he was still a respectable distance.

"Fine sentiments from someone who bound himself to Arcanium, where Bell starves you like an ascetic." The sides of the door groaned under her grip. It made her think of mattress springs and rocking cars. Her legs shook so badly that she stepped back into the grass.

"That's different. It's not temptation I seek to avoid, but death. I can't eliminate it, but it can be limited — reserved for those who trespass on this circus, performed as a function rather than a need."

"I didn't trespass. So why was *I* punished?" She wanted to strip off her dress, too tight, too constricting, the slight bit of skin still covered in desperate need of air.

"You were just in the wrong place at the wrong time," he said quietly. "Or rather, Bell put you there. He set me free in your direction. He made you the perfect beacon. The women and some of the men of this circus scream for me every night, too. I can barely sleep for the clamor. But only Sasha can share my bed, and that doesn't ease the ache. I followed the sound of your cries from afar, as piercing as any of the cast of this circus. You haven't stopped calling me, Neve. You're *begging*. You know what you want more than you'll allow yourself to admit, or else you wouldn't be backing up to me now. You wouldn't want me to fill you deep, spread through your body, my pleasure coursing through your bloodstream, your pleasure bursting in your brain. I would take your words, little girl, and yield my own to you. No more talking when I can barely think. Grant both of us that grace."

"Stop doing this." Her feet rasped over dead grass. Breath came in short gasps that clouded the air in front of her. Tears threatened to burst through the dam. Everything on edge. Everything pulling her to him. She blamed him, but she was the one holding the rope and hauling herself backward.

"I can't." He sounded as though her rope had closed around his throat. "This isn't me, little girl. This is you and me together, and I don't think we can fight it…much…longer. It's inevitable, Neve. Please. Please don't make us suffer anymore. Just…let me…"

Her head fell back from a sharp wave of pleasure through her body and hit his chest.

The contact was electric, violent as sparks where they met. She slumped, boneless, against him and moaned, "Yes."

Whether intended as permission or exclamation didn't matter.

He smoothed massive hands down her shoulders, and with them, the straps of the dress. He exposed her shoulders, folded down the jersey until it slipped over her breasts and snapped back underneath them. She covered his knuckles as he palmed her breasts. An ever-shrinking part of her mind attempted to push him away, but his touch was magnetic. She thought she'd die if he stopped now, that he would tear skin away if he tried to remove his hands from her.

They could have been the cluster of humans from the haunted funhouse, surgically sewn limb to limb, or the aerialists cursed together. With their contact came clarity, primitive complexity in the drumbeat of their hearts pressed close, his chest to her back, his pulse in his palms over her breast.

Neve thought she heard other sounds, other shouts through the caravan area, some muffled through walls, but soon all she could hear was the rushing in her ears and the rumble of his moan when he dipped his head to kiss up her neck. Their legs tangled as they moved forward to the open door of her trailer. She stumbled but he kept her up, lifting her from the ground and holding her up against him by her breasts alone.

She slammed her hands against the sides of the door, but not to stop him. She ground back against the front of his trousers. God, she could feel his cock, larger than average but nowhere near as large as she knew it could become.

He snaked one hand down from her breast to her thighs, drawing the hem of her dress up as he ground right back. Mikhail cupped her through her underwear, rocking the heel of his palm against her clit but fingering her slit through her panties, dampened even more with fresh arousal. Bell had to have woven magic into her clothes as well, because the way she fought lust all day long, she should soak through anything she wore.

"Not here," he groaned into her ear. "Inside. I take trespassers out in the open, and you're not one of them. When we're finished, you will be glad this was more private."

He turned her around then lifted her up. She wrapped her arms around him, her head falling to his shoulder with a whimper as though she were in pain. He climbed into the trailer, slamming the door behind him.

The strongman was too big for the space she'd been provided. Really, the only place he'd fit was the bedroom. He had to move sideways through the aisle, lifting her, shifting her, and she adjusted her legs or arms as needed as she tasted the tattoos and salt on his shoulder, biting the flesh to reassure herself that he was real, solid, that he wasn't just a man-suit over statue, the way he felt. Her teeth dented the skin.

They couldn't make it to the bedroom. He hitched her up to bend her legs over his shoulders then fell to his knees, his feet in her bathroom and her back against the wall that made up her wardrobe.

"Now that you've invited me, we have all night, little girl. This will help." He left the same dents in her soft inner thigh that she'd left on his shoulder.

He wasted no time pushing her dress up her hips then tearing her panties away. The elastic snapped against her skin like a switch.

Neve's wails filled the small space as he closed his mouth over her clit. She rocked her hips, practically climbing the wall as she arched and pushed her clit against the tight, velvet heat. He wrapped his arms around her thighs so she couldn't wriggle away, his dark, tanned skin seeming even more so against her blue-veined paleness. She held her forehead with one hand as though to keep herself upright. With her other hand, she threaded her fingers through his hair, locks of it tickling over her legs when he moved.

She groaned as he lifted his head from her clit with a wicked smile to stare up at her.

Neve struck his shoulder blade with her heel. "Don't stop. You were begging me a minute ago."

"You were saying no a minute ago," he said. "Now I know I shall be satisfied. When first we met, I promised you that I could make love to you all night. Shall I show you?"

"If you make me wait all night before you let me come, I'm going to kill you with my bare hands. My nails aren't as sharp as Lady Sasha's, but I'm a desperate woman, and your eyes are right there."

He smiled, the darkness of his sockets glowing again, but the tendons of his neck and shoulders were so much more relaxed than before. "Would you claw these pretty garnets just because I didn't give you what you wanted immediately? I think someone needs to learn patience. Four weeks is nothing, Neve. You'll have years of this. I've had a hundred and twenty-seven."

"Fuck." She didn't think she'd ever said the word just as an expletive, but it felt good in her mouth, though not as good as him.

He dipped down to run his tongue between her folds, flicked the tip at her clit to make her twitch.

"When you swear, it doesn't sound natural to you. I like it. Say 'fuck' again, and I'll let you come, little girl."

She banged the back of her head on the wall in frustration, screwing her face tightly against the nagging warning that she should tell him to leave and he'd have to go, invitation be damned. She could end this, fill herself with the tentacle toy until she bit through her pillow, go to sleep unsatisfied like she had the last four weeks, her still valid wedding ring digging a groove into her cheek.

But she'd asked him in, and although she should make him stop, she just didn't want to anymore, not with every last sexual knot, like pebbles under her skin, loosening under his touch.

How many other people had come into the circus like this, knowing what they should and shouldn't do, but giving in to it anyway when they realized there was no point in fighting? How long had it taken them? She didn't think she got extra points for each week she'd resisted, given that she'd tied herself to the incubus before she'd even been brought in.

How had each of them eventually justified themselves? Maybe they'd decided that as long as they were in the company of bad men, bad demons, bad demigods, they should just embrace being bad themselves.

She felt sick. She'd been an analytical believer all her life, but she couldn't remember the last time she'd encountered an ethical or moral dilemma quite this intense, and she'd voted in several election years. She wasn't used to having no clear choice before her, wasn't used to knowing that she wouldn't be able to do what she thought was right, wasn't used to wondering whether she'd ever been right at all.

But her body adhered to simpler principles on the hierarchy of needs. It wouldn't let her say no, and she was inextricable from the meat sack in which she'd been born. She couldn't tell her body that to cling to the incubus was to succumb to a fallen state rather than fight it. Fight it for what? For her soul, already caged in Arcanium and made to sing a song of pleasure rather than praise?

What was forgiveness when there was no sin? Sin was as much part of the design as salvation. To believe anything less was to ignore the beginning of creation.

Neve closed her eyes and shook her head, but her hips lifted as though to plead for Mikhail's mouth once more. "Fuck. Don't stop. Whatever I do, don't stop."

"I usually only take orders from Bell and Sasha. But that, love, is an order I like."

He moaned as he closed his lips around her clit and the folds that cradled it, his tongue pressing, sucking, the vibrations and sensations combining into a devastating force that narrowed all her thoughts away from theology and morality to the nexus of her legs.

Everything became about the ever-tightening coil from her clit up her spine to her mind, where she could only keep shaking her head to keep it from exploding. She had no such luck where he sucked her pleasure from her. She pulled his hair, arched away from the wall until she was balanced on his shoulders while he kept a firm hold on her thighs. He didn't let up, didn't let her fall—except in her mind, where she fell like water over a cliff. Sweat dripped down her back, leaving cold, wet places on her dress. He kept the orgasm rolling, rapids over sharp rocks, as she rode his tongue.

Finally, Mikhail stood and tossed her onto her bed in the same motion. He stretched out an unnaturally long tongue to clean off anything she'd left on his trimmed moustache and beard.

"Take off the dress, little girl. You don't need it anymore tonight."

She pushed it over her hips rather than try to bring it over her head.

The lights were on in her bedroom, which meant that, quite unlike their first night, he could see all of her, and she could see almost all of him.

He could see how she wasn't perfect like a succubus, her breasts larger because she was soft everywhere, her thighs and ass big and strong from softball games and strength training. Her family's buried Irish heritage had returned full-throttle in her, which meant bright blue veins, pale freckles over her shoulders, nose and forearms. She had flesh folds, ivory stretch marks, bulges, colors to her translucent skin that women like Maya and Valorie never had to deal with. Kitty's skin was golden underneath the chestnut, and the Spider's own paleness was like matte porcelain, broken only by the ink of her tattoos and the occasional mole. Neve couldn't even point to her hair as some bastion of ginger pride, given the mess it was at the moment. She couldn't imagine any of it being anywhere near as sexy as the man who stood before her — sex personified, which was kind of the point.

Yet the strongman pulled his hair back, staring over her in the light as though he could eat her up from toes to hair roots. He stroked over the front of his leather trousers with a strangled groan.

"That didn't almost kill me," she said, sitting up on the comforter. "I couldn't move the first time, could barely talk. You thought I was dead."

"My mouth will flay, but it doesn't have to kill. You came, but if I were to leave, you would discover yourself unsatisfied. You will not be truly satisfied until I come inside you. And if you were any other woman, *that* would kill you, no matter what I did to hold back."

"That's awfully penis-centric."

The strongman actually laughed. "It's simply how incubi feed from women."

He crawled onto her bed, his gaze like heat on her breasts as their weight brought them down, still defying most gravity at this point but showing signs she wouldn't be so lucky for much longer — except time seemed suspended here, with Kitty looking young even though she was supposed to have been in Arcanium for over twenty years.

Under Lord Mikhail's devoted attention, Neve gathered her breasts in hands too small to contain them. Flesh plumped between her fingers, pressed together for cleavage that drove straight men crazy. Then she held them up by her nipples, rolling them between her fingers. They hadn't needed help to become the hard buds they'd pretty much been from the moment the incubus had entered her bedroom four weeks ago, but there was an undeniable nerve connection between her nipples and her cunt that seemed to ache with pain as much as with pleasure.

It was strange to do all the things she'd done with Joseph — things she'd done because they were expected of her and because she'd thought he'd like them — and have them actually mean something for her. To understand that some of the things women did for their husbands were for themselves.

"Is it the same between incubi and other men?" she asked, curiosity returning with the brief respite provided by his mouth.

"I nearly killed a man from a hand job alone."

He batted her fingers away from her breasts, humming with pleasure as they yielded to their weight again. He replaced her hands with his, massaging the hard, bright pink flesh, the areolae wrinkled from tightening. He pressed the tip of his tongue to one of his canines, dog-tooth sharper than the rest, as she automatically parted her legs to alleviate the sudden tension he brought there.

"Gay and bisexual men are more at risk with an incubus than women, because any contact with my cock or theirs makes them susceptible to my feed. Bisexual men and women are in the most danger from sex demons in general — far too many ways for both succubi and incubi to feed from them."

"Who's safest?"

"Lesbians. They won't respond to an incubus, and there are really only two ways for succubi to kill them, and plenty of ways for them not to. There are succubi in relationships with women who have no idea what they are. The demons just refuse certain kinds of sex. It's nothing to do with a moral or preferential hierarchy. A feed simply requires specific genital contact for it to satisfy the sex demon."

"So as long as you keep your pants on, I'm safe."

"You're one of the few who is completely safe from my cock, love, and that makes you invaluable to me."

For some reason, talk of killing her wasn't as problematic as it had started out, perhaps because it truly seemed out of his hands and because she still wanted him so intensely that she felt hollowed out. But being called invaluable rankled in a way she couldn't quite pin down with all of her blood pinking her nipples, flushing her cheeks and dilating as many blood vessels as it could in her cunt, her folds, her clit.

She covered his mouth with her hand, but she bit her lip as he nipped at her fingertips and crawled over her to make her lay back. If he just wouldn't talk, she'd be able to get through this. She'd be able to sleep satisfied tonight, kick him out afterward, tear away everything that smelled of him, wash herself of his scent, slip between cold sheets and curl up with her legs against her belly to hold in the inevitable sickness of guilt, the cold of the platinum ring on her finger the coldest of all.

Mikhail made the built-in headboard groan when he closed his hand over it, leaning his hips forward to bring his leather placket against her breasts. The leather was so tight that he couldn't exactly fuck them, but she gathered them in anyway, shivering. Even through the leather, the path of his cock tingled over her bare skin, as though each individual hair follicle could sense how close he was and reached for him.

"Open the leather." That deep purr had returned, too tender to be a growl, too dark to be gentle. "Take out my cock, little girl. You invited me in, but if you need my cock, you must open the last door. I won't have you pretending that the wicked demon took you against your will."

Neve hated him a little as she brought her fingers to the front of his trousers, undoing the laces that held him in, unthreading them until the placket folded to the sides and she could reach in. Free him.

A whimper whined past her lips as he swelled to fill her hand with each stroke, his pre-cum alone enough to smooth the way. He pulled the trousers down his thighs. They peeled off the rest of the way seemingly on their own.

He surged when she raised herself up to take the head of his cock in her mouth, the glistening flesh impossible to resist, the musky scent and taste of him better than anything she'd ever had. When he pushed in, his cock slid over her tongue, hit the back of her mouth then slipped into her throat without any obstruction.

They groaned in tandem, and Mikhail grabbed Neve by her hair to push her down to take his whole giant cock. Her throat miraculously expanded to take him all the way. She could still breathe without effort, but when she touched her neck, she knew just where the head of his cock had reached. She'd cough, heave, struggle to breathe even though she could anyway, if it didn't feel so freaking good to have him deep in her throat, almost as good as in her pussy.

She shouldn't have been able to open her mouth wide enough, and her lips should have hurt to stretch. She should have bitten him. Instead, he growled like a beast at the way she licked, swallowed, rubbed her throat to caress the head through the flesh of her neck. He pulled his hips back to bring the head to her tongue before sliding himself down her throat again. With her free hand, she furiously stroked around her clit, more turned on by him fucking her mouth than she'd thought it was possible to be. The pleasure was like pain. It was impossible to conceive of it until it was experienced.

"No. No time. I want in your pussy, little girl. We have years for me to possess your mouth. I'll entice it in other ways, I promise." He withdrew completely, and now she gasped, now she coughed, her diaphragm heaving as though her body had only just realized what he'd been doing to it.

Mikhail laughed as he crawled back. He hooked his arms under her knees to spread her legs farther, testing the limits of her flexibility.

"God, I've wanted back in you for a month," he groaned. "Your dreams stole into mine, your desires like a fog in my head, with nothing to show for it."

His cock was at its full thickness and girth now, the head broad at her entrance, but he angled his mouth over hers to take it more gently, without the same distorting magic of his cock. It felt more like just a kiss in comparison, something that was made better from an incubus' touch but not within the realm of the impossible. She much preferred the kiss, opened her mouth for him of her own volition, wrapped an arm around him to scratch over his hard muscles as he pushed his cock in.

She wallowed, grasped, reveled, stroked her clit and wrapped her legs around his. Nothing felt more right than when he stopped talking and she stopped thinking, when their bodies were flush together and he was inside her, when she surrounded him.

He didn't make her wait. He didn't make himself wait. He clutched the headboard with one hand and pulled himself in—tireless, relentless—his cock entering her over and over, pushing again and again into impossible places that nevertheless yielded to him. He kept going until she cried out, her back curving to bring her hips up against his, her cunt clutching as though milking him. He broke from their kiss, and his cock seemed to pulse and grow even bigger…as though it needed to, as though she could possibly take any more. But she did, digging her nails into his shoulder and keeping the pace on her clit to drive her orgasm through the heat that filled her where it shouldn't have.

There it was again—the sense that something in her head stopped, that everything stopped, for a second or two, perhaps ten. She didn't lose time so much as skip it entirely. He was still above her, still inside her, when she came back. She had no way to know for certain whether she'd been out and for how long—just a knowledge, a certainty, that something had been lost.

Neve panted, relinquishing the oversensitive pleasure of her clit to wrap her other arm around him. She fancied his tattoos had a texture, though everything about him was smooth over the inhuman hardness underneath.

And speaking of hardness…

Lord Mikhail stayed hard in her, opened his red-tinged black eyes to peer down at her with an indeterminable expression. He watched her until she blinked. Then he ran a crooked finger along her cheekbone, an impossibly gentle gesture for such a large, strong man.

"Hello, Neve. It's good to see you again."

He drew her up to meet him as he dipped down to kiss her again. She was still sluggish, emerging from whatever his feed had done. No longer a starving man consuming his first meal in weeks, he kissed her with slow, sweet deliciousness that warmed her all the way down to her toes. She twitched as though waking up when he moved inside her again, shallow thrusts that caressed her inside, caressed her outside with his skin a whisper against hers.

He slowly eased them over, with him on his back and her resting against his chest, straddling his hips. She felt like this had been a yoga pose at least once, her knees this close to her chest, but she was too comfortable on top of him to adjust to a more typical position.

"I've not begun to tire yet, little girl."

Neve knew the moment he'd gathered magic against her again, because she suddenly stiffened, all tension returned, her folds pulsing, clit pulsing, cunt pulsing. The aching was back, desire everywhere she was soft, everywhere he was hard.

"Don't you see how wonderful this can be?" he said. "Isn't this tension so much better when you know it is fleeting?"

"Mikhail, please stop trying to make this okay. When you talk, it just makes it worse." But as she raised herself up, it pushed her down to the base of his cock, and she choked on her words. She brushed his small, dark brown nipples with her fingertips, and when she tweaked them with her thumbs, he made a happy grunt that extended into a groan as she rolled her hips.

"I apologize. Speaking to women like this is not my forte."

"Like this?"

"When women don't know what I am, when they aren't inclined to resist, I am the artist. It is part of my hunt to lure them in with pretty words. But Sasha is the only woman I've spoken with properly for over a hundred years, the only one I can speak with after sex. Even as the Arcanium strongman, I am not required to talk. For the longest time, all I ever *had* to say to women was everything I needed to get me into their bed. And that was all they ever wanted from me. What am I supposed to say?"

"How about nothing?" She licked the hollow of his clavicle, tasting salt and flesh, licked up his throat, kissed under his jaw. "Just stop. And if you're going to make me feel like this, don't keep it this strong. Fuck me, please."

"Ride me." He cradled the nape of her neck, but he didn't guide her until she had kissed up his chin of her own accord. "Rise up and work your pussy all over my cock. Let me see you, Neve."

She did as he told her, bracing herself on his abdomen instead of his chest to keep herself as upright as possible, as distant as she could be while still spitted on his cock. She breathed in his magic, swam in it, raised herself up and let gravity bring herself back down again. She sheathed him to the hilt every time, her wetness and his cum making an unbearably wet sound every time she took him in. But she couldn't stop now, didn't want the pleasure of his cock against her inner walls to stop, not when every stroke was as good as one of her old orgasms.

Her breasts shook and swung, not appreciating the violence with which she bounced over his cock, but she couldn't care. She rolled her hips and ground down, took him as hard and deep as she pleased, until another cry ripped from her throat and another shared orgasm heated through her and left her boneless, a collapsed, dead-weight body over his, not that it fazed him.

"I promised you all night, Neve. I am unreliable in many things, but I keep my promises."

Chapter Seven

He eventually wore himself out long after she'd been left nearly catatonic, though she kept her nails hooked in him, quivered when he brought her to orgasm. By the end of it, she felt as though she'd been systematically skinned inside and out with a fine razor, all nerve endings exposed and stimulated over and over and over and over… Each time she thought she couldn't stand more, he'd shift the angle, kiss her again and the fire would rekindle.

His cock could have continued, but he pulled one of the blankets out of the drawer next to him and folded it between them so that he was no longer in contact with her.

Despite that, her dreams during the few hours of sleep she managed were such that the two of them somehow pushed the blanket beneath them and came together while unconscious. He was still asleep when she woke up, his movements too slow to be anything but unhurried somnambulism. She clung to his shoulders, pressed her face to his chest, breathed in the sharp, musky incense of his skin. She hid herself against him, canting her hips to his patient, bleary rhythm.

He woke to climax, tangling his fingers through her tangled hair, the dreamy motion of his hips quickening and strengthening until he sank completely in, semen pulsing to join the rest, and his feed upon her nearly pulling her back into the dream from which she'd emerged.

Mikhail hummed as he finished, her own orgasm fluttering around him. He eased his fingers from her hair to comb through the mess he'd help make.

As soon as she was able to move, she shoved his chest.

Her intention had been to shove him away from her, but he was so immovable, she shoved herself back from him, which worked just as well but was still unfair, since this was her trailer, her bed.

"Neve?"

Poor man sounded confused.

She used the distance she'd made to help her as she rolled off the bed. Neve hoped the golems knew a good dry cleaner, because sex was damn messy. She was used to only doing it once at a time, but she'd lost count of how many combined orgasms they'd had — with a corresponding amount of semen that seemed like serious overkill, unless it performed a different function for incubi other than carrying sperm. At this point, though, her biological curiosity was so far on the backburner, it couldn't have boiled water.

She'd cover herself with a blanket, but his side was the one with the blankets, and she didn't want to ruin another one.

"I need you to leave. Please."

Mikhail sat on the edge of the bed. "I don't understand. Did I do something wrong?"

"You can't stay. I'm exhausted, dehydrated and in desperate need of a shower."

"Neve, what's wrong?"

"Please, don't call me by my name." She massaged the bridge of her nose. The headache from dehydration needled the place between her eyes and behind them, little pinpricks that threatened to throb. "Just…go. Get out."

"I don't understand. Were you not satisfied?"

Neve laughed, though nothing was funny. It was a good thing she wasn't expected to smile for the customers or else she'd really be in trouble. "Oh yeah, I was satisfied. I'm feeling almost normal now, except for not wanting anything to touch me and most of my circus days being nothing but hands. Except for feeling like a cumbucket." Yet another word she never used, but there wasn't anything more accurate. "Except for the two hours of sleep where I basically had sex dream after sex dream, and I'm squelching and sticking and there's enough semen in here to get a harem pregnant. I just really need you to leave."

"I don't understand."

"You said that already. I hate to be impolite. Really, I do. But I have nothing left, and I couldn't be clearer about you needing to leave. Maybe in a few days, I can be clearer as to why, but right now…" She picked up a bookend in case that made her point, even though she'd have to disinfect it later.

What a little girl holding a bookend was supposed to do against a strongman when her fastball had barely made him blink didn't matter. He stood, retrieved his trousers from the floor. He, unlike her, seemed to have emerged from the night unscathed, traces of their various bodily fluids nowhere to be found.

Brow knitted, Mikhail ducked out of the bedroom. He paused at the top of the stairs. "Thank you. My mind hasn't been this quiet in months."

"You're welcome." She guessed she meant it, but she wouldn't be able to appreciate it either way until she'd had a long, hot shower.

As soon as he was out of her trailer, striding out in the morning with the usual steam rising from him in curling billows, Neve gathered all the blankets that could have possibly been soaked through and dumped them outside. She couldn't see anyone else out there looking at her, so she didn't know if she flashed someone in the process, but right now, she just couldn't care.

* * * *

Her mood didn't improve after the shower, though she spent longer in there than most mornings. She ate apple slices, cheese and summer sausage from the mini-fridge instead of going for breakfast under the big top. She wanted these precious few moments without anyone around, anyone close to her.

But more than having alone time, somehow she knew... Maybe it was because of Misha and Carlo hurrying to one of their trailers last night, unable to wait. Or Kitty telling her that the sex demons' sexual tension affected the entire circus.

It only stood to reason that a release of that tension would also affect the circus. A whole night of releasing tension...and again this morning... What had everyone done while the incubus' magic had surrounded her, insinuated into her like a parasite, spread its tentacles to suck the self-replenishing life from her then burst in shared climax? She was all too aware of what they'd probably done, and the last thing she wanted was to go out into the circus where everyone knew what she'd done and for how long and how intense it had been — as though they'd been peering through the windows, too.

When she couldn't stay in her trailer any longer without getting to Kitty's tent too late for makeup, she pulled on one of her negligees — the jersey dress was on the lawn with her linens. It wasn't her usual costume, pink silk with lace cutouts, and her bra and panties showed through the thin material, but if Bell had wanted her to always wear the jersey, he should have given her more dresses to choose from. The grasping hands in the funhouse would cover most of her body anyway.

She kept her head down, but she was fortunate not to meet anyone or have anyone bother her on the way to Kitty's tent.

No such luck when she entered it.

"Holy crap, woman, what did you do last night?" One of the twins — Neve couldn't tell which because she couldn't read their necklaces from the entrance — swiped invisible sweat from her forehead. "I haven't had a night like that in years. What are you? Insatiable?"

"I don't think anyone in the whole damn circus slept," the other twin said. "Everyone looked completely trashed at breakfast this morning, either because they rode the waves or because they weren't able to."

"I'd stay away from Bell if I were you. He's snippy as a feral tom. You know, I don't think he's been without a woman in his bed for over twenty years. Did he have anyone before Valorie, Kitty?"

"There was a period when he didn't, but not long. Before Valorie, he had the woman who was the illusionist before he took the position." Kitty braided the twins' pigtails together as she talked. She glanced up at Neve, assessing. Like the twins, her face was drawn, although the color in her cheeks and light fur over her face concealed the worst of the dark circles. "Don't worry about him. He knows how to handle himself. I'll get to you in a minute, sweetie. Feel free to grab some cold-press coffee from the fridge."

"Lord Mikhail had the circus going so hard," the second twin said. "Seth and Lars actually did their personal gay thing with us there, which was weird and wonderful. They're out and everything now, but they were so embarrassed this morning. Hey!" The second twin pressed a hand where her hair met her forehead. "What gives?"

Kitty finished off their hair without another word, pretending an invisible gnome had yanked their braids instead.

Valorie ducked into the tent and headed straight for the vanity, where she put on her own rhinestone-studded, glittery harlequin face. She acknowledged Neve with a raised chin and smirk but, thankfully, that was all.

Maya came in next, wincing a little as she walked, but she, like the rest of the women in the tent, appeared thoroughly satisfied, thoroughly tired. She still had trouble looking Neve in the eye, her posture telegraphing guilt, even though Bell was more at fault.

Seeing her in her Mad Red Queen regalia gave Neve a twinge of nausea anyway.

"Thank you," was all she said in Neve's direction, but that was enough to bring a flush to Neve's cheeks again. She bent over her knees to hide her face while she waited for Kitty to call her up.

The girls seemed to figure out something was wrong and didn't say anything to her about it again. Other women who popped in and out didn't add to the humiliation, so there must have been some mouthing words and miming when they came in, but Neve didn't look up to make sure.

"Your turn."

When Neve stood, only the Spider was at the vanity, putting heavy kohl on her lids then painting two more eyes under her real ones to create the illusion she had four.

Kitty started by pinning Neve's hair away from her face. "You want to talk about it?"

"No."

* * * *

The funhouse hands worked over her as fervently as they did when she wore the jersey dress, so now she knew it didn't matter which costume she wore.

Those hands quickly restoked the fire Lord Mikhail had extinguished. She'd known it was only a matter of time before the arousal returned, just as it would only be a matter of time before Lord Mikhail showed back up on her doorstep, but she'd hoped she would have longer than a few hours.

She nearly cried, tears hot and stinging in her eyes with betrayal at her own body for not letting her have any peace. At Joseph for wanting her to be like this. At Bell for transforming her into this — because heaven knew he could have interpreted that damn wish any way he damn well pleased. At Lord Mikhail for only making it worse while he at least got a good feed. At every single person who passed her while she writhed against the hands, because she didn't have to fake the horror of being pulled into an unseen abyss.

Weeks, months, years, decades of this insatiability stretched before her like a prison sentence, more and more a version of hell as time went on. Sure, it wasn't pain, but it was a lifetime of discontent, and there was nothing within her own power to do about it. She had to depend on the kindness of friends and strangers. But she didn't *want* to.

And this was all she was ever going to be to friends and strangers alike — a cypher either way, a living sex doll whose body had weight and substance, but did anyone realize she was inside it, too? She was a commodity to be consumed, a pretty thing to look at. She couldn't even impress them with some feat of physical prowess or accident of nature like the performers or freaks. Bell could make the arms seem alive with his magic, so he didn't actually need a woman in this tableau. She might as well be a mannequin.

Her brain liked to feel useful, but there was nothing for a scientist to *do* here. Being pretty was its own accident of nature — and its own curse. It certainly had been back when she hadn't been interested in sex, yet that had pretty much been the only reason men had wanted to be within her sphere. It was even more of a curse now that she was interested in sex, now that she had virtually unlimited access to sex she knew she'd enjoy.

Because I'm incidental to the whole equation.

That's why she was so ticked off at Mikhail and Bell. That's why she'd woken up satisfied yet still frustrated. That's why she hated everyone right now. But it didn't matter to any of them, because she had big boobs and sexy lingerie whether she was happy or not.

Neve wished she could get a hold of the chainsaw. Maybe the bone saw. She bet people would notice something other than her body then, too concerned with what she was doing with theirs. She wasn't morbid or violent by nature, but a regular diet of horror movies had given her brain access to some gnarly weaponry for her fantasy life when she had idle destruction on her mind. Blood spattered in stark patterns on the walls of her imagination.

That got her through most of the day of guys groping themselves and the Gentleman having to move along nearly a dozen men trying to do things to her they shouldn't.

Above all, she didn't make eye contact. She pretended they were the fourth wall and she the performer who couldn't acknowledge it. Eye contact made the more brazen of the men think they had her permission. She dared them to use that logic in a zoo. When they reached for her, she would twist away, but she still wouldn't look at them. Whether they thought her glaring at them was encouragement that she wanted them or encouragement to annoy the crap out of her, the result was the same. The tightening of her belly called the Gentleman every time.

She wasn't sure whether she was more anxious at being touched because they were doing it without her permission or because, if they did touch her, she might let them do whatever they wanted anyway. Neve didn't know whether a man had to be an incubus to make her feel good. Bell hadn't been an incubus, and the brush of his fingers had been enough to set her skin off. And all these damn hands on her...if any of them went under the edge of her underwear, she didn't think she'd resist much.

At a certain point late afternoon or early evening, there was a brief lull in the number of guests coming through the funhouse, as there sometimes was. She hoped it was close to the end of her work day, hoped the prospect of a good seat in the big top tent had drawn guests away from the funhouse. She'd never drunk more than a glass of wine now and then — and a cocktail even more rarely — but she suddenly had a taste for vodka that she wasn't interested in developing more fully. Mostly, she just wanted to sleep in a clean bed with clean sheets and room to stretch. And if she had to have sex dreams, she'd rather have them alone and wake up without another person there, even if her body would prefer something warm.

This circus was going to drive her insane, and Neve didn't think she was exaggerating. How was she supposed to make Arcanium work for her when what it demanded of her went against everything she used to be?

A man rounded the corner, walking alone, which was enough to make him unusual. People didn't come to the circus on their own. People came on dates, with their family, with a group of friends or some variation thereof.

Neve hadn't been single often, but it had been enough to know that most places were incredibly lonely by oneself, with all kinds of reminders that alone wasn't okay. Particularly at restaurants. God forbid a woman want to be seated alone at a table rather than at the bar or getting her food to go.

The world was built around relationships, and people tended to go into haunted houses in groups. Part of it was for safety in numbers, but scares also worked better that way. Fear was as contagious as humor — which was why horror movies used screeching violins the way sitcoms used laugh tracks and why the funhouse had its own soundtrack throughout the building.

The man strolled through, hands in the pockets of his tan trench coat, his black fedora low over his eyes as he watched his feet kicking up, as though he heard music to dance to instead of screams. He glanced up at her the way a person taking a pleasant walk looks up for roses.

Square jaw but fine features that reminded her a bit of the fey masculinity that made up Bell's unique attractiveness. Pale, but with a touch of enough sun that it wasn't like hers or the Spider's. Dark hair, clean-shaven. Eyes so blue they glowed through the shadow under his fedora. He wore a suit under the trench, his black shoes matte and foreign. Hardly the ensemble one should wear to an outdoor circus rife with sawdust, grass, ice and mud. Yet there wasn't so much as a smudge on his shoes or a drop of moisture from an icicle on his trench coat.

He stopped in front of her.

She twisted and writhed against the hands grabbing her, caressing her parted legs, pulling her arms up to present her breasts at their best angle. But as stimulating as the hands were, as much as she understood the image that Bell had wanted to create, she didn't think she'd felt quite as sexual under a strange man's scrutiny as she did right then. A sexual object, plenty of times. But a sexual woman…?

He looked at her. At *her*. Not just her body, although he appeared to appreciate that, too, taking in the sight of the hands reaching under the brief skirt of the negligee, cupping and squeezing her breasts, pulling her hair. But he returned his gaze to her face, searched her there as well, leaving her uncomfortable under the scrutiny even when she wasn't looking back at him.

But then she couldn't help but meet his eyes, victim of her own curiosity. His hands were in his trench pockets, but they weren't moving, so he wasn't trying to surreptitiously jerk off. She couldn't even tell if he was turned on, because the trench coat mostly hid the front of his trousers. The dilation of his pupils and the color in his cheeks could be easily explained by the dark funhouse or the cold weather, because otherwise his face was perfectly serene.

A slight smile curved his lips, and that weird glow to his eyes drew her attention until she couldn't look away even if she wanted to.

He didn't blink.

Writhing and twisting against the hands seemed more and more deliberate the longer their eyes met, until her desire was at an exquisitely excruciating peak — not the old agony, but a new, fresh hell, the way it had been when Bell had first given it to her with a kiss. She couldn't figure out how long the man met her eyes, how long she stared back at him, but he had to have lingered too long.

Yet the Gentleman didn't come.

One of the hands at her breast pinched her nipple. Neve cried out, her surprise joining with the screams and moans of her personalized part of the soundtrack. Another hand stroking up her thigh trailed along the line of her folds then back up to her clit to press in delicate circles. She tightened her fists over the wrists of the disembodied arms holding her up. She pulled her body taut, onto her tiptoes, simultaneously trying to arch her body into the touch and away from it. Confused. So turned on that her cunt clenched in undulating rhythm—not quite an orgasm, but a preface to one.

The man in the fedora still didn't blink, but his gentle smile widened at her reaction—as though he was the one who had made it happen.

A hand drifted up from her other breast to close around her neck, not squeezing—more like an elegant choker over her neck than a collar. She still looked the man in the eye because she couldn't look away, but her breathing came more shallowly, and her brain had gone strangely blank except for what the hands were doing and the image of the man in front of her.

"It's a pleasure to meet you, new girl. I hope you'll favor me with a few moments of your time when our next opportunity presents itself."

He turned to continue down the corridor, as casual leaving as he had been entering. It was a few minutes before another group passed into the corridor. By that time, the hands had returned to where they were supposed to be, and she was turned on like crazy, wondering whether she'd fallen asleep standing up and dreamed the whole thing.

When the hands released her and the soundtrack turned off, Neve fell to her knees.

"Please," she whispered. She tried to pull the limp hands back up her body, even though they'd changed from living limbs to rubber—the carriage turned back into the pumpkin. If she could just have another orgasm at someone else's hand, even a disembodied one, something to shut this desire off for another few hours, she might not have to go to sleep in such an awful state.

But without the magic moving them, the hands were no more effective than sex toys.

Neve slammed her fists on the floor, screaming, kicking at the limp props that had fallen like fishing nets around her. She felt entitled to the tantrum, because she doubted Bell would let her take a hammer to his kneecaps, although that would certainly improve her mood.

The Gentleman stepped around the corner to make sure she wasn't being attacked, but once he determined she was safe, he wisely left her alone.

An order of fried mushrooms and a small personal pizza from the odd chef later, she felt a little better.

Magic or not, though, the chill in the increasingly wintery air was a little much for all the bare skin she showed. When she started shivering, she left the lights and marginal warmth of the food court and headed around the back of the big top to reach the caravan the long way, in case the performances ended and people caught her walking around looking the way she did without anything else to cover her—too vulnerable to any man who pressed himself upon her right now for her own comfort.

She had a feeling her arousal wouldn't be quite this bad without that stranger—real or dream-made—bringing it up to a fresh pitch.

The first ecstasy was supposed to be the pinnacle, with everything after a series of graduated disappointments, nothing ever as good again. That was reason for drug overdoses, serial killers and adult discontent, with all the firsts taken up and first feelings never replicated. The way Bell had made her negated that principle. Every high was just as sweet and aching as the last, although over time, if the arousal wasn't satisfied, it turned stale. Now she was at the new pitch all over again, sweetly intense in such a way she *wanted* to enjoy it, except she knew it wouldn't stay sweet, and even if she saw it to its conclusion with someone, the relief would be all too temporary. Her arousal hadn't been designed to end, which had quickly taken the wonder of it away, hadn't it? Because arousal was just another kind of stress, and stress wreaked havoc because it wasn't supposed to be felt forever, only in short bursts.

She was a committed monogamist and introvert who'd never had this problem before but whose body had been redesigned into hyperpromiscuity. 'Slut' felt more honest, but the social connotations were even worse than the name that felt even more accurate, although it wasn't used clinically anymore.

Nymphomaniac.

It was like being on drugs all the time that left her as irritable as she was frustrated, but what the hell was she supposed to do about it as long as she was still married, as long as that still mattered to her as a matter of principle? What was she supposed to do about it when her mind rebelled at the very notion that she fall into bed with anyone just to get this itch scratched, although she wasn't sure there was any practical reason to rebel? Was there calamine lotion for this?

So deeply wrapped in her thoughts against the cold, Neve saw the man with skin like stone stepping out from the backstage exit, but her reaction time wasn't what it should have been. She walked straight into him, feet stumbling over his and hers until their legs were a tangle, though he'd caught her by the shoulders. She fell face first against his chest, clutching at his upper arms to catch herself, to pull herself standing again. Like most of the men in Arcanium, he was naked from the waist up, which meant she was suddenly surrounded by warm male scent and firm skin.

Lord Mikhail looked like flesh and felt like flesh-covered stone. Victor felt like flesh, but with the texture of pumice stone.

"Hey, sorry." Victor helped her regain her balance, held her shoulders tightly until she was standing on the ground rather than on his toes. "That was my fault. You were so determined in where you were going, I should have moved rather than expect you to. I guess I was distracted, too."

He was hard. Not just his athletic body. The fairly strong erection in his tight trousers felt normal to her, more normal than the strongman's. But he felt strong to her, too, with kindness in the sound of his voice, surprisingly apologetic in comparison to most men she encountered. There were any number of attractive qualities behind the stone color and texture of him, friendly eyes and smile, appealing structure…

And she was against his body, a body that wanted sex as much as hers did.

Temporary insanity—that was the excuse she was going with—although that insanity was going to be a heck of a lot less temporary if she could expect these feelings for the rest of her tenure in Arcanium.

Neve slid her hands to his chest, stood on her toes and pressed her lips to his. She parted them soon after the first kiss to lick the line of his lower lip. Then she pushed his chest, crowding him, until his back struck the thick canvas of the big top tent with a sound like he'd hit a wall.

His exclamation was muffled, but the surprise didn't last long. He smoothed his palms down the back of her negligee to the hem that stopped barely an inch beneath her ass as though tailored to her unique measurements—most short skirts rode well above appropriate, due to the appreciable size of her hips and backside. He dug stone-strong fingers deep into the flesh he found, gathered her up in handfuls, sliding the skirt up in the process, until only her panties and his leather trousers were between them. She lifted her leg at his urging, curled it around his hip to bring herself against his contained cock, which gave her something to rub her clit against with increasing urgency. The moans he muffled in her mouth intensified, and the sounds of her pleasure climbed higher and higher the faster she worked her hips against his.

Because it was working, even through clothes. What they were doing brought her up, up, up, promising the sweetest release if she could just…

"Wait, wait, wait." He let go of her leg, which slid her slightly down his body and made him groan at the sensation against his erection. "Not that I'm not enjoying this, but if there ever was a case of tripping and falling into sex, this is it. I don't think we've spoken to each other once, not even to say hi."

She hit his shoulder with her fist, but not hard. "God. Of all the men in this damn circus, I have to stumble into the one who actually asks if I'm okay with it."

"Actually, most men in Arcanium are like that. Minimizes the number of times the Ringmaster whips us."

"I'm pretty sure most men would think the fact I'm humping them like a bitch in heat was grounds enough to assume I wanted sex."

"But you don't — or at least not the way most women want sex."

She hit him again, this time a little harder, but though he grunted, he didn't keep her from doing it, nor did he stop her from forcing herself away from him, step by step. "How can you even tell?"

"I don't know. I just had the impression that you were humping in an angry way. My penis can't tell the difference, but I can. It's like hate sex, which can be pleasant in its own right, but we don't know each other well enough to have anything to fight about. We literally haven't exchanged two words until now."

"I'm sorry." She pulled on the roots of her hair, as much to hurt herself as to alleviate some of the tension accumulated around her temples. "I didn't mean to attack you like that. It was all so much, and then you were there, and... And I'm listening to what I'm saying and not liking it one bit. There's no reason for me to jump your bones without warning just because I'm horny and have the female equivalent of blue balls all the time — as though you're just there for my relief. Cheese and crackers, this is what I always hated men doing to me." The headache hit her just as the understanding did. "It didn't matter who you were, just that you had a dick that would actually work on me, a warm body instead of a toy. I'm so *sorry*."

And now the dam broke, tears streaming down her face. She didn't think the day could get any worse, but there were still hours left, so she knew better than to say that aloud.

"Hey, don't cry, okay?" When he stepped forward, she stepped back, keeping the distance between them because she still didn't trust herself.

And she wasn't any less angry about it, angry at herself for being as reductive as all the people who came through Arcanium to stare at her boobs, the men who'd tried to buy her drinks then got mad when she told them she wasn't interested, her husband who'd only wanted a wife if she was happy to fuck him.

"I wasn't exactly unokay with it," Victor said. "I was just concerned because you seemed unhappy, and as a matter of personal pride, I don't want the women I'm with to be unhappy. And look, here we are, talking. We've said more than two words to each other now."

"No, I really shouldn't have done that. I'm still not used to dealing with these…feelings, for lack of a better word — nerve endings and places in my brain all awake and firing electricity in ways they never did before. I'm not used to fighting it all the time, but I shouldn't have taken it out on you just because you were a man and happened to be there. It's inexcusable."

This time, when he stepped toward her, she didn't back away, and she allowed him to brush the line of her jaw with his knuckles. "Don't beat yourself up too much. We all have to learn that around here, some more than others. I wouldn't have said no, by the way. And I won't say no if you still want to. I have a small trailer, but it has a bed that works, and we can go back…"

He gave a wry smile when she ducked her head, ashamed, furious with herself for wanting to say yes, at Bell for making her this way, at the strange man in the trench coat who'd brought her up to this intensity with nothing more than a change in the hands' routine. Furious with freaking everything.

"You don't have to feel bad about saying no, either," Victor said. "If you don't want to, that's all right. I'm not taking any of this personally. The Spider was aloof as hell for months, and she still has as much of a no-touch policy as Lady Sasha. In fact, you remind me a lot of her. A bit ambivalent, are we?"

She nodded. She didn't know him well enough to spill her guts, but ambivalent was a terribly understated, if accurate, way to describe what she was going through.

"Look, I'm going to back off now," he said, "because you look in dire need of space. You don't ever have to follow up on this, but I'm going to let you know that if you ever want sex from me, you just have to ask. You only surprised me, and I wanted to make sure you were okay."

"Thanks." She supposed the message she was sending with her body was a curious mixture of 'Why, yes, I'd like to fuck right now, thanks' and 'I don't think I'll ever be able to look even in your vague direction again.' But mixed messages weren't clear enough for Arcanium, given how rigidly its men seemed to follow the rules. "I'm going to take what little is left of my dignity and go back to my trailer now."

"Also a valid life choice. Neve, right?"

She nodded.

"You know, there's not a man in Arcanium who would say no to you if you asked."

She didn't have the heart to tell him that was the problem.

Neve started back toward the caravan. Victor's footsteps crunched behind her. She knew he wasn't following her. They were simply going toward the same place.

The tension built up, awareness of each step from each of their bare feet in the dead grass, knowing he was still hard and she was still horny. She didn't know if Victor had a Plan B for the night, but he was single and comfortable with casual sex and she wasn't.

Neve didn't think that mattered anymore, because she couldn't keep going like this. She wasn't the woman she'd been. She couldn't hold herself to the same standard any more than she would a person with brain damage who'd suffered an irrevocable change in cognition or personality.

Under the Christmas lights, Neve turned around and faced him. He didn't walk into her like she'd walked into him, and he didn't appear surprised that she'd stopped.

"Your bed, not mine, and just the once. Then I want to go back to my trailer to sleep alone. Are those terms acceptable?"

He appeared both bemused and amused at her brusqueness, but he nodded.

Given their respective states from where they'd left off, they didn't even make it to the bed, and neither of them removed their clothing. They fell to the floor of his trailer before Victor was able to close the door behind him, one foot braced on the grass and his knee on the steps up. He pushed her panties to the side, and she opened the front of his trousers. He fucked them up into the living room aisle then took a second to hook the doorknob with his foot to give them a fleeting vestige of privacy. She barely gave him that second before pulling him back down.

She panted underneath him in the aftermath, stroking his back as he kissed her neck. His thumb brushed her nipple through the negligee and bra. He hadn't even gotten her out of the bra.

When she stopped running her hands over him, he pushed himself back onto his knees and reached for a dishcloth so she could clean between her legs. He offered her a drink, but she shook her head.

"Do you want me to walk you to your trailer? Mama raised a gentleman."

"No, thank you. I'm tired."

"Okay. Good night, then. Hope you enjoyed yourself as much as it sounded like you did."

She stopped at the bottom of his steps before opening the trailer door. "Don't you mind being used?"

"Not in the slightest."

Chapter Eight

With nothing else to do the rest of the week, she read the books Bell had provided, knocking them out with speed that could only be explained by a lack of Internet connection. She hoped these books weren't the only ones she was allowed to have as long as she lived at Arcanium.

Sometimes during the afternoons, she headed into the big top tent. She hadn't yet seen a full performance, but watching rehearsals was close enough to the real thing. She was regularly impressed.

Victor mostly played foundation to Valorie and Lennon's tumbling, although he did quite a bit of it himself. Neve had been avoiding him—because she was ashamed of herself, not of him—but she liked to watch him flipping through the air as much as she enjoyed watching Seth and Lars practice—although Seth and Lars practicing was significantly sexier than the tumbling. Part of their whole concept was defying the laws of gravity because of the way they were magically connected. The aerial act itself was less spectacular than the conceit, which was the premise of the whole circus — Is it real or not? And does it matter, as long as it looks amazing?

Maya's high-wire act was predicated on the fact that she couldn't fall, so there were all sorts of things she could do. She wasn't quite at Kitty's or Neve's curviness, but as Joseph had pointed out, she was top-heavy, and she was built with more curves than the usual skinny, petite miss who would walk the high-wire — because thinner legs were easier to keep closer together, and the less sway a woman had to her walk, the better. Valorie's would have been the better frame for high-wire and tightrope walking, but she was already an aerial contortionist, and Maya doing flips, handsprings and freefalls in circles, plus assorted other balancing acts, was much more impressive.

The fire-eater practiced his act as well, complete with juggling, fire fan dances and tumbling that ended with flips through flaming hoops.

When Lady Sasha and Lord Mikhail entered the big top, everyone else mostly cleared out, not inclined to stick around while the sex demons stoked each other and anyone close to them. But Sasha and Mikhail needed to practice what they'd planned for the weekend. Based on what she saw in rehearsals, everyone regularly changed their routine. After so much same old, same old, she supposed they had to keep things fresh.

It kept things fresh for the audience, too. A new guest wouldn't know that anything was different. He'd just get a good show. But a regular attendee would appreciate the variety, all the more reason to return again and again. Neve hadn't been surprised to learn that there were Arcanium groupies and fan clubs, and not just because some of the circus folk were prone to sleeping with outsiders.

Mikhail knew she was there in the bleachers, watching them, but if Sasha did, she gave no indication. She and Mikhail did their routines, talked when they wanted to change something, repeated moves until they agreed it had the desired effect. They emanated, but not as strongly as during the actual performances, when Neve could feel them all the way from the food court. Lady Sasha kept their interaction entirely professional, and Lord Mikhail respected her wishes. As soon as rehearsal finished, Lady Sasha went one way, and after a wistful look into the bleachers wherever Neve was sitting, Lord Mikhail went the other way. It was amazing how much a demon could look so much like a kicked puppy.

On the afternoon Bell sat next to her, though, there was bounce in Mikhail's step, and a smile touched the corner of his eyes, if not anywhere else in his expression.

Bell straddled the bench, one foot higher than the other due to the elevation of the bleachers, his elbow on his higher knee. It was a performance of nonchalance, but with him, sometimes it was difficult to tell what *wasn't* a performance. She didn't face him, continued to watch the sex demons performing, but she caught the arrangement of him out of the corner of her eye, and his presence had an attraction all its own—different from the kind Mikhail had on her, but undeniable.

"Tonight, Arcanium is going downtown for a Funhouse event. The nature of what we do during the events pushes enough boundaries that we'd be unlikely to manage them without the patronage of just the right people, but the Funhouse is quite near and dear to my dark, little clockwork heart, and I'd very much like you to be a part of it. It's the reason I brought you into Arcanium in the first place. I think it would suit you, if you let it. But it's your decision. Attendance is mandatory for all working cast these days. Participation has never been."

"What boundaries would you be pushing, exactly, that are farther than the haunted funhouse?" she asked, sitting almost primly, which was more a function of the bleacher benches than naturally good posture. However, her lower back stiffened at what he might be asking of her.

"Come now, Neve. A dedicated horror fan such as yourself knows better than to think the circus funhouse pushes all the boundaries that it could. The things we do during the events are not strictly legal the way what we do during circus hours are, when I suggest, intimate, tease but ultimately hold back. Patrons pay a flat fee for our time at Funhouse events. Some of the things we do during that time, though completely consensual and unpaid for, may be perceived by outside parties as something entirely different."

She finally turned to look at him, incredulous and unsure why she was still so incredulous. "Are you saying what I think you're saying?"

"Not quite." A boyish grin much like his old one returned to his face. "The Funhouse is what we already do in the circus, but amplified, truer, what everyone wants it to be and what I envisaged for Arcanium from the beginning. You know perfectly well I've no interest in prostituting out my people. Money's merely adequate compensation for the entertainment we provide, and people expect me to ask for it."

"Sounds an awful lot like prostitution, Bell, and like you made me for the sole purpose of pimping me out. Or else you're not explaining it very well."

His smile faded, but not into anger. "How would you like the hands on you to do more?"

Bell seemed to feed upon her reaction—as though he knew about the strange man in the fedora and what the hands had done while he'd watched, as though that had been designed as the teaser for this little request.

"The Funhouse is where the horror of Arcanium meets its eroticism, a place for people to encounter the true Arcanium that awakens after they leave. It's what I would have Arcanium be if not for the censures and strictures placed upon an operation like mine, as well as upon the individuals that make up so many of my people. Do you think you are alone in how you feel now, in your resentment, guilt, confusion? Arcanium was built to set that free."

He slid himself closer, still perched like a sprite.

"Imagine the Serpent King, the Spider, the mermaid, the werewolf, the Creature, the Tall Man, the Horned God, all laid bare for everyone who ever had a flicker of curiosity for what hid under the leather and latex. Imagine the Ringmaster laying his whip upon the back of someone who begged him for it rather than begged him to stop. Imagine the horror and intrigue of limbs removed, the man or woman completely vulnerable. Imagine the carnal awareness of a body's insides as well as its outsides, writhing in what appears to be pain but could also be pleasure. Imagine what lurid horrors we can bring to life when we're simply given the room to allow these terrible fantasies to come to fruition."

Without his smile and with that off-kilter attraction engrained in his being, she was all the more aware of the sheer performance of him. He fit into his role like a glove, human visage nothing but a costume, although she hadn't seen so much as a pair of black eyes from him. He wore arrogance, casual flexibility and fey beauty as though he'd been vacuum-sealed into a latex bodysuit, but there were places here and there where the illusion threatened to peek through, if a person dared look close enough to notice. The wideness of his mouth when he smiled, showing too many teeth. A fleck of gold in his hazel eyes. The golden band around his strong upper arm. The set of his shoulders and neck, simultaneously tense and relaxed at the same time. It was all of these things and none of them that betrayed him, but peering too closely hurt the eyes, like staring too hard at an optical illusion.

Krishna had held the universe in his throat. Neve wondered what sort of universes Bell's façade concealed.

"The Funhouse is a chance to explore those terrible fantasies safely. I have ways of keeping the law from interfering. The only rules and laws that matter are mine. That means you don't have to be a part of it, although I'd hoped you would consent to being an exhibit and perhaps yield to your nature enough for a performance."

He took her hand, turned it to run his fingers along the lines on her palms as he had done in the fortune teller tent. Neve wished she could pretend he was hypnotizing her, but sincere passion bled through every smooth, charismatic word.

"You don't need to decide now, my dear, but I'd like you to see it before you convict me of procuring and pandering, before you think yourself a whore for me." He passed his thumb along the blue threads of the veins in her wrist. Her breath caught, her mouth parting slightly at the static electric sparks from the contact.

He brought his other fine hand to her lips. So attuned was she to his touch, she could practically feel the texture of the ridges and whorls of his fingerprint.

Bell leaned in, but he was the one to veer away, lowering his head so that his forehead pressed to hers. Neve closed her eyes tightly, hating herself because she knew that if he'd kissed her, she would have welcomed it and everything more. Because he was warm and beautiful, and sex with him would be like his kiss, sweet and impossibly intense. It was all somehow worse knowing how good his kiss had made her feel before she'd understood what a manipulative bastard he was, before she'd known what he'd made her.

"I apologize. I would say it was unintentional, but I won't lie. Misguided. Careless. Ill-advised." He retreated, pushing himself back on the bench. "Think about it, Neve. Think about what your own dark heart desires, about what the true Arcanium can do for you. You have until this evening, when you'll see what Funhouse has to offer."

He swung his legs over the bench and stood.

Neve wanted to ask him something, but the question hooked into her tongue behind her lips, and she didn't dare open her mouth again.

Because she didn't ask, he didn't answer. He nimbly descended the bleachers bench by bench rather than down the stairs. She clenched the edge of her own bench, her lips wishing she hadn't let Bell turn away.

* * * *

Neve knocked on the Spider's RV door. With daylight growing dim and the golems scuttling around like the worker ants they were, Neve didn't have much time left, and she'd reached the end of her own considerations without arriving at a satisfactory conclusion. The rules of decision-making — and *Who Wants to Be a Millionaire?* — now suggested she ask a friend for advice. Neve didn't know the cast well enough, although most of them were perfectly nice.

She did, however, have peers — people in the same situation she found herself in — and the Spider's name kept coming up.

The Spider opened the door, wearing a black terrycloth robe and nothing else. She blinked with obvious perplexity.

"Were you expecting someone else?" Neve asked.

"I wasn't expecting anyone. Oh, the robe? No, nothing like that. There isn't much I can wear. That used to bother me, but now I barely notice." She tucked the sides of the robe more firmly around her. "Did you need something?"

"Is it all right if I ask you some questions?"

The Spider looked no less perplexed. "Okay… Would you like to come in? Ignore the mess. My housekeeping skills have suffered some. Something to drink?"

The last part was said ironically, because the mess the Spider spoke of was a vast collection of whiskey and bourbon bottles on the floor in the tiny living space. The scent hit Neve just as she entered, and the sight struck her just as hard.

Far be it from her to criticize someone else's house, though. "No, thanks. I don't drink much."

"Must be nice." The Spider sipped from the glass she'd obviously been nursing before Neve had arrived.

"Sorry. I don't really entertain, and I take up a lot of space when I sit. There's room in the cab or in the bedroom. Which would you prefer?"

"The cab," Neve said quickly.

The Spider's grin was wry. "Don't worry. I'm not that kind of spider."

"It's not you." Just the mention of a bed, knowing the woman was naked and that Neve might as well be, triggered an automatic reaction she'd rather avoid.

The Spider crawled into the cab after Neve, squeezing herself through the narrow opening and settling with her back legs splayed. The logistics of multiple limbs as fully developed as hers had to be difficult to manage. Yet the Spider still made sure her drink didn't spill.

"People don't come to me for questions. That's usually Kitty's job."

"I don't think Kitty can help me," Neve said. "She doesn't have the same conflict. Based on what I've heard, you might."

In spite of Neve's suspicion that this wasn't her first tumbler, the glint in the Spider's eye was shrewd, assessing, as sharp as her teeth. "Religious objections?"

"Sort of." Neve didn't think there was a polite-society way to talk about it, so she stopped trying. "All my life before I came to Arcanium, I was uninterested in sex. My parents weren't strict about my Christian upbringing, but I was firmly in the 'no sex until monogamous marriage, no divorce' camp, although I wasn't really fundamentalist or evangelical about it. It was the way things were supposed to be, and it wasn't a trial, with a whole deadly sin not even part of my repertoire, you know?"

The Spider laughed, loud, harsh and dark, but not cruel at all. "Sorry. That wasn't directed at you. I'm afraid I had a more fundamentalist upbringing, but I took on every last deadly sin in spades before I was even a legal adult. Funny how we ended up in the same place, isn't it?"

"Bell bringing me here basically broke every principle I followed," Neve said. "I'm still technically married, though my husband talked about divorce before Bell took me. After what Joseph did with Maya, I probably would have gone along with it eventually, but I'm still married in the eyes of God and the state. I never thought my religious objections were that strong until they were challenged. But now I want sex all the time, with anyone at all, and damn it, I hate this. I hate feeling like Bell and Mikhail are following the letter of Bell's law while still forcing me into having sex I'd rather not have. But my body wants it—*needs* it. I can't say no. And I don't know what to do. I assume you must have made a decision at some point—principle or pleasure. I was wondering how you balance that."

The Spider took a generous swallow of her drink then set it down in a cupholder. "Principle or pleasure—I like it. The short answer is that I don't balance it. I had to decide to give up the principles, not that they were particularly useful to me before Arcanium either. I'm with the Creature because he's kind, because he gives me something I need and because I think I love him, strange as we are. On the rare occasion I do fuck another member of Arcanium, it's because *he* asks me to, so I can give him what *he* needs, and it satisfies a few of mine. Is it biblical? Not in the least. You need to decide if that's your line."

"What if I don't know?" Neve asked.

"If it's not biblical principle, what about having indiscriminate sex turns you off? Why resist it at all?

No one else here does. Most of the people in Arcanium have no compunction about sleeping with man, woman or human-like beast — and given I lie with something that calls itself the Creature, who's better than any man I've encountered, I can hardly throw stones. Kitty calls it taking comfort in what comfort you can find. Maya calls it purgatory. For me, I never had a chance at resisting, and if Bell modeled your…appetite after mine, I don't know that you have a choice either."

Neve combed her hair back, scratching at her scalp in the process. Was it the voice of God, the little angel on her shoulder, that told her not to commit adultery, not to sleep around, not to spread her legs for anything and everything? Was it the voice of Society, that melting pot of thoughts and beliefs that drew most from the American undercurrent of Puritanism and Protestantism, with its fundamental suspicion of women and poor opinion of men?

When an image depicted lust, it showed Aphrodite rather than Eros. Jezebel, the Whore of Babylon, the whisper campaign that Mary Magdalene's demons had been sexual and that she'd been the woman at the well with many men under her belt… Though, given the stereotype of the promiscuous, voracious red-haired woman, the secular world she'd grown up in was just as responsible for her hesitation as religious upbringing.

But the more Neve examined her life, the more she thought religion didn't have a damn thing to do about it.

It formed the surface of her objections, not the foundation. Heaven knew she didn't let religious objections stop her from other actions, other beliefs, no matter what the Bible said. She had her own principles, some of them biblical, some of them just plain human decency.

Abstaining from sex had a practical element that didn't apply in a magic circus where most of the consequences had been removed precisely so that people could have as much sex as they wanted — and with whomever they wanted. As far as Neve could tell, Bell's vision for Arcanium was decadence rather than temptation of the soul. Depending on who was right on the question of religion, the difference might not matter, but Neve was just a woman, and a woman could only do her best. Take comfort where she could, like Kitty said.

And still Neve hesitated. Struggled to resist. Hated herself for giving in. Hated the ones with whom she gave in, even when they were considerate, kind.

Which she supposed had been the Spider's reason for asking.

If her point of principle wasn't that God frowned down at her in paternal disapproval whenever she had sex with someone who wasn't her husband, why did she feel like shit?

"Was your objection religious?" Neve asked.

"Don't model yourself after me, new girl. I ran away from my fundie family straight into the arms of a sexual predator who turned me into what Bell turned you into. I'm such a tangle of victim grooming, post-traumatic stress and religious contempt that when Bell first brought me in, I'd basically accepted that I was the worst sinner and destined for hell because I couldn't stop myself from doing what my conditioning told me to do. These days, with the Creature there for me to relieve those impulses with someone I actually like, I don't struggle with the same ambivalence."

Ambivalence. That was the word Victor had used.

Neve stared at the Spider's glass of whiskey. The color reminded her of Bell's eyes when he was turned on. "Men have wanted one thing from me most of my post-pubescent life. I escaped their worst impulses, and it's sick that I'm actually grateful for that. I managed to stay clothed through everything they tried, but I had to fight for that. They'd get so angry at me, like I'd taken away their favorite toy, not like I'd made an independent decision about my own self, my own body."

"I was trained to be what men wanted me to be, to enjoy what men wanted me to be," the Spider said. "But just because I felt pleasure and just because I was turned on didn't mean it was what I wanted. I turned tricks that my ex called art. I was his unpaid prostitute. And I swore I wouldn't let Bell do that to me when I entered Arcanium, but I ended up doing it to myself. I think that's why he doesn't push me to play his Funhouse games. I'll pose for him. I'll be his sculpture, but I won't perform. I won't do that again—not yet, and probably not ever. I thought Bell would know better than to do to someone else what was done to me, but that goes to show you never really shed all your naivete. He's not malicious, but nothing's beneath him."

Neve rested her elbow on her thigh, her chin on her fist, meeting the Spider's eyes. The irises were black as a demon's but warmer. There was all manner of cynicism and rue in the set of her jaw and lips, but Neve thought she'd never seen more compassion. "He wants me to perform."

"I know what stops me," the Spider said. "What stops you?"

Neve resisted the urge to tear her gaze away, to protect her vulnerability from being seen. What reason did she have to hide that from the Spider? She'd been through the same things. Worse things. She could take it.

"It's been reinforced time and again that men like what they see, and I can't discard that data based on my own biases," Neve said. "Sometimes I think I could just lift my shirt, ask for a million dollars and retire in a week. I'm the pretty thing in a glass case, and people pay money to stare because it gives them a chance to imagine having me. Bell wants me to be that pretty thing, and sometimes he wants to open the glass case to let other people play with me because I'm a pleasing shape, because I'm that fantasy for them. And now I enjoy their fantasies, whether I like it or not. I'm the perfect plaything. But I'm also a damn intelligent, ambitious woman, but do any of the people playing with me care? No. Because I'm just their fantasy, their doll, as lifeless as a sex toy, and I don't matter. I'm a receptacle for their pleasure, something to lose themselves in, the sum not of my matter and mass but of my empty spaces. And I'm not okay with that."

The Spider's lips thinned but curved in a gentle smile. "I guess we've arrived at the principle."

"Do you know how hard I worked to get good grades, to remember everything I needed to remember, to get into a good school with scholarships, to graduate then continue schooling until I got my doctorate? I'm Dr. Freaking Neve Kimble, but the only place anyone thinks Dr. Kimble isn't my husband is at work."

"If it makes you feel better, all the people of Arcanium are objectified like that. It's a consequence of the performing arts, particularly of a freak show." The

Spider shifted her second set of legs. "Just because you're freakishly beautiful doesn't make it any less relevant. We're not meant to be seen as people. We're supposed to be interesting to look at. People can decide to get to know us better, but the very premise of Arcanium is visual. It's dehumanizing, but it's nothing personal."

The Spider made to protest when Neve picked up the tumbler and took a quick swallow of the whiskey. Neve made a face, but it went down her throat hot and strong. The Spider mouthed 'okay then' and didn't stop her when she took another quick drink.

"I always wanted to be so much more, though," Neve said. "I didn't wear garbage bags, but I covered my body, rarely wore anything more revealing than scrubs. Never wore much makeup. But when I wore a lab coat, strangers still wanted me to put on a pair of hipster glasses to satisfy their 'hot nerd' fetish. That's the way it's always been."

"People will always see you first. That's something you can't control. For most people who pass through this place, they won't be around long enough to know you beyond what they see." The Spider eased her tumbler out of Neve's hand, drained it herself then put it back in the cupholder. "Believe me. I've been through this, darling."

"How do you handle knowing that all someone sees when they look at you is sex and not you?"

"I handle it by being scary as hell." The Spider touched the tip of her tongue to one of her sharp eyeteeth. "As someone who's afraid of so much, it's nice to see fear from everyone else now. The teeth, the claws, knowing I could kill them if I wanted to... People passing by me sense it, even if they can't put a finger on why. And the Creature knows me by my own fears. Bell knows me with his magic. With all the people who pass by then forget you in the next thought, it helps to have at least one person who *knows* you, who will look at you and see more than just your body."

"I'm not the horror side of Arcanium," Neve said. "I'm only the sexy side."

"Then you'll have to find something else. If you don't want to have random, casual sex with anyone who touches you, then don't. But if you really have no true moral qualms about it, then you need to find something. Even if you find fucking while married to someone else to be an ethical dilemma, you still need to find something, because your sexuality isn't going to stop just because you're stubborn. You, Mikhail, Sasha and Bell all need to find something, if just to give the rest of us a chance to breathe." She arched her eyebrow slightly to show she was kidding, but not really.

"Any recommendations?"

"I think Bell wants more from you than what he's given. You won't have to go looking too hard for his plan. It'll find you eventually. It might find you like a swarm of killer bees and the taste of honey on your tongue at the same time, but it'll find you just the same."

Neve was really beginning to understand why the Spider drank. "What should I do at the Funhouse? He wants me there. He wants me to be…this."

The Spider's second pair of arms inside the robe bulged against the terrycloth like emerging parasites. There was something compelling about the way the Spider was clearly uncomfortable, but Neve recognized that particular form of discomfort well by now.

"Maybe it's time for you to figure out not what God wants, what the rest of the world wants, what Bell wants or what Mikhail or every other man wants from you," the Spider said. "Maybe it's time you figured out what Dr. Motherfucking Neve Kimble wants. Then figure out what you need in order to take it without regret."

Chapter Nine

The cast gathered in a handful of caravan trailers, a semi-trailer following behind. Hors d'oeuvres would be provided at the venue, but the golems passed around some easy food to eat while they traveled.

"Trust me." Kitty handed Neve bottled water and a sandwich. "You'll need it."

Neve was in Kitty's trailer, which carried more women than men, despite the fact everyone seemed less concerned with gender separation the rest of the time.

She still refused to be on a bed. The conjoined twins and the Spider took that honor. Neve wore her white terrycloth robe, but she still felt there weren't enough layers between her and the intrinsic suggestiveness of a bed. Caroline, the youngest member of Arcanium — although since no one aged, it was hard for Neve to tell whether Caroline really was the youngest or just looked like it — offered to let her sit on the small dining bench, but Neve took a spot on the floor instead. She wanted to stay uncomfortable. It was a good distraction from her nerves and the vibrations of anticipation her body decided was desire. Arousal was arousal. Her body saw it all the same way.

After about an hour, the golems pulled up to the loading dock of an empty warehouse. Neve was used to feeling underdressed in the circus, but the rough alley made her feel overdressed instead, and she suddenly had to worry about tetanus. She was so used to going barefoot in the circus, like many cast members, that she hadn't even thought to bring shoes.

"Do you meet in abandoned warehouses often?" she asked.

"Not often, but we've been to this one before," Kitty said. "It isn't abandoned. From what I understand, it's a tax shelter of some kind, and we're not the only esoterica the owner hires to fill it. I think they do some other kind of urban haunted house in October."

"You mean we're not the only ones who do that?"

Kitty laughed. "You'd be surprised how often extralegal extreme horror pops up. We're far from the only show in the country."

The interior of the warehouse was more or less clean as they entered through the loading bay and climbed the concrete stairs to the third floor. Dust was more of a problem than splintered crates, nails or squatters. The golems poured in first with their industrial-size mops and swept through like fairy godmothers, turning on lights, clearing dust away, hanging black tarpaulin over windows and setting up ceiling-high partitions into a winding, labyrinthine pathway. They were quiet and efficient.

At the top of the stairs, Bell greeted a man who wore an expensive charcoal-gray business suit—hardly the kind of person Neve would have seen as someone interested in esoterica, but she knew from experience that the scene took all sorts.

"Most of you have met Samuel Amendola before," Bell said, "but we do have some new blood. Samuel is the one responsible for us being here today. He provides the venue, he sent out the invitations and he's paying for our time. He's brought with him quite a few friends — some business, some personal — for this private party. Everyone has been apprised of the rules and will wait on the second floor until we're ready for them to ascend. We have the whole third floor to ourselves. Thank you, Samuel. We'll see you at ten."

"Very much looking forward to it." Mr. Amendola gave an officious bow that Neve didn't like. He peered over the small crowd of performers and freaks with lust that was startlingly possessive. Neve held the top of her robe to keep his gaze from crawling anywhere on her.

From the way the third floor was laid out, smooth concrete broken with cinderblock columns to provide structure, the ceilings and floor below were thick enough that she could barely hear the party Bell had said was going on below. If laughter and loud conversations hadn't drifted up the open staircase, she wouldn't have known that guests were already there.

Still unsure what Bell had in mind for her, Neve stayed out of everyone's way, even as the performers and actors shed their outer layers and tended to their makeup, which Neve would do if she had any idea what she was supposed to look like. Bell went with each exhibit into the maze, one by one. She thought he might be doing something to finish them off onsite, because when they left, most of them weren't particularly horrifying. She didn't doubt Bell was capable of making them so.

Neve sat in a corner, watching what little she could see now that the golems had set up all the temporary walls and the black curtains that separated cast and crew from guests. She ruminated over the same things that had been running through her head since the afternoon. It certainly didn't help that Bell had left his intentions for her a mystery. How could she decide what to do if she didn't know what she'd be agreeing to?

Kitty and Victor each asked whether she was all right, and she nodded to both. Because she *was* all right. Bell wasn't going to ask her to literally kill someone and get off on doing it. He wasn't going to make her do anything that was destructive or that would hurt someone—more than they wanted, which was again something she knew from personal experience. He wouldn't make her do *anything* if she didn't want to. But she was here, so she might as well at least play haunted exhibit like she did for the circus—unless Bell's vision was just too horrible for words, and she doubted that would be the case, because he'd already know what she'd refuse.

'How would you like the hands on you to do more?'

Maybe not a shot of whiskey, but a glass of wine sounded good right about now. She sighed. That way lay madness and mind-numbing agents. It was far too easy to settle into a routine of oblivion. The empty bottles in the Spider's trailer proved that.

"You're the last one, my dear." Bell stood above her, holding out a hand to help her to stand, which she took. He wore his usual leather trousers, but also a loose, thin, white cotton shirt. Neve hadn't thought he owned anything that covered his upper body. "I'd like to start you from the very beginning. You've never attended a Funhouse function before, and being a part of the haunted funhouse doesn't quite prepare you for what we do here."

He eased the robe down her shoulder. She untied the knot at her waist to allow him to remove it from her like a gentleman with his lady's coat.

She still wore her wedding ring, which Bell didn't comment on. She assumed that at least some of the people who would be joining them were also married — and likely not with their partners at this event, based on her unkind assumptions about people in the higher echelons of business and other power structures. But infidelity was also a powerful fetish, even when it was mere illusion. Guests to the Funhouse wouldn't know the difference, and she wasn't ready to take it off, even if she'd basically agreed to adultery. But at this point, that adultery couldn't hurt her husband, which was the only reason she let Bell lead her to the edge of the black curtain that separated the green room from the rest of the floor. He pulled it back and gestured her through.

The guests wore outfits that wouldn't have been out of place at a cocktail party or high-end charity function. Little black dresses glittering with jet beads, long slinky backless gowns, tailored suits with silver pinstripes, shining patent leather shoes, stilettos that would make a dominatrix weep with envy.

Neve caught sight of a few fine leather vests under suit jackets, and in some cases, corsets or harnesses. Chokers that were actually collars. Bracelets that could become handcuffs. Braided decorative belts that could become a flogger in less than a minute. Most of the guests were merely done up, suggesting little more than a fat bank account, but there were enough people displaying unconventionality that Neve was even more curious. What kind of business did Samuel run? How had he come to bring business associates into something like this? How had Kitty put it? *'Extralegal.'*

Fringe sexualities weren't inherently shady by any means, but this whole setup was. And Neve was a part of that now.

All seventy-five or so people turned when Bell led her through the curtain.

The guests stared at her with expressions that varied from hard and unforgiving to indulgent, kind to lascivious. She wasn't wearing anything under the black silk negligee that could only be called a dress in the most generous sense. Bra and underwear would have interrupted the cutout of lace that led from under her arms down to the hem, which reached less than halfway down her thighs. It was one thing to be covered with groping hands, but she felt entirely naked under these strangers' scrutiny. It was somehow worse that they were all clearly rich. It made her feel sold.

Bell hooked his arm through hers when shyness and a dose of fear made her hesitate, the curtain swinging against her leg.

"You look lovely. I think we can lose this, though." He pulled the rubber band from her hair, which flipped down from the loose bun she'd made and fell to the small of her back. Bell tousled it to drape over her shoulders and wave with its own shape.

Golems walked through the clusters of guests with champagne on trays. Bell grabbed a flute and handed it to her.

Samuel Amendola stood with a small cluster of other men with watches just as ugly as his, some wearing wedding rings of their own. "A charming young woman, Bell. Were you intending to introduce her?"

"Not to you," Bell replied, with a deliberate snap of insult that had Samuel as well as his guests laughing. "She's new to the circus, and I wanted to show her what we have in store for the rest of you. If you would indulge me for a little while longer, I promise it'll be worth the wait."

"It always is," one of the other men with Samuel said.

"Especially if she's a part of it." Another one of Samuel's companions reached out, hooking a lock of her hair in his hand.

Bell smoothly insinuated himself between the men and Neve, ever polite but not allowing anyone to confuse politeness with permission. He clicked his tongue in disapproval. "No touching. Not yet, and certainly not without an invitation."

"And here I thought she was the invitation," the man replied.

Samuel took the man's wrist and pulled it back. "I made it clear, Allen, that there are consequences to intemperance. If you can't follow Bell's rules, you might as well leave now, for your own sake."

The arch loftiness of his manner didn't quite hide the tightness in his shoulders as he held Allen back. He'd encountered 'consequences' before, then.

The petulant curve to Allen's lips suggested he didn't take Samuel or Bell seriously enough, but he yielded, his attention alone bridging the gap between him and Neve.

"It's a privilege to have us here," Bell said.

"A privilege we paid for," Allen countered.

"A privilege nonetheless. I agree to bring my people only under certain conditions. You may think you're safe. You may think you can get away with anything, with your lawyer on call and a secure Swiss bank account. But once you step through that curtain, you're in my territory, and none of the people here nor any amount of money or bribe to the law will save you from me. Are we understood?"

Had anyone but Bell said that while wearing black leather pants and holding the hand of a scantily clad woman in a crowd of wealthy associates, he would have been laughed out of the warehouse and probably beaten within an inch of his life by very expensive security personnel, perhaps with homophobic epithets rained down upon him. He was wearing eyeliner tonight, his dense curly hair gleaming close to his head, and with his body covered, it was more difficult to see his strength. However, he was so much less delicate than he appeared, so much more in control than his wardrobe suggested, and it was impossible for him to hide that completely within his human façade.

Allen finally nodded.

"Good. Now if you can wait a few more minutes, I need to introduce Neve to what she's going to be a part of." Bell brought Neve forward again, kissing her shoulder in a proprietary way. He looked up at Allen as he did so, as though to show that he could but Allen couldn't. But even so, the place where he kissed her awoke the rest of her skin, a stone in the pond of her desire. "You can enjoy the sight of her then. Excuse me."

"You're not helping," Neve whispered at him as they reached the split in the black curtain that acted as the entrance to the Funhouse.

He pulled her through into the near pitch darkness within. His white shirt was just about the only thing she could see, but in a matter of moments, she could feel plenty. He slid his arm around her waist and brought her against him, slowly, gently, though no rude erection pushed against her abdomen.

"I'm uncomfortable with this," Neve murmured. His breath was cool against her lips, so he wasn't about to kiss her, but she couldn't help but feel like she was still being scrutinized and that he could see much better in the dark than she could.

"I keep expecting you to slap me, but you're so very polite. There's no need to be so nice, my dear."

"I'd slap you now, but I can't find your face."

He laughed, pulling away and hooking his arm in hers again. "I appreciate that you agreed to join me here, despite your reservations. I think the same enthusiasm you have for the haunted funhouse will be served well by this one. Shall we?"

"How exactly is it going to be different from the haunted funhouse, other than my not being able to see? I'm barefoot, but some of those women were wearing scary high heels. They're going to need to know where they're going."

"There are pieces of glow tape to delineate the path. For someone so observant, I shouldn't have to point them out to you."

"Them's fighting words, Bell." She wasn't feeling playful, but he was keeping her mind off of what had been bothering her since he'd invited her to the Funhouse. Pretending she was confident made her feel more confident, and it changed the way he interacted with her, even if he could see beyond the bravado.

"Drink your champagne, Neveline, and relax. It's like your funhouse, but better."

She swallowed the rest of the champagne. Bell plucked the glass from her fingers. She didn't know whether he set it down on the path or made it disappear. She just followed the ghost of his shirt through the darkness and around a corner. The line of the partitions stopped at a black platform, where red lights shone down upon a figure Neve didn't immediately notice, because it was just as black as the rest.

Then the figure lifted its head, and Neve saw the dark blue flame at the ends of her hair, purple in the red light. The Spider had been airbrushed — or magicked — completely black from head to toe. She rose on all eight limbs, wearing nothing but a satin underbust corset with red lace detail over her abdomen.

The Spider moved with the kind of jerky grace of the tarantulas she liked to keep with her in the creepy-crawly tent. She was all angles, long legs, long arms, long fingers, except for her exposed breasts, which were full for her frame, especially when there was nothing to contain them. Neve tried to be circumspect when she checked, but she confirmed the Spider wore *only* the corset. Neve hoped the airbrushing was magical, because she could only imagine the dedication and discipline to have every last bit of her painted, even to the inside of her lips and over her labia.

The Spider tilted her head, reaching one sharp-nailed hand out to stroke the pointed tips along Neve's jaw, drawing her closer. The Spider trailed her fingers down the shadow of Neve's cleavage to the bodice of the dress, curling a claw in to draw her still closer, until Neve had to grip the edge of the platform. The Spider looked directly in her eyes, and though she didn't speak, Neve heard her as though she had Bell's telepathy.

'What does Neve want?'

Neve didn't let herself think. Or rather, she ignored every thought, even as she leaned in to close what little distance the Spider had left. She moved slowly enough that the Spider could have stopped her, even if she wasn't capable or willing to speak, but instead, the Spider angled herself to meet Neve's shy kiss.

She'd never kissed a woman before. She wasn't sure how she felt about it beyond the pleasure of a kiss, the way anything could shiver over the surface of her skin like a tongue of fire blossoming through fumes. If she hadn't been standing and the Spider bent on the platform at an awkward angle, Neve might have parted her lips, explored more.

When Neve broke the kiss, the Spider had both of her right hands flipping Bell off. The Spider grinned, kissed Neve's cheek then retreated, lowering herself almost flat again with impressive flexibility.

Bell kept his gaze on Neve, though he didn't say anything until they rounded the corner. "Interesting."

"Just don't."

"I don't mean because of the undeniably erotic image of the two of you together, especially in that light. I mean that the Spider chose you to kiss. When she doesn't have her spiders, she prefers working without a partition, because she's still mildly claustrophobic. But she won't let anyone touch her, which is why the Gentleman waits unseen in the corner in case he's needed. She's spare with her friendship, sparer still with desire. I knew you'd gone to her to discuss your decision. I believed it wise. I hadn't realized you'd made such an impression."

"I think you're the one who made the impression, modeling me after her—which she's angry at you for, and so am I." Though she doubted that devastated him.

"And is that what you wanted, Neve?"

She didn't answer him, continued instead down the path until the next break in the partition.

This time, the two performers stood in a glass case, blue light pouring over them. Seth and Lars were bound together in a deep kiss, their bodies naked, their legs interlocked, their hips so close together that their cocks weren't visible—or at least that was what Neve thought, until she stopped in front of the glass case to stare.

Their skin melded, molded together, sinking into the other's body everywhere their skin met. When Seth lifted his hand from Lars' shoulder, for a moment the skin struggled to stay in contact, stringing like molasses, the blend of contrasting flesh tones like the mingling of watercolors. Even their mouths were trapped together, their lips pulled tightly against the other whenever they'd withdraw from the kiss—as though their curse had intensified beyond mere contact, making them closer than ever, closer to one body than two. It was as hot as it was horrifying.

"It may look awful, love, but they, like you and the Spider, are here of their own volition, and they agreed to this particular horror," Bell murmured in her ear, although he didn't touch her as he watched over her shoulder. "I promise they quite enjoy themselves as long as they don't have to see who's watching them. They're more open with their affection than they once were, but they haven't grown used to other people enjoying the sight of it."

She licked her lower lip, shifting from one foot to the other. She rethought her decision not to wear underwear under the dress.

"Come along."

The next glass case sent light wavering into the hall. The mermaid swam close to the glass, though when she saw Bell behind Neve, she swam back again, glaring with large, iridescent eyes. She was topless, the way most mermaids were when not in a children's story. Frills ridged over her shoulder blades, and webbing stretched between her fingers and under her arms. The gills on her neck opened and closed. Her lips were blue, but only because the patches of scales along her cheeks and down her torso were also a light blue and green. Professional mermaids were nothing new, but even a woman who knew how to use a fake mermaid tail underwater needed to breathe. There were no obvious places for a woman to breathe above water, no human ways to breathe underwater. Guests from outside Arcanium would wonder what the trick was, as they did with every aspect of Arcanium. And as usual, there wasn't a trick.

Neve continued on, leaving the wavering lights behind her.

This was the second time Bell had followed her through a maze. It occurred to her that he rarely got to watch someone experience his circus in real-time. She sensed Bell's hunger for her reactions and wished she didn't feed him so well, but she couldn't help it. She liked haunted houses, she liked freak shows, and she was now in the perfect position to like sexual exhibitions as well.

The next tableau had been set up on a low platform, no glass partition. Carlo was bound, naked, to a St. Andrew's cross, the bindings black leather and false legs attached to the stumps of his thighs.

Misha didn't look any healthier than usual, but he appeared pleased that he didn't have to swallow anything. Instead, he started pounding nails into the false legs, which spurted blood as though they were real.

Carlo arched, his erection unflagged. But he shouted as Misha took a toothed cock ring and snapped it around the base.

"Carlo's a little bit of everything," Bell said. "He and Misha alternate from Funhouse to Funhouse on who gets tortured, but Carlo gets to have his legs chopped off before he's sodomized, which is always a satisfying visual, and he never tires of it. I've gotten more use out of him than anyone would give him credit for…although Misha can swallow anything, which makes watching a dildo the size of Ciarán's cock go down his throat also quite satisfying. You know a little something about that, don't you, love?"

"Stop." Neve didn't need to be reminded of how much he knew, what he'd experienced in his secondhand way. "If you're going to be cruel…"

"I'm not saying it to be cruel. There's nothing wrong with a throat yielding to an incubus. Jinn in general can find their way into just about anything with ease when they choose to make it sweet. If it gives you some sense of balance, I've had my own throat around the cock of another jinni myself."

Carlo was weeping and moaning at the same time, but Neve actually looked away from him to stare at Bell. He raised an eyebrow.

"I don't know why that surprises you. Most jinn are shapeshifters one way or another, which makes the shape of one's genitalia quite inconsequential. I prefer surrounding myself with fierce women because they are so rarely appreciated, but when I choose the company of men, I'm partial to equally underappreciated men who don't try to dominate me. I decide if I allow them to, just as I allow the women who choose my bed to decide."

She blinked.

"I still don't know why that surprises you. But you've experienced something I've never been able to try myself. I'm as subject to the destructive effect of a sex demon's feed as any other creature. Until you came along, I had never experienced the other side of an incubus' feed from a human woman's perspective. I'm quite envious of you, love."

Neve had no idea what to say to that.

Bell gestured her onward.

Lady Sasha was next, in a glass case set on a pedestal. The succubus reclined on a reticulated python that had to weigh over two hundred pounds and filled almost the entire base of the container. Three albino ball pythons were wrapped around her body. Yellow-white scales slid and clung along her firm breasts. Muscles flexed around the curve of her nipple. A thick body moved between her legs to cover her, although it hardly seemed like modesty.

Lady Sasha wore very little as a rule, but it was amazing the difference made by removing the last strips of leather from a figure like hers. She lay there like a pin-up parody of a Genesis painting. All she was missing was an apple, although she'd painted her lips a cherry red.

Neve kept a certain distance from the case, unsure what Lady Sasha thought of her, especially as angry as she was with Mikhail.

The succubus turned her head, opened her dark eyes. The irises were red, not a glow in shadows like Mikhail's—more like garnets under white light. She moved under the slithering serpents around her, stroking along the firm bodies as she lifted herself upright. The python underneath her didn't seem to be bothered by the shift in weight.

There was ferocity in those eyes that Lady Sasha didn't soften with a smile. Neve didn't necessarily sense animosity, but she still backed away. Lady Sasha's fierce gaze followed her until Neve turned the corner, trying to catch her breath and crossing her arms over her breasts to cover her nipples. They were hard as diamonds against her forearms, and the silk only stimulated them more.

Neve ducked away from Bell's hand when he touched her shoulder.

"On Oddity Row, she's compelled to be pleasant. Though she's kind enough for a demon, she's not nice and doesn't particularly like being nice."

He didn't pursue contact again. The bastard knew exactly why she didn't want him to touch her now.

It certainly didn't help that Lord Mikhail was next on display.

He was dressed like a warrior out of a video game, but one that objectified men as much as its women, with harnesses and armor meant to enhance rather than protect the appearance of his physical strength and Atlas figure. He was an executioner in gay culture leather, but the harness around his cock was what drew the eye.

Leather wrapped around his scrotum and the base, keeping his erection impossibly large, hard and curved under a leather-edged blade that extended beyond the head of his cock. From the sides of the leather cock ring, two more leather-edged blades curved outward. He wore leather gloves with razor claws over his nails. The helmet through which he wore his long hair in a tail covered the lower half of his face like a muzzle, but with serrated blades like teeth over his mouth.

He was delicious, his dark skin gleaming and tattooed, at its best from every angle, and at every angle dangerous as hell — a not-so-subtle warning of what he was that so many would still ignore if he pulled them in hard enough.

He could have been a wax sculpture, except for his breathing and the way his eyes followed her as she backed away from him as well. There was ferocity in his own gaze almost identical to Lady Sasha's and also without any outright animosity. His cock twitched, pulsed, making the blade over it glint in the light.

Neve thought getting away from him would help, but his magic followed her, and it had apparently reached the conjoined twins on their own platform as well.

The twins were blindfolded, gagged, their arms tied over their heads. Rope bound their ankles wide apart to spread their legs and give them no purchase or solid ground to brace themselves. They were poised in a seated position above an indifferent machine that slowly pushed thick red dildos into their pussies.

The pale tumbler wore a mask that concealed everything except the glee in his eyes as he walked around the girls with the remote in one hand and a flogger in the other. Even though the dildos were slow, the twins were already writhing with the same fervid need that had wrapped itself so firmly around Neve's own desire.

Lennon winked at her as she passed, grinned underneath the leather mask. The stretch of the leather over his smile made it decidedly creepy. Lennon flicked the flogger over one of the twins' breasts. When one twin flinched, the place at the base of their spine where they were connected meant both of them jumped. The twin's skin went white where the flogger had struck her then flushed into pink lines. He trailed the tails over their shoulders, the bulge in his loose leather trousers prominent, not contained like Lord Mikhail's.

"Seth and Lars used to scene with them, all four bodies melded together, and Lennon used to swim with Melanie in the mermaid tank, but I think they prefer spending the Funhouse events apart, despite their entanglements the rest of the time. The Funhouse is a chance to step out of the usual boxes…into other boxes, true, but different ones. Arcanium is so similar from week to week. These parties allow for some variety. If you ever have an idea for a change here in the Funhouse events or in your usual funhouse tableau, do not hesitate to ask. I don't want my children bored."

"What do *you* do to keep from getting bored? Figure out how to make the people who've been with you longest miserable? Bring new people in to make new people miserable, too?"

He took her by the wrist and whirled her through the dark until she hit a corner in the makeshift hallway. The partition shuddered, but it didn't fall or collapse. When she raised her arms to protect herself, he grasped her wrists like cuffs and pressed them against her shoulders, which pushed her deeper into the niche.

"If you're still miserable here, Neve, you've no one to blame but yourself." This time his breath brushed hot across her cheek and over her ear, close. "The price for bringing interesting women into my circus is that those women are often their own worst enemies, but while I'm no hero, I'll thank you not to make me your villain. You were the one who wanted to know what this was like. I've gifted you with opportunities, protections, sensations that most women and even some men would kill for, and all you can do is condemn yourself for what you have because it's new, strong, something you were unprepared for. Instead of attacking me, why don't you take the Spider's advice, love? Why don't you just fucking take what you want?"

Neve leaned her forehead against his, tilting her head to bring her mouth closer to his until she could almost taste him. "What makes you think I want you?"

He closed the brief gap between them with a surprisingly gentle kiss, moving his hands from her wrists to the walls on either side of her. He broke the kiss with a groan when she ran her palm over the front of his trousers.

"What is it with demons and dicks? Is it a man thing?" Neve asked. "You know, average is perfectly fine."

Bell laughed as Neve worked his leather trousers open one-handed, but his laughter caught when she wrapped her fingers around him without warning. She didn't have anything for lubrication, but he didn't seem to mind as she stroked over the shaft. She advanced, stepping between his legs, forcing him to retreat in an awkward dance, because she still stroked him with a too-tight grip. Even so, he threaded his fingers through her hair and caught her lip in a tender bite.

"Demons are larger to intimidate. It's the nature of the beast, darling."

"Why do I doubt female demons have the same inclinations?"

They passed the platform of the human knot that usually resided in the haunted funhouse. They were still missing parts, but now mouths and hands were sewn and working over breasts, balls, clits, cocks, their bodies oiled and slick, a surgical orgy in progress — and by all appearances, as pleasurable for the people in the knot as their time in the haunted funhouse had been terrible.

Bell stopped her against the wall, holding onto the edge of the partition before the tableau as he thrust into her hand. Pre-cum was now more than adequate, as though he'd called it forth, and although he wasn't as big as Mikhail became, he was still well above average, which would have made her nervous prior to becoming part of Arcanium.

"For most female demons, the only thing they need for intimidation is mere aggression, to take what they want and not need a man to do it, but wanting him anyway. Also the nature of the beast, I'm afraid."

"Am I intimidating you, then?"

He brushed one of the broad straps of her dress to the side, exposing the swell of her breast almost to the areola, but he seemed in no hurry to bare her entirely. Instead, he claimed the line of her collarbone with his thumb, nearly bruising the hollow, as though he could hook her if he wanted to. "I said 'most'."

"Oh, yeah, because you're so special, so different. You like a good, strong female because that means you're better and stronger if you get to have her. And you treat her like crap because it reminds her that she's here at your behest. It's still an ego trip, just like this whole clockwork circus, or else you'd set us all free, let us all be voluntary, instead of working us until you're ready to let us go."

"I'm not making you do *this*." He tried to kiss her, but she turned her head.

Neve didn't stop him, though, as he lowered his mouth to her neck instead. That felt almost as good — tasting over her pulse, down the cord to her shoulder — as they stumbled back into darkness. He made no effort to hold back his moans. Why would he, when he was getting exactly what he wanted from her and he could let anyone know it?

She was the one to shove him into the wall this time, her hand over his cock quickening. He was hot to the touch, as much of a furnace as Mikhail, his cock hotter than the rest of him but his tongue feverish under her jaw. Sweat formed at her temples, at her lower back, and she squeezed her thighs together.

"You're right. You're not making me do this. You also can't make me finish it." She abruptly pushed herself back, using the fabric draped over the partition to wipe her hand. No one would see the damage in the dark. "Suck on that. Suck on that yourself if you want it done."

"You bitch." But he laughed again — laughed and panted with his trousers open on either side of the cock sticking out, hard and needful. "If I were the vengeful sort, you just put yourself in a terrible position, because I'm the one who decides whether you come tonight."

"What else is new?" She brought her strap up, adjusting her dress back to normal. "Maybe now you'll understand a little of what you did, what you've made me feel ever since you granted my wish."

He carefully tucked himself into his trousers fully erect, which left a good portion of the head still over the waistband. He covered it with his shirt as though he was barely bothered, which just made Neve more annoyed. He hadn't spontaneously lost his erection to make himself more comfortable, though, and that assuaged some of her annoyance.

"I'm more than familiar with the sensation of dissatisfaction," he said, "of lust without an outlet. I've been fighting the influence of the incubus and succubus far longer than you, and although it's been a while since I've had a dry streak, I have gone quite a stretch without sex, you know, even when I didn't have to."

"I get it. You can have whatever you want whenever you want it, and you're only without what you want because you choose to be, because you're *such* a nice guy."

He caught her by the hair from behind, pulled her back gently but inexorably, gathering more of her hair in his hands until her neck strained from how far back he'd pulled her head. He bent over her, peering at her upside-down.

"Like Sasha, my dear, I'm not nice." Bell kissed her forehead then abruptly released her. She bent her knees to catch herself before she collapsed on her ass.

The Tall Man sat on a stool in the next glass case. The Short Man stood on a platform next to him so that he was half a head taller than his companion. Neve bit back a rare expletive at the erection the Tall Man held in his thick-clawed hand. Both men were in full demon mode—sharp teeth, black eyes and certain parts of their anatomy quite exceptional in comparison to humans. Although the Short Man was giant in proportion to his height, he seemed much more manageable when next to the Tall Man's erection, easily twice the size of Mikhail's, which was already impossible. Sure, it fit in his giant hand in a proportional way, but still... How did a penis like that even work? Was there enough blood in his body for his heart to pump through it?

"Why don't you ask them to find out?" Bell sauntered by her. His demeanor suggested a complete lack of the distress and frustration that she'd tried to give him. Now she wanted to slap him again.

The Short Man jerked his cock more quickly as he peered down at her, his grin wide and wicked.

Neve blushed as she realized he probably had an excellent angle down her dress from where he stood.

The Tall Man turned his ponderous head toward her as well, as though he'd only noticed her once the Short Man did. His teeth were so large that they pushed his lips out. When he opened his mouth, he looked like some kind of prehistoric predator, like a dire wolf or a sabretooth tiger. Yet his black eyes were surprisingly placid, his only apparent tension held in the hand moving just as ponderously over his massive cock.

"Neve?" Bell called from the other end of the hall.

But she looked between the two men, the two demons, Mikhail's magic surrounding her like thick fog as though he'd sent it after her in particular. What she'd done with Bell hadn't come to any fruition, and fruition was all Mikhail's magic wanted from her.

She shrugged the straps off her shoulders, pushed them down until the fabric over her breasts folded away. The ruching under her bust kept the dress from sliding down. She watched the two demons intently, watched their reactions to what she let them see.

Moss grunted, nearly doubling over as he swept his hand in a blur over the shaft. Semen spurted over the glass, spilled over his hand.

Ciarán narrowed his eyes into slits like black ink across his face. He found his own faster rhythm, startling for a hand of his size, and he spread his legs wider as he leaned toward her.

Moss muttered something Neve couldn't understand as he continued to stroke his own cock through the last thin flows. Ciarán gave a series of groans like the Earth itself moving. Moss grinned, needle teeth glinting as he whispered one more unintelligible thing.

The Tall Man snapped his cock into his grip, closing his eyes entirely as jet after impressively thick jet of cum struck the glass right in front of her.

Bell signed in exasperation as he stepped next to her. When he waved his hand, the cum on the glass disappeared as though never there. Moss threw back his head to laugh. Ciarán's lips curved, pulled back to reveal the full measure of his inhuman teeth.

Bell took Neve's forearm to lead her on. "Was that really necessary? Not that I'm disappointed you're having fun, but now Moss and Ciarán are going to have to work twice as hard to build another erection, and as you've probably noticed, Ciarán's takes a bit more effort."

"You didn't have to lead me through either funhouse. You could have just put me where you wanted me, turned the key and set me off like a wind-up toy. If you didn't want me to do things like this, maybe you should have made me different. Or not done anything to me at all."

"Then you'd still be married to the man who fucked another woman not minutes after trying to fuck you behind my tent, which would have been much better, I'm sure."

"He was only with her because Arcanium's a honeytrap," Neve snapped.

As soon as they were around the corner and in front of the Creature — chained onto his knees, with his wings forced into their full twenty-five-foot span by hooks buried in the leathery skin — Bell shoved her into the light. She flinched when he reached for the straps down her arms, but to her surprise, he yanked them back up her shoulders. The fabric didn't completely cover her breasts until she adjusted them, but it was clear he'd wanted them to.

"You think Joseph only fucked Maya because of the succubus? Without Sasha plying her trade, your husband still wouldn't have said no when Maya made her move. Even if she hadn't gone after him that day, if I hadn't granted the wish — which I'm incapable of doing, by the way, when I hear one — it would have taken only two weeks before he'd found someone else. By the time you realized he was having affairs, he would have slept with five different women."

"You don't know that."

"I know it as surely as you stand here now." Bell had raised his voice, though he wasn't quite shouting. "What is this, Neve? I thought we'd reached an agreement that, of my many faults, saving you from your husband wasn't one of them."

"What are *you* doing, Bell? Why are you wasting your time with me like this? Why allow me to do what I did to you? Why take the time to put me through the Funhouse so you can watch my reaction? Do you really think I'm going to come up to you, sway out of my dress and beg you to do for me what my husband couldn't? Do you think that because Maya is ignoring you and everyone else is paired off, as long as we have similar figures, I might be an adequate substitute?"

Bell stepped forward, pointing at her with such restrained anger that Neve nearly cowered. "No. I'd be lying if I told you I didn't want you warming my bed some nights. But if you think for one second that I made you the rebound when I didn't even know Maya was going to leave... What I want from you is nothing like what I wanted from her."

His fine cheekbones twitched from clenching his teeth as he attempted to rein himself in. "I'm not wasting my time with you. If you want to tease me every day without bringing me to completion, I won't deny you. If you never slide between my sheets, I won't ever force you. There's no subterfuge here, no nefarious plan. I wanted to show you the Funhouse because I believed you would appreciate it, and you do."

The Creature had stopped pretending to be a prisoner. He watched them, snapping his head from one to the other as though watching a tennis match.

"And just as I didn't change you for my bed, Neve, I certainly didn't change you for Mikhail's, regardless of what Lady Sasha believes. I thought *you'd* enjoy Mikhail, not the other way around. If you haven't liked what he gives you, why don't you instruct him on how to properly serve a woman like yourself? Or you can continue distracting yourself with Victor. It's no skin off my nose, love. I enjoy playing games, but not I'm not playing *you*. Believe it or not, Neve, I simply enjoy our time together, and I want you to be happy here. Is that a fucking crime?"

Neve blinked. She was pretty sure the Creature did, too. Because Bell almost sounded like he was hurt. She wondered whether Maya's absence was getting to him more than he thought.

She crossed her arms under her breasts. "How did you not know Maya was going to leave you?"

"I'm not actually omniscient. I seem so to a human being, but there are gaps in my knowledge. Seeing things profoundly relevant to my own fate is one of those gaps. The closer someone is to me, the less I see their future in relation to mine. It's why Arcanium still needs watchdogs, along with the fact I can't be in two places at once."

He made himself small. Neve knew that much. He was two or three inches taller than her, just under average for a man, too lithe for most to see his power, and Neve couldn't help but think it had to take a certain kind of man to choose to underwhelm, to camouflage himself as unthreatening. There were two kinds of men who did that — those who used it to give themselves the perfect moment to strike when no one expected it, and those with no need to strike. Neve suspected he was a bit of both, and she suspected the latter was the one standing in front of her, because she'd given him every last chance to strike, and he still seemed to take offense that she thought he would.

Bell didn't say another word as she considered him, didn't glower or even sulk, didn't get defensive, didn't loom. He was a puzzle box she turned over and over in her mind, unsure if solving it would release the cenobites or not.

Finally, without saying anything else, she approached him and tucked her arm around his elbow again.

"How'd that taste?" Bell asked over Neve's shoulder.

"Barely enough to spread over my tongue. She's wary, Bell, but she's not afraid of you."

Bell covered her hand in the crook of his elbow. "Good."

Neve looked over her shoulder at the Creature as he put himself back into imprisoned animal mode. "What was that about?"

"Just getting a second opinion. We should complete the visit and set you up in your exhibit now. We don't necessarily have to rush through the rest, but we really shouldn't stop again. Under less formal circumstances, you'd be able to take your time, but I sent the Ringmaster to the front to entertain, which I'll have to compensate him for. He intensely dislikes direct interaction with guests. I want to relieve him as soon as possible."

"If he dislikes people so much, he might have chosen the wrong profession," Neve said.

"There are perks, and as a rule, he rarely has to deal with people he'd rather be torturing in a similarly fashioned dungeon." Bell eased them away from the werewolf, enclosed in a metal cage framed like an open Iron Maiden. In the haunted funhouse, he wore pants. Not so in the Funhouse event, where he'd been stripped completely to display his hairiness and the strangeness of his transformation. His cock and scrotum were shackled like the rest of him, and he surged against the chains strapping him into the cage. He'd also been muzzled in metal, which concealed his teeth but not his seeking tongue.

Neve stopped a few feet behind Bell. "Is he a prisoner or not?"

"He's on probation. He's calm enough when released but quite an animal in the sack. He's sometimes put on the circuit if he's been a good boy."

"The circuit?"

"You'll see. There has to be some mystery in life."

"That's where you want me, isn't it?"

His silence in the darkness was answer enough.

Maya rested on the next platform, reclined supine on an inclined bench and wearing only a pair of black panties. Her gaze followed Bell and Neve until they were right in front of her. Bell stepped onto the platform, trailing his fingertips up the valley of Maya's spine.

She rolled her shoulders to shrug him away. "I agreed that you could hurt me, Bell. But don't think I agreed to it because I wanted everything back. This is for the Funhouse. That's it." She turned her head around to face the back of the wall. "Save it for the audience."

"Of course," he said quietly. Bell turned to a surgical tray of hooks, rings and a coil of silver chain. "Maya's a genuine masochist with an appetite for contrition. Sometimes she chooses scarification. Needleplay. Branding. In this case, corset piercing. I have a potion that heals wounds as though they were never there. It gives me and the Ringmaster a perpetually blank canvas, and Funhouse regulars believe we're not truly hurting her, because her skin remains flawless from session to session."

"The Ringmaster?"

"He'll whip her during tonight's entertainment."

Neve furrowed her brow, staring at the back of Maya's head as though she could send concern through the woman's scalp. "You mean that great big bullwhip he uses in the haunted funhouse? I've seen them used only once in a scene, and it wasn't the way the Ringmaster uses it."

"He's still pissed I won't let him wield the glass-knotted whip in the funhouse anymore," Bell said.

"Do you know the damage it does? Not just surface damage. It can crack ribs, traumatize organs. I don't understand how that can feel good, and I don't understand how you can let it happen…"

Maya turned back around, offering a weak smile to Neve, although she wouldn't acknowledge Bell as he stepped down from the platform. "Whatever damage he does can be undone. It's not about feeling good. Sometimes I don't want to feel good. It isn't like the scenes you might be more familiar with. Safety and sanity aren't concerns here. Only consent. Nothing's happening that I didn't choose." She nodded toward the darkness ahead. "Go on. Don't worry about me."

"She's been doing this for years, and she's still healthy, not a single scar on her that she didn't want to keep. She'll be fine." Bell guided Neve with his hand on the small of her back, but he stared at the brushed concrete floor instead of at Maya, keeping his head down until they'd turned the corner.

Neve bit back the impulse to ask if he was okay, but Bell straightened, inhaled sharply as though to bring himself back and hide the feelings deeper. He clearly didn't want to discuss it, and she wasn't his therapist.

The Horned God was next. She'd never heard him say a word, and on the occasions he ate with the rest of them, he sat with the demons. His eyes weren't black and his teeth weren't sharp, but he bore several racks of antlers—one set on his head, one on the tops of his shoulders and one emerging from the back of his shoulder blades. He was furred from the V of his hips down, his penis visible through the thicket of thick, white hair but not as proudly shown off as many of the others', and not erect.

He was just an oddity, his skin so gray it was almost blue, his nipples pierced with delicate silver rings, his white-irised eyes wide and unblinking. There was something terribly penetrating about those eyes, as though they could see more deeply than the impenetrable eyes of the demons.

Neve cried out at the next glass-case tableau. A man done up in thick leather over his ripped fireplug body held the head of the carousel engineer, Caroline.

Just her head.

It had been severed halfway down her neck, sinew swaying from the bottom, the uneven place on her spine and opening of her throat visible from the base. Her blonde and blue-streaked hair was wound around the thick man's hand so that her head poised just over where his cock would be.

The rest of her body was on the other side of the tableau, on her knees while a whipcord-thin man strapped head to toe in similar thick leather felt up the naked body of a headless woman.

Caroline twisted around in the shorter man's hand from where she'd been nuzzling the leather over his cock. She smiled. The headless body waved to Neve.

"That…that…" If Neve hadn't known any better, she probably would have assumed there was some kind of mirror making it seem like two women were one. Knowing it was real was what made it so awful. "That's not okay, Bell."

He laughed. "It was her idea. We moved the torture carousel to later in the event because she wanted to do this in the Funhouse instead."

Valorie came tearing through the halls in a translucent white latex bodysuit, with only nose holes for her to breathe. She skittered like a ghostly, possessed demon in an impossibly contorted body, her mouth open and eyes rolled back. Neve gave another little scream, but it wasn't nearly as terrible as Caroline's literally beheaded body being used, which bordered on necrophilia and reminded her of a disturbing series of true crimes.

The next tableau showed Christina, the Human Torso without any limbs, roped up with rubber tubing. The places where her limbs had been reduced to nubs appeared more cleanly removed, the visible interior not flesh but mechanical, as though she were an android who had been mined for spare parts. She sparked with malfunction as she struggled against the tubing holding her aloft.

On his knees, the tattooed man was nearly unrecognizable because his whole body was airbrushed a light green. She only recognized him because he'd kept his piercings, which looked even stranger on a man made to look like an alien. Troy teased Christina's biomechanical folds with his split tongue, both sides surprisingly dexterous.

The man in the next glass case could hardly be called a man. If Neve had thought Caroline was the most disturbing thing the Funhouse could offer, she stood corrected.

He wasn't just another Human Torso, although he was missing his limbs. His had been severed farther up his legs and arms, leaving him nothing but a torso alone. There were obvious scars where he'd been stitched together.

A tube had been inserted into his throat to allow him to breathe, another one lower for feeding, because his nose had been removed and his mouth had been sewn and healed shut. His eyes had been removed, the eyelids grafted closed. His ears had been removed and covered. He had the barest features of a face, his skull left intact but everything else scarred over, and not in the clean, featureless way of the Gentleman.

What was left showed signs of having been a man once, with black tattoos all over his skin, his chest and abdomen those of someone who had clearly wanted to look good, a five o'clock shadow over his chin and scalp.

He'd been left only his head, torso, cock, balls and anus. A silver plug had been inserted into his ass, and a golem in a tight nurse's dress, face mask and the usual deadened eyes of her kind worked lubricated, gloved hands over his genitals without enthusiasm. The lube glistened over his nearly purple cock.

In case anyone thought the man was nothing but a rubber mannequin, his muscles twitched when the nurse stroked over his lower abdomen to his navel, and when she focused on his tight, dark sac, his cock pulsed and moved as though blindly searching for what had given it pleasure. He shook his head, tried to arch. It was like watching a man wearing a straitjacket in a sensory deprivation room. Touch was all he got to experience, and he fought to feel it.

"My God, Bell. What did you do?"

"Why not ask what he did?" Bell's voice was exceedingly pleasant and exceedingly cold. "We sometimes display the Blob in Oddity Row if there's a cool breeze, but otherwise, we mostly bring him out for Funhouse events, because it's the only time he gets to come these days. It's not like he can take care of it himself or ask someone else, can he? I'll eventually give him some of his senses back, perhaps once he's gone completely mad and earns the mercy of a clean slate. But I explained plainly what it was he would do in my Funhouse, and he wants to be here. He told me himself. So don't you 'my God' me."

Bell brought her to the next glass-case tableau, this one empty except for a luxurious four-poster bed turned down in red silk that wasn't practical at all but looked amazing. The walls had been draped in red velvet like the oddity tent curtains. The entire feel of it was like some gothic fantasy boudoir, lit by a pair of golden lamps on either end.

The glass wall slid to the side.

His lips brushed her ear as he ran his hands down her arms. "This is your stop."

Chapter Ten

"I don't see any hands." Moths battered Neve's cold, hollow insides, nervousness briefly overtaking the effect of the rest of the Funhouse journey.

"You will," Bell said. "Do you trust me?"

"Not nearly as much as you seem to want me to."

"Do you trust me on this?" He gently nudged her onto the platform. "Do you trust that you'll enjoy this as much as everyone else will?"

Neve turned around at the hiss of the glass closing back to make a seamless wall, and for a moment, she couldn't breathe. But the glass case didn't have a top, and it didn't reach all the way to the third-floor ceiling. She was getting plenty of air. Her lungs just hadn't convinced her brain of that.

"Neve." Bell pressed a hand to the glass. She automatically placed her hand against his. "This is almost exactly the same as the haunted funhouse. Guests stare at you all day, wondering what it would be like to touch you, to feel what you're feeling. This is no different, except you'll be allowed to feel so much more, and they'll be allowed to linger. But they can't touch you, and you can always close your eyes. Trust me. Trust that I intend to give you nothing but pleasure tonight."

Neve took a deep breath through her nose, exhaled out her mouth, again and again until her lungs worked like normal. She nodded.

"Then climb into bed like a good girl."

He trailed his fingers down the glass as she backed herself to the bed then crawled under the covers. The silk was as heavenly as her dress over her skin, no prickly static to disrupt the experience. Just cool silk caressing what smooth limbs they could cling to.

"Now close your eyes and try to sleep, good girl. No monsters under the bed tonight. I'll see you later this evening."

Neve forced herself to close her eyes and keep breathing, unsure what was supposed to happen and when. When she shut her eyes, though, she saw the things in this Funhouse that were the most terrifying in their quiet cruelty. Bell had never pretended he couldn't be cruel. Her stomach churned as she wondered whether that was okay with her.

A wave of warm calm swept from head to toe in seconds, leaving her nearly asleep.

"Relax, Neve. One day you'll understand why I do the things I do."

She rested there, her hair splayed out on the pillow, one hand next to her hip and the other curled next to her face, which was turned slightly away from the corridor. She'd pulled the covers over her chest so that only the black straps of the dress could be seen, but the way the silk clung to her, her form was still clearly discernable.

Her brain flashed between Caroline's severed head, the Blob's twisting body, Valorie's silent scream, the way she imagined Maya's back would look after the Ringmaster finished with it, but it was as though Bell plucked those thoughts from her head like apples until her mind was quiet again.

The Funhouse had its own soundtrack—like the haunted funhouse, but with fewer screams. A string quartet played something haunting and slow in a minor key, but underneath it, almost too soft to hear, were low moans, soft groans, as though from a distance or just behind one of the curtained partitions.

When stray cries, murmurs of conversation, distant laughing and moans that doubtlessly came from the Arcanium exhibits who were unapologetically having sex rather than just being sexual accented the soundtrack, Neve knew the Funhouse event had officially begun.

All of this happened while she slipped away, untethering from consciousness, aware but not paying much attention. By now, she was used to sleeping in spite of sexual tension, so there was no reason for that to keep her awake now.

A hand wrapped around her ankle.

There was no one else in the bed with her, nowhere for anyone to hide. The silk had been flawless when she'd climbed in, no holes for anything to creep through.

At her twitch, the hand slowly made its way up her body, mapping the contour of her leg, over her knee, her thigh.

The disembodied hands that groped her in the haunted funhouse were human, but what moved over her bare leg now, teasing the sensitive inner thigh before retreating to less vulnerable flesh, didn't feel normal. The fingers were too long. She wasn't positive, but she thought there might have been an extra set of knuckles. It was how she imagined the Gentleman would feel like if he had the inclination to touch, but the texture was different — not quite slimy, not quite brittle, reptilian but not rough, smooth without being scaly. Her dream-trapped mind couldn't pinpoint the exact quality, but it was unmistakably wrong.

The same wrong kind of hand smoothed its way up her other leg. She drew her knee up in a bleary attempt to shake it away, as though it was just a spider crawling over her, but it followed her up, cupping her knee then squeezing the length of thigh.

She moaned, shaking her head, her brows knitting.

"Relax. The sex demons will send out another burst of magic any minute now. You're doing wonderfully."

The strokes of the strange hands softened into a massage, urging her along with Bell to relax, go back to sleep.

Another pair of hands wrapped around her waist. Long-fingered like the others but with nasty claws at their tips, they gathered the dress up her thighs, ran over her abdomen with eerie possessiveness then found their way to her breasts. When she lay on her back, her breasts tended to gravitate toward the sides, but the dress kept them somewhat contained and the strange hands did the rest, testing the yield of her flesh, claws pricking at her cleavage.

Her eyelashes fluttered as she shifted against the hands exploring her body more personally, more intentionally, than the hands from the haunted funhouse. She caught a glimpse of mountainous knuckles under the silk as the hand massaged her breast, the other clawed hand overlapping with the long-fingered hand on her leg as they caressed her thigh.

A sound escaped her, a harsh exhalation she couldn't control, as she tried to turn over. But the peace had officially been disturbed. Her bed writhed with the phantom hands slowly savoring every part of her body they could touch, as though whatever they reached was the most arousing piece of her. At this point, she could easily tell when disembodied hands were aroused — a kind of tension or restraint required not to squeeze her too hard in excitement.

But the clawless hands didn't hesitate when she tried to roll onto her side. They clamped down on her legs and yanked her onto her back again.

Neve's eyes flew open.

As soon as they knew she was fully awake, the clawed hands slid up to grasp both breasts in a firm, almost painful grip. The silk sheets fell away, exposing black, crackled hands connected to arms that emerged seamlessly from the sheets on either side, as though a demon beneath the mattress reached up without barrier to caress her.

There was a terrible tearing sound as the clawed hands tightened their grip, but instead of rending her, they tore the black silk of her dress until her breasts were bare. The rip extended down past her navel, pushing the covers farther down.

The other pair of hands emerged from under the covers now, with mottled bluish-green, scabrous fingers that dented the meat of her thighs until she squirmed.

And from the corner of her eye, ghostly figures watched from outside the scene. Most of them were already in a state of undress by now after everything they'd witnessed earlier in the maze. They watched with their noses pressed to the glass, fogging it with their breath until someone urged them back so everyone could see. Some turned away — Neve assumed to return to a previous tableau — or continued on, but a few stayed, observed mercilessly as the demons laid claim to her.

Allen stood there, his hand in his open trousers. She couldn't see anything anatomical, but it was perfectly clear what he was doing. That wasn't breaking the rules here, but Neve had to look away, pained at the reality of a supercilious ass like that taking pleasure from what was happening to her. She closed her eyes, shaking her head again, playing along with the fantasy but also oddly raw after being pulled out of her half-sleep.

The hands on her legs gripped her thighs hard enough to bruise, but the thumbs were gentler, caressing where her thighs pressed together as though to coax them to open. They disturbed the trimmed curls at the juncture, making her abdomen, mound and thighs break out into gooseflesh. Neve bit her lip as those thumbs brushed closer and closer to her clit, which peeked out from the top of her folds even with her legs closed.

Meanwhile, the clawed hands had also taken a more delicate turn now that her breasts were out for it to enjoy, as though the mind behind it couldn't quite decide what to do with her now that he had her at his mercy. When his claws rubbed together, they made a sound like sharpening knives.

Then those claws descended upon the peaks of her breasts, closing in on the areolae, which puckered and darkened, her nipples hardening almost out of self-defense rather than arousal. But as the claws plucked at her, dangerously sharp on such sensitive places, the pink deepened to near red on the tough, pebbly flesh. She pressed her thighs more tightly together against the relentless sensations sending lightning bolts from her breasts to her clit, which throbbed with every pinch and pull of those wicked claws.

With a high moan, she brought her own hands under her breasts as the claws pulled her nipples taut. When the claws released her, she caught the tender, menaced flesh with her softer palms, but quickly brought her thumbs and forefingers to her nipples to press her own nails into the flesh.

Neve lifted her hips helplessly toward the teasing fingers so close to where she wanted them. Her folds tingled, full between her thighs, but she wasn't quite ready to part her legs for everyone on the other side of the glass to see her so shameless, although she knew she only delayed the inevitable. She wasn't going to be able to keep her legs closed for this, and hell, even if she did, the hands would find their way in from underneath.

Another pair of hands, human-like but skeletal and gray, grabbed her wrists and yanked her away from touching herself. She'd still been pinching her nipples, and the sudden jerk pulled them to the point of pain before she could release her breasts to quiver back against her chest. Neve cried out, struggled against the hands on her wrists, but they forced her fists back onto the pillows. The claws tapped her breasts in a clear gesture — *naughty, naughty.*

Then another pair of hands — black and shiny as a spider and bigger than Ciarán's, with claws like those of a wolf — emerged from the red silk, dwarfing the long-fingered hands on her breasts and legs and seeming to quell them as well. They stopped stroking and teasing her and instead joined the skeletal hands in holding her down as the broad black hands flexed their fingers, displayed themselves to her like a warning.

One giant hand curled its fingers to brush her cheek in a parody of tenderness. It played its nails over her lower lip, plumped from her biting it. The other giant hand slowly lowered itself to her abdomen. The clawless hands on her thighs roughly pulled her legs apart, spreading her for her audience, who watched so intently they almost didn't breathe, perhaps because she was having trouble with that herself. She trembled with such violence that it could only be genuine. The hand on her abdomen spread its fingers, taking possession of everything it touched, then slid down to her mound.

At that moment, Neve felt a surge of desire so strong through her that it overshadowed the pain of the claws on her nipples, the bruises the other hands had left, any lingering modesty. The hand at her face closed around her neck just as she raised herself to meet his fingers descending between her legs. They brushed over her clit but weren't concerned with it. All the demon wanted was inside.

Two giant fingers pushed rudely into her cunt, which offered no protest or obstacle, entrance smooth from a combination of what the Funhouse exhibits and fucking with Bell had already done to her and what the other hands had continued.

Hers weren't the only moans filling her ears as the demon penetrated her, probed her, pushed as deeply as he could, curling his fingers to own her before she could adjust to so much inside, so dexterous, so big. His claws added a line of pain to the sensation, like a wasp sting on her tongue during a kiss, turning some of her moans into screams. He brought his hand down from her neck after a squeeze that made her vision blur then groped her breast, small in his massive paw.

She fought against the hands holding down her wrists and legs, but their grips were as unyielding as iron. She didn't know whether she was fighting to get free or fighting to offer herself more fully to the demon who took her, didn't know whether she screamed out of pleasure or pain, whether the stinging was one or the other or both.

What she couldn't mistake was that, underneath the moans and cries she couldn't control coming from her mouth, the sound of his fingers moving inside her made clear how wet she was. She didn't know whether the people on the other side of the glass could hear it as loudly as she could, but they'd be able to see.

"You're the strongest in the room, little girl. I smell you, hear you, feel you, feel what you're feeling, feel what you want those hands that aren't mine to do to you. You're irresistible. It only makes what I send so much stronger in return. I thought I could control this. I thought I could fight how much I — "

That wasn't Bell.

The voice in her head was much deeper, wilder, a vibrating rumble that brought tears to her eyes. She thrashed under the prison hold of the hands, which struggled to keep her down as the giant demon hand beckoned for her orgasm.

It ripped through her as though he'd clawed straight through. Liquid splashed over the demon's hand and on the silk as her hips bucked off the bed. The thick fingers continued to plunder her, forcing her orgasm into pain and back. Her cunt clutched at him in desperate need. Neve bit her pillow, her screams grating and scraping through her throat.

Applause followed, but Neve could barely hear it through the roaring in her ears and the familiar groan in her head. She felt his orgasm, too. He sent the waves of it through the Funhouse, leaving only heightened desire in its wake, because in a glass case and with a blade affixed to his erection, he couldn't satisfy himself or kill anyone with his feed.

The hands didn't stop or disappear. She didn't expect them to. This was a continuous exhibit, presumably until everyone had made it through and had their fill of whatever repeats they wanted. The haunted funhouse was a place of perpetual dissatisfaction, all teasing and no follow-through, but this was the exact opposite. And apparently the demonic hands qualified not as sex toys but sexual partners, because the end of her orgasm was followed by sheer relief that none of the dildos or her own hands could give her.

It didn't last long, with the sex demons emanating like nuclear reactors, but the tension that had been building up since Victor had snapped. What followed was new tension, new desire, new lust, and she could live with that, even though it came on just as strong.

As the crowd that had gathered around her moved on, either to whatever lay beyond the Funhouse maze or to previous exhibits, the fingers inside her eased out all too slowly, forcing her awareness of every stretch, pull and caress of him until he emerged. And as his fingers lifted away, her wetness made a thick, fluid line between them and her cunt. The hand stretched those fingers out to show off how she'd made his shiny skin glisten even more.

"*Again…*" Mikhail pleaded. "*Please don't stop.*"

She didn't know whether he could hear her, but she tried to think in his direction. "*Stay away. Stay out of my head.*"

"*Your desire screams even louder than you do. It's all I can do to not shatter the glass and break down the walls between us to bury myself in you and feed until I no longer know hunger. But I can't not hear you. Your desire is so much stronger than my control, and it* begs *for me… I can't…stop…this…*"

Another wave of need hit her as strong as a twenty-foot wave, obliterating the satisfaction the demon hands had given her as though it was nothing but a castle in the sand.

Thick fingers coated with her arousal entered her mouth mid-moan, forcing their way in against any muffled protest. With the desire hot and thick inside her like a summer storm, she shook her head as though trying to refuse, but she also sucked him in, breathed in the strong fragrance of her own scent, swallowed her own salty taste. Underneath it, she tasted the demon as well. Bell had been thorough in his creation, down to the undertaste and aroma of smoke and uncooked meat.

"*Do that all you want, but stay out of my head.*"

"*You opened the gate, Neve, not me.*"

She couldn't keep having a conversation with Lord Mikhail and handle the sex magic and demon hands at the same time. As the demon's filthy fingers filled her mouth without any magical aid, its other hand drifted between her legs again, this time avoiding her pussy, which still felt as though it gaped, the air cool against the wet heat.

He instead focused her clit, pinched the front of her folds between two fingers, plumping them and trapping the blood inside. The smooth side of a claw teased the hypersensitive flesh. There was no body to laugh at her, but Neve still sensed amusement in the way some of the other hands eased their hold on her. The long-clawed pair found her breasts again, pinching her nipples as well between the razor edges of his claws. They all seemed to delight in making her wrench and writhe, which only made it worse.

Please please please please…

The long, scabrous hands from the beginning parted her legs until her heels were on the edge of the bed on both sides. Then, as though afraid the larger hand torturing her clit would notice, they slithered in, thin finger by thin finger, until she was nearly screaming again. They stretched her inside, pulling her open more and stroking all angles of her cunt.

The demon in her mouth forced her head from side to side, demonstrating his dominance. The hands over her breasts might have actually been giving her little cuts at this point, but she wouldn't know, wouldn't care. And still the hands at her wrists kept her pinned.

The hall on the other side of the glass was nearly empty. She had an audience of one. Neve could hardly believe that all of this was going on and almost no one was interested, which briefly distracted her from the intensity of her own need.

The man on the other side of the glass stood near the back of the corridor out of reach of the light, an apparition she could barely make out until he touched his hat in greeting and stepped forward.

He wasn't wearing the tan trench coat this time. A trim leather jacket clung to his slim frame. But he still had that fedora, and she couldn't forget those uncanny bright eyes or the enigmatic amusement that lit his whole beautiful face with the subtly of candlelight.

She tried to sit up, suddenly embarrassed that someone she recognized was watching her. All the hands forced her back down again, redoubling their efforts to thoroughly overstimulate and distract her.

He wasn't touching himself, and she couldn't tell whether he was aroused. But there was a quality to his face, to his consideration, that transcended simple interest and entertainment. When he realized she recognized him, his boyish grin broadened, but his amusement didn't transition to humor. He wasn't laughing at her. And as more gaunt fingers found their way into her pussy and the pulsing pinch over her clit became too much to fight, his smile melted away, leaving his beautiful face something thinner, darker, hungrier than it was before.

He was looking into her eyes when she came again.

The giant fingers retreated from her mouth. Neve gasped for breath as the fingers inside her continued to fill and stroke her inner walls, and still more entered. How many fingers did this particular demon have, and how many more could she take before it became painful?

The man continued to survey her, savor her, as the hands over her clit and inside her pussy once again stretched out her orgasm thin and tight to the brink of agony before letting her come down. The giant demon hands released her clit. It throbbed terribly as blood moved through the flesh again, which circled her cunt right back into a pleasureless orgasm that clenched around the thin, spidery fingers inside her.

The man nodded — in acknowledgment, gratitude? Then his grin returned, and he sauntered around the corner.

Only when he was gone did other people start passing by her tableau again, and the hands reprised their assault on her senses in tandem with waves of the incubus' lust.

She had no idea how long any of this took, but the hands eventually slunk away from her body, retracting back into the bed as though they'd never been there but for the rumpled sheets and what some might kindly call her 'disarray'.

Neve closed her eyes. She slumped, replete and panting, against the mess of silk around her, completely uncaring that her dress was ruined or that she was the very definition of 'ridden hard and put away wet' and felt like it, too.

She was briefly alone and untouched. After too many orgasms to count — what were the odds a woman could have that problem twice? — and at least eight hands on her at all times, she was quite through with contact.

The glass at the front of the case whispered to the side. Bell had removed his shirt and had since taken care of his erection one way or another. To Neve's irritation, Lord Mikhail stood a few paces behind him, still in his 'sex kills' costume, still hard and emanating, although he seemed to be semi-successfully reining it in.

"If you climb out here, you'll feel ever so much better." Bell clasped his hands behind his back, as though he was just passing through and incidentally rendering aid.

Neve groaned as she sat up. All of her muscles ached, and there was an unspeakable wet spot underneath her. The straps of the dress draped over her arms, the dress itself fluttering on either side of her breasts. She brought the sides together, more to maintain a semblance of dress than of modesty.

Her legs were weak, shaking. Bell stepped onto the platform to help her down. Upon crossing the threshold, all the juices, sweat, salt and blood disappeared and her dress stitched itself back together, leaving her as un-disarrayed as she'd been when she'd entered the Funhouse maze.

"I may kill you both," Neve said.

"You'll feel better once you've eaten," Bell said. "We haven't started performances yet, and you don't have to mingle."

"What do you mean, we haven't started performances yet? What the hell was I doing?"

"Too much, love?"

She punched his arm, and she wasn't gentle.

"Ow. I told you there was something you could do in the circuit in addition to the Funhouse exhibits."

"Right now, all I want to do is wear sweatpants, wrap myself in a fleece blanket and eat pizza rolls while I watch a movie. But the only one of those you let me have in my trailer is the blanket."

"I'll get some pizza rolls for the freezer and an e-book reader with a streaming program. And if you wanted pants, all you had to do was ask. As long as you limit use to when no one from the outside can see you. We have a certain mystique to maintain, after all. But we have to finish out the night, and I told you that you'd enjoy the performance as well, didn't I? I promised. Lord Mikhail, please escort Neve to the buffet and show her where she can recharge without any of our guests accosting her."

Neve skirted away from Mikhail as he held out his hand. She was so done with hands.

Bell placed his own on her shoulder. "He's fed, my dear. He'll be little trouble to you for a little while."

She glanced from Bell to Mikhail, who was one of the few people who could appear dignified and stoic while done up in that ensemble. "Who died, then?"

"Lady Sasha broke the ban," Mikhail replied, "for tonight alone. She wasn't any happier about the effect I was having on her than you. We've fed on each other, which should give us a brief respite even in the midst of this cacophony. I won't hurt you, Neve, and my control is no longer so tenuous. Please."

"If you're going to perform, you'll appreciate a little help, but the effect of his touch won't overwhelm," Bell said, uncharacteristically gentle.

Putting her hand in Lord Mikhail's sent fresh electricity through her worn-out circuits, though the leather of his gloves kept the contact from being direct. Even so, it wasn't half the impact of what he'd emanated at the beginning or when he'd tried to convince her to fuck him. He pulled at her, as though hooking threaded needles through her palms, but it was bearable.

"How much are you holding in right now?" she asked.

"How long can you hold your breath?"

"One minute ten seconds in the summer, when I swim. Is that how long I have?"

"No. That's how it feels to hold the magic in," Mikhail said.

"Can you really do this?"

"After feeding as I did upon Lady Sasha, yes. Trust me."

"Haven't been given a reason yet," Neve said.

"Let me give you a reason."

Against all her better instincts, she tentatively wrapped her fingers around his hand and allowed him to do the same.

"Good. I'll let you crazy kids get something to eat while I handle logistics. Excuse me." Bell climbed through the rumpled bedroom then ducked through a folded back panel that Neve was positive hadn't been foldable before.

"Am I the last exhibit?" Neve asked.

"The explosive finish," Lord Mikhail replied.

"I can't hear anyone."

"They're on the other side of the red curtain."

Lord Mikhail led them to the red curtain at the end of the maze. He held the velvet up for her. She let go of his hand to duck under.

The murmur of people talking among themselves as though once again part of a fancy cocktail party instead of a sex-and-horror show was louder than the curtain should have been able to conceal.

One of these days, she was going to ask Bell how all the magic worked, but for now, she could accept that there were rules and laws quite different than the ones under which she'd always worked. Almost nothing was impossible, just statistically improbable, and Arcanium had rendered certain impossibilities to a statistical possibility of one. Not simple at all, yet simple as that. She could spend decades in Arcanium out of scientific curiosity alone, if all these orgasms didn't give her a stroke or make her punch someone powerful in the face first.

People turned around to look at her, people with diamond cufflinks and ruby necklaces. She didn't doubt part of the attention came from being followed by Lord Mikhail, but it struck her like acid.

Neve held her head up and avoided everyone's gaze the way she did in the haunted funhouse. After everything they'd seen of her and the suggestive way some of Arcanium's people were mingling, they might have wanted to do more than talk if she made herself approachable.

The room, which was really just the rest of the third floor, had been set up in two sections. The red curtain opened to the elevated lounge, arranged with modern couches that snaked in S shapes to accommodate many people at once while cast entertained them from display platforms that took the place of coffee tables.

The other half of the room had been set up like an amphitheater descending from the lounge. No cheap bleachers here. The platforms were sturdy and didn't creak, and the seats were just as luxurious as those in the lounge.

It was easy to pinpoint Arcanium circus folk in the crowd. Even the simpler outfits were more elaborate than the traditional elegance of the guests. Maya had pulled on a full feathered skirt and black corset. Kitty had gone her usual furry fairy route with a glittering copper gown, brown corset and doves done up in her intricate hair. Valorie had changed from her ghost latex into a white lace body glove. Victor wore a crown of crystals with a complete lack of irony that Neve somehow appreciated even more. They all sat with their patrons, laughed, ate, flirted. Kitty sat on a large man's lap. She was pretty sure Victor was talking dirty with the woman he was drinking with.

The Spider had chosen not to mingle. She was bound with white rope to a web hanging angled from the ceiling. The fire-eater had been strapped into a pneumatic harness that made him look like a partially turned dragon. He breathed fire from a platform on another side of the room. A few other Arcanium cast members had taken places on platforms, including Misha, doing his sword-swallowing act with innuendo he could never suggest when the circus was open, and the Rotting Man, whose naked body she'd never wanted to see and now couldn't unsee.

Two of the clowns, Comedy and Tragedy — who Neve hadn't expected to be here tonight, given that the clientele was entirely adult — had been chained in pretty but sturdy silver to the columns. Their monster mouths were open all the way to their ears, displaying teeth that Neve hadn't seen on anything but deep-sea predators. Given that kind of anatomy was impossible to fake without CGI and not even Bell could CGI reality, Neve didn't know how people could possibly think it was funny feeding them with their bare hands, but the clowns didn't seem to mind, and no one's fingers were bitten off.

To the right, Caroline stood at the center of what looked like a hell-dimension version of her carousel, with the men who'd been fucking her separated head and body as two of the mounts. She wore all patent leather, from the police hat to her stripper boots. Decapitation appeared to have done nothing to dampen her spirits, because she happily switched and caned the thighs and asses of every man on the seven-mount carousel. Christina was riding Troy, who had looped himself into the reins and who laughed madly through his bit every time Caroline got him. The Cyclops and three other prisoners made up the rest of the herd, done up in sub bondage and, in the case of Caroline's shorter, stronger man, horseplay. A few female guests rode them for a laugh.

To the left, the odd chef manned an open bar and buffet table of both odd and normal delicacies.

There were curtained rooms along the sides of the amphitheater that looked almost like box seats. More curtained rooms lined the back of the lounge against the red curtain. Based on parties Neve had been to with Joseph, it didn't take long for her to realize what those rooms were for.

"Is there a law here that *isn't* being broken or bent beyond recognition?" Neve muttered. "I'm *really* not sure how I feel about this."

"You don't have to do anything with our patrons that you don't *want* to do. Lady Sasha and I are quite adept at walking among them without getting accosted — with the right dissuasion." He brandished the blades on his gloves and nodded at Lady Sasha, who wove between the many people in the lounge completely naked, but with a pair of king cobras wrapped around her body like a harness, hissing in warning when anyone dared get too close.

"Where am I supposed to hide a knife or a snake in this outfit?"

Mikhail laughed, a booming sound that ricocheted eagerly against the concrete. "Let me be your blade."

So he'd protect her from them. *But what protects them from me?*

She could sense it in this wide room. Pulsing through the laughter and chatter, in the bubbles from the champagne, in the hiss of skin and fabric. Everyone had adjusted their dresses and trousers so that anything they'd exposed in the maze was back to socially appropriate. But there was a hand on a woman's thigh. Under the top of a bodice. Over the front of a man's trousers. Up the back of a jacket. All these hands everywhere, and by now she knew a little something about hands everywhere. Moans under the creepy quartet music. Pills being passed from jackets — prescription or illicit highs, the promise of youth all night long. For every person in Arcanium who said no, there seemed to be another who would say *yes, please*.

And for all that she wanted to say no, she was literally terrified that she'd say *yes, please* without hesitation. She tried not to show it as Mikhail walked with her to the buffet table. Standing in front of fried grasshoppers, salmon pate sandwiches and blinis, she was reminded how hungry she was after all the exercise the demon hands had put her through.

She'd never been much of a foodie. Joseph had cooked most of the meals, and when it had been her turn, she'd depended on simple staples. But some of the restaurants and food events they'd attended had at least proved to her that her palate could be broadened. She filled a small plate with one of everything that didn't look like it had once been an insect or arachnid, though she wasn't averse to trying them eventually.

An older man with receding hairline but a face rife with character came up next to her with his own plate, choosing among caviar and cheese options. "It's a cold night, and that's a very short dress. Would you like my jacket?"

Neve glanced nervously at Mikhail behind her, who was picking up toothpicked samples with that delicate dexterity that had surprised her before. He nodded, but she wasn't sure what he was giving permission for.

She opted for being polite. "I'm fine. Thank you."

"My friends and I are sitting on that part of the couch over there." The man nodded to a group of four other men, who were talking together and eyeing her as their friend spoke. "There's room for you."

"No. I really think I'm done for the night. I'm here for the food." She started around the table toward the bar for a drink.

The man caught her upper arm. He wasn't rude, and he didn't hurt her, but Lord Mikhail set a heavy hand on the man's shoulder. The man immediately released her. Lord Mikhail turned away as though nothing had happened and as though he wasn't wearing assless chaps.

"Enjoy your evening," Lord Mikhail called as the man made a wise retreat. "Do not fear saying no to them, Neve. And you don't have to be polite. They'll only call you a bitch — and that but once."

"What do they say when you say no?" Neve asked.

"They don't say much to me. Even when they desire me, I frighten them. People fear what they most want. When I'm not hunting, I do nothing to discourage this. The Lady and I are only here if someone breaks their contract."

"And to salt the mines," Neve said.

A smile. "Do you want to stay in the lounge, or would you like an escort to the green room?"

"I'd like to just sit and not be disturbed. Is that possible here, or do I need to go to the green room?"

He gestured to one of the high tables by the bar, made for two, then broke away from her to get his own drink.

"That was quite a show, darling. Everything I've come to expect from Bell's Arcanium and better." Samuel, accompanied by his associate Allen, had sneaked up on her from behind, whether intentionally or not. She had no doubt, however, that waiting until Lord Mikhail was no longer at her side had been intentional.

He held out his hand as though in a business meeting. "Samuel Amendola."

"Neve. I don't really have a title here."

Allen stripped her with his eyes but Samuel didn't. He wasn't even briefly looking at her cleavage, displaying controlled behavior Neve had only noticed in long-time coworkers and her bosses, at least the ones who wore lab coats instead of suits—men who'd learned how to work with women as equals. Neve liked working with men like that, so she didn't mind shaking his hand, although she remained wary.

Samuel kept hold of her fingers, lifted them as though he would kiss them, but the lift was the only salute he gave. "Have you worked in circuses before, or in another profession?"

There was only a little hesitation before asking about other professions—a comma rather than an ellipsis, which carried less disapproval, and he didn't leer at the suggestion.

"I've never been part of a circus before. I originally worked in a pharmaceutical research lab."

Samuel raised a bushy white eyebrow before sitting in the chair next to her. "You don't say. Were you always interested in the circus arts? Dreamed of running away to a circus?"

She'd wanted space, but actual conversation was something she'd been without for a while.

"Not in the least. Arcanium sort of…happened to me." Neve wondered how to play her past. Obviously, the truth wouldn't do, but she'd never been good at making up stories. "I was going through relationship problems. Some women hit the gym. Some get a haircut. I apparently joined a circus."

"So that ring on your finger… Is that by habit or is the relationship on hold?" Samuel nodded toward her left hand. "You chose a rather unconventional venue for mere separation. Are they aware of your relocation?"

Neve raised her left hand to stare at her wedding ring. In terms of fidelity—and being realistic with herself about the nature of Arcanium as well as the nature she'd been given—the diamond had become nothing more than pretty carbon. She wasn't going to get divorce papers signed, but there was no reason to dwell too much on technicalities if she'd be declared dead a decade or so. She sighed then twisted the ring off and moved it to the third finger of her right hand, which was less symbolic than it seemed—the fourth finger on her right hand was smaller than the left.

"Habit," she said softly.

"I didn't intend to bring up unpleasant memories."

"You couldn't have known." She checked his left hand. No ring and no tan line where a ring would be. In the winter, that wasn't a given sign, but he was darker-skinned, like Mikhail, and she thought the contrast would have shown better on him. Allen still wore his wedding ring. All the more reason to keep ignoring him. "How often have you hosted the Funhouse?"

"This will be my third year. I have several properties here and there that have served as Bell's canvas. We used to be a group of twenty, but we've since grown — invitation only, like a secret society." Samuel grinned with amusement at himself. "As secret societies go, I suspect we're more esoteric than most, but at least we're not meddling in the affairs of the world."

"Why meddle in the affairs of the world when you can meddle in other kinds of affairs?" Neve ducked her head. "Sorry. I didn't mean for that to come out as sarcastic as it did."

He placed a hand on hers on the table. "We do what we do. When I was young myself, I used to imagine running away to join the circus. They lost some of their edge when they discarded unapologetic strangeness and danger and focused more on gymnastic feats. Admirable in their own way." He peered over the lounge, where Valorie was showing off her contortion skills and where Seth and Lars engaged in displays of tandem strength. "But Bell's Arcanium is special. It's the highlight of our year."

"Did he suggest a sex show or did you?" Neve asked.

"Who are you to judge, girl?" Allen laughed, gesturing over her.

"I've done private parties before, but they were the kind partners went to and where you didn't pay for the performers," Neve said. "I'm only judging a little. You're judging a lot."

Samuel's smile widened. "This is Allen's first party. He doesn't quite appreciate it the same way I do."

"And how do you appreciate it, exactly?" Neve asked.

"I'm a widower, have been for ten years. I never remarried, but I crave company like any man. In my circles, you tend to cross paths with the perverse and mercenary, but it's not very interesting. Not at all. Deep in the heart of it, I feel other men like me forget that companionship is the commodity, not the people. When Bell insisted that all carnal accompaniment would be performative or else strictly consensual, that appealed to me more than knowing I could have anyone and anything I wanted."

Samuel gestured to his friend. "Allen doesn't quite understand that. He thinks the contracts give us loopholes rather than limitations. But even after your performance in the maze, I appreciate that if you're here with me now, talking with me, it's not because you were coerced by your boss or some misguided effort to keep me happy. And if this conversation is all you do with me, I welcome it."

Allen rolled his eyes. "You're a romantic old fool. Who sponsors and attends a sex show for the conversation?"

"He'd be surprised," Samuel murmured to her before taking a drink.

"Well, I know I'll be disappointed if she's not in the circuit," Allen said. "I'm saving myself for that, unless you're available for a private room now?"

"Pass. Even if I weren't exhausted, hard pass." Neve kept expecting some kind of repercussion for being rude, but no fiery hail rained down upon her head, and no man slapped her unwilling mouth.

"You're a shrewd businessman and a pig, Allen. Have another drink and think about what you've said," Samuel said, with the same light, casual air with which he'd introduced himself.

"I'd rather think about other things." But Allen took the advice to get another drink, looking instead to other cast members in the lounge.

Neve watched him leave. "He's never going to catch a circus woman like that."

"I believe any companionship he pays for tends to be of the sort with whom he's paying for something else entirely."

"And what do you pay for?"

"I've no interest in remarrying, Neve, dear, but I enjoy the company of a young woman, the better if she has something to say."

She slid her hand from under his. "I'm not sure how to feel about that, Mr. Amendola."

She really didn't. The sensation of his very human hand on hers and the raspy warmth of his worn voice was doing things that made her spine feel as bubbly as the champagne, and she didn't know whether to be angry at her body or Samuel or Bell or whether she should just follow her sex-crazed instincts. Practically speaking, she was worn out, but she'd bet her entire indecent wardrobe that she could lead Samuel to one of the private rooms, draw the curtains, have him and still be able to resuscitate her arousal for a performance.

"Samuel, please," he said. "If I'm making you uncomfortable, do feel free to find yourself more welcome conversation. I'm grateful for the time I've had."

He was easily in his sixties, vital but old to her, with thick hair and leathery skin. She'd never been a May-December romanticist, but age hadn't been a significant factor in her pursuit of a partner back when sex hadn't been high on her list. Did it matter now that sex had taken a different place on that list? Her *body* didn't care, but what about *her*?

"Tell me, my dear, what did you do in pharmaceuticals?" he asked.

"Research and development. Slow, methodical and often disappointing, but I liked my work, especially since I wasn't the part of the team that handled trials. I always felt that would be too much pressure. I worked with theory and formulas, contributed to preliminary testing — nothing where lives might be lost. I also never had to sell what I helped create. I've been told I'm too blunt for that."

Samuel smiled. "If you liked your work, why abandon it? Life in a traveling circus may seem exciting from the outside, but does it compare?"

As long as she was understating the truth… "I might have been a bit hasty with my career change."

"Is there anything about Arcanium that keeps you here?" His implication was clear, but she appreciated he didn't say it. An orgasm could be faked. Just because it looked like she'd been thrilled to pieces didn't necessarily mean that she had been.

She tentatively placed her hand on his, afraid that she was just doing what men like Allen expected her to do, afraid that Samuel was being charming to get what he wanted, afraid that it didn't matter because she was going to do this anyway.

"Bell does what he can to keep me. Plenty of pretty things. New people. Excitement. Samuel, I confess, I haven't been completely honest with you, and I'm not very good at telling lies or letting myself get away with them."

Samuel glanced down at her hand on his, at her fingertips brushing over the prominent veins. He tilted his head. "Well, I can't pretend I have the same compunctions — I am a businessman, after all — but if it's against your principles, who am I to stand in the way?"

She was thankful she was barefoot, because she thought she'd wobble if she were wearing heels. She slid off her chair then urged him to stand as well, which brought him almost flush against her. The friction of his suit through the thin silk made her breath catch and her eyelids flutter.

Neve threaded her fingers through his hand. After a deliberate press of her hips against his, she slowly drew him with her to one of the privacy booths at the back of the lounge. She avoided Allen's heavy gaze and resisted the urge to flip him off.

But she caught sight of Mikhail. Without a word, gesture or expression, he set his drink on the bar then strode behind it to a less ostentatious series of curtains that Neve assumed led back to the green room. She ran her tongue along her teeth watching him leave.

"Part of the reason I left my old job to join Arcanium was because my relationship with my husband had changed. I'd changed." She pulled them into the black booth, which was lit only by a small, old-fashioned lamp on a table. She tugged the rope that held the curtain open. It swung closed, blocking the view of everything on the outside, but it wasn't nearly as effective as the red curtain at blocking sound.

Everything in the room except the red curtain was black. It looked like the booth of a bordello.

"People change in marriage," Samuel said. "Newlyweds often forget that. They marry not one person but a hundred, one changing into another year by year, sometimes transforming over the course of months or weeks or days." His gaze finally began to wander over her body. He could have touched her then but he didn't. He waited, curiosity a glitter in his eyes. "What changed for you?"

"I developed…appetites that I'd never had before."

Neve hadn't ever tried actually using charm on anyone who wasn't her husband. All the sex she'd had since joining Arcanium had just fallen into her lap whether she'd wanted it or not. She tried now, hoping that any amateur mistakes she made would be endearing to a man who'd doubtlessly been flirted with by women more professional than she.

"He betrayed me, but I know now that he never would have been enough." She kept her voice quiet as much for effect as for keeping anyone on the outside from hearing. His suit jacket spread as she undid the buttons. His breathing came more heavily, pushing his chest against the spotless, pressed, white shirt.

"Why do you think Bell let me in, Samuel? I have no special skills. I don't juggle. I don't tumble. I'm not especially flexible. I don't do tricks with animals. I'm not keen on heights. Why do you think Bell brought me into Arcanium?"

"Why?"

A low moan escaped her. Desire magnified that compelling raspy quality in his voice, his question like nails clawing at her skin in desperation, though otherwise seemed so composed. Neve stroked down the front of his trousers, found where he wasn't composed at all.

"Because *nothing* is *ever* enough." She curled her other hand around his neck and pulled him down to kiss her. Despite his patience, he met her with the sudden passion his reply had revealed.

She unzipped his trousers, slipped through the opening there and through his boxers to take his hot cock in her hand.

Neve tore her mouth from his, pulled him back by his thick hair when he started to kiss down her neck. "I have one question to ask, Samuel."

"Anything."

She held his cockhead in her palm, massaging around his slit with her thumb.

"Is this why you spoke to me tonight?" She stared directly into his eyes with such intensity, he stopped trying to look at all of her at once. "Did you think your kindness would get you more than your friend's crudeness? Did you deliberately approach me with him to make your honey seem sweeter against his vinegar?"

He panted, brows knitting in either confusion or in an attempt to stall as he considered how best to reply in his own favor.

"Your answer won't affect what I do," she said quietly. "I just want to know."

"I wanted to have sex with you." Samuel traced the line of her collarbone to the strap of the dress. "What man in his right mind wouldn't? But I approached you to know you, without any expectation, nor did I set out to seduce. This, whatever this is, is a happy accident." He brushed her lip with his thumb, licked his own lips at the touch. "I told you. I prefer paying for company, not sex."

"Well, you paid for company. Are you paying for sex?" She gave him a particularly intense squeeze up the full length of him.

"No. You could walk out now, and I wouldn't say a word against you." But his pained expression and the way his cock pulsed and continued to grow in her hand suggested he'd be sorely disappointed.

She couldn't know how much of what he said was honest and how much of it was to get her to continue. She'd told him she would regardless, but he may not have believed her any more than she could entirely believe him. He sounded sincere, though, and he'd tasted like an Old Fashioned, smelled of old leather and good shampoo. She raised herself onto her toes to kiss him again.

She shrugged off one strap of her dress to bare her breast, but she stopped him before he could slide his hand up her leg, before he could tumble them onto the loveseat provided.

"No," she murmured against his mouth. "Just this."

She pulled her hand from his trousers, spit into her palm then slipped back in. She wrung him in the same hand to which she'd switched her wedding ring, alternated between kissing him as though she wanted to swallow him up and watching his face. She'd learned how to give her husband pleasure by watching his reactions, learned to love watching him come undone because of her, even if she couldn't share in his pleasure. But now, watching a man's pleasure gave her just as much pleasure as she gave him.

Ever since Bell had changed her, she hadn't had a single human being. Victor was the closest, but he'd been altered by Bell enough to not to count. This man was without question a man, with a man's imperfections, a man's weaknesses. Having him against her, kissing her, swelling to fill her hand... All of these things set off an electrical storm that had so little to do with magic or demons that she suspected it was as close as she was going to get to normal.

He couldn't read her mind to know what she wanted before she knew she wanted it. Any stamina was either age or pharmaceutically induced. He didn't have a whole arsenal of spells and tricks to get her into bed with him. He wasn't the most attractive man in the world, not even the most interesting. But he was real and he was human and he was a man, and touching him was like touching a tree after stripping away the bark.

She pulled him down over her on the loveseat, wrapped her legs around him as she continued to stroke his cock and over his sac to the sensitive flesh behind. With her other hand, she pushed him down her neck to suck her exposed nipple.

He wasn't anything like Mikhail or even Victor. Years with his wife and paying for company had taught him confidence that had been well-earned, but he was so very real. And somehow, she was not. All she could think of was *more*. She felt as wicked as the demon hands that had left their invisible marks all over her body like brands, as though they'd passed their corruption on to her.

Samuel came over her hand, pulses of semen striking his trousers and her dress. His groans mingled with hers between their parted mouths as he gasped out his orgasm and tried to keep kissing her at the same time. She hadn't come, but at some point, it had stopped being about that.

"I'm sorry," he panted. "I'm sorry. I didn't mean to..." He cupped her folds over the dress, trying to take care of her, but she eased them both upright on the couch and gently pushed his attempts away.

"That was what I wanted. I don't... I mean, I'm not..." She didn't know how to explain the line she'd drawn in the sand, knowing that the slightest breeze might shift it or make it disappear. "Pleasuring you was all the pleasure I needed."

It was a cheesy, fake line, but it was as true as the rest.

He brushed her hair away from her face, peering as though trying to understand her. "I hope you didn't think you had to do that because I hosted the event. I hope Bell didn't put you up to this."

"No," Neve said quickly. "No, I chose this."

"Okay," he whispered. "Are you all right? You appear...stunned."

She nodded.

"Okay." Samuel adjusted the strap back over her shoulder, the silk back over the breast. Tentatively, he leaned in and she met him for a slow, simple kiss. "The staff are outside to help us clean up?"

She nodded again.

"Shall we?"

Neve hadn't quite understood the term 'Walk of Shame' before now. Although she'd just given Samuel Amendola a hand job and it had been her choice, she felt people's judgment, their assumptions about her that seemed self-evident, given the state of her dress and the front of Samuel's trousers as well as the cleansing wipes that he used to tend to himself back in the room and the ones the golem gave her to clean the worst of the cum off her dress.

Mikhail was out in the lounge again. He'd changed out of costume and into a suit of his own, with a red-wine-colored sweater under the jacket and his long hair bound back. He'd taken a seat near the carousel, and he watched her as he sipped something in a tumbler, darker amber than the Spider's whiskey.

He watched as she came out of the booth, saw her as everyone else saw her.

Watched as she stood in indecision at the high tables, where her food had been half eaten.

Watched as she turned away from everyone and walked as casually as she could to the dressing rooms — away from how everyone saw her, from what she knew she was, from what she couldn't help but become.

* * * *

"You didn't have to do that."

Bell knelt next to her and wrapped a fleece blanket around her shoulders. Well, he'd said all she needed to do was ask.

She continued to sit there against the column, concrete floor painful against her ass, but she didn't want to move. "You're awfully hands-on with me, Bell. You never struck me as all that interested in anything but the circus, not the care and mental balance of your people. Why the exception?"

Bell crossed his legs to sit next to her. "This is usually Kitty's job, but she's been busy when you've needed help. And I do care about my people, Neve. To care for my people is to care for my circus. You're no exception. Besides, I find myself with plenty of free time these days," he added dryly.

The Ringmaster glowered down at them as he passed by, his red leather jacket swinging around his trousers like that of a darker Captain Hook. "You disgust me."

"Fuck you, too," Bell said in a perfectly conversational tone. "Go get ready to whip Maya. That should improve your mood."

"What's his problem?"

"He thinks I'm far too soft with my humans. If I didn't let him whip people all the time, and if he didn't have Kitty to keep him grounded, I believe he would have left Arcanium long ago. Or perhaps I underestimate him." He wrapped his arms around his crossed legs and rested his chin between his knees, deceptively flexible. "He's only had Kitty the last eighteen years. He's been with me for sixty."

"How long has Arcanium been operating?"

"One way or another for about two hundred and fifty years. I've been a con man of con men for longer."

"The con being that it's not a con?" She felt less numb now. The magic that kept her from getting too cold couldn't compare to the comfort of actually being warm. She took the edges of the blanket and pulled them tighter around her like bat wings.

"That's always been the humbug, long before P.T. Barnum made it his game to show genuine fakes. It amuses me." He twirled a lock of her hair around his finger. "You really didn't have to do that. That's not why you're here."

"Yes, it is."

"I'm not lying to you, Neve."

"You don't get to make someone driven to have sex with almost anyone, even after being finger-fucked into oblivion, then say that you didn't make me to have sex with your patrons."

"You didn't have to stay in the lounge. If talking with Samuel made you uncomfortable, both I and Mikhail emphasized that you could deny them anything."

"You didn't make me the kind of woman who would deny them anything."

Bell turned her face to him. "Hey. What you did was *your* choice. Even if you feel you can't control how much you want sex, you still have the choice who to have it with. I didn't put you in the Funhouse so that you could give my patron his perk. He's never taken advantage of one of my women during the Funhouses he's hosted. You're the first he ever had in one of the privacy booths. I don't know what else I can do to convince you that Arcanium is meant to be your playground as much as mine."

She closed her eyes. "I suppose you want me to do the performance now."

"I swear, woman, I could slap you sometimes. Yes, you'll enjoy the performance, but I reiterate for the five hundredth time that you're not required to do it, just as you were never expected to engage in any sexual activities with our guests. Maya and Kitty make no bones about only choosing men they want, not men who want them. Neither Valorie nor the Spider ever have sex with guests. Victor usually *only* has sex with guests, so you were a bit of an anomaly there, too. I promise, Neve, that you need not do anything you don't wish to do. I didn't interfere with what you did with Samuel because it was what *you* wanted."

And what do you *want, Neve?*

Neve climbed to her feet, leaving the blanket behind. She looked down at the wet spots on her dress. A few moist toilettes hadn't done much to help, and she was pretty sure it was as ruined as other things that had miraculously been repaired before. Until then...

Bell tried to say something as she took hold of the hem, but whatever he'd had in mind trailed off when she brought the dress over her head.

The fire-eater — still dressed as a dragon shifter — and the Tattooed Man had been holding a conversation, but both of them abruptly stopped. Lennon, the Serpent

King and the Creature all paused what they were doing as well.

She tossed the negligee onto the blanket and stood there naked as the day she was born in front of everyone in the green room.

What do you want?

"Where do you need me?" Neve said. "Let's do this."

Chapter Eleven

It was as though no one had ever seen a naked woman before, despite being part of Arcanium for so long — and some of them older than the New Deal. Even the Ringmaster spared her a glance, perhaps considering what his bullwhip could do to what she'd exposed.

Lennon didn't attempt to be circumspect about sizing her up as he stretched behind the wall that concealed the amphitheater backstage. "That's a good look for you. You should do it more often."

Neve felt oddly free without clothes designed to make her sexier. She was a human body, her meat vehicle burdened with hungers over which she had no control, just like everyone else. She was human from hair to hide, and her brain was as much a part of that body as her body was subject to her brain. Appealing to her brain apparently led to her yielding her body, and any contact with her body lit up her brain. It wasn't folly to try to separate them, but at this point, she wasn't sure there was anything to gain by trying.

What did she want?

Demon, jinn and human couldn't look away. The Spider was right. She was the one with the power here. She could walk among the people of Arcanium or the Funhouse guests as naked as Lady Sasha, without even a pair of snakes to protect her, and no one could do anything unless she allowed it. They could want her all they liked. Their cocks could grow, harden, point straight at her. Their balls could turn purple and explode. They still couldn't have her.

She'd already decided that she wouldn't screw the guests. She'd walked the tightrope with Samuel, but he hadn't been inside her. He couldn't boast that he'd had an Arcanium performer, at least not honestly.

But she would perform. Guests could look at her. Guests could jerk off to her. But she'd remain a fantasy. Maybe she could afford to make a few exceptions, but she'd rather form a reputation closer to the Spider's — *look, but only touch yourself.*

What she wanted from the people of Arcanium was still undecided, but when it came to these events and the haunted funhouse, that's the way things were going to be.

The show had to go on, and her appetites wanted her to be part of it. She didn't know if these Funhouse events would give her enough relief or the fortitude to resist the cast the rest of the time, but it was worth a shot.

Bring…it…on.

She twisted the wedding ring on her right hand. Naked but for diamond and platinum. She should have a necklace.

"Like this, my dear?" Bell came up from behind, lowering a silver choker in front of her face then bringing it tight against her neck and clasping it.

"Do I want to know if those are real?" The base of the choker was light, the jewels small, but two clear, glittering pendants dropped over the jut of her collarbone, and a third larger pendant dropped down to accessorize the valley between her breasts.

"Money isn't an object for me. The only reason I charge is because people like to pay. They'd think what I offered was worthless if they didn't part with their money to have it. Lady Sasha sometimes wears this. She has a whole costume set, but she agreed to let you wear the necklace."

"So I *don't* want to know if these are real."

"They're conflict-free, whatever they are." She heard his amusement as he adjusted her hair over the back of the necklace. "We do have gowns or lingerie you can wear, you know."

"What the hell are you doing, boss?" Lennon said, hitting Bell's arm with a grin.

"Will they just get torn off me like a heroine on the cover of a romance novel?" Neve asked.

"Likely. They're easy to repair, though, as you're aware."

"I'll pass."

"Very well." He ghosted his fingertips down her arms and kissed her shoulder. Her flesh marbled at the touch, and she almost leaned back against him, but he stepped back, adhering to her preference rather than her weakness. "Are you sure?"

She nodded.

"Then you'll be placed on the wheel. As a novice, you'll be excused if you back out once you choose your fate, but I wouldn't advise it."

"Bell, what exactly is it I'll be performing out there?" she asked, finally hearing the warning in his reconfirmations.

"It's a game of chance." Bell pulled a silver half-dollar out of nowhere — certainly not from any sleeve — and traveled it over his fingers one way and back. "You might not even be chosen to perform tonight. But you won't know with whom until after you choose a door."

"It's 'The Lady and the Tiger,' love," Lennon said, "but the lady might also be a tiger, if you know what I mean."

"I get it," she replied. "I don't choose who I have sex with. I just choose the door. Then I have to submit to whomever — or whatever — is on the other side and give our guests a good show in the process."

She'd be a lot more nervous if she hadn't gotten off too many times to count under ministrations of hands that couldn't be anything but demonic. But she couldn't pretend the idea didn't also make her feel like she'd swallowed a cold squid, because it meant she couldn't be selective. She couldn't deny someone in the circus just because she didn't like them. Actually, she *could*, but it would ruin the show, and since she'd decided the show must go on...

"I'll see you soon." Bell regarded the image of her in the jewelry and nothing else with lust he made no effort to conceal. "The Ringmaster runs the ring during the circus performances, but I emcee for the Funhouse."

As soon as Bell left, Lennon flipped onto his hands, turning so he faced her with his feet up in the air. "You angling for the boss's bed now that Maya's out of the picture?"

"No. He's not the only one who can see me naked, you know."

"I'm well aware of that, love. Just asking."

The impulse to hold her arms over her body was almost unbearable, but it would be a fool's errand, given how much of her there was to cover, and now everyone had seen everything anyway. And even more Arcanium members were coming backstage. Kitty, Maya, Valorie, Victor and a good number of the rest had returned, each as surprised by her nudity as the last. She supposed they were used to Lady Sasha being naked, but everyone else wore *something*, even if it wasn't much. Or they were like the Spider in her body paint or the Horned God, able to walk around naked without appearing so.

Well, she was wearing diamonds — or something that looked like diamonds. She really was afraid to check.

Kitty beckoned her over to where Maya, Valorie and Caroline were also waiting. "Daredevils over here."

"Only women?" Neve asked.

"Sadly, our audience is heavily straight, with a male majority," Kitty replied with dry hatred Neve hadn't heard from her before. "While invitees are informed of our broader spectrum and simply walk past what they don't like in the maze, we find that when we go too homoerotic in our performances, there can be backlash. Not when women do it, of course. Just men. It's backlash we can handle, but we'd rather avoid it altogether."

"Generally, they like the 'damsel in distress against the terrifying monster' scenario," Caroline said. "You know, the Universal horror posters of fainting women and ravaging villains. They like it when a victim succumbs, like what you did in the maze. Nice work, by the way."

Neve blinked. She kept having to remind herself that Caroline wasn't as young as she looked and that she'd been doing this for a while. "Thanks. Do you mind playing the victim?"

Caroline laughed. "Not at all. It's scary at first, because you rarely get to see the demons and monsters of Arcanium in full evil mode, but no matter how evil or scary they look, they're still in it for our pleasure as much as theirs. It's fun. And Riley and Colm get all riled up watching it, too, because they're possessive but it's also really hot, so I get ravished twice. What's to complain about?"

"In a nutshell," Maya said, shrugging.

"Besides," Valorie said, adjusting her lace body glove, "when you're more or less exclusive, it's nice to have a change every now and then, just to shake things up."

"Speak for yourself." Maya unlaced her corset and untied the skirt of feathers. Two lines of large gauge rings in inflamed skin striped her back. Silver chain had been attached to the rings in a crisscross corset pattern. They jingled lightly when she straightened.

"Speaking for the exclusives, like I said," Valorie said. "So you're just going directly to pain tonight, huh?"

"If the monsters want me, they know where to find me afterward." Now she was almost as naked as Neve, wearing only underwear again. Kitty brought her a pair of silver shackles, and Maya snapped them around her wrists in front. Kitty hooked the leather leash to the chain between the shackles.

"Is it just me or are we suddenly overdressed?" Valorie quipped to Caroline.

"What exactly happens now, aside from female human sacrifice?" Neve asked.

"Maya goes first." Kitty helped Maya put her hair up—a whip that left welts could also cut hair. "Bell gets them all to participate in counting her blows, gives them a taste for the blend of violence and sex they've come to expect."

"That doesn't sound very healthy," Neve said.

"Remember that they think it's fake." Maya winced every time the flesh of her back pulled on where the rings had pierced through. "Plenty of healthy people enjoy fake violence. Hell, plenty of healthy people enjoy real violence when it's contained, controlled. If the Ringmaster wasn't intending to draw blood, would you still question it?"

Given her background and own enjoyment of stinging things, Neve shrugged to cede the point.

"Once the Ringmaster drags Maya off," Kitty continued, "Lady Sasha does a snake dance to warm everyone up. Lord Mikhail is usually a part of that dance, but tonight, he's working the crowd from the seats. Seth and Lars will do a version of their aerial act. That's as close as they're okay with us going homoerotic, as long as it's athletic—very Greek of them. Then Bell will bring out the wheel of chance, and whoever it lands on, he'll introduce. Then you pick a door, which selects a monster."

"Then you do the monster," Valorie said.

Kitty nodded. "Depending on how long each performance takes, Bell picks either two or three women. Bell will close it out with a hypnosis session that puts members of the audience with each other to humiliate and thrill them, because as you said, Neve, nothing brings people together like collective humiliation. And nothing keeps them quieter about it outside the party. It usually ends with some kind of orgy. Then we retire to our cots or our own clandestine meetings back here or out there with them."

"Then the golems wake us up with everything ready for us to leave, just in time to arrive at the circus and eat breakfast before it opens," Caroline said. "At least you didn't come into Arcanium during the Halloween season. That can be brutal."

"Sounds like fun." Neve scratched her scalp. Even though she'd been magically cleaned, she wanted a shower. She wanted her own bed, empty. And she still wanted a movie night with comfort food and comfortable clothes. "So is it just the three of us or are you coming back for something else, Maya?"

"I'm just the whipping girl tonight," Maya replied. "Sometimes Kitty participates."

"But exhibitionism isn't my kink at all." Kitty started combing Caroline's hair. "I'll sometimes go out to the audience and invite someone to a booth, but I'm not a performer. Even people who think it's hot to fuck me tend to point and laugh at the Bearded Lady in public because they think they're supposed to. After all, what's funnier than a hairy woman getting some love? I'm not interested in playing jester. One of these days, I might have more options." She tugged at the braids of her beard. "But for now, I prefer to take my sex in private, where my partner doesn't feel compelled to pretend they don't want me."

"Usually the twins perform, but I don't see them anywhere. Oh, here they come." Maya raised her hand in greeting. "Now it's an actual game of chance for the rest of you. Is Christina playing tonight?"

"Not tonight," Joanne said. She and her twin wore filmy beige fabric wound around their bodies like a sarong to show where they were bound and that they were clearly not wearing underwear. "She and Troy are shacking up on one of the cots, at least once Troy's through with his part."

"Christina plays maybe once a year. Sandra used to play sometimes, too. People kept expecting the demons to break her like a twig," Valorie said. "Then our Skeleton wished herself out healthy and took the Fat Man with her as a bonus for being such a good voluntary, so Bell's been on the lookout for both. Be thankful you didn't wish to lose weight. It would have been a real shame to lose all this."

Valorie pinched Neve's side. Neve danced away from her, laughing because she was deathly ticklish, not necessarily because she thought it was funny.

"If the menfolk could play, it would be an even better game," Valorie added, "but alas, we're not yet at a time when straight men won't catch the gay by looking at a man touching another man's dick."

"So we're all that's left to sex up the demons and monsters of Arcanium," Caroline said brightly. "It's a terrible burden to bear."

"And the rest of you are okay with random Arcanium demons, not ones you pick?" Neve asked.

"Sure, why not?" Caroline said, shrugging. "They still follow the rules and you're guaranteed a good time, no matter how creepy they get. I mean, you know how it is, having sex with a demon, right?"

Kitty didn't yank on Caroline's hair the way she had with the twins, but she nudged Caroline's head.

"Whatever." Caroline dialed down her enthusiasm a tick. "From what I understand, they have the power to make it really fucking bad or really fucking good, and the way Bell has it set up here, it's always the really fucking good — for our benefit and to keep them from doing too much damage. Because now I'm thinking about how it would be to take Ciarán without magic. Yowch."

"And they're pretty good about making the scene about whoever you want to." Maya lowered her head. "You know, doing a show for your person — or people." She nodded at Caroline and the twins in acknowledgment. "Me, I mostly just like Arcanium's demons. Even the clowns have kind of warmed up to us, which is weird as hell after avoiding them all these years. I guess we have you to thank for that, Caroline."

"Except for Murphy. Murphy's still a grouchy bastard who doesn't want to play outside the hive, bless him." Caroline waved at Comedy and Tragedy as they went through the door with the rest of the monsters.

Valorie gave Caroline a slight push as though to test that she was a human being and not a robot. "You're weird. Must be to make up for the fact that you're the most normal woman in Arcanium."

Valorie's hair was already in braids and loose from its bun, so Kitty came up behind Neve and started brushing her hair then twisted it up and wrapped it around a comb.

"Trust me." She patted Neve's shoulder. "The necklace is worth showing off, and you won't have to worry about it catching on the collar or getting tangled."

"Thank you." It was odd to thank Kitty for preparing her as a symbolic sexual human sacrifice, but Neve admired practicality.

Kitty let two stray locks frame Neve's face so she didn't look too done up, diamonds or not. "Are you sure about this?"

Neve suspected Bell had a hand in Kitty doublechecking.

"Not in the least. But I'm not going to get any less frayed tonight, even if I do nothing. The only way for me to know if I like this is to try. I don't appear to have a choice in being a nymphomaniac, but if I have to be, I think I want to be the best damn nymphomaniac in this circus."

Maya dissolved into a fit of laughter that she tried and failed to turn into coughs.

Valorie crossed her arms with a crooked grin. "You have some fierce competition. You ready for it?"

"Bring it, Contortionist Barbie."

That just made Maya laugh harder. Kitty slapped her rear, but she couldn't hide her own grin.

Caroline narrowed her eyes in contemplation. "How do you even measure that?"

"Believe me," Neve said. "I'll come up with a way."

* * * *

Neve couldn't see anything from backstage. All she could do was listen to Bell announce each act.

The Ringmaster had a rich, booming voice, rounder and more resonant than Lord Mikhail's, though similar. Bell had none of that. He spoke quietly, intimate and seductive, hypnotic without soothing his audience to sleep. He brought the same intensity to the microphone in his role as emcee as he did to his fortune teller readings. Every person in the audience probably felt like he was talking to them.

Neve pressed her forehead against the partition concealing the monsters in an attempt to cool her skin when Bell called Lady Sasha to the stage. Since the beginning of the show, the sex demons had subtly increased their magic—only those who knew it was magic would recognize the building excitement and arousal for what it was. Once Lady Sasha took her place, however, and the harem music began, she took firm hold of everyone she could reach, and Lord Mikhail apparently did the same. There were moans coming from the audience, and moans behind her from the cast who had retired for the night but who'd found a partner to while the magic through.

Kitty had ushered the Ringmaster—who'd carried Maya offstage with him like a child—away with her somewhere private to tend to Maya's wounds. It had been strange to see the Ringmaster hold someone so tenderly and show a modicum of kindness, although his face still appeared to be stone-carved malice. There'd been no other way to carry her, though, with thirty blows applied to her back and thighs, rings ripped out and flesh torn to shreds. She'd been in no shape to walk. Her eyes had been half open in a daze that hadn't been anywhere near an expression of bliss.

Neve didn't understand the impulse to be struck like that, especially in front of an audience. It went well beyond the realm of S&M, so unrelentingly sadistic Neve couldn't wrap her head around why it was allowed at all. Whipping someone into shock had to be harm by anyone's standards, no matter if it was voluntary or not. But the other women, while concerned, didn't appear frightened by the extent of Maya's injuries.

It wasn't Neve's back, though, so she let it go to deal with the snake pit in her abdomen. She'd already had sex in front of everyone, so she didn't know what the big deal was in her brain, why this was different just because it included a demonic partner rather than living props that looked and felt like multiple demonic partners.

Lady Sasha left the stage and stepped into the green room where the rest of the cast milled about, her cobras entwined in new patterns around her. Cast and crew skittered away from her, as much from the smoldering frustration in the set of her jaw and burning red eyes as from fear of touching her. Naked, she strode to where the golems had laid out the cots, separated into small rooms by curtains like in hospitals — privacy by sight rather than by sound and presuming most people wanted to sleep.

After Seth and Lars' performance, they exited the stage with Lars' hand on Seth's shoulder as they rushed into the back. Joanne and Jane grinned. It was hard to believe they'd ever been successfully closeted, especially given the states of their tight, elastic pants, which concealed nothing. Theirs had to have been one of those secrets everyone knew but kept for the boys' sakes.

"Well, my dear friends," Bell said into his microphone, "I think it's time we move on from foreplay. What do you say?"

Applause followed.

"Would you like to play a game?"

Louder applause, more individuals discernable through the din — presumably from those who had been to one of these events before and knew the game in question.

Misha rolled out a primitive contraption most people would recognize from any cheap carnival—a wooden wheel outlined in metal pegs, which the arrow would click against when the wheel was spun. The circle had been split into four wedges, each with a drawing of one of the women available—presumably done by Troy on the fly, since each event would have a different cache of women to choose from. He managed to capture each of the girls in a sketch, in a style that suggested he'd done most of his own tattoos.

"Who shall we see first, hmmm? Ma'am, please come up here. Tell us your name—no last names, let's pretend we're anonymous here—your sign and your most secret kink, please."

The audience laughed, but so did the woman who took the microphone.

"My name is Ingrid. I'm a Leo, and I love a good massage."

"Come now, Ingrid," Bell said. "A good massage isn't a kink. It's a given."

More laughter, but also a female groan that suggested Bell was giving her one.

Neve licked her lips, her body suddenly aching. She clenched her teeth against the desire. The more she fought, the worse her arousal would become, but then again, that would get her in just the right place to take whatever random monster was assigned to her, if any.

"Share with me, Ingrid." God, he sounded like quick sex in a closet. "What's your secret fantasy?"

"I want to be blindfolded," Ingrid said, hesitant, but urged to divulge both by applause and by Bell's natural influence. "Blindfolded in a strange place, so I don't know who's taking me."

"Maybe we can arrange that tonight. One of my girls is going to have a stranger in a stranger land here soon, too. Why don't you give that wheel a spin, Ingrid, love?"

The tick of the arrow on the pegs was too fast to be Neve's heartbeat but felt like it anyway.

"Ah, our spirited twins. Joanne, Jane, it's time to come out and face your fate."

"See you on the other side." Jane saluted the other girls as she and Joanne pushed against each other's backs in order to stand.

Neve sighed, but she could only be so relieved when not being selected meant she had to deal with the anxiety a little longer — or a lot longer. She didn't know how long the twins would last.

"Our wonderful audience may wonder why the girls are pictured together, other than the obvious," Bell said. "I could be cruel and have only one of them ravished while the other is spared, but let's face it, folks, that just wouldn't be fair. Where one goes, the other follows, and I simply can't bring myself to separate them from the monster in store. All the more for him, yes? My creatures can more than satisfy them both until all four legs can't hold the two of them up."

Enthusiastic applause. Wolf whistles. The early sounds of moans again, like the maze and haunted funhouse soundtrack. Some people were already getting started just at the sight of the twins and the suggestion of what was to come.

"Ladies, you know what you have to do. Our strongman is here to keep you from trying to run. Wave to them, Lord Mikhail."

Oh God. That meant Mikhail would be close to the stage, maybe even in the front row. She wouldn't be able to ignore him. Neve brushed her hand over her breast, cupped herself, rolled her nipple between three fingers but forced herself to stop.

"You have two doors. Behind each door is a monster, but it's up to you the kind of monster you choose. Some are downright sweet, I'm sure."

Laughter.

"Go on, Joanne, Jane. Choose. There's nothing left to do but choose."

The lights dimmed. Music rose up to meet the anticipatory silence.

"The music is cued to match the monster," Caroline whispered. "They all have different rhythms, different personalities."

Valorie closed her eyes to listen better. "They got Ciarán and Moss. Damn it. I was hoping for them."

"Wait, both Ciarán and Moss?" Neve said. "You can't separate Joanne and Jane, but how come the twins gets both?"

"They don't separate either," Valorie replied. "They do everything together. It's similar to Seth and Lars' curse, if I had to guess, except it's not a curse."

"I always thought they were... What do you call it? Some kind of symbiotic relationship," Caroline said.

Valorie snorted. "More like Dr. Jekyll and Mr. Hyde. Ciarán's the kindly, horny old superego and Moss is the nasty bastard id." She shrugged when Neve raised an eyebrow. "They grow on you. And though Moss *is* a nasty bastard, he's not awful or anything. He's the one to go to if you like dirty talk."

"I like dirty talk," Caroline said happily.

Valorie gestured at Caroline. "Exhibit C on why Resident Nymphomaniac is a difficult title to win."

"I have an edge," Neve said.

"Which is?"

"It's what Bell made me."

"Well, he's very good at that, isn't he?" Valorie said.

"Fishmonger," Neve muttered.

Valorie laughed. "That's putting it kindly. I've read *Hamlet*, too."

"Thank God," Neve muttered.

"Don't thank God. We get so very bored around here sometimes. *The Complete Works of Shakespeare* was something I challenged myself to read in a year. It took me a little over that, but I'd already read some of them in middle school and high school, which helped."

"Do you still have it?" Neve asked hopefully.

"It's a doorstop, but yeah. You're more than welcome to borrow it. I probably won't read through it again."

"Do you have thoughts on it?"

"You mean, does good William give me the feels? Sure he does, sometimes. Why? You want to start a book club?"

"Hell, yes," Neve moaned, resting her head against her forearm, unable to distract herself enough from the sounds of what was going on during the performance and in the audience. There were vibrators. Vibrations and moans and groans and sighs and grunts and growls, and a steady stream of profanities from Moss.

Valorie bit her lip against a grin. "Well, when you put it like that, I suddenly feel like a bookworm."

"Me, too. I actually took a class on Shakespeare in college. I was going to take another one, but Arcanium happened." Caroline spread her arms. "As Arcanium happens."

Valorie rubbed Neve's shoulder. "You going to make it there, Nymph?"

Neve nodded, let out the shaky breath she'd been holding. "It would help if you would tell me what to expect, what monsters might be waiting for me behind those doors."

"Telling takes away all the fun. You're just going to have to wait and see, new girl."

Neve groaned.

"Screw your courage to the sticking place," Valorie said. "It's almost over for the twins."

Definitely almost over. The twins sounded exactly the same, so even though their rising moans weren't always in rhythm, they overlapped and magnified the sound above the intensifying music, which had a pounding drum foundation.

She couldn't stop imagining what it was like for Ciarán and Moss to have sex with both twins at the same time when the place where the girls were conjoined limited their positions. She came up with a number of scenarios, all which she then imagined herself in solo, with the giant demon looming above her and the small demon eye-level with her hips, at a perfect height…

An animalistic howl rose, joined by a rebel yell from Moss. The girls sounded like they were crying, but the sex magic cocooning itself around Neve had never been more intense. If there were a female version of a gloryhole, a cock just sticking out of the floor, she'd have screwed herself silly by now, but there was nothing but her own fingers, which she already knew wouldn't work.

The drums stopped into almost complete silence, broken only by the twins' hiccupping gasps.

Ciarán carried Joanne and Jane out from the concealed backstage area, looking like the demonic version of himself from the glass case, with his prehistoric teeth. Most human Tall Men wouldn't have been able to carry a pair of girls like them, even though they were probably light enough individually. Humans weren't meant to grow that big, and weight could wreak havoc on a skeletal structure that hadn't been designed to support them. But Ciarán did so without effort. He could probably qualify as a strongman himself, as a giant and with his prodigious, visible, vascular strength that belied how gently he eased the twins to the floor. Moss wasn't far behind, grinning like the cat who'd gotten the cream, the catnip and all the sardines in the cupboard. He wiped his mouth with the back of his hand, making clear what he had done for at least one of the twins.

Jane laughed weakly, patting Ciarán on his forearm. "Thanks, big guy. We may never walk again."

"Our pleasure." Moss slapped both girls on their asses then grabbed hold of Ciarán's hand. Ciarán hauled him up onto his massive shoulders. Moss saluted the other girls waiting in the wings with a wink, as though saying, "*Next time.*"

"Double, double, toil and trouble. Delicious, wasn't it?" If the response to Bell was more subdued, Neve thought it wasn't for lack of enthusiasm but because of occupied mouths and hands. "Think you have the appetite for more?"

The audience managed to make themselves heard, even if the cheers had a certain strained quality.

"You, sir, please come to the stage. No, leave your shirt off. We're all strangers here, even when we know each other, yes? You know how we do things. Name, the age you feel you are and your deepest, darkest fantasy. And remember, I'm psychic, so I'll know if you're lying. That's all right, sir, you're supposed to be intimidated, but I promise I won't bite. Not you, anyway."

"Hello. My name is Magnus, thirty. And I, uh, I want…" Magnus drifted off in palpable embarrassment.

"Magnus…" Bell's voice became unbearably personal again. Neve could almost feel his breath against her ear, over her neck. "Every single person here today has a deep, dark fantasy they shudder to air aloud. Every single one of them. Some of my people have imaginations that swirl with the wickedest filth they dare not speak. A waste of a good opportunity, in my opinion. Do share, sir. I'm all a-quiver for someone to conquer their fear in this house of horrors."

"I, um, I pay a girl to tie me up, slap me and call me a dirty old man, a tub of lard, waste of breath. I pay for it every week. I don't even have sex with her. She just meets me in the apartment I rent as a playroom and humiliates the shit out of me. I'm not allowed to come until I free myself, which is well after she leaves."

"There now." Bell spoke in a soothing purr, and Neve couldn't help the sound that escaped her. Caroline giggled. Valorie covered her mouth in her continuing but failing attempt to hide her smile at Neve's discomfort. "Freeing, isn't it, sir? As a reward, you get to help fate choose the next victim. Spin that wheel."

The arrow on the pegs ticked violently then slowed to a stop.

"It seems fate seeks a little flexibility. Our contortionist, Valorie, she of the biting wit and sharper knives. Come out and join us, love. Don't worry. We won't make anything easy for you, no matter how far you stretch."

Neve struck the partition with her fist. "Lord have mercy."

"Bell doesn't do mercy. Peace out, bitches." Valorie stood in a single fluid motion. For such an unforgiving outfit, there was absolutely nothing it needed to forgive on Valorie's lithe, angular figure.

"Just the two of us now," Caroline said. "You look like you're in pain."

"I wonder why." She clenched her teeth, but not in anger.

"Wait. *Are* you in pain?" Caroline stood, concern in the furrowing of her fine eyebrows, but she seemed unsure whether to approach. "Is there something I can do?"

Neve shook her head. "If the next round isn't me, I don't know what I'll do, but I'll find somebody. God, you'd think I'd had enough, and then Mikhail goes and—" She pounded the wall again, releasing a rush of air.

"Dude, I rescind my claim for Resident Nymphomaniac. I didn't know it was that bad. At least it explains that one night."

"Sorry about that." Some of her blood managed to flush her cheeks rather than making everything between her legs feel hot with sexual infection. It felt like an illness, like something she could pass on or something that had been passed on to her—from fucking Mikhail, from kissing Bell, from furiously having sex with Victor, from leading Samuel away. It felt like something was *wrong*...

"Hey, no worries. The golems had to do some extra cleaning on the carousel, that's all. Everyone had to sign a nondisclosure agreement, so anything else you heard about it is all just rumors."

Neve was surprised into a laugh.

"Hello, darling. This is a treat, having you join us for the entertainment tonight. Valorie doesn't always partake, ladies and gentlemen, but it takes more than a monster to make her afraid. If you're so fearless, love, pick a door, any door. The one on the left is the creature that the twins denied. Behind the other, whole new horrors. Choose wisely. There's no turning back."

Something that reminded Neve of the music Lady Sasha danced to, a snake charmer's melody set to a richer orchestra, filled the room. But there was no way Valorie had opened the door to the succubus.

"Sounds like she chose David." Caroline pronounced it 'Daveed'. "That should be fun."

"I don't think we've met," Neve said, trying to distract herself.

"You probably have. He works in the haunted funhouse, but outside his 'costume', he's barely recognizable. Have you met the Serpent King yet?"

"The man with the snake's body?"

"Yeah. The body is just an accessory, not an all-the-time transfiguration. David himself is diphallic, totally natural. I think Bell only did some cosmetic work on the two penises…penii…"

"Either one works." Well, she'd wanted a distraction. Now she was distracted by the thought of two working phalluses at once.

"The two dicks. How's that?" Caroline grinned. "Other than Kitty, he's the only oddity who was somewhat famous before being brought in. And he's part-time, although Bell's been trying to him in here full-time. He's contract work, like me. We're not trapped and we still get all the benefits. It's nice. So is he. Also, he's fucking hot. Really passionate, eager to please and eager to be pleased at the same time. Totally loses himself in the role of the Serpent King. The act is almost like a tango. I think he does some porn on the outside, too — not that it speaks to his acting skills."

Neve laughed again, the sound almost a sob. Caroline was trying, she really was, chattering to keep Neve upright rather than internalizing the pleasure that was like razorblades under her sensitive skin. And it was working, despite the throb of magic that still swirled around and through her, unrelenting in its assault.

"I don't think I've ever seen anyone like this before," Caroline said quietly, finally deciding to rub Neve's back. Neve flinched away. Caroline held her hands up as though to reassure her that she wouldn't try that again. "Carlo, sometimes. I always assumed Lady Sasha suffered in silence, and Lord Mikhail looks like he's in pain at the worst of it. But never this bad. The only people who look this bad are the ones actually in pain."

"It'll calm down when it knows it'll get what it wants," Neve said. "I hope."

Valorie and David lasted longer than the twins with the Tall and Short Man, which made Neve suspect they weren't just having monster sex but engaging in a performance that demonstrated their respective oddities and the inherent sexiness therein. She hadn't ever witnessed Valorie rehearse with the Serpent King, but who knew what kind of private rehearsals happened outside the ring?

And Neve would be going in without a single rehearsal, without knowing *anything*. She didn't even know whether she could perform well or whether she'd won people over in the maze through sheer enthusiasm rather than poetry. She didn't know whether she looked good when she was having sex or whether the idea of having sex with a willing woman was enough for people to overlook any deficiency.

By the time she reached the stage, she didn't think how she looked having sex would feature very high on her list, but that didn't stop her from worrying about it while she still had some of her wits with her.

"Thank you, Valorie, darling. I believe it goes without saying, friends, but just in case it doesn't… Please, do *not* try any of this at home. We are not liable for whatever strange positions the paramedics find you in. You laugh, but I count at least three of you who have made just such an emergency room visit."

The Serpent King slithered from the enclosed backstage with Valorie happily naked in his arms. He smiled a serpent's pointy grin. In the haunted funhouse, Neve had interpreted that happiness as evil glee, but closer to him, the wickedness seemed to be a trick of structure, a ridge over his eyes that drew the shape of his brows down in perpetual disdain. However, his laughter was pure human, despite the thirty-foot stretch of thick muscle and bone that comprised his tail.

"New blood," he said as he set Valorie down. "I remember you from the funhouse. Nice to see you in the line-up. Nice to see you in general." He stared her up and down with obvious delight, though whatever penile oddity he had displayed out on stage had been effectively hidden once more within the cloaca. "Hope to meet you more personally real soon. Don't be a stranger."

"It looks like we only have time for one more gruesome attack upon such virginal purity." The audience that wasn't otherwise engaged laughed.

"You, sir. Come on up and help fate choose between the blonde and the redhead. I love your jacket. May I? Oh no. Oh dear. With leather pants underneath, I just end up looking like an eighties reject instead of a badass." Bell gave the first silly laugh Neve had ever heard from him, and damn if it wasn't one of the more endearing things he'd done. "You keep it. Now, you know the drill. Name, relationship status and a deep, dark secret desire you wouldn't dare tell anyone else."

"Sure. I'm Locke, mercifully single and open to new relationships."

Both Neve and Caroline looked up at the same time, even though both of them knew they wouldn't be able to see who spoke smooth as melted butter, so much so that Neve could almost taste it. And with the phantom taste came a sudden desire to lick melted butter and sugar off a hard body.

"I don't know if everyone heard you, Locke. You mind repeating that? Oh, no, wait. A few people in the back collapsed onto the fainting couches, so I'd say your message definitely got out. Does anyone have a ruler? I think it's time to measure cheekbones, because I'm feeling threatened. Oh, and he has dimples, ladies and gentlemen. I'm afraid I can't compete."

Locke was still laughing like a little boy himself when Bell pointed the microphone at him. "Well, I'm not competing with anybody. I'm just here to have a good time."

"How's it been so far?"

"Illuminating."

"I like that," Bell said. "But don't think you can get out of sharing your darkest desire. I'm not easily distracted."

There was a protracted silence. Then, his low register husky and warm, Locke said quietly, "I don't have just one."

"Damn, he sounds like one of those guilty kisses you only take in the dark, doesn't he?" Caroline breathed.

"You don't have to give the whole list, Locke. If I were to start myself, we'd be here till Valentine's Day. Just a peek into that twisted psyche. That's all we ask."

Another silence. "I like watching people in beautiful pain. Crying and begging for more. I very much enjoyed watching your Ringmaster with the Maya woman."

"So do I, Locke. So do I." But a note of distance suffused Bell's heated reply. "Thank you for trusting us. Give that wheel a spin. Will it be our enterprising carousel engineer with a taste for dominating bad boys or the newest cast member of Arcanium? She still hasn't quite found her place, but fuck, that woman is game for just about anything."

The ticking noise felt like it would end with an explosion this time if Neve didn't get what she needed.

"Excellent spin, sir. Neve, darling, would you come out, please? I think it's time to fully initiate you into our esteemed, eccentric circle."

"Awww, I wanted to go, but you seem like you need it more." Caroline brushed the stray locks of hair away from Neve's face so that she didn't look like she was having as much trouble as she was. "Knock 'em dead. Remember to have fun. And try not to die between here and the scene. All right?"

"I'll make every effort." Neve braced herself against the partitions as she made her way to the opening that led to the stage.

Immediately upon stepping onstage, howls and wolf whistles expressed appreciation for her brief choice of costume. Neve allowed her eyes adjust to the light then took a deep breath and stepped out to join Bell to the right of downstage. She walked with a sway, her breasts quivering with each step. Locke was heading toward his seat, but he stopped halfway up to stare.

He'd taken off his jacket to let Bell try it on and held it draped over his shoulder like a model in a magazine, but his wide, blue eyes under the telltale fedora were fixed upon her, as though stunned. And in being stunned, that hunger she'd seen outside the bedroom tableau returned in full force. Blue was too cool a color for what smoldered behind.

Lord Mikhail was in the front row, his arms crossed over his chest, biceps bulging against the arms of his jacket. Unlike many of the men within view, he hadn't undone the front of his trousers, but his large cock pressed against the seam of the leg, the fabric forcibly holding it down the way his leather pants did. His eyes and eye sockets had gone black in the dimmed light.

Neve tried to ignore both men and went directly to where Bell held out his hand. She took it, let him draw her next to him, pressed her hip against his and kissed the corner of his mouth, a greeting more than anything sensual. Then, on impulse, before Bell could raise the microphone to speak again, she turned his face back to her and parted her lips to kiss him more fully, slow, sensual, their tongues meeting in light, smooth brushes over their lips as the audience cheered.

He was the one to ease back, albeit with some reluctance. He brought the microphone between them. "Makes a man wish he was a monster, doesn't it? Now, this was your first Funhouse. What did you think?"

"I think it's not over yet. Did you think you'd won, Bell? Did you think I'd fold just because I was tired? I'm nowhere close to finished, and I don't think you've given everything you have yet." She took his earlobe between her teeth and sucked lightly. She was rewarded with a soft moan, barely loud enough for the microphone to pick up, but she thought she'd surprised him a second time tonight, and apparently, he liked these kinds of surprises. "I dare you to really scare me, Bell. I really do."

"Dangerous to dare, love. I hope the rest of the monsters behind the doors heard you and step up to meet it, even if they'd planned to go more gently on the new girl. You don't need gentle, do you, Neve?"

His hand had been on the small of her back, but he slid it down to squeeze her ass, and she was surprised to feel the prick of claws like the ones that had left livid scratches on her body. Bell had never showed his claws to her before. She hadn't even known he had them. This time it was her turn to moan, and she was pretty sure the microphone caught that one.

There were other sounds she could hear while on stage that the partitions had mostly blocked — sounds with which she was so intimately familiar because she'd either done them or had them done to her by now. When she looked beyond the first row, it was more difficult to see what was going on, but she saw enough. The orgy had already begun, but in the midst of everything they did, most people's attention was nevertheless fixed upon the stage.

God, those sounds. They used to repel her unless made by her husband or for him. Now it was a reminder of what was happening to other people who weren't her, and suddenly, all she wanted was to forget about the monsters behind the doors and just grab Locke from the stair, beckon Mikhail from his seat and pull Bell down over her right on stage. Three pairs of hands and three cocks sounded like just the right amount.

Bell slapped her right cheek as though to jolt her from her reverie. The heat in his smile suggested he'd seen exactly what she'd been thinking about. "Maybe another night," he whispered in her ear. Then he brought the microphone back to his mouth. "Don't get distracted, love. What you're looking for is behind one of those doors, and I think the rest of the audience agrees with me — I've been looking forward to this all night."

People managed to stop what they were doing long enough to clap if their mouths were busy, holler if their hands were busy. The cheers followed her to center stage, in part a reaction to her turning her ass to the crowd.

Door number one and door number two. Right-handed people were inclined to choose the right door, and that's where she wanted to go. She turned instead toward door number one. Every step to the door pulled her on the rack, tighter, tighter, tighter, but wrapped around a dense core rather than apart in four directions. Even the act of taking hold of the doorknob felt obscene.

As she opened the door, the lights went a bluish green. Soft, minor key string music overlaid with a waterphone emitted from the speakers.

In the darkness on the other side of the door, a giant mass shifted.

Neve backed away, nerves hitching on the roads of her arousal.

A slick tentacle struck the ground. It left a trail as it slithered back into the darkness.

What the actual fuck?

Neve stumbled back, straining to see what was in the shadows.

Five more tentacles stretched out into the light. Three of them were smooth, black or dark gray — difficult to tell in the dim light — but two of them were thicker and lined with grasping suckers. At the ends of the larger tentacles, there were seven smaller tendrils, like boneless fingers.

The tentacle arms raised up and grasped the sides of the opening to pull the body forward.

At first, Neve wasn't sure that what came out had ever been humanoid. All she saw were masses of tentacles like Gorgon hair, sliding, grasping, glistening with something too thick to be water and too thin to be slime. But then it opened its black eyes, like barnacles deep in its face, and parted its mouth. Each tooth narrowed to a point so sharp it could have been carved, like the teeth of a lantern fish. And it had legs, large powerful legs the same color as its tentacles, which was why she hadn't noticed them at first, not until he'd crawled all the way through the doorway and had room to stand.

He was twice the height of the doorway, which Mikhail would have been able to walk through and Ciarán would have had to duck. His body was a slick anemone, a cluster of deep-sea worms, a biological paradox. Tentacles unfurled and twisted in constant movement, the darkness of his body difficult to see through them, like staring at a blurry photograph and trying to see sharp lines. He was a creature from another dimension, not the alien that Troy had pretended to be but something truly anathema to her reality. Each step shook the floor, and his tentacles struck the concrete with wet slaps, rubbed against each other with sounds too much like what came from the audience, awful and arousing at the same time. He was very much a humanoid figure underneath the tentacles, but they always drew her eye away.

Neve scrambled back until her heels hit the first step up that led to the first row.

"Now, now, Neve, no running," Bell said softly into the microphone. "That's not the game."

The being lowered himself at center stage. He leaned forward to reach his grasping tentacles toward her with a low moan that wasn't of desire but an attempt at a voice, like the opening of a giant stone door in a cave.

"Are you scared now?" Each word was extended, nearly deafening. It wasn't so much that he was loud as the vibrations were violent, shuddering through her like the big bell in a bell tower.

She could run. Mikhail would try to stop her, she supposed, but if she were truly afraid, she doubted Bell would force her to take this...thing on. But though her surface mind rejected the sight of this being almost completely, she couldn't help the slow, damning swell of curiosity.

This was a creature feature kind of horror monster, no question, the sort that wouldn't be out of place in an eldritch bestiary. There was nothing like it in the haunted funhouse, and there had been nothing like it in the Funhouse maze. She hadn't seen him on Oddity Row or slithering through Arcanium after the circus closed. Yet although she might not have been introduced to everyone in the circus yet—after all,

David and the Blob had been new to her—she felt almost certain she knew him.

She cautiously stretched her hand out to touch one of his reaching tentacles. If his suckers were similar to those of a squid or octopus, that could spell danger for her, tearing her skin and drawing blood. But Bell wouldn't send something like that out here to take her. Capable of violence, yes, but not something that would actually do damage she hadn't signed up for.

The tip of the tentacle she touched curled around her finger with frightening strength. It was like a prehensile tongue, although not quite as slippery.

The comparison made her bite her lower lip against the reawakening of her desire. Fear immediately receded.

The being's mouth curved upward in a glittering, terrible smile.

"Who are you?" she whispered. But he shook his head, still smiling like a shark.

His tentacles beckoned her in, parting over the front of his body to where his dark, slick cock arched up—big and as strong-looking as the rest of him, the head pointed, bottom ridge of the shaft frilled.

The arcane assortment of dildos under her bed suddenly made sense.

The being's laughter filled the room as her face flushed a hot, burning red that probably extended all the way down to her chest. Then he jerked her in by the hold he had on her finger, and she tripped forward into his waiting tentacles. They wrapped around her, quick and unstoppable as pythons. Whatever coated him slicked over her, and again, she was reminded of tongues—tongues that licked around her arms, her waist, her legs, shifting all over her body.

She shouted as he whipped her around like a carnival ride, adjusting his hold by raveling and unraveling his tentacles over each part, disorienting her.

Before she knew it, she faced the audience again, gasping and trying to find something to hold on to, but he shifted his tentacles from her grip every time. She was at his mercy, held up from the floor and nothing under her control. There were more wolf whistles as the being spread her limbs to display her, inspecting her with a prod here, a brush there, then curling around her thighs to part them farther and expose her cunt to everyone's gaze.

Mikhail was still there. He clutched at the front of his trousers as though he wanted to tear them off—or perhaps as though he wanted to tear his cock from himself, crush it in his strongman's grip.

The being rolled his tongue against his teeth in a deep, clicking purr as he brought his tentacle arms, with their seven smaller finger tentacles each, to her torso. They curled around her, suckers pulling on her skin as though searching—over her abdomen, near and over her navel, over the skin above her mound, up between her breasts then over them—leaving red marks where they'd been. If his suckerless tentacles were like tongues, the suckers were like mouths. The comparison was all the more apparent when they blindly found her nipples. The suction was nearly excruciating, yet her clit throbbed with every suck.

Before Bell had granted her wish, she'd had no doubt she was somewhat masochistic based on what she and her husband had discovered during experimentation. But that masochism hadn't been connected to sexual desire.

Now she couldn't deny that her masochism effortlessly extended into that realm. Between the demon hands and the being's suckers, the only conclusion she could draw was that she was indeed turned on by pain—this kind of pain, the kind that walked the line of pleasure but wouldn't give her the satisfaction.

"You don't need gentle, do you, Neve?" Bell whispered in her head.

"No," she murmured. She jerked against the tentacle grip over her wrists and ankles. She shook her head sharply, closed her eyes. "No, no, no…"

The being hesitated, his suckers still working over her nipples but his tentacles otherwise still.

"Don't stop," she pleaded. "Whatever you do, don't stop. Just take whatever you want. Just…oh, fuck *no*."

His laughter was an avalanche in her ears. He curled his tentacles away from her then snapped them in vicious rubber band slaps over her abdomen and breasts, leaving new flushes over the red sucker marks. She swore a blue streak she didn't know she had in her, but the being cut her off when he brought his greedy suckers back to her breasts. She fought the tentacles around her feet and ankles for entirely new reasons, tired of being bound, wanting to hold instead of being held and moved back and forth against her will. Even as she writhed into the suckers at her breasts and teasing her mound without getting close enough to her clit—*oh God, what would that be like?*—she dug her nails into the tentacles, trying to get them to let her go.

She cried out as the tentacles spun her again, this time tilting her head to face the floor, her profile to the audience. Her breasts weighed heavily against the tentacle arms, but he held her more or less steady around her waist and thighs. He released her wrists and ankles, as though he'd known what she wanted.

Neve kicked, though, and shouted as he flicked his thinner tentacles across her buttocks. It reminded her of her favorite flogger, but with more of a sting because he put more power behind it.

She wrenched with every blow until tears joined whatever secretions he produced to glisten on her skin. But when she whimpered, it was because her folds, her pussy and her clit weren't touched or sucked, not so much as caressed. And with dozens of tentacles in her way, she couldn't tend to it herself.

She could only imagine what her backside looked like when he was finished. He smoothed his cool secretions over her ass, raised her up to stroke the tears from her cheeks, although that did nothing to clean the mess.

When he pulled his suckers from her breasts, she screamed. It hurt, yes, but she felt almost like she was throwing a tantrum. She was at the end of her night and she couldn't take any more, damn it. The whole night had been a tease — worse with Mikhail there, emanating at her like a black sun sending out radioactive waves with every little solar storm. The scream grated through her vocal cords.

A tentacle shot into her cunt without warning, nothing but its secretions — and hers — to protect her as the tentacle shoved in with the force of a fist. She cried out, wrenched again against the tentacles before her body realized it hadn't hurt.

The tentacle undulated, arched within her, but not on her G-spot, which was all the more maddening.

That tentacle was joined by another — smaller, thinner, entering her just as rudely and as a counterpoint to the thicker one fucking her. It found a different place that wasn't quite like the G-spot, but which still had her wriggling in spite of feeling full.

She dug her nails into his arm again as a third tentacle squeezed in with the other two. This one swished over her G-spot like a cat's tail. The fullness stretched her blood-swollen flesh taut, her pleasure tauter.

The being brought yet another prehensile tentacle up to trace over her lips. He didn't have to force anything. She opened her mouth and took him deep as though swallowing a cock. She suspected this being had some of the magic the other demons supposedly had that allowed improbable sizes in tight spaces, but that didn't stop her from feeling strained.

Even though his tentacles took her from either end, as unpredictable as the liquid music of the waterphone, she rocked herself forward and back to her own rhythm, using her strength and her grip on his tentacle arm. His groan shuddered through her in low vibrations so strong, her clit thought they were close. She moaned her orgasm helplessly through the tentacle in her mouth.

Just when she thought she couldn't take any more, that this was going to be the sexual overstimulation that sent her tumbling into the realm of unconsciousness, the tip of a tentacle traced from the base of her spine, between her cheeks, to just between her legs, circling the last unpenetrated orifice she had left.

She immediately tensed. He had to have felt it around what he'd already put inside her.

He pulled her upright again and into the seething cradle of tentacles against his body, facing her toward the audience. His gigantic face loomed above her, his teeth a disquieting lack of distance from her head. Tentacles wrapped around her breasts, not quite squeezing but pulsing their grip, and the suckers returned, needy little mouths.

She knew what he was going to do before he did it. Her eyes widened as he finally brought one of his suckers right over her clit, keeping blood in the little organ no matter what he did elsewhere.

She'd only done anal once and hadn't liked it at all, but the being's tentacles were thin and slippery, and every time her thoughts were coherent enough for her to try to raise herself up away from that probing limb, the suckers over her nipples and clit would just suck harder, distracting her until the tentacle had curled like a parasite in her ass, moving with its own rhythm like the rest.

As soon as he thought she was ready, another two tentacles made their way in with the rest until she was completely full, her skin covered in his slick secretions like oil, on pornographic display for every person in the room. She shivered as she fought off her second orgasm, which climbed so hard and fast that she was afraid it would pummel her from the inside.

Mikhail reclined on the couch by himself. So many spectators had moved up to the first row for a good look, but no one dared sit next to him when he looked like he'd kill anyone who tried. He wrung his erection with so much force, it couldn't have felt good, but he didn't stop, didn't blink.

The being's cock came up between her parted thighs, and she let go of the tentacle claiming her mouth to grab the equally slick erection. Her hands felt small around the shaft, but she caressed the head and pumped both hands over him, her grip as firm and punishing as Mikhail's, unintentionally finding the same rhythm until the being growled again.

Neve clamped around the tentacles, her orgasm a rain of punches inside, her body like a fist to whatever had slithered within. Her eyes rolled back and her eyelids fluttered, taking away the sight of Mikhail staring. She came so hard, she managed to make the tentacles sway from the rocking of her body as she tried to intensify everything at once—the tentacles in her ass, the tentacles rubbing every last spot left in her cunt, the suckers over her clit and her nipples, the tentacle in her mouth, the tentacles all over her body like tongues, the cock in her hands. Her own liquid sprayed the tentacles moving in her cunt, not that it made a difference. Her muscles nearly cramped from the tension that wouldn't release, wouldn't stop, kept hitting her over and over and over as long as the sucker over her clit didn't let up.

Finally, the being groaned one more time as the music reached its conclusion. The cock in her hands pulsed, visibly twitched. Thin, whitish fluid closer in consistency to his secretions than semen struck her cheek, her breasts, her arms, her stomach, before the pressure made the rest a fountain down his shaft.

Neve thought it was over when the tentacle in her mouth and the suckers pulled away to let her orgasm run its course, as thick tentacles emerged from her cunt, leaving her empty and a complete mess from head to toe. The refined nudity Kitty and Bell had arranged had been rendered cheap with the being's fluids.

Then, the tentacles in her ass still curling and uncurling in a horrible, wonderful way she still hadn't decided whether she liked, he turned her around to face him and brought her gaping pussy to his still-spilling cock. He'd already found all the places that made her squirm, knew exactly how to angle her so that the frilled ridge rubbed over them. He stood up with her like that, the floor far away from her now. He spread the many tentacles around his head as he slowly slid her down his cock, deeper, deeper, as impossibly deep as Mikhail would go. Deeper.

With her mouth no longer stoppered, her moan was long, loud and humiliating.

"Goddammit, Neve, ride him. Fucking ride him, gorgeous creature. Take that monster cock deep. Make it yours. Grab those fucking tentacles and ride him."

At this point, she didn't know whether the desire burning under her skin was more hers or Mikhail's, but he'd officially lost control of his sex magic, which took the room by torrential storm. She did what Mikhail told her, undulating and writhing over the being's cock and tentacles the way she had those strange dildos for days. She filled herself up, her moaning almost constant except when she had to breathe. Her whole body had become one giant sex organ bent on pleasure and unafraid of anything except not being able to come again, because she wasn't done, somehow wasn't done. Something still yearned inside her, because when someone and something wanted her, she could never be done.

It was a kind of hell, but it was also liberating to not think about what she should want or what she should be, to accept the constant ebb and flow of pleasure, accept that it wouldn't stop.

She looked over her shoulder. In the rows behind her, Rome could have been burning, but the audience was fixed only upon its pleasure, and that pleasure no longer had rules. If there were women, the men had the women, but in the absence of one, they pleasured each other—these sensitive men who couldn't watch another man getting fucked by a male monster.

A man was on his knees in front of Locke, who had somehow miraculously stayed dressed. She still couldn't see his cock, because it was buried down an older man's throat. Locke shoved his erection into the man's mouth, but he was transfixed, clenching his teeth, the hollows of his cheeks twitching.

Bell sat on the edge of the stage, his bare toes in a crouching woman's mouth. He was clearly aroused but the only quiet in the storm, his eyelids heavy in feline pleasure.

Mikhail stood then lifted the sofa and slammed it against a column. The legs and frame splintered like balsa wood. He staggered away stage left as though he'd been shot in the stomach. Watching wasn't going to help. Her coming wasn't going to help. Everyone around him coming wasn't going to make a damn bit of difference to him. No one could give him what he needed without dying except Sasha—who Neve doubted would do it a second time tonight.

And after the effort Neve had made to avoid having sex with him again after that long night, she'd made it clear she wouldn't do it again either…all so she wouldn't be exactly what she was right now—nothing but holes to fill over and over again, to scream and moan because that's what the things inside her wanted. Because Mikhail would take it all if he could. Every man would. If she collapsed dead, they'd still all be satisfied.

She turned back to the being, stared into his unfamiliar elder god face with certainty he could understand her. "Enough," she whispered. "End it."

She let go of one of the tentacles above her to rub around her clit. It hurt now, but she also rode him harder, rocking to ensure all the places that needed to be stroked were stroked, rocking until she squirted again and his cock surged inside her with another flood. They rained down on the concrete floor.

The being knelt in it without a care. As he eased himself out of her, he wrapped her in more and more tentacles, bringing her closer to the body she couldn't see. He slid back to the open door, taking his prize into the darkness with him as the reprised music concluded.

Chapter Twelve

As soon as the door closed, the being tangled around her began to shrink.

She didn't fight to get out of his grip. The tentacles receded on their own, and she couldn't possibly be filthier without taking a dive in a septic tank. The secretions didn't smell fishy, so she didn't mind it as much as if she'd taken said dive. Besides, she was comfortable in whatever held her. Strangely enough, it was a welcome change, because the tentacles didn't feel like hands.

Eventually, they all fell away except for two pale arms and a slight, wiry man over her who was heavier than his height suggested — dense, then. Pale, slight and dense. He nibbled her ear.

"Well, love, that's what I call a show." Lennon laughed, panting slightly.

Somehow, a five-foot-seven British tumbler had become the gargantuan Lovecraftian being that had stuck her from every end as though she were nothing but a tiny voodoo doll.

Neve pushed herself up onto her hands and knees as Lennon rolled to the side onto his back, groaning and shaking his head. He still didn't look human. His pale skin was nearly chartreuse, and the hair that had been shoulder-length and black was still a writhing nest of tentacles. His eyes were black all the way through, his teeth sharp. But the demon beside her now wasn't anything close to what he'd been during the performance.

"I haven't gone wriggly like that in half a century, darling," he said. "But I never step down from a challenge."

She must have still been looking at him strangely, because he laughed again. "Water demon. When Bell brought the mermaid in, she challenged me, too. Without tapping into my demon side properly again, she would never have been satisfied. But as it is, we have our torrid little affair, and Bell gets a slimy monster on command. Just not usually that many tentacles." He gave a flourish like taking a bow. "You're welcome."

Under the influence of fatigue, her first impulse was sarcasm. But after everything she'd been through, after everything she'd done, she could hardly throw stones, much less barbs.

"Thank you."

His expression suggested he hadn't expected actual gratitude. He curled a finger and caressed the corner of her mouth. "Go see Bell about getting cleaned up there. I think I'm going to take a dip in the mermaid tank."

Her limbs shook, but she managed to stand. "I'd do that again."

"Really? Just give me a few minutes. I think I've got it in me to wriggle out again…"

Neve giggled and punched his chest. "Not now, wiseass. Another Funhouse. I'd do that again."

"I like your thinking, ginger. Get along now. Daddy has to rest for a moment."

"Okay, now I'm saying 'ew'."

Lennon grinned. "Interesting where a nymph like you draws the line. You hiding a cigarette anywhere on you, love?"

"You would know." She pressed her thighs together as though it would somehow convince what was between her legs to feel less open, but her body was bouncing back in its own sweet time. Intellectually, she knew she was already close to normal, but she still felt like she'd been rearranged.

He playfully slapped her ass. "Have a good night."

Neve made her way out of the backstage darkness, although she didn't see who she would have been having sex with had she chosen door number two. He or they had probably left after she'd picked Lennon, knowing she was the last damsel in the show.

Bell hooked her by the back of the necklace and swung her around the doorway into the green room. "You, my dear, are a naughty girl."

"I've heard."

Bell undid the clasp and held the necklace over her shoulders. It was covered in dripping strings of Lord knew what. "Well, that's… You didn't choose the door I thought you'd choose."

She couldn't hold it in anymore. The whole awful, fascinating, exhausting night came out in a rush of giggles and choked sobs.

"Oh, sweetheart, come here." He stepped around her then pressed her face into his shoulder. The same magic that had cleaned her off after Samuel swept over her again and rendered the necklace sparkling again, left her dry and not smelling of tentacle goo and Cthulhu semen.

As soon as she could stop sobbing and laughing and could find a breath, Bell wrapped the fleece blanket around her again. The diamonds were long gone, but she liked the fleece better.

She sniffed hard and shook her head. "Sorry. I'm fine. Really."

"You did me proud. Go get some sleep. We don't necessarily have an early morning with the golems doing most of the work, but we do have to get up, and no one is going to want to."

"Mmm, delightful."

Most of Bell's people who hadn't joined the orgy outside had already retired to the green room or the cots. Caroline reclined in the lap of her larger man while the thinner one kissed her neck. Ciarán and Moss were speaking to each other, in no apparent hurry to go to bed. The clowns protected all points of entry for the cast's sleeping chambers. No one would be allowed to climb into anyone's cot unawares.

"I need to go back onstage in a minute," Bell said, "but I sent the fire-eater out to distract the crowd so I could take care of this. Would you take on the Funhouse again, Neve?"

"Ask me again next Wednesday after I've recharged. I could stand it if no one touched me for another month, but I'm going to have to deal with hands for another three days in a row." Neve shrugged. "I'd perform again, but I don't know about doing everything in one night. Just because I *can* orgasm indefinitely doesn't mean I *should*. That should be an Arcanium needlepoint. Does Kitty embroider?"

* * * *

The cots were set up in makeshift rooms, about four cots to a room. They could be pushed together for those who wanted to sleep with someone else — or multiple someone elses — but a cot was good enough for her. The problem was that most of the rooms were taken by at least two people, and those two people were usually doing things that weren't conducive to anyone else getting any sleep.

The only room where sleep was actually happening was in the room where the Ringmaster slept with Kitty tucked against him and with Maya tucked against Kitty. Maya's back appeared as flawless as it had started, with none of the effects of Bell's piercings or the Ringmaster's whip. Neve didn't linger, intimidated almost equally by all three for different reasons.

By the time she found an unused room, it was near the curtains the golems had set up to block the windows. They flapped inward from the wind outside the building. Between the fleece and her natural immunity to the cold, she didn't mind winter drafting over her while she slept as long as she could sleep in relative peace. The cast as well as the audience were making noise, but the audience had many layers of partitions between them and Neve, and the cast was more discreet, perhaps in consideration of those trying to rest.

Her head had barely hit the pillow, though, when she shot up again, eyes wide and panic shooting through her chest.

She'd seen Lady Sasha in her own private room with her cobras, but she hadn't seen Lord Mikhail.

Neve ran through the curtained hallway. She just managed to catch Bell before he went back to the stage.

"Where's Mikhail?"

Bell didn't say anything for a moment, blinking slowly as though in consideration. "He was in a state where he couldn't be trusted. I let him fly to hunt. I allowed Sasha to go as well, but she elected to stay in."

"He's going to kill someone," Neve protested.

"Yes. That's what he does."

"But he doesn't have to. He doesn't *want* to."

"Whether he *wants* to is irrelevant. It's what he does." Bell tweaked her nose in a gesture that was oddly intimate. "And he doesn't *have* to, but Sasha won't fulfill him again."

Neve bit her lip. He knew perfectly well what her dilemma was, but he didn't hurry, even when the fire-eater came through the stage door, smoke rising from his mouth and nose like steam rose from the incubus' body.

"You might catch him before he leaves," Bell said, "but I'm not going to call him back, Neve. I won't force him to remain because *you* don't like the outcome. Him being here is like chaining a starving dog in a butcher shop, and when he's like this, it's best to let him fly, especially if you're done for the night. Excuse me, I really do need to go now."

Bell stepped through the doorway again.

Neve spun around to search at the open end of the building on the other side of the Funhouse maze. At first, she thought she'd missed him, but after running past the working bathrooms, she caught sight of him at the edge of the floor, naked and as strange and strong as he'd been at her window.

Though he didn't have wings and she'd never seen him fly, Mikhail bent his legs in a clear preparation to launch, expression contorted with reluctance.

"Wait."

Until she called, she hadn't been sure she would. But she kept seeing him in her window, seeing him over her, the disappointment that had passed over his face when he'd finally moved to take her, to feed upon her.

Lord Mikhail froze at the edge.

This part of the third floor had a few feet of concrete between them and all the action. It was quiet, peaceful rather than eerie, the sounds of the city at night a welcome change from the outskirts Arcanium tended to frequent.

"Where are you going?" she asked.

He clenched his teeth over and over, balled his hands into fists. "Bell gave me leave to hunt. What difference does it make to you?"

"You really don't want to, do you?"

It wasn't just desperation masquerading as anger. He was actually angry, without the restlessness that would betray need instead. When he turned around, however, his massive cock was still erect and a deep, furious, purplish red, sagging under its own weight yet defying gravity.

"I can't wait much longer, Neve. What do you want?"

She let the blanket drop to the floor then took his fist, led him away from the edge.

"Neve…"

"Don't." She gently pushed him against one of the concrete columns.

"You didn't want—"

Neve knelt in front of him, shaking her head. Just taking his hand had awakened her all over again, her desire a tireless engine—far more tireless than she was. After Bell's cleansing spell, she barely felt used except for some residual aches and the sense of being stretched.

"You don't want to kill anyone," she said, "and I don't want anyone to die."

"There's always someone who has to die. When a man or woman trespasses, I'm more than willing to kill."

"And innocent women in their own rooms, their own beds?" Neve trailed her fingertips up his thighs. They twitched at her touch.

His lips thinned. He covered her fingertips with his, stopped her. "I never understood how others could do it without regret. It is a useless death—a life snuffed out, all because she chose to be fucked by me. And with all my power, what choice does she really have? It's what I am, but I have never liked the waste."

"I'm tired," Neve said. "Really tired. I don't want anything rough, okay? All I ask is that you take what you need, no more. Come as soon as you can, feed as much as possible. Can you do that?"

He stared at her, the glow in his eyes a dying fire, the rest of him inscrutable. "I won't take long," he said finally.

She continued to stare up at him as she brought her hands around the base of his cock. He was so hot she thought he'd burn her, but he didn't.

Mikhail gritted his teeth again, but a brief groan made it past his lips. The back of his head hit the column, the tendons of his neck tight, as she slid the head of his cock over her tongue and closed her mouth around him.

One would think he hadn't been with a woman in years rather than hours. She had no impulse or desire to put on a show after exaggerating her responses all night — not by much, but enough to exhaust whatever muscles made expressions. Nor was she interested in any kind of gymnastics her tongue could offer him. But with contact made, even the bare bones of fellatio had its own vibration, strumming through her in waves she couldn't hear but she could feel.

He brought his fingers to her hair, sliding them through the taut strands, tucking into the bun. He tried to push her deeper, but she resisted the impulse to swallow him all the way in, though she knew she could and that he wanted her to. When she withdrew, he hissed as though in pain.

"No," she said gently. "Not deep, not forever. Just what you need. Okay?"

Lord Mikhail nodded, eased his hold on her hair, waited without a sound for her to take him in again. This time, he didn't close his eyes. They were slits as he watched her stroke over his shaft and move her mouth over the head of his cock.

His hands tightening again over her head and his quickened breath told her he was close.

"Beautiful. Need."

His teeth were bared, body taut and contoured with mounting tension. She stared back up at him, wondering if she'd heard him at all. Her abdomen twisted with uncertainty, but she increased the suction around the head and tightened her grip around the rest of his erection.

"*Need.*"

Arousal flooded her as he spilled into her mouth. He pulled her lust to its peak in tandem with his to feed upon it. She clamped her mouth around him, drawing his pleasure into her, her orgasm like stepping into a hot bubble bath. Her low moans and his prolonged, animalistic growl broke the silence, as though Arcanium couldn't help but penetrate every corner of the floor.

She sank inch by inch down his cock, taking in more to chase the sweet pleasure down. Her vision clouded and blurred, so she closed her eyes, sinking down, down, down — not needing to breathe, just needing him inside her, needing him deep.

Mikhail did as she asked and drained as much from her as he could through her mouth, which wasn't as effective as her cunt, and she'd known that. She just hadn't wanted anything else between her legs, hadn't wanted to feel as intimate with him, as possessed, as she had the first night or that long night. In that respect, she succeeded, but she still felt like his blood pumped through her body, that some of her thoughts were his — not necessarily that she was overhearing them, but as though their thoughts overlapped.

She didn't pass out, but she went blank for a moment.

Lord Mikhail withdrew from her mouth with the delicacy of removing a sword from a wound. He cradled her head then crouched down to rest her on the blanket.

She wasn't sure, but she thought he mouthed *beautiful.*

He stood guard over her while she recovered, his cock mercifully soft now, much less intimidating in size though still impressive.

Once she was able to stir, he lifted her head so he could wrap her once again in her blanket. When he picked her up in his arms, none of his skin touched hers.

Mikhail carried her back to the makeshift sleeping chambers, finding her another quiet room and setting her down on one of the cots. With careful hands, he unwound her hair from the comb, which eased her forehead and scalp.

He didn't say another word, just brushed her mouth lightly, tracing the seam of her lips. Then he backed out of the partitioned room to leave her alone.

Neve's story continues in the next book of the series, Haunted.

Want to see more from Aurelia?
Here's a taster for you to enjoy!

Arcanium: Haunted
Aurelia T. Evans

Excerpt

Wednesday after the Funhouse found Neve where she'd never expected to be.

"I think this is the weirdest thing I've ever done," Valorie said, setting down her wine glass.

"I feel like we're going to get in trouble," Caroline said, "for doing something so…"

"Normal?" Neve poured herself another glass of red then settled cross-legged on one of the cushions in Kitty's tent, which was the largest tent that wasn't the big top and somewhere the men weren't likely to interrupt during the week. "I wasn't the one who came up with the idea."

"Still, an Arcanium book club. Is this even allowed?" Caroline asked.

"Maybe if we discuss books while tied up in shibari bondage?" Maya offered.

"I'm tied up enough. I don't need that here." The Spider had refused a wine glass, opting instead for the flask she'd brought in. The woman knew what she wanted.

"Me too." With hands rather than rope, which meant Neve didn't have to worry about rope burns, but sometimes her wrists still bruised a little, depending on how hard she struggled when guests passed by.

After the Funhouse event, the golems had provided coffee and breakfast for the road, and once in the vehicles, the cast could sleep a little while longer, but they'd still had to stumble out of the caravan and get themselves done up for the circus opening in an hour. Neve hadn't had a good chance to breathe, away from things touching her, until Monday. With the promise that there wasn't another Funhouse event for another three weeks, she'd take all the no-contact time that she could, even though the hands in the haunted funhouse had aroused her all over again. It was curiously relieving not to act on her desire for a few days, despite the distraction, and to have something like this to do instead.

"It's a good idea." Kitty had brought her knitting, which made the set-up even stranger. "I'm surprised we never came up with it before. It's been thirty-five years since I've been in school. I used to read a new book every two days."

"It hasn't been so long for me," Caroline said. "But it was nice to read something that I hadn't before. And have the *time* to read it, you know?"

"It's been about twenty for me. I don't remember the last library card I had," Valorie said.

Neve shrugged. "Anything to knock some books off my reading list. Thanks, everyone, for agreeing to it. We get so much physical stimulation around here. Yes, that kind, but also all the physical demands like contortion, tumbling, climbing... It's been really nice to engage in some intellectual stimulation for a change."

"Boredom is one of the biggest problems in Arcanium that no one ever talks about," Kitty said. "We're so concerned about the interpersonal interactions, setting boundaries and keeping ourselves and each other safe. But even when everything is as it should be, we can only fuck each other so much. Intellectual stimulation has been nicer than expected. Is it strange I thought of the world in the book as the weird one, where they don't have to think about human-demon peace talks or circus politics? And is it bad that I laughed at some of these characters thinking they're outsiders?"

"I think everyone feels like that," Neve said. "Perfectly normal people feel like that, because everyone has at least one thing that isn't 'normal'. The Internet made finding other people with the same weirdness easier. But people are so quick to call you out if you're even the slightest bit not normal."

"Normal is overrated," Joanne said.

"Normal doesn't exist," Kitty pointed out, literally using the pointy ends of her knitting needles for emphasis. "It's entirely relative, and no one fits all the criteria of *any* normal, which makes the fact that people enforce it even more frustrating. If normal means average, a lot of terrible things are normal. If normal is simply the measuring stick, it's a pretty narrow stick, and no one needs it rapping their knuckles every five minutes."

"Weird is overrated, too." The Spider, like the twins, took up a lot of room, so they got their own chairs. She stared at her flask, which Neve was pretty sure had been emptied. "Normal is Stepford. Weird is Arcanium."

Since no one else asked, Neve did. "What's wrong with Arcanium?" She could think of plenty of answers to the question, but she couldn't know which the Spider would pick.

"Arcanium isn't the worst that weird has to offer," Kitty said quietly. "It could be so much worse, Elizabeth."

"That's why it's hell." The Spider picked up her book and turned it around in her hands. They were pretty much finished talking about it anyway. "It sucks you in, makes you complacent. You're okay with some of the people. You can live with it. There's room for love. But you still can't leave. And it could be worse? That's true of literally anything. Well, I'm sitting in fire ants, but it could be worse, I could be dunked alive in an acid bath. And here's the thing… If it can be worse, who's to say it won't be someday? As much as things around here stay the same, Bell gets bored just like us, doesn't he? And we all serve at the pleasure of Bell Madoc. What happens when Bell's pleasure changes?"

"And on that note…" Neve swallowed down the rest of her wine, grimacing reflexively.

"I'll toast to that," Maya said. She drank the rest of her wine as well. Kitty gave her an odd look.

"Hear, hear," Joanne and Jane said together, raising their glasses.

The Spider, her work there done, labored to her feet. "That's enough from me. Same time next week? Valorie brings the wine, I'll bring the harsh dose of reality?"

"Sounds like a plan," Neve said.

The Spider stopped at the door. "In case you couldn't tell, Neve, your boyfriend's outside, and I think he's here for you. Proximity's a bitch, so I'm going to go get this handled. Goodnight."

"Really?" Neve leaned forward to try to see through the open flap, but he wasn't in her line of sight.

"You mean you couldn't feel that?" Caroline asked. "It's like the temperature went up ten degrees ever since he arrived."

"I always have those temperature fluctuations. If he's not deliberately emanating, this is how it is all the time."

"Oh, sweetheart, I'm so sorry," Caroline said, only half-joking.

Joanne and Jane shifted uncomfortably on their ottoman. There wasn't any other way for them to shift, but despite their jokes in Kitty's tent after Neve's first night with Mikhail, both twins appeared troubled that the subject of humor was right outside the tent.

After a moment, Neve remembered that Lord Mikhail was supposed to have been obsessed with them at one point. Joking meant that he wasn't anymore, but their expressions made Neve wonder whether they'd ever completely move on or whether moving on was just a coping mechanism in a contained environment.

Neve rested her wine glass on the vanity, for lack of anywhere near her to put it. "I'll go take care of it."

"Is that what they're calling it these days?" Valorie said.

"Actually, yes, sometimes?" Maya said.

Neve followed the Spider out of the tent. Elizabeth headed right toward the midway, her walk steady — either she could hold her liquor and a flask wasn't enough to render her tipsy or four legs were better than two when the earth decided to move.

Mikhail stood to the left, leaning against the big top canvas, which was as thick and taut as a wall.

Neve raised her eyebrows in surprise.

Ever since Bell had promised her more comfortable things to wear while ensconced in the circus and out of sight of anyone on the outside, she'd happily schlubbed around in her new collection of sweatpants, leggings, customized sports bras, cotton shirts and oversized jackets. House clothes, things that were intended for comfort rather than sexiness. She was wearing a T-shirt dress, oversized sweatshirt jacket and leggings — hardly the stuff romance was made of — and happy for it.

Lord Mikhail wore the same suit from the Funhouse event but with a tucked white shirt underneath. His hair had been tied back, exposing lines on his face that Neve swore hadn't been there before. And his hair — which had always been black and wild, gleaming as though moussed — was liberally shot through with dark gray and silver that also salted the hair on his face.

"What prompted this?" He was even wearing shoes. She hadn't known the circus strongman had shoes.

"Do you like it?"

"Excuse me?"

"I cannot control every aspect of how I look in this form, but I can alter some of my features and I can dress like a gentleman." He stepped forward, almost shy, and spread his arms to present himself.

"Congratulations?" He looked like he could punch someone's head off and make wise investments at the same time. It was a good look, but it was such a far cry from the leather daddy he usually played, or even the upscale hired gun ensemble he'd sported at the Funhouse event. And the gray hair…

"Isn't this what you want?" he asked.

"What I want? Why would you think I wanted these things? They look wonderful, Mikhail, don't get me wrong. But why did you feel the need to change what didn't need changing?"

"Because you will not allow me to have you except in the direst of circumstances, but you gave yourself in an instant to the wealthy man."

Neve didn't think she was capable of blinking so many times per minute, but she still wasn't sure all this was actually happening and not from something Valorie had slipped in the wine. "And you think the reason I gave him a hand job instead of you is because he was older and wore a suit? I also let Lennon take me in twelve different ways when he was full-on Lovecraft, but I don't see you turning into a wriggling monster with copious mucosal secretions."

Mikhail lowered his arms in frustration. "But if it is not those things, then tell me what I should be for you and I will become that man."

"You don't get it, do you? You don't mean to be this awkward. You *really* don't get it." Her ambivalence about Lord Mikhail suddenly became clear. "You don't understand why I'm not falling into your arms, why you don't get to have me whenever you want, because I'm *capable* of withstanding you, even though it's difficult. You don't understand why thinking that all you need to do is tick off some boxes so I'll want to have sex with you is reductive, insulting and one of the chronic systemic diseases in the dating scene. Which is why I was so glad I was out of it."

Neve scoffed, running her fingers through her hair and shaking her head. She was smiling, but more from a lack of adequate expression for her bewilderment. "You really don't understand these things, and I think I know why."

Mikhail glowered, but he hadn't stormed away. "Enlighten me."

"I've been on the receiving end of your seduction, so I know as well as anyone how flawless it is. But that's all you've ever had to do — turn on the charm and get your way. After that, everyone dies. You know how to seduce a woman, but you've never had to figure out what to do afterward or what to do with a woman who doesn't want to be with you all the time."

"I know what I want, and I know what I need," Mikhail said. "If it's a matter of pleasure, you know I can fulfill you. Why do you hesitate?" Annoyance drew his eyebrows together, the furrow between them comically pronounced. "Why do you laugh?"

She tried to stop giggling, but every time she looked at him in costume as a mature, wealthy patron, it kept getting funnier and funnier.

Absurd. That's what this is.

Still shaking her head, she went around Kitty's tent and into Oddity Row. If he was making the other women uncomfortable, she wanted to lead him away. As she'd hoped, Mikhail followed, likely confused about why she'd laughed, why she'd left or both. In any other place in the world, she might have been wary about turning her back on a man of Mikhail's size and strength when his intentions were so clear. Strange to have Arcanium be safe in that regard when it wasn't in so many others.

"It was not my purpose to amuse you," he said.

"I know. It was your purpose to sweep me up and fuck me for the sole reason that you want it and I want it, and I'm the only one available right now."

"There's nothing wrong with that. I thought you were a practical woman. What could be more practical than yielding?" When she stopped walking away, he cupped her elbows and rested his cheek against her hair. "What is the purpose of fighting what you desire, Neve? There is no *reason*."

She briefly savored the immediate electricity of contact, her nerves seeming to sway her closer to him. Then she continued toward the food court, Mikhail on her heels. "Just because the reason is emotional doesn't mean the reason is invalid, especially when attraction is composed of many elements — one of which can be mutual respect, for instance."

"I respect you. I wouldn't pursue you as I do if I didn't respect you," Mikhail said.

"And the fact that I'm one of two people you can have nonfatal sex with in Arcanium, that's what respect means to you? Not killing me? That's not something you decided. That's something that was done to me that you can take advantage of. Lady Sasha is your equal, Mikhail. I'm just a piece of ass to you. A piece of meat."

"Now it is my turn to laugh at you." He didn't. He didn't even look like he wanted to. "You keep expecting me to be human, but I'm not. You *are* a piece of meat to me. That doesn't mean I do not respect you or desire to please you."

"So you can have sex with your meat," Neve said.

"It's what I am!" It was the first time he'd ever raised his voice, and she put one of the food court tables between them by reflex. He stopped short at her reaction and held his hands up to calm her like she was a spooked horse in his barn. "It's what I am," he said more gently.

"It's not what you are. Do you see Lady Sasha losing her mind?"

"Succubi don't have to work as hard, and in Arcanium, she has much more meat available. She will never be as desperate as I. Her food source is secure. You like science, yes? That's what Bell tells me. Do you need an ecology lesson from an alternative species?" He gestured to the picnic table, a surrogate student desk.

Neve complied, sitting down and spreading her fingers on the wooden top. "Your class, professor."

"Almost every creature of this planet is created with three primary needs—food, shelter and proliferation. One might argue that food is more important than the other two, which are often sacrificed in pursuit of it. Incubi and succubi, as demons go, are hybrids with much in common with humans. We're born of fire, but we can also be born from a human womb. Some of the demons here in Arcanium are fortunate. Not all demons need food or shelter or need to procreate. But Sasha and I, though immortal, are driven to feed, driven to spread, and driven to protect ourselves, just like human beings. Where we differ is that the sex drive and the drive to consume are one and the same."

Neve opened her mouth, but Mikhail raised a finger to signal that he wasn't finished. He sat down on the edge of the table and met her gaze. "You are part of a comfortable world, little girl—or you were. But even in this comfortable world, you are still driven by these needs, although you have shifted how they are achieved. Your ancestors spent most of their energy and waking hours hunting and foraging. This eventually transitioned into subsistence agriculture, then bulk agriculture. Once a small handful of people became responsible for keeping the rest fed, the others no longer needed to pursue the source of sustenance as stringently and could take on other tasks in return. A system of barter for goods and services was eventually replaced with a currency stand-in that drives commerce today. All the work your people do, at its most fundamental level, is for the purpose of affording food, shelter and sex. It is a single-minded pursuit cluttered with frivolous distractions to pretend you are no longer so primitive. If I seem single-mindedly bent on sex, Neve, it is because I am. I want to feed, little girl. I *need* to feed. Just tell me what *you* want, what *you* need in return, and I will give it to you."

He was right. It was a fully pragmatic way of approaching relationships — biology and transaction. And he wasn't wrong, as far as Neve could tell. He just wasn't all the way right.

"Say 'subsistence' again," Neve said.

It was Mikhail's turn to blink.

"You're a lot more eloquent when you're trying to convince me to have sex with you. This part you're really good at. You should teach more often, sir. 'Pursue the source of sustenance as stringently'? You really are trying to get me into bed."

Mikhail narrowed his eyes in suspicion. "You're laughing at me again."

"I'm not laughing at you. I'm amused at myself." Neve climbed up to sit on the tabletop, putting herself more level with him. "That kind of single-minded pursuit of sustenance, as you call it, makes sense in scarcity, but the reason other things have taken the limelight is because our food sources are no longer so scarce, if you have the money for it. In addition, your food source in Arcanium is managed by Bell, creating false scarcity, and in your case, a false sense of imminent starvation. The fact is, one of the main reasons I haven't been humping everything in sight upon arriving in Arcanium — although getting used to it was hell—is because I know it won't kill me. If you've been doing this as long as you have, how on Earth have you not learned to manage the cravings that you *know* will be satisfied and won't kill you if they're not satisfied *now*?"

"A human's sex drive isn't the same—"

She held up her finger to interrupt him. "How long can you hold your breath?"

He stared at her, although he kept whatever thoughts passed through his mind a mystery. But he understood what she was really asking. "Indefinitely," he muttered.

"If I were to touch you now, would you hold it, or would you use that contact to get what you want?" Neve hovered her hand a few inches above his, close to the bared skin of his wrist. Cufflinks glinted at the buttonholes. She had to credit his attention to detail.

He raised his fingers in response, interlocking them with hers. For a moment, lust she hadn't felt since that all-nighter shot through her, as dangerous as a jolt of electricity. It stole the breath from her lungs and made her wonder, underneath that lust, whether this was it, whether she'd have to cut him off entirely, like an Arcanium restraining order. Then, after sucking all the air from her lungs, he pulled everything—or most of it—back, the way he'd done at the Funhouse. He panted briefly, closing his eyes from the effort. When he opened them again, they were black, glinting red, but touching him was only a little different from touching someone else she was attracted to.

"See?" Neve licked her lips and crept her fingers over the veins and tendons of his wrist.

Mikhail swallowed thickly, his hold wavering but staying strong. "Would you have me hold my breath indefinitely, then?"

"Would you?" She pulled her hand away and felt along the sleeve of the jacket, the texture its own seduction over her palm without his added help. "What if I told you that if you did, I wouldn't mind spending time with you, providing you human company? Everyone who isn't Lady Sasha avoids you. But if you're like human beings, surely you also have a drive for company that isn't just sexual."

"A sexless relationship. Is that what you seek from me?" Mikhail said. "From an incubus?"

Neve shrugged. "Not necessarily, but why the hell not?"

She'd apparently rendered him speechless.

"You talked about sex drives. Well, most of my life, I didn't have one," she said. "My desire for nonsexual interaction with men hasn't diminished just because my desire for sexual interaction has increased. But turning into a voracious nymphomaniac *has* made it harder to have nonsexual interaction with men, because once they know they have a good chance, they pursue, and I have to fight not to give in. And I want *more* than that, damn it!" She hit the table with the flat of her hand, angry out of nowhere—at men in general, at Bell, at Mikhail, at herself. "I want someone—*anyone*—to look at me and not see the sex they want to have. Is that so much to ask?"

A large strongman flinching was an uncommon image. "I don't think you want me to answer that question."

Neve slid down the table a few feet away from him. The distance between them seemed wider than that. "Is that so?"

"There are four levels by which an incubus experiences attraction," he said quietly. "When a human is attracted to us but not us immediately to them, their attraction incites our own, triggering our magic to intensify the attraction. Two, we can create attraction in cases where neither we nor the subjects are immediately attracted to each other — with the exception of those with an incapacity for attraction." He nodded to her. "Then there are the people who we find attractive on our own, but they initially do not. Then there are those attracted to us and we to them at the moment of meeting. That connection explodes with tension, as you well know."

He deliberately stepped around the table closer to her. "Every time I look at you, I want you. I can mask the effects, but I can't make them disappear. And I feel what other men want from you. With very few exceptions, no, no one can look at you without wondering what it is like to sleep with you. Women's responses are either more nuanced or come from a place of envy. But you cannot alter how fundamentally attractive you are — across multiple generations, multiple cultures, multiple centuries of trends. You are timelessly sexy, Neve. If you're looking for nonsexual male companionship, perhaps you should seek out a gay best friend."

What he said gave her too many feelings, one after the other — contradictory and on completely different sides of the multiplanar spectrum of emotions. Flattery, irritation, a primal sexual heat at being so wanted rather than just needed, despair at the confirmation that she was a perpetual sexual object to strange men even outside the objectifying context of Arcanium, fury, pride, depression, grief, pleasure, nausea, gratitude...

She tried to keep all those emotions out of her voice when she said, "You really think I'm beautiful? You don't just want everything that breathes and has breasts — and sometimes even those are optional?"

"If I had my way, Neve, no matter what restrained me, I would break through it just to bring you against me and have you in your bed, in mine, in whatever bed is closest — and only a bed, because we could stay there more comfortably all night and all morning like we did. Even though you wanted nothing to do with me when you first saw me on Oddity Row, I saw you and wanted you with a power that you couldn't have known before Bell got his hands on your wish."

Still careful, he closed the distance completely. He traced the frame of her face, curling her hair around his finger, then released her with visible effort — still holding back the effect of his magic as well as he could, only a stray wisp brushing her like fragrance passing on the wind. "I called then. You didn't hear me, but when you called for me from miles away, I followed you. I've had many women, and I thought many of them beautiful. You are beautiful, too, Neve, but beautiful in a way that makes it hurt to desire you, to desire a woman who doesn't want to want me. I don't understand why or how you resist so stringently."

She *didn't* want to want him. To give in to him now would undercut everything she'd just said. But even without the full measure of his magic pulling her under like a riptide, he was wearing too much and so was she. Her mind projected the image he'd given her of him taking her back to her trailer, filling up the small hallway, filling her bed, filling her, or kicking in the door of someone else's home and throwing her on some random bed just to wrap himself around her and sink into her all night. Or his bed. She'd never visited his trailer, a whole place that would carry his scent deep in its matter, the way everyone's houses eventually did.

For a moment, she thought she understood what it was like to hunger for sex like a succubus — as physical a craving as for food. She wanted his taste in her mouth.

"Not a sexless relationship." She coughed, because it had come out in a whisper. "But does every encounter between us have to be about sex? Am I really just going to be the resident Arcanium slut and that's it? Is that all you can be for me? Is that all *I* can be for *you*?"

"What do you mean?"

"When I considered men to date, a bare minimum of what I did with them was sexual. I enjoyed contact for intimacy rather than to satisfy some sexual tension. I married my husband — my ex-husband — because I could talk with him, laugh with him, cry with him, cuddle close to him, stay up all night binge-watching TV shows with him, visit museums and national parks with him. And the entire fucking thing dissolved because I didn't like sex with him."

Hate-filled resentment, surprising in its once-again abrupt vehemence, gave her the strength to back away again. "Haven't you ever wanted anything more than sex from the women you had sex with? You called their deaths a waste. That's why you came to Arcanium. Even though you're an incubus with a drive to consume sex, isn't there more to your life? And if there isn't, do you want there to be?"

Mikhail lowered himself to the bench of the picnic table, his legs comically angled because of his height.

The age smoothed from his face, the gray from his hair, until he was just himself—or whatever counted for himself in this particular form. "Yes."

Neve inhaled deeply. She'd been unaware that some part of her had been holding her breath. Then she sat next to him. "Bell clearly had the two of us in mind when he made me impervious to whatever makes your feed fatal. But I don't want to fall into bed with you just because you won't kill me, okay? I suggest, just as an experiment, that we suspend sex unless we're both desperate—the point at which Bell would send you out of Arcanium to hunt. You think you're nothing but a mindless animal, that you're just made for sex and strength, but I've actually really enjoyed talking to you. You're charming. You can be considerate. You're not afraid of multiple syllables or evolutionary biology, overly simplistic though it can be. Maybe it sounds radical, but what if we just…dated?"

Mikhail's expression appeared angry, but the blackness and red glow to his eyes faded until his irises alone were black. "Dated."

"Dated. Did things that weren't just sex. You were waiting outside the newly formed Arcanium book club. Kitty knits. Caroline watches shows with her men. Troy draws and tattoos out of his trailer. Besides attacking helpless men and women and practicing choreography with Lady Sasha, what else do you do? I know you don't pump iron to look like that, and I've never seen you jog around the fence line like some people here. Is your entire life truly nothing but the pursuit of your next meal?"

"I, um…" Mikhail appeared completely taken aback by the question. It occurred to her that, like his awkwardness trying to figure out what kind of man she wanted to fuck because he'd never had to put that much energy into making himself desirable, he'd never reached a point with a woman where she'd asked him what he liked to do — standard small talk for a first date, but small talk he rarely had to employ. "I like nature series and documentaries."

"That explains a lot. Stephen Fry or David Attenborough?"

"Attenborough, although both are calming. I… Are you honestly asking whether I want to just sit and watch nature films with you then *not* have sex?"

"Yes. The actual person's version of 'Netflix and chill,' because who wants to get it on while watching *Breaking Bad*? *Hemlock Grove*, maybe."

"I don't know that one."

"Not a fan of horror, big guy?" She slid a little closer to him until her knee touched his. That was all, but he still appeared completely confused by her signals.

"We live horror here. I see no reason to perpetuate it in my escape."

"Fair enough. So, what say you? If you don't want to get to know the woman you're having sex with without killing her, you don't have to. And if you don't want me to know the incubus haunting me, you can keep yourself a mystery. It's your decision. But if dating isn't your scene, then you need to stop creeping on me and doing all kinds of sexual gymnastics to try to get me to sleep with you all the time. We'll chalk our sexual encounters down to legitimate necessity, each of us taking impersonal advantage of the other then moving on. I don't know about you, Mikhail, but that doesn't sound appealing to me. Sounds more like going to the doctor to get vaccinated."

"But no sex."

"Your focus on that suggests it's a sticking point...or a deal-breaker."

"I've so rarely encountered people attracted and attractive to a sex demon who request that they not have sex," Mikhail said. "If no sex is to be had, would what you ask of me be mere friendship instead?"

Neve patted his thigh. Again, he looked down at his leg as though it were covered with alien lifeforms. "There's nothing 'mere' about good friendship. I have—had—male friends. The difference is in chemistry—a desire for closeness, for contact that doesn't automatically lead to sex. It's keeping our clothes on while stripping away the layers to the mind." She shook her head in amusement. "Many men are presented with this journey and choose a different path. They wouldn't think any less of you for refusing."

Mikhail looked out toward the midway, where some glow-in-the-dark features were luminescent from a whole day of recharging. "If I say yes, must I offer you flowers?"

"You may. It's not my preference, though."

He scowled, but though his frustration could snap a metal wire and his anger could melt a stop sign, his expression was less dangerous. "Very well. But may I kiss you tonight? I haven't been able to since that night, and you've done many things since then that made me want to kiss you." He rested his knuckles against her cheek, but though it could have been aggressive, all he managed to portray was tenderness. "Just a kiss, I promise."

When she licked her lips again, they and her mouth seemed bone dry, despite the fact that she'd been salivating ever since she'd stepped out of Kitty's tent.

"If you break your promise, you break so much more than that promise. Do you understand?"

Lord Mikhail nodded as he leaned in, holding his breath still.

He brought his hand to her neck, almost as though to choke her, and she flinched automatically, but he just smoothed his huge palm up her neck, caressing the length of her throat with his thumb in a gesture both possessive and unbearably intimate.

He stayed gentle, as chaste as a centuries-old incubus could be, his magic simmering under his skin. It tried to reach for her, but he kept it leashed as well as he could as he kissed her, parting his lips to savor hers. All her focus narrowed to that contact. Her nature made it electric enough, the same as it had been for every other man she'd touched, save for a thin extra layer of arousal that threatened to shift inside her — like his cock in her cunt — if he let his control slip even a little.

But other than that, kissing him was like kissing any other man, and it was still honey-sweet and sultry, early autumn instead of midwinter.

When he pulled back, both of them gasped for breath. Neve knew why she had, but Mikhail still appeared surprised by the whole affair.

"Is that how humans kiss when they date?" Mikhail asked.

"I think you're confusing dating with romance. Sweet romance, anyway. Some like their romance spicy. Some don't want romance at all."

"And you?"

"A little bit of all three. I'm going to stop this now." She retreated back around the table, which was a better barrier than willpower. "Not because we wouldn't both enjoy the outcome if we stayed here, but because we've agreed...or I thought you had. Do you agree, then? There's no pressure to date, Mikhail. It all seems very weird, even to me. This whole evening has."

Mikhail crossed his arms, this time in contemplation. "Must I hold my breath indefinitely?"

She shook her head. "I'm looking for a partner, not just a sex partner. I want dating to eventually lead to sex as a natural consequence, not as an immediate given. With my appetites, is that unrealistic?"

"No," he said quietly. "It's merely...unprecedented."

"Dating with sex is unprecedented for me, so we're both in unfamiliar waters."

"Beware, little girl. Here there be monsters." A tentative grin.

"You don't say."

"I'm willing to try." He stepped around the table, but all he did was offer his hand to shake.

Which she did.

As she turned to head back to the caravan, he slapped her ass hard.

When she spun around, shocked, he raised an eyebrow. "A little spicy, no?"

She couldn't restrain a smile. His tentative grin broadened, caution in his black eyes, but also wonder.

Home of Erotic Romance

Sign up for our newsletter and find out about all our romance book releases, eBook sales and promotions, sneak peeks and FREE romance books!

About the Author

Aurelia T. Evans is an up-and-coming erotica author with a penchant for horror and the supernatural.

She's the twisted mind behind the werewolf/shifter Sanctuary trilogy, demonic circus series Arcanium, and vampire serial Bloodbound. She's also had short stories featured in various erotic anthologies.

Aurelia presently lives in Dallas, Texas (although she doesn't ride horses or wear hats). She loves cats and enjoys baking as much as she dislikes cooking. She's a walker, not a runner, and she writes outside as often as possible.

Aurelia loves to hear from readers. You can find her contact information, website details and author profile page at https://www.totallybound.com